Table Of C

CW01429587

Cases

11) *Piotr Maksimowski (1950), Beaconsfield, s Bucks*
12) *James McKay (1928), Glasgow, Scotland*
13) *George Wolfe (1902), Tottenham, n London*
14) *Frank Stokes (1958), Gosforth, Newcastle-u-Tyne*
15) *Robert Galloway (1912), Walsoken, Cambs*
16) *Milton Taylor (1954), Worleston, Cheshire*
17) *Manoeli Selapatana & Panaotis Alepis (1858), Swansea, Wales*
18) *Stanley Boon & Arthur Smith (1939), Hindhead, Surrey*
19) *John Hill & John Williams (1885), Weobley, Herefordshire*
20) *Ernest Jones (1959), Lepton, Huddersfield*
21) *Arthur Osborne (1948), Southowram, Brighouse*

22) William Knighton (1927), Ilkeston, Derbys

23) George Chalmers (1870), Braco, Perthshire, SCOTLAND

24) Joseph Fee (1904), Clones, Co Monaghan, Ireland

25) Oliver Newman & William Shelley (1931), Edgwarebury, n London

26) Thomas Wheeler (1880), St Albans

27) Martin Coffey (1946), Manchester

28) Vivian Teed (1958), Fforestfach, Glamorgan, Wales

29) James Gillon (1928), Lower Beeding, Sussex

30) Percy Barrett & George Cardwell (1919), Pontefract, w Yorkshire

Case 1
"Del Fontaine's Final Round On The Gallows"

~A Boxing Tragedy~

**Raymond Bousquet (31)
aka 'Del FONTAINE'
[1935]
MURDER
of
Hilda Meek (19)**

" .... you said you wanted me to die with you; well my dear you are going to die with me for a change ...." Part of a letter written on the day of the murder by the killer ....

"Some time ago the girl had her fortune told by a Gypsy, who said she would be murdered within three years." 'Del Fontaine' ...

A familiar story of a young girl interested in a famous older man – In the mid-1930s, Hilda pursued 'Del Fontaine', a famous French-Canadian boxer, when he came to England – eventually she tired of him; but by then, he'd become obsessively jealous about her – in the end, he shot her and her mother at their home in South-East London in July 1935 …. as he sat in the police-station, he recalled that when they had first met, they went to a Gypsy, who had read Hilda's fortune, and told her, she would be murdered in three years time – they had met in the Summer of 1932 ….

Before the Summer of 1935, only a handful of people would have heard of **Raymond Bousquet, a 31-year-old French-Canadian from Manitoba**; by the end of Autumn, he had been headline news in Britain …. However, before as 'Del Fontaine', the British boxing public knew him well …. he was something of a star …. In a ten year career starting in 1925, Fontaine, had fought 102 times: he'd won 53 of them, including 36 KO's …. He was most notable within boxing for winning the Canadian middleweight boxing championship in 1926, and again in 1931 …. He'd first fought in Britain at the *Royal Albert Hall* in Kensington in west London, when on April 7th, 1932, he'd won by a KO against Londoner Frederick Smith …. Fontaine's boxing style was described as aggressive and crowd-pleasing, but with a poor regard for defence …. Over the next three years, Fontaine faced many of Britain's most successful middleweight boxers, including Billy Bird, Jack Casey, William 'Gypsy' Daniels, Tommy Farr, Jack Hyams and Harry Mason. From his initial arrival in Britain, Fontaine's fight record was good with 23 wins, 4 losses and 3 draws; but from November 1933, his form took a terrible reversal, with just 4 wins, 16 losses and 2 draws ….

Fontaine had a wife and children back in Canada; but as a boxer, he was never short of female attention, including from teenage girls, and in the summer of 1932, an almost seventeen-year-old London girl was desperate to meet Fontaine …. attempts were made to persuade her otherwise; but she persisted, and began openly seeing Fontaine in early 1933; by the Summer of 1935, the now **19-year-old Hilda Meek**, seemed to have really got her man; by then he was made most welcome at her family home at **60, Aldred Road in the Kennington area of Walworth in South-East London** ….
However by June 1935, it was clear that Fontaine's professional career was failing, and Hilda, through her dad, was trying to arrange for him to work in fairs …. On the third of the month, Hilda wrote to 'her man', who she thought was back in Canada …. She said how much she missed Fontaine, and was miserable without him …. she thought the plan was for the Canadian to arrive back in Britain in the third week of June …. The letter ended with 13 kisses ….

However much the youngster may have been in love with Fontaine, the boxer was not always sure about the relationship: he had his doubts about young Hilda …. In one letter, written after June 3rd, Fontaine blamed the teenager for pursuing him – saying that before he met her, he had hardly ever been in a pub …. He claimed that Hilda had told him she was eighteen, when they first met; and he thought her older than that …. obviously, he quickly found out her true age, as a few months later in 1932, she had a 17th birthday party …. Their *sexual* relationship had been no concern of the law from the start; but as a well-known boxer, he felt he be would in trouble being with someone under-18 in a pub – certainly with the press and, of course, were it made public, then his affair might get back to Canada …. Fontaine also complained that he had to keep giving money to Hilda and buying her presents …. By June 3rd, Fontaine had, indeed, returned to England, and was in lodgings not far from Kennington in Camberwell …. He also complained that Hilda was not keeping her 'promises to him' ….

Another letter written at the same time by Fontaine, complained that Hilda had 'wrecked his life'; and had turned everyone, including his wife in Canada, against him …. he said 'you have damned my soul', and that she had ruined his 'future in the ring' …. he added that eventually through seeing the teenager, his boxing career had nose-dived, and worst of all, he now found out that Hilda was looking at other men …. so Hilda's letter of June 3rd had, as she perhaps thought, been forwarded to Fontaine in Camberwell [As it turned out, Fontaine, had been continually in England since his return from Canada in July 1934[1]], as on June 1st, (1935) he had fought and badly lost in Kettering.[2] Fontaine had to retire hurt: then worst was to come on June 17th in Newcastle-u-Tyne: he was KO'd …. During the fights, Fontaine suffered concussion and now he claimed his 'head turned' - Fontaine informed Hilda, that because of her, he would probably never fight professionally again …. He claimed to be 'punch drunk', and didn't know what he was doing half the time …. Fontaine blamed Hilda's mother partly for their problems – he said that Alice Meek had encouraged Hilda to take older men for their money, and that she, herself, wished she were young again, and could do the same ….

After Fontaine's return, he did meet up with Hilda – where she confirmed that she was looking to see other older men – the boxer complained that she had broken the promises in her letter – but the teenager simply replied that 'promises were there to be broken' …. However, Fontaine, began also making threats to Hilda, telling her, that she would not be going to any more night-clubs any more …. During one meeting, Hilda, told Fontaine, that she had spent a previous afternoon in bed with another man …. Hilda said she intended sleeping with this man again the next afternoon, and that just recently, she had been coming back at two in the afternoon …. drunk …. it was clear to Fontaine, that Hilda, was on the road to becoming a prostitute …. Fontaine said he was perplexed by Hilda's change of thought – at the beginning of June, she said all that mattered was happiness; now she said none of that mattered – this new man, said he could get Hilda anything she wanted ….

In an attempt to frighten Hilda Meek further, Del Fontaine, now wrote in a letter on Wednesday, July 10th, that he had bought a gun

---

1   …. presumably he didn't always want Hilda to know he was in Camberwell, and told people that he had gone back to Canada ….
2   http://boxrec.com/en/boxer/13697

(as we shall see he had previously mentioned having a gun): they had planned to meet up later in the evening, having also met in the morning, when he would give the teenager the letter …. In it, he said: "You have made a wreck of me, you have wrecked my happiness, you have wrecked my life, I will make sure you don't wreck any other's life' …. Fontaine said the gun was bought by him in Montreal in 1934, and, somewhat strangely, he told Hilda, there was no point trying to trace the seller …! Fontaine claimed, that in April, whilst he was drunk in a hotel room in London with Hilda, that she had tried to put a shilling in the meter to gas themselves, as they were both so unhappy …. Fontaine ended one letter to Hilda with the words: " …. you said you wanted me to die with you; well my dear you are going to die with me for a change …." As a failing boxer, Fontaine, felt he had been tricked into staying in Britain …. Hilda had not stood by her man …. He claimed he was not so much jealous of the other men, but it was the fact, that he felt, he had been played for a fool by Hilda ….

However, despite all this, Fontaine and Hilda agreed to meet at 7.00 pm at a pub in Camberwell on July 10th …. What happened next became headline news throughout Britain the next day …. shots were fired, young Hilda, came running out the house; when the police came, it was reported, she was dead in the street next to her mother, who had also been shot …. they were lying under a lamp-post; but that was just journalism …. Despite being seriously injured, Mrs Meek (43), screamed out: "My girl has been shot!" Neighbours came running – there was chaos in the street: Hilda was dead; but Mrs Meek was still alive …. at that very moment, Hilda's dad, Samuel, had come along from where he worked next door in a hotel: he had been summoned by one of his younger children, an eight-year-old …. he frantically pushed his way through the crowd to see the tragedy …. Eventually, he managed to get inside his house – by now his daughter's corpse had been brought in too …. Minutes later the police arrived, and passers-by told them, that the pair had been gunned down in the street …. it was most shocking …. Miss Meek had, in fact, been shot in the house; staggered out into Aldred Road, was shot at again, but this bullet missed: her mum followed and was herself then shot …. Incredibly, a doctor attempted to perform an operation on the mother in the street: a bullet was seen by the crowds to be taken out of Mrs Meek's stomach …. At one-thirty am, she was given a life-saving operation in Harley Street, which involved her husband giving blood …. One neighbour had told the press, that Miss Meek, had collapsed laying face down in the gutter with blood gushing from a wound in her left-side …. such were the crowds in the street, the *Daily Mirror* noted:

"THEY WATCHED: OUTSIDE the home in Aldred Road into which tragedy had stalked huge crowds were gathered last night. Ice-cream vendors, patrolling the street, did a roaring trade."

It was a warm Summer's evening, and within feet of the shooting, many young children were playing games …. Despite media reports, Del Fontaine, had, in fact, taken the body of Hilda back into the house, the door of which was now locked, when it shut: he had to ask a by-stander to get the key out of his pocket to let him in!

Under arrest in the front-room was …. Del Fontaine: he was on his knees kissing Hilda; an automatic pistol was placed on the table, after he'd taken the remaining bullets out: Bousquet claimed he placed it there – however, a police-officer claimed they grabbed the gun off him, and that he had to be pushed back onto a sofa; and that he had not told them it was safe to come in, as he also claimed – he quickly told officers his real name, and he was whisked away to the nearest police-station, telling the arresting officers: "It's all right. They both deserved it!"…. Searched, Bousquet had a letter on him explaining the night's events …. The boxer said he arrived at the pub at 6.40 pm and Hilda was already there …. He said they went to nearby Denmark Hill and had a drink …. they soon returned to Camberwell, and after about an hour, they decided, that they had had enough of pubs: Bousquet said he had only drunk three pints …. However, as they decided what to do next, Hilda, said she was going home to fetch her mum and Bousquet should remain there …. Towards eight-thirty, the Canadian became annoyed at waiting and decided to make his way to Kennington …. On arrival at Aldred Road, fifteen minutes later, the front-door was locked; but Bousquet had a key and let himself in …. Mother and daughter were not overly-surprised to see him …. as he entered the front-room, the boxer could hear the phone receiver being put down – Hilda was on the phone to someone .... All seemed quite normal – Mrs Meek said she was, indeed, coming out; but needed to put her make-up on; Bousquet went to the toilet .... When he came back – yet again Hilda was on the phone; but he could hear the words: "I will meet you at 10 o'clock. You know where."

In a jealous rage, Bousquet, picked up the phone and shouted down it, that 'she's not going to meet you!' .... Unfrightened, Hilda, told the other person to forget what they had just heard, and to be there .... With the phone put down, Bousquet told Hilda, that she would not be going anywhere this evening, except with him .... he explained to the police, that the final letter written to Hilda, had been given to her in one pub, but she ignored it; she then read some of it in the street in between pubs, and chided the boxer with the words, that he was too much of a coward to do anything about her seeing other men, or indeed using a gun: he was all talk .... Bousquet said Hilda repeated this in the front-room, so he shot her: a first shot missed ...! When Mrs Meek began screaming, the Canadian said, that she would get some of the same ...!

Mr Meek told the police that he had always got on very well with Bousquet – he had been to watch him box a number of times – he did not think that the boxer had been effected *mentally* by bouts, but that he had a very painful rib, that had been broken, and still required constant medical attention .... One of the arresting police-officers claimed that in the police-station, Bousquet, said: "By the way boys, don't think I'm crazy, because I'm not. She was supposed to be mine ...." He then added: "Some time ago the girl had her fortune told by a Gypsy, who said she would be murdered within three years." 32] It seems Bousquet thought he had killed the mother too, as he allegedly, also said: "They are both dead as I fired at their hearts."

The officer leading the inquiry was Detective-Inspector William Quinlan – on the following day, he searched the living-room and found *three* empty cartridge cases and one live cartridge: in the wall by the fireplace was a bullet – it had gone through an armchair before hitting the wall .... a second bullet was embedded in the fireplace .... However, the bullet that killed Hilda was found in her body meaning Bousquet had fired at least three times in the house ....

A Mrs May Duffett, Bousquet's landlady in Camberwell, told DI Quinlan, that since February, Bousquet had been constantly complaining about headaches, and that she thought he was suffering from depression, but that this improved after he saw a doctor …. She said that since then, she feared for the Canadian's mental state, and no longer allowed her son to share his room ….

An important witness that DI Quinlan wanted to interview was Alice Meek – however, it was several weeks before she passed out of danger, and was able to speak to the police …. she explained, that she had been staying with some relatives in Bristol in early 1933 – on her return, Hilda introduced her to Bousquet …. she said that Bousquet and Hilda spent many evenings together, but never stayed out late – most nights 'Del Fontaine', as the family knew him, left their home by nine-thirty …. On Sunday mornings, the couple would go to a Catholic church in Camberwell …. She said two weeks before the murder, one morning, Bousquet, mentioned that he had a gun at his lodgings – Mrs Meek told him to be careful, as it was now a crime in England to possess such a weapon, but the boxer seemed distinctly unconcerned …. Bousquet did not elaborate as to why he needed a gun …. Mrs Meek said that until that morning, she simply regarded Bousquet as a nice young man, who was a bit lonely in a foreign country – she didn't consider the age difference between him and Hilda a problem – Bousquet seemed a quiet man …. *He* did, however, seem somewhat insecure about their age gap, and was clearly jealous of her being around other men …. for example, he did not like her working as a waitress in Oxford Street …. It was getting to the point, where Bousquet, did not want Hilda to talk to any males and increasingly females as well …. Mrs Meek said that Bousquet fired two shots at her daughter in the room and again just outside the doorway in the landing by the front-door …. Having, herself, been shot by the Canadian, she didn't immediately loose consciousness, for she could recall Bousquet carrying Hilda back into the house …. Until all this happened, Mrs Meek, told officers that she thought of the boxer as a single man – she and her husband had no idea, he had a family back home …. She did point out that this was what Bousquet had said, and they had believed him …. although he must have told Hilda he was married, as it was in one of the letters to her - "wrecked his life" etc.

Naturally enough, Raymond Bousquet, was examined by a psychiatrist whilst on remand at Brixton Prison, and a report was compiled on September 5th, two weeks before his trial. Bousquet, himself, denied that he was mentally ill, or that he had ever suffered from epilepsy …. He spoke of his boxing career, and how badly he had been 'knocked about' in his last fights …. Not only concussion, but Bousquet had also suffered from insomnia, a staggered gait and double vision …. since his period in custody, the last two conditions had greatly improved, and he appeared to have no sleep issues at Brixton …. According to the medical team there, Bousquet, had showed no signs of insanity at all – however, when the time for his trial approached, he did appear to slip into a form of depression ….

On **Monday, September 16th, 1935, Raymond Bousquet, appeared at the Old Bailey before Justice Porter in a trial that lasted less than a day** …. In opening the case for the Crown, the prosecution stated that Bousquet must have fired three times at the victim – the first two shots missed, the third, which hit her was on the doorway to the hall; and then the last outside hitting Mrs Meek …. The defence declined to call the prisoner to give evidence, and there were only three witnesses for the defence: the first was Bousquet's manager – David Edgar, who said that in the boxer's last fight in June, Bousquet was so badly injured that he had fought in a crouching position, and subsequently all the blows to him landed on his head …. Mr Edgar said in his last fight, Bousquet's head hit the floor, and there was blood coming out of his ear …. Edward Lewis, a former boxer, explained to the jury the effects of being 'punch-drunk' - he said that Bousquet was not, in his opinion, medically fit, to have fought in June …. The third witness, a Dr Tennenbaum, said he believed the prisoner did not not know what he was doing, when he shot the victims ….

The jury, which included one woman, clearly felt Raymond Bousquet, did know, what he was doing …. they were out for just 20 minutes, and there was no recommendation to mercy with their verdict of guilty of murder. On October 14th an appeal was dismissed; and Robert Baxter and Thomas Phillips were hired to execute the boxer on **Tuesday, October 29th, 1935, at Wandsworth Prison at**

9 am …. The report the Home Office had, has Bousquet firing *four* times at Hilda Meek …. They were also informed, that there was no suggestion that Bousquet didn't know what he was doing, and he had used a firearm, including firing it in *public* - something that could not be tolerated in urban areas …. There was no reprieve ….

Case 2

"The Arundel Street Murders"

William Shaughnessy
(1951)
Murder
Of
His Wife Alexine And His Daughter Joyce

Illustration 1:
William
Shaughnessy

A murder case that prima facie seemed clear-cut: a matrimonial row that ended in a husband strangling his wife. However the killer tried to cover his tracks and in the course of events a daughter was murdered also; but the father was never charged with that murder and officially the case remains unsolved.

It was with a classic piece of police jargon that the Portsmouth City Police suspected that William Shaughnessy had killed his wife, **Alexine (42), a French-Canadian, and one of his daughters Joyce (20)**, when on the evening of **Tuesday December 19th, 1950** they said they were seeking a man who might be able to help them with inquiries into a double murder at 319 Arundel Street in the city.

The address in Arundel Street was a rough and ready second-hand shop; some might say what was on sale was rubbish, but it provided a living for 48 year old **William Shaughnessy** and his family.

The family included a 16 year old son Ronald who at tea-time on the nineteenth returned home to a horrible and terrifying tragedy: his sister Joyce was dead in her bed in a room on the first floor. Perhaps the shock acted as an anaesthetic for the young lad immediately dialled 999.

Within minutes the Portsmouth C.I.D. had arrived and they routinely searched the house and the distraught Ronald received another shattering blow, for pushed into a cupboard under the stairs was his mother's body! From a cursory glance it was obvious she had received blows to the head; later it emerged she had been strangled too.

Det. Supt. S.J. Lamport head the inquiry and he requested that the Home Office despatch a pathologist. Within hours the world famous Dr Keith Simpson was examining the murder scene.

On the following morning detectives routinely questioned the neighbours to build a picture of the family, as young Ronald was too distraught to be interviewed. Next door at number 317 lived Mrs I.A.

Moore who said that the Shaughnessy's had only moved in October and that William Shaughnessy seemed like a nice chap, though all-in-all the family kept themselves to themselves.

Joyce Shaughnessy was an extremely attractive brunette, who did not have a steady boyfriend, though she had been writing to an Australian sailor. Mrs Moore said it appeared that the business was not to successful and only a handful of people would go in.

However despite their neighbouring walls being thin, Mrs Moore said she heard nothing of an irregular nature. Similarly Mr A.J. Robinson who owned a watch-makers opposite to number 319, said that he could not detect anything untoward. He said, : " They were very quite neighbours. They came over to the shop on a couple of occasions to get some small jobs done. The Mother said they were hoping to make a go of the business and were going to do a bit of tailoring and making suits. The business was opened about six weeks ago, but I don't see how they could have done much trade. "

The couple had moved from the Portsmouth suburb of Copnor, where their previous neighbours described the family as , : " normal happy family. "

So if Mr Shaughnessy was the killer, why did he not kill Ronald and his three other children- Shirley(14), William junior(9) and Irene(8) ?

Those younger children were taken to an old family friend Mrs MacKinnon, who told of the heartbreaking task of not being able to answer the question of, : " Will Mummy and Daddy be with us for Christmas? ", from the youngest daughter, Irene.

As far as everyone could tell William Shaughnessy was a decent family man who had served the country in the war in the Merchant Navy, before he was invalided out.

Shaughnessy had another daughter, the married Mrs Zena Knight, who was bed-ridden with tuberculosis. She could think of no conceivable reason why her father would kill two people in his family.

Surprisingly the police could not find Mr Shaughnessy, and to the shock of Mrs McKinnon he appeared up at her house in Copnor on December 23rd. At about 6.00 p.m. he entered her house and said, : " I have not done it " and that a man called " Sam " was responsible. Mrs McKinnon did her best to comfort him and then called the police.

Questioned and charged with murder of his wife, William Shaughnessy did not make any statements and denied he had killed anyone. When he appeared at the Hampshire Assizes in Winchester in March 1951 before Mr Justice Byrne, the defence was simply that William Shaughnessy was " Not Guilty ": some other person, a killer at large, murdered Alexine and by implication Joyce Shaughnessy. As was the case before the Homicide Act(1957), the defendant only faced one murder charge, in this case, that of his wife. However he was never charged with the murder of his daughter.

The prosecution was led by Mr John Scott-Henderson, K.C., the Recorder of Portsmouth and Mr Robert Hughes, whilst Shaughnessy was represented by Sir Ewen Montagu K.C., the Recorder of Southampton and Mr Norman Brodrick.

Mr Scott-Henderson told the jury which included one woman that on December 18th, Shaughnessy went to a pub in Fratton Road at mid-day and at 2.00 p.m. he went into another pub an had several drinks: witnesses would say that he appeared to have a lot of money. Then at just after three he went home and murdered his wife.

Describing Mrs Shaughnessy's injuries, Mr Scott-Henderson said, : " .... she had some 10 wounds on the head which varied from a half-inch long, to two and a quarter inches. There were cuts but they were not so serious that they would fractured the skull. They would probably be sufficient to cause loss of consciousness .... then her own stockings had been taken off and both used to strangle her. "

Mr Scott-Henderson then said the body was taken and put into a cupboard under the stairs. Whenever any of the children came home they were all told that there mother was away: the two youngest were sent to the cinema, and Joyce and Ronald were taken to several pubs.

At one pub a girlfriend of Joyce joined the group and said Shaughnessy had a lot of cash. When they returned home Shaughnessy said to Ronald, William Junior and Irene that he was going to take them to London. When he returned in the afternoon of December 19th, one assumes, he killed Joyce, having first sent the children out first. During the morning in London, Shaughnessy had said that his wife had gone to Birmingham.

On the question of the mysterious " Sam ", Mr Scott-Henderson said it was a " cock and bull story ". Shaughnessy had told Mrs McKinnon that he had left the shop and left the key in the door. When he returned his wife had been killed and raped. Shaughnessy told the police that he found his wife in a pool of blood. He said, : "

I had put Mum where Irene could not see her .... I could see she was dead and then it occurred to me to put her in the cupboard under the stairs. "

It emerged that the Shaughnessy's were renting the shop from a Mr Stanley Witt. He told the court that the -10 owed on November 16th was not forthcoming. After several requests and letters Mr Witt was promised -20 on December 16th. Mr Montague for the defence tried to suggest that the shop required repairs, but all Mr Witt would say was, : " I have been told so many lies by the individual, I was wondering what the next one was going to be. "

Shaughnessy's nine year old daughter Irene told the court that she was repeatedly asked to leave the house and to go errands. Recalling that fateful day, Irene told Mr Justice Byrne, : " I did not see my Mummy again that day, and I have not seen her since. "

At 6.45 p.m. on December 18th an insurance agent Mr William Spendlove came to the shop. He said Shaughnessy was quite normal and not agitated in anyway.

After the drinking spree on the eighteenth Joyce was ill, but on the nineteenth when her brother Ronald asked to see her, his father said she was too ill; Ronald never saw his eldest sister again.

Ronald told the court that his father had been to prison on several occasions but he and his mother were outwardly happy.

On the second day of the trial the Crown presented evidence as to how Alexine Shaughnessy actually died.

A girlfriend of Joyce, Miss Eileen Ayton said after the drinking bout in the local pubs, she stayed at Arundel Street until 11.15 p.m. It emerged that the impromptu party was because Shaughnessy's brother Frank was visiting from Canada. Eileen intended to spend a girls night with Joyce at the shop, but because Joyce was ill because of too much to drink, she left. Had she stayed ....

Dr Keith Simpson place the time of death of Mrs Shaughnessy as on the afternoon of the eighteenth. Mrs Shaughnessy's black stockings had been tied around her neck twice. In addition there were 10 wounds to the head which would have rendered her unconscious, and which had been inflicted in quick succession. It was suggested by the Crown that a poker had been used.

In fact late on the eighteenth a local policeman P.c. R. Smith had seen the shop door open and inquired inside; William Shaughnessy emerged to say it was unlocked as his son had gone to get a taxi for Eileen Ayton.

Having departed from the rest of his family in London on the nineteenth, Shaughnessy spent two nights with a casual acquaintance, whom he had met in a pub in the Elephant & Castle.

It was Det. Insp. H. S. Payne who worked out where Mrs Shaughnessy had actually been killed: in a back bedroom.

To add a touch a further drama before William Shaughnessy gave evidence the court was told of an unsolved murder in the city in 1947. In August of that year a prostitute was found strangled in Charlotte Street in a bombed area. Det. Supt. Lamport told the court that the girl in question was strangled with a lanyard(short-cord). The senior policeman told the court that no lead had ever been made.

In the witness-box William Shaughnessy said he had lived in England until 1926 when he had emigrated to Canada, when he remained until 1933, when he was deported. Since then he had never had a regular job, apart from his war-service.

He then told the court his account of December 18th saying, :

" I went out just before 12 o'clock to the New House pub. I had a pint and got a pair of trousers from Mr Cook, which I agreed I would mend for him ....

Irene and my wife were in the house. It was just about twelve. I did not stay long and went to the Dog & Duck until 2.00 p.m. and then went home.

The sign on the door, which should have been open was showing " CLOSED " .... I went inside and turned the sign around to " OPEN ".

I found my wife .... lying on her back. All I could see at the time was blood on the floor by her head.

When I saw that I was sick and just stood looking at her .... I took it for granted that there was no-one else in the house.

I did not want my little girl(Irene) to see my wife in that condition and know that she must be dead.

It occurred to me to take my wife upstairs and lay her on my bed. I did not do it because the children were always going in and out of our bedroom ....

I did not think of calling the police, because I wanted my children to remember their mother at all times as a live woman. "

Shaughnessy then told the court of how he sent Irene out on several occasions and then recalled the evening's events in the pub, and where he had stayed before returning to Portsmouth on December 23rd.

In a loud booming voice he said to the court, : " I did not hit my wife on the head, or strangle her. "

Cross-examined by Mr Scott-Henderson, Shaughnessy denied there was any marital problems over the non-payment of the monthly rent. He further added, ; "

My wife has always been a good wife to me. I have told a lot lies in the past, and I had not only stolen, but there were instances of false pretences and forgery, but she always stood by me. "

Asked why he did not attempt to revive Alexine, when he first found the body, he said he knew she was dead, and he didn't call the police, because he didn't want to upset his children.

Unfortunately for Shaughnessy all his answers to Mr Scott-Henderson on his behaviour after he had found his wife were so unbelievable, and he could not explain why the poker was so clean: Shaughnessy said he did not know.

Shaughnessy was further trapped by the judge. Mr Justice Byrne asked him, : " When you sent your children back to Portsmouth, where did you tell them to go ?- " To the shop", came the reply.

Mr Justice Byrne then pointedly and suggestively said, : " Your whole object of putting your wife's body in the cupboard was so that the children would have no knowledge of what had happened .... ? "

Somewhat non-plused Shaughnessy replied, : " Yes ".

In a final desperate throw of the dice for Shaughnessy, Mr Montague told the jury that the back of the shop was a bombed site, and that a person could gain easy access to the back of the shop: Anyone could have gained an illegal entrance.

In his summing-up, on March 13th, which lasted two and a quarter hours, the judge told the jury that was wrong to say that the prosecution had to show a motive to help prove the crime of murder; It was highly likely that there was an argument between the man and wife.

The judge posed the question of why would Shaughnessy keep sending his daughter Irene in and out of the shop, unless he had something to hide.

Finally in cases where evidence was circumstantial, then the jury should look at all the circumstances, including Shaughnessys's behaviour *after* the death of his wife.

After a retirement of an hour and 40 minutes jury had their verdict: they had no doubts, William Shaughnessy must have murdered his wife. Accordingly Mr Justice Byrne told Shaughnessy that he would, : " Suffer death by hanging. "

Shaughnessy then said, : " Never in all my life have I struck my wife . " He then left the dock on his own and was taken below.

On April 23rd the Court of Criminal Appeal(Justices Cassels, Hilbery, and Oliver) dismissed the appeal.

On May 9th, 1951 Albert Pierrepoint assisted by Harry Allen hanged William Shaughnessy at Winchester Prison.

The obvious foot-note to this crime was the murder of Joyce Shaughnessy. Her father was never charged with her murder, and no references was made to it during the trial, which was odd, because usually the Crown would ask the trial judge to present evidence of other killings to substantiate the actual murder charge.

Curiously after Shaughnessy had been executed the police said the murder of Joyce would remain on file ....

Case 3
"The First Use Of A Palm-Print In A Murder Trial In England"

James Robinson
(1955)
Murder
of
Mrs Mary Dodsley

Had James Robinson killed his victim two years later he could not have been convicted of murder let alone be hanged.

The case also notable in that it was first time that a palm-print was used in evidence.

There were whispers in the court. The jury had been out for over six hours. It was 1955 and usually in murder cases a verdict was brought in quickly. Everyone agreed this must surely be one of the longest deliberations in English legal, history certainly in the Midlands.

Another 30 minutes and at last the jury retired. Yet the drama had not ended with the usual verdict for the foreman had stunned the court with a verdict that seemed a contradiction.

He said: "We find the prisoner guilty of murder, *committed unintentionally during a crime of violence, namely rape.*"

Courts are normally very conservative places and anything out of the predictable usually throws them out of line, and for a few agonising seconds, no one was quite sure what the jury had decided. To the layman how could a man be guilty of murder if it was unintentional?

Quickly the judge, **Mr Justice Jones**, restored order and asked the foreman to say simply whether they found the prisoner guilty or not of murder and deliver it in that form. The foreman nodded and replied: Guilty of Murder.

The prisoner was then asked if he had anything to say. He shook his head and the judge told him he would 'suffer death by hanging.'

The details of how a man could be guilty of murder he never intended goes back to December 1954 and to a law from the 16th century.

It was a cold crisp morning on **December 16th, 1954** and the neighbours in Old Road, the Nook, Skegby, near Mansfield were surprised that **83-year Mrs Mary Dodsley** was not up and about as she normally was. Some feared the worst that nature had taken its course, but one of them noticed something slightly odd - a kitchen window was open.

Mrs Dodsley lived alone in a large detached house called the Hollies, which was set off the road, and had been a farmhouse before its conversion.

Two of the neighbours climbed through the window and began calling out. They received no reply and going upstairs in the bedroom they found Mrs Dodsley laying on her back on her bedroom floor in her nightdress. There was no apparent cause of death other than nature, but as a matter of routine the police were called.

The two constables who arrived took a quick examination of the body and although there were bruises around her face and on her chest it did not look as if foul play had occurred, although her nightdress was pushed slightly up her legs. However like the neighbours they were concerned by the open window.

The police thought perhaps Mrs Dodsley had suffered a heart attack during a burglary and had fallen. However the house was untouched, despite local rumours that Mrs Dodsley kept large sums of money in the house. Furthermore no effort had been made to open a large safe. It was to be the post-mortem that was to reveal that a terrible crime had been committed.

Held later that day, it revealed that the old lady, 83 years old, had been the victim of a sexual assault, and that her ribs had been broken, and that actually cause of death was suffocation.

Along with crimes against small children this type of crime injects an extra boost into the police's efforts to catch the person responsible, and all the Mansfield police came in for duty to help.

The absence of any apparent burglary and the sex-motive lead the Chief Constable of Nottinghamshire, Mr J.E. Browne, to call for Scotland Yard's help, who despatched Detective Superintendent Ball of the Murder Squad and Detective Superintendent Maurice Ray of the Fingerprint Department. When details of the sex attack were revealed it was believed a mentally unstable person might be responsible, as it had been a Full Moon.

The local police interviewed all the neighbours and asked for any courting-couples to come forward. The isolated country lanes around

Skegby were well known for lovers to meet, and the police promised that they would be discrete. However a week later no one had been arrested.

The police discovered that Mrs Dodsley had few living relatives and that one, a brother-in-law, had not visited in her months.

At the house Superintendent Ray found a number of fingerprints, all of which proved to be legitimate. However Ray also found a palm-print on the top of a window slit in the kitchen.

Following routine investigations in the neighbourhood the local CID were suspicious of a 27-year labourer at a local turkey farm. **James Robinson** lived in Sylvan Crescent, a five-minute walk from Old Road. He lived with his mother and sister and was known as a heavy drinker and was noted for being drunk on many occasions.

When the local police's suspicions were passed to Supt. Ball he took a gamble. At first Robinson denied any knowledge of the murder, despite it being widely report in the area. Then Ball took a gamble and arrested Robinson on suspicion of murder, which enabled him to have Robinson's palm-print taken. It matched the print from the kitchen window. Robinson still denied ever going to the Hollies, although he now admitted he knew of Mrs Dodsley.

At the end of **March 1955** James Robinson **appeared at the Birmingham Assizes.** Despite the apparent overwhelming evidence that he had been in the Hollies, **Mr J.R. Bickford-Smith**, said Robinson would plead 'Not Guilty', in that, "He was not responsible for the hideous happenings which took place there."

In the witness box, Robinson said that on December 15th, he had been out to work and returned home at six. At about eight he went to the *Rifle Volunteer* pub and stayed till closing time.

Mr Bickford-Smith then asked him: "Did you go to the Hollies that night?"

Robinson replied emphatically: "No Sir.", and he gave the same reply when asked if he had killed Mrs Dodsley.

Mr Bickford-Smith said that it was not disputed that Robinson was in the pub until eleven o'clock, and so he called Dr M.A. Lecutier, a pathologist to tell the court when he believed Mrs Dodsley had died.

The doctor said that he believed that Mrs Dodsley had died 'between nine and ten p.m.' He explained to the court that he had come to this conclusion from examining the contents of her stomach. Mrs Dodsley's last meal was said to have taken place at five and the doctor estimated she had been killed ' four or five hours later. '

Early **Mr Robert Vaughan, QC,** for the Crown had told the court the evidence against Robinson.

Firstly the counsel explained the law that if a person killed an another during a serious crime then even if the death was unintentional it was quite clearly murder. He explained to the jury that this was called 'constructive' or 'felony' murder and had been part of English law since the 16th century.

He then called Professor J.M. Webster a Home Office pathologist.

Professor told Webster told the court that in his opinion Mrs Dodsley had been asphyxiated, which had been cause by two factors. Firstly that Robinson had lay down on top of her and put his hands around her neck.

He then said that he found no forensic evidence of rape, but that the victim's vagina was bruised. The last point was taken up by Mr Bickford-Smith.

Under the law whilst rape is a serious offence, and in 1955 was called a felony, *attempted* rape and indecent assault are simple offences, called at that time misdemeanours. Hence Mr Bickford-Smith's point was that if a death resulted from *attempted* rape or an indecent assault it could not be murder under the constructive murder rule, unless there was the specific intent to kill.

At this point the judge cleared the court and decided to clarify the point with the jury. He told the jury that Mr Bickford-Smith's point was legally quite correct, but that the constructive murder rule was part of the common law and was not written down. He said that since the 16th century the law when the crime was ' involving rape ', was that if death took place 'during rape' that was sufficient to prove murder. Thus even if there was no evidence of actual rape, it could still be implied the crime took place 'during rape'.

Returning to the Crown's evidence, Mr Vaughan called Mr Charles Hedlin of the Home Office's Forensic Science Laboratory in Nottingham, who said that having tested the lino in the Hollies' kitchen with one of the accused's Teddy boy shoes, he was in doubt they were one in the same.

Following this evidence was the another piece of damming evidence against Robinson. Superintendent Ray told the court he had found Robinson's palm-print on a kitchen-window. He explained the absence of any fingerprint saying that Robinson would have pushed up the top of the window with his palm.

Mr Vaughan also called a Home Office pathologist who said that determining the time of death from the contents of a stomach was not an exact science and that he estimated Mrs Dodsley had been killed between 11.00 p.m. and one in the morning.

In his summing-up Mr Bickford-Smith told the jury that if they accepted the evidence of Dr Lecutier then Robinson was innocent. Then he said that if they accepted the evidence of the palm print they would be convicting a man for the first time on a capital charge on such evidence.

Finally in his direction to the jury, the judge said that he must add caution to the palm-print. He said even if it were Robinson's that did not prove that he had been in the house. However it must pointed out that Robinson simply denied ever being near the house. How would he explain the footprint on the lino?

With reference to the actually attack on Mrs Dodsley, the judge said that the manual strangulation was not sufficient to prove an intent to kill, so if they believed Robinson had attacked Mrs Dodsley, it was for them to decide if the attack was 'during rape.' Only if they were sure Robinson intended to rape Mrs Dodsley could he be guilty of murder.

Having been convicted on **March 29th, 1955,** Robinson appealed and on May 9th was escorted to London for is appeal. Much was made of the fact of the first use of a palm-print. The appeal court observed that without it Robinson might not have been convicted. However as with all evidence it was for the jury to decide on its validity. The appeal was dismissed and Robinson's new execution date was fixed for **May 24th, 1955 at Lincoln Prison**.

In the death-cell Robinson maintained his innocence. In a letter to his mother he said: " I never did this crime….

I believe the day will come when they do find the guilty one…. As you know and all Skeby knows, I am innocent. "

Although it was widely accepted that Robinson had not intended to kill Mrs Dodsley few people in Skegby and Mansfield had any sympathy for him and he was duly hanged by Albert Pierrepoint and Harry Allen, without any local protest. As one neighbour said: "We felt he got what he deserved. Obviously we are sorry for his mother."

Ironically had Robinson been convicted two years later he could have only been guilty of manslaughter. Under Section 1 of the Homicide Act (1957) the doctrine of constructive murder was abolished.

Case 4
"The Roehampton Torso Murder"

"Oh my God, it's a human being." - The discovery of a female human body, albeit just it's torso, in a stables in Roehampton, south-west London.

" Ladies and Gentleman, I wish you all a very good night. I have a great deal more to say, but I am so bad I cannot say it." - Daniel Good's final address to the Old Bailey.

Daniel Good
[1842]
Murder
Of
Jane Jones

Daniel Good

Famous early Victorian murder, but as yet not done by the magazine. So at last, what the Times described as a 'murder of a most frightful and appalling nature', can be fully revealed….. The case was perceived as being badly handled by the new Metropolitan Police and directly lead to the creation of a plain clothed 'detective branch', and the forerunner of the modern CID…. The diabolical killer, Daniel Good was caught by an amazing co-incidence in Tonbridge, Kent…

<u>**Timeline:**</u>

8.45 pm: Theft in Wandsworth High Street
9.15 pm: Constable Gardiner and two shop-boys arrive at Granard

Lodge, Roehampton
9.30pm - 9.45 pm: Constable Gardiner and others break out of locked stables
10.00 pm: Constables Hayter and Tye arrive.
11.00 pm: Superintendent Bicknell and Sergeant Palmer arrive.

It was getting dark on the evening of **Wednesday, April 6th, 1842**, and two men, with completely different attitudes to life, were in Wandsworth High Street, south west London. Constable William Gardiner [V Division] was on his beat, when at about 8.45 pm, a shop-boy, Samuel Dagnell, ran to him to report the theft of a pair of trousers, in a pawnbroker's shop. The owner a Mr Collingbourne, said that an 'Irish Coachman' who he knew had taken a pair of black trousers, after buying a pair of black knee breeches. The boy said he had seen the man put the trousers under his overcoat, and then under a cushion on his pony and trap. Mr Collingbourne argued with the man in the high street but the Irishman, at first feigned ignorance of the matter, then became abusive and drove off.

Another shop boy, Robert Speed from across the street witnessed the argument and both he and Mr Collingbourne said they knew the man, who was described as 'swarthy', and that that he worked as a coachman in a large country house in Putney Park Lane in Roehampton and about two miles away to the west. Constable Gardiner enlisted the two shop-boys and they made their way to Roehampton. Today the area is very well-to-do, and the lane still exists but in 1842 it was the very edge of London and still quite rural. The house they wanted was called Granard Lodge, and was owned by an East India businessman, Mr Queeley Shiell. He and his wife were elderly and in the mansion lived their son John, his wife and four children. They employed about a dozen servants, including the 'swarthy Irishman'.

The officer rang the doorbell and was told by a servant, that the man in question would be found in the stables area, a few hundred yards away. There were two blocks, and one had an upper area which had been converted into four bedrooms for staff. In two of them were the Irishman and a son of Mr Shiell's chief gardener and bailiff, Mr

Thomas Houghton. However that night the son, John, had been staying in his father's room, which adjoined this stable building. The area had a gate and when the bell was rung, a thin, dark, sinister looking man in his forties answered…

The man had with him a young boy. It was Speed, the shop-boy who asked whether the coachman was in, to which the man replied, in a distinct southern Irish accent: " I am the coachman, **Daniel Good**." This was the signal for Constable Gardiner, who stepped forward to arrest the coachman for theft. Attempting to confuse the issue, Good said he had bought a pair of breeches, which he had, but hadn't paid for them, which he did. He then offered the money to the officer to give to the shopkeeper. However since the allegation of theft centred on a pair of *trousers*, Constable Gardiner said he couldn't do that. Good agreed to come to Wandsworth, but the officer said he would like to search the pony and trap, the stables and Good's room. Good, casually said, he didn't mind. However he soon changed his attitude, when the officer and the two boys went to search another stable on the south side of the yard.

Good stood by the door and began shouting. The commotion was heard by Mr Thomas Houghton, who when the situation was explained by Constable Gardiner, told Good to stand aside. Lead by the officer, lantern in his hand, all six entered this stable. When the officer shown his torch into a corn-bin, Good became agitated, pleading to be taken back to Wandsworth to settle the 'debt'. Speed was told to guard Good, but this did not stop the Irishman from 'helping' in the search by moving hay. Good was then moved out of the way, and the search continued. Mr Houghton then moved on to some bails of hay, and in the semi-darkness and in the light of the officer's lamp, prodded something soft, which he thought was a dead goose…

In the next second, Daniel Good had vanished into the night. The cunning Irishman had also locked the other five in the stable. The men tried to break the door down with hay forks, but failed, and so returned their attention to the earlier find, which they assumed was an illicit plucked goose, that Good had stolen from the estate and hidden. As the men looked into the hay bin, they thought it was too big to be a goose. The next thought was it was a dead sheep or pig. When the lantern was shown right up, the shop-boy, Samuel Dagnell cried out: "Oh my God, it's a human being." The other boy, Robert Speed, turned it over and saw it had breasts.

It was a truly revolting sight for all there was, was a female torso: no head, legs or arms, and even worse it had been disembowelled, with the entrails hanging out. With great determination the men broke out of the stable, but it took 15 minutes. It was another 20 minutes until two locals officers, Constables Hayter and Tye arrived. Constable Tye then took a pony and rode to Wandsworth police station, whilst Hayter, said he knew Good well: he was a devious man. Constable Hayter also had seen a broken fence and footprints heading across the then fields, eastwards towards Putney and Wandsworth and parallel to the Upper Richmond Road.

At about eleven o'clock, a Superintendent Bicknell and Sergeant Palmer arrived at Granard Lodge from Wandsworth, and took charge of the case. A fuller search with more lanterns was undertook. Near the body was a large pool of dried blood, and in another stall was a blood and urine soaked mattress. It was rolled up into blankets and tied up. In the stable, in a locked room, when opened, was a 'very fulsome smell', similar to that of burnt pork. In the room was a grated fire, and Mr Houghton pointed out how full it was, with coal and wood – two wheelbarrows full, he estimated. He then recalled seeing smoke the day before and what he thought was the smell of burning horsehair.

Later Mr Houghton's son, John, told police he too had 'perceived a very uncommon smell', and this was at about six-thirty in the morning. He asked Good if he had been singing horses, to which he replied he had drunk too much the night before, and had been roasting cheese to help him recover. Young Houghton said he had heard the sound of cracking wood, and when he asked Good about the fire, the coachman replied he was drying out harnesses. In the fire were human bones, including two pieces of skull. The stable later revealed, two strips of petticoat, a bloody knife, saw, and by the fireplace, a blood stained axe. Dr Alfred Allen, a local practitioner told police the dismemberment had been done after death, which had occurred, approximately three days before. Apart from, part of the bladder, most of the stomach area had been removed.

Granard Lodge itself was empty at the time of the discovery, as the family intended to move to Piccadilly in central London and had decided to have an Easter break. Thus the police believed with only the servants around, they may have had much more time on their hands, especially as the previous weekend was Easter. John Houghton told the police no one liked Good, as he was of a bad character, and thought of, as highly dishonest. However he said he heard nothing unusual from the weekend onwards. He denied being drunk, and said he was a heavy sleeper.

Daniel Good had worked for the Shiell family for some two-and-a-half years, and often brought women and girls back to the stables and would offer them tea in the harness room. Young Houghton said one girl, a barmaid from nearby Wimbledon, he had seen in the stables about half-a-dozen times in the last year. He said she last stayed the night about a fortnight earlier, possibly explaining the mattress. Another woman had also visited regularly in the last 12 months, but Good had told the Houghtons, she was a sister. The woman had also looked after the young boy, who was Good's 10-year-old son, also named Daniel.

Daniel junior told the police that his 'Aunt' he called 'Mother' to please her, and that he had lived with her in Marylebone, but she regularly came to the stables. He had last seen her on Easter Sunday, when he went to church in Baker Street. When he returned, his 'Aunt' had gone, and a neighbour looked after him until Monday, when his father picked him up from school, and told Daniel junior his 'Aunt' had gone into service and would not be back for six months. He spent the night at the stables on Monday, and at friends of Good's on Tuesday night. On Wednesday, father and son went to Woolwich, south east London, and the boy noticed his father had a box with his 'Aunt's' blue hat in it. There they met a woman called Susan Butcher, who Daniel Good told his son was a cousin, but she wanted him to call her 'mother', which when he did, he was allowed to drive the pony and trap back from Woolwich, as they dropped the woman off at New Cross. The woman was in fact the barmaid from

Wimbledon. It was on this return journey, that Good stole the trousers, and the little boy sat on the cushion, with them underneath as they fled from Wandsworth High Street.

So who was the woman in the stables? It wasn't Susan Butcher, the Wimbledon barmaid. The Houghtons said that the other woman, Good's 'sister', had called herself 'Jane Good'. The Houghtons were sure they hadn't seen her since the end of March at Granard Lodge, but inquiries showed, that she was alive and well on the evening of the Easter Sunday, and obviously Daniel junior had seen her on that day too. It appeared that the woman was also known as '**Jane Jones**'. It seemed beyond any doubt this was the woman whose torso had been found in the stables. And where was Daniel Good?

The search for Good was later documented by the Metropolitan Police in an official report headed: "Outline of Steps Taken By The Police". It stated that at 9.30 pm all divisions of the Metropolitan Police were informed about the discovery and a description of Good. However this was regarded with scepticism, as Constable Gardiner and the others didn't break out until, at least, that time, and it seems more likely the circulation began when Constable Tye arrived in Wandsworth, so at least an hour later. The report said all police stations in the Metropolitan Police area knew of the case by four am, but the next shift began at six.

By this time, Good had made his way to Jane Jones' lodgings, slept in her bed, disappearing with a large box, a bundle of clothes and her bed. He left Marylebone at 5.15 am, seen by a policeman! Somewhat harshly Constable Gardiner was dismissed from the force for allowing Good to escape, and this policeman was also in trouble. At five am, a Sergeant Stephen Perdrian, saw the cab in South Street, even noting down its number: 726. The officer saw Good hand a trunk to the cabman, but this information was not acted on until four-thirty pm, when the police wanted to know where the cab had gone. So it seems highly unlikely that at five am, the ordinary police on the beat knew anything about Daniel Good.

Jane Jones lodged with a Mr and Mrs John and Jane Brown, who ran a grocer's shop in South Street. She had a sign in the shop saying:

"Mangling Done Here by J. Good". She was thought to be about 40, 5' 2" and was described as 'neat looking' and not 'stout'. She had lodged with the Browns for about three years and had called herself Mrs Good soon afterwards, and the boy had stayed with her for the last two years. The room was rented in the name, and paid for by Daniel Good. Good, himself, had told the Browns, that the boy's 'real' mother had died, 18 months before. It seems Good regularly visited Marylebone, although not so much after he began working in Roehampton. Mrs Brown said she had last seen Jane Good on Sunday afternoon between two and three, and she had been wearing a blue hat. She told the police that Mrs Good was worried and that she was going to Roehampton, but if she took Daniel junior, her husband would 'massacre' her. Mrs Good was apparently greatly perturbed about what her husband wanted. She had thought some three months prior that she was pregnant, but it was not the case.

Sergeant Perdrian traced cab 726, and reported that at 5.45 am on the seventh, Good and the trunk had been dropped at a livery stables in Dorset Place, Pall Mall East. A second cab took Good to the *Spotted Dog* pub in the Strand, where he deposited his luggage under the name of 'William Stanley.' According to a barmaid at eleven-thirty am, Good and a woman left with the trunk. Good was described by a cook in the pub as 'restless and tired', and Good told him he had been on a railway journey all night, although he did not know what railway. The cook heard Good tell the woman: "That bugger won't trouble you no more."

Sergeant Perdrian traced the third cab which had gone from the Strand to number 4, Flower and Dean Street in Spitalfields, in the east of the city. On Friday morning, the officer found the room occupied by a Mrs Mary Good, aged 59, a fruit-seller in Bishopsgate. Neighbours said she was Daniel Good's wife, and that the couple had come in, in the late morning, but left again mid-afternoon with the trunk. Mrs Good returned and agreed with the officer, she had been in the *Spotted Dog* and then said, it was the first time she had seen her husband in seven years! However on Thursday afternoon they had gone to a coffee shop at five pm, and Good had vanished. Unsure whether the real Mrs Good was an accomplice after the murder or worse, he told her of the Roehampton crime, and she immediately said Daniel Good was a 'villain' and hoped he'd soon be arrested and hanged.

The trunk and other items had been taken to a pawnbrokers nearby, after Mrs Good had vouched for her husband, saying he had just returned from sea. Some of the other items were female clothing. Despite the apparent good work of Sergeant Perdrian, he was censured for travelling to Spitalfields and making inquiries without informing the local division. However by Saturday, the whole country was captivated by the case and what the *Times* described as the " The conduct of the Metropolitan Police... marked with a degree of looseness and want of decision, which proves that unless a decided change is made in the present system, it is idle to expect that it can be an efficient detective police, and that the most desperate offender may escape with impunity."

Meanwhile the Metropolitan Police carried on. Good's description was circulated on Wanted Posters. He was said to be about 46, 5' 6" tall, very dark complexion, black hair, long features and bald at the top of the head; walks upright, was dressed in a dark Great Coat, Drab Breeches and Gaiters and Black Hat." Hope fully he had not fled the kingdom. Naturally there was a great deal of suspicion about the Irish in London. One was observed by the police visiting Mary Good and a cloth was put across the window, as the pair conversed. The police believed secret messages were being passed, and this linked back to Good. Watches were also placed on the home of Lydia [Susan] Butcher in Woolwich.

At just after midnight on Saturday, a young man knocked loudly on Mrs Good's door, but she refused to answer. He had a large bundle of papers under his arms, and when he left the house, he was promptly arrested. At the police-station he complained bitterly about the police, saying he was a solicitor's clerk, offering her, his employer's services. He was released with a warning about doing business at such a late hour. The case had excited the professional classes greatly, particularly as officially the body was still to be identified.

Legally the body of Jane Jones was identified when two neighbours said, she had a mole on the right side of her neck, in such a shape etc., as was on the torso, and on April 15th, the body was buried at Putney Parish Church. Incredibly, somehow, the torso had come into the hands of a local publican, who displayed it for money, on the previous Sunday. The thinking classes were doubly shocked as it was commonly thought, albeit probably incorrectly, that Jane Jones had been four months pregnant at the time of the murder.

One item found at the stables was a travelling box on the pony-and-trap. Opening it up, Constable Tye said the smell was revolting, and since pieces of flesh were found at the junction of the Lower Richmond Road and Putney Bridge, it was believed that the victim's entrails were taken there by Good, presumably late on the Easter Sunday night. Showing his craving for money, Good didn't destroy Jane Jones' clothing completely, and had given some to Susan Butcher and his real wife. It also transpired on April 5th, he had stolen three shawls and a fur tippet from a shop in Marylebone.

Mary Good had said she had married her husband some 25-30 years prior near Cork City, whilst they were both in service. Three years later they came to London, when Good left her. She was not the mother of Daniel junior, although she knew of his existence. The *Times* discovered Good had been an Army Officer's servant, and had served in the wars in Spain, between 1808 and 1814 and was in receipt of an army pension. At the age of 18 he returned to Cork and married Mary who was aged 31. It was said his real name was either Sullivan or Dinovan. He poured his heart out to Mary and told her, they'd be happy together again. It appears he didn't confess to murder, although the police were greatly suspicious of Mary Good.

An experienced ex-soldier, Sergeant Stephen Thornton was dutied to watch her home. The man who visited daily, was an Irishman, Richard Gamble, and he was followed everywhere, but didn't lead the police to Good. A Mr Dixon came forward to the police to say that an Irishman called Daniel Good had been in his father's service as a coachman, and had received a seven year sentence for theft of property as a servant, a very serious crime at the time, but this had been commuted and the man served about 18 months in Millbank Prison, London.

On April 16th, an Inspector MacGill, who was based in Sidcup, on the very edge of the Metropolitan Police area in Kent reported to Scotland Yard that he had visited a local farm since Good had worked there as coachman. Inquiries at Elmstead Farm, lead to a Mrs Head, who had shared quarters with Good. She described him perfectly down to his dark black eyes. She said he had been beaten up by their employer, a Mr Fitzgerald, and she had bathed and tidied up the wound, which was over the upper left lip under the nose. Good, she said spoke Gaelic, French and Italian as well as English, but could neither read nor write very well.

Despite this the police had a letter written to Mr Shiell from Good. It was very badly written and almost unintelligible, but the gist of it was, to ask Mr Shiell to care for Daniel junior. In it he said his 'dear wife' had died five years before. He said he was a devout Catholic until he met Susan Butcher and that she was ' the cause of all my trouble and misfortune'. Another letter said Good would commit suicide by throwing himself off Waterloo Bridge. A body of a man was found in the Thames at Richmond, but it was not Daniel Good. But the letters seemed to suggest in no doubt that Good was responsible for the torso.

By now Daniel Good was a national anti-hero, described as a 'fiend'. He was 'seen' all over England, often 'dressed as a woman'. It seems however he slipped out of London on Sunday, April 10th, and headed for what was then rural Kent. On that day he visited a barber's in Bromley, dressed as a bricklayer. The hairdresser, a Mr Anthony Foyle, was suspicious of the dark stranger, who insisted on being seen to, in the darkest part of the shop. Intentionally Mr Foyle began to talk about the 'Putney Murder' in a loud voice and then other customers joined in. Good refused to be shaved, when Mr Foyle said what he'd like to do with the murderer. Nevertheless Good paid for the non-shave, and typically became embroiled in a slanging match with the barber as he left. Mr Foyle said he didn't think Good was a bricklayer, as they rarely had the money to be shaved regularly, so Good backtracked saying he'd just started looking for a job in Kent as a 'brickie', and in his previous job he had to shave every day, and preferred to be without a beard and moustache.

Good left Bromley for Sevenoaks and then made his way to Tonbridge arriving at 11.00 pm at the *Bull* pub. Next morning at five-thirty he went to the *Angel* pub in the town and asked the landlord where the work was. There was a great deal of building in the town at the time, and Good quickly found a job at the railway station, building cottages nearby. Good was very quiet but knew the job. He found lodgings that night, but the landlady, a Mrs Hargreaves said he was restless in the night, and terrified whenever he could people moving about. Then after a few days, Good quietened down and settled into his new job.

On Saturday [April 16th] he had done a full week's work and perhaps emboldened by the thought he was safe, he responded to conversation from another labourer, a Mr Thomas Rose. Rose, an ex-policeman, thought Good looked familiar, and amazingly he regularly had pounded the beat down …. Putney Park Lane. Perhaps injudiciously, Mr Rose said: "Your name is Daniel Good." He must have known of the murder. However Good replied his name was 'James O'Connor'. But the ex-policeman had him. He told him he had seen him Putney Park Lane, and even named his employer. He even added that Good 'knew young Houghton!'

Incredibly after what had happened in the stables, Mr Rose went away to fetch the police, telling other labourers to watch Good! However a Constable Humphrey quickly came to the building site, and two others, Ludlow and Peckham soon arrived. However despite the obvious procedure of taking Good to the police-station, they invited him for a drink in the *Angel*! There, common sense, prevailed, and Good was handcuffed and his room searched. There, coachman's clothing was found, whilst in the bar, Good was in possession of a black muslin petticoat, stained in blood. Soon a large crowd descended on the *Angel* and Good was quickly taken to the police-station. There he claimed he was 'Richard Hall' and 'innocent'. He was taken by pony-and-trap to Maidstone Prison and on the way asked for a shave, which Constables Ludlow and Peckham refused for obvious reasons. However at the *King's Head* pub in Mereworth he was allowed some beer and food.

At seven pm that night at the prison, the governor pronounced him to be Daniel Good. Conveniently Good removed his hat and combed over his bald patch. The next day he was to be taken back to the capital. The journey was long and potentially dangerous for so many people lined the route, shouting and throwing objects. At Greenwich, he was taken from a civilian coach and put in a police one. Escorted by police on horseback, Good arrived at Bow Street magistrates at eight pm. Perhaps exhausted by his ordeal, Good began talking.

He admitted he was Daniel Good and that Jane Jones had been with him on Easter Sunday, but he claimed he didn't know how she died. He seemed to enjoy the attention and spoke of his daring escape from the stables and his jaunt into Kent. Then after some coffee and bread and butter, he fell fast asleep at three am. Meanwhile an Inspector Nicholas Pearce and Sergeant Thornton had arrested Mary Good and Richard Gamble for 'receiving stolen goods'. The press were not best pleased accusing Scotland Yard of picking on the two, because of their failure to find Good immediately. They pointed out Mrs Good had asked the police to take the articles away herself.

However this only angered Scotland Yard even more and incredibly on Monday morning [April 18th] Mary Good and Gamble were also charged with murder. Understandably she became very angry and agitated and had to be physically moved from the cells to the court. At 10.30 am Daniel Good was charged with Jane Jones' murder, followed by the other two. By now the press were becoming more sympathetic to the police praising their efforts. Dressed as a coachman, at Good's next appearance in court, he was dressed in the blue overalls of the prison.

This appearance on Thursday, April 21st, was a committal hearing and Bow Street was packed, including many MPs and aristocrats. Some 33 people were called to give evidence. Good frequently cried during the hearing, especially when his 10-year-old son gave evidence, and he was allowed to shake his hand. After the daylong hearing, the Chief Magistrate, Mr Hall committed Daniel Good to stand trial at the **Old Bailey on Friday, May 13th. Good was to be afforded three judges: the Lord Chief Justice of England, Lord Denman, and Justices Alderson and Coltman, in a trial that last**

just 11 hours.

The trial began at ten am, and again the court was packed. Included there was the new Queen's, 69-year-old Uncle, the Duke of Sussex. **The case for the Crown was put by the Attorney-General, Sir Frederick Pollock, assisted by Messrs Waddington, Adolphus and Russell Gurney, whilst Good was defended by Mr Doane.** The charges against Richard Gamble were dropped on the following Monday, but in the dock with Good was his wife, Mary. Such was the law at the time, the pair were indicted 32 times, to cover every possible way the murder could have been carried out. After Good pleaded 'not guilty', the prosecution now intimated that Mary Good would face the lesser charge of 'being an accessory after the fact of murder'. Mr Doane then requested Mrs Good be tried later, this was granted, and the lesser charge was, in fact, later also dropped on Monday too.

The first witness was Dr Allen. He told the captivated court that the torso was almost completely drained of blood. He would not say she was definitely pregnant, which seemed to be the case, because he noted that she was rather 'plump', particularly her bosoms. Another doctor, called Ridge, also thought, she had been pregnant.

A number of witnesses then told the court of seeing Jane Jones on the Easter Sunday. One saw her, arm-in-arm with Good at Hammersmith at 3.45 pm. Twenty minutes later the landlord at the *Coach & Horses* pub in Barnes, said the pair drank gin and water, and the woman was referred to by Good, as his sister and Welsh. Back in Roehampton, at four-thirty they had afternoon tea with a friend of Good's, a Mrs Fanny Hestor, and the woman was said to be his sister-in-law. During this conversation, Mrs Hestor spoke about Susan Butcher, and this upset Jane Jones. They left and naturally she demanded of Good, who this girl was. At six-fifteen, a policeman saw the couple on the Upper Richmond Road, near the junction with Putney Park Lane, with the woman haranguing the man, but him apparently quite docile.

At seven pm they were in the *King's Head*, Roehampton drinking gin, and the landlord had the impression Good was trying to get the woman drunk, as she was trying to push the drinks away after a while. It appears that the pair finally reached Granard Lodge at about seven-thirty and made their way towards the stables. However they were stopped by Mr Shiell's footman who asked Good to take some post to Putney. Good said he would take them to the *Green Man* pub on Putney Heath, and at the same time would see if an acquaintance would take his son to Ireland. That was the last time Jane Jones was seen alive.....

Sir Frederick suggested that the motive behind the murder was the time Susan Butcher had spent in the stables. She, it seems, had wanted or agreed to marry Good. He had told her parents, his wife had been dead for five years. One problem was that Good was a Catholic and she didn't think she should marry one, but Good intimated he could become a Protestant, if that's what it took. In the witness box, Miss Butcher said she had never had sex with Good in the stables. She confirmed Good had given her a number of items of female apparel, including the blue hat, but she had no idea, under what dreadful circumstances, their availability had come about.

For the defence, Mr Doane said the prosecution had not shown that Good had killed his 'wife'. He may have dismembered her, but he suggested he did this *after* she had committed suicide. Mr Doane pointed out the "disgusting and horrible circumstances of the mutilation of the body" were not part of the murder charge. However so sure was Sir Frederick of his case, he declined to sum up, and this allowed Lord Denman to address the jury. He said he was not sure what motivation Good may have had to murder Jane Jones, but if she did commit suicide, surely that would have suited his purpose, so why go through the dismemberment ritual. After just thirty-five minutes deliberation, the jury found Daniel Good guilty of murder. Now no longer restrained by the rules of the court, the judge clearly indicated what he thought the motive was. Having sentenced the coachman to hang he added:

" There is no doubt that it is owing to the indulgence of your inclinations for one woman after another, that being tired of the unhappy deceased and feeling that you could not enjoy to its full extent, in your view, the fresh attachment you had formed, that you resolved upon destroying the unhappy woman...."

Lord Denman added he was in no doubt in his mind that Good had lured Jane Jones to the stables to murder her, and had plied her with the drunk to accomplish this. He was also sure robbing her of her "little property" was also part of his plan. His final words to the condemned were: "It is absolutely necessary that your life should be forfeited to the laws of God and man."

But true to the end, Daniel Good wanted an argument. He claimed Miss Butcher was always drunk, and to blame for his 'wife's' death. Rather unusually he was permitted to make a speech from the dock. He said that having left Mrs Hestor's, Jane Jones spoke of suicide. At the stables, Good said he decided to lock her in, to prevent her harming herself. When he returned she had cut her throat with a razor and penknife. Good said he threw the knife off Hammersmith Bridge. He said on Monday morning, a man who he knew casually came to the stables trying to sell matches, and Good said he explained what had happened and the man suggested concealing the body. The next day the man returned and with an axe and knife, dismembered the body. The man was supposed to return on Wednesday and dispose of the remains by throwing them in the river, but he never came back. He claimed he told Miss Butcher everything and she still kept the blue hat, and didn't go the police. Good ended his speech with a bow to the court and the words; " Ladies and Gentleman, I wish you all a very good night. I have a great deal more to say, but I am so bad I cannot say it."

Good had apparently meant 'bad' as tired. But far from any sympathy, Good seemed even more 'evil' to the press and public alike. Nearly everyone assumed the mystery man was a lie, and that Good had tried to drag a good and simple English barmaid into the crime. Despite the late hour, large crowds had gathered outside the Old Bailey and cheered, when they heard he was going to be hanged. It seemed likely that in her drunken state, Jane Jones had removed most of her top clothing, as the black petticoat was bloodstained, and the rest weren't. She was probably on the mattress when Good hit her with the axe.

Daniel Good's **execution date was set for Monday, May 23rd, 1842 outside Newgate Prison**. As was usual with such high profile cases, the crowd was said to be largest ever seen for an execution at Newgate. The multitude began arriving at eight pm the night before. They watched at three am, as workmen put the gallows up, a task that took some three hours. Good had a restless night, fully waking at five am. When first visited by the prison Governor, Mr Cope, he exclaimed: " I am no murderer." At seven, Good devoured his breakfast. He had less than an hour to live and at 7.45 am the Sheriff and Under Sheriff of Surrey, Middlesex and the City of London, pressmen, prison-officers and others came into the death-cell.

By now very emotional and shaking anyone's hand who would let him, he thanked the Reverend Carver for his help. However he would not confess. A few minutes before eight, Governor Cope gave Good some wine to drink, then the **hangman, William Calcraft** tied his hands with rope, pinioned them behind his back, and took off the condemned man's white coachman's cravat. However he still had the appearance of a servant, although he was noticeably thinner and looked quite ill. As the death procession left the prison and onto the gallows, Good was still trying to 'shake' hands with people. The prison bell was tolled, Reverend Carver uttered the religious tones of the funeral march, and this seemed strangely to drown out the chanting of the mob in Good's ears. Once outside Good was overcome with terror. Slowly, 'more dead than alive' he climbed the steps to the gallows. The noose was placed around his neck and he shouted: "Stop Stop!" Good told Calcraft he wanted to address the crowd, but the hangman pulled the lever and the Irishman was dead. Good 'struggled very little'.

In the death-cell, Good wrote three letters. One thanking a number of people in authority for their kindness whilst he was awaiting his execution. However he still blamed Miss Butcher for the death of Jane Jones. He claimed the mystery man was a match-seller from Brentford. Another letter was sent to a couple, who, Good hoped would adopt his son. The third was to Mary Good, wishing her the best of luck, and that anything he had was to go to her.

A month after Good had been executed, the Joint Commissioners of the Metropolitan Police, Colonel Charles Rowan and Richard Mayne sent a letter to the then Home Secretary, Sir James Graham, suggesting the setting up, of a plain-clothed 'Detective Force'. Within the month, two inspectors and six sergeants had been established. By 1846 two constables from each division were trained in 'detective work'. However there was much political and popular resistance to what was seen a French-style 'secret police' and even in 1868, there were only 15 detectives out of a force of 8,000! The figure today is 32,500 Police-Officers, of whom, approximately 15% work in the CID. In addition there are 1,300 Police Community Support Officers [PCSO], 1,900 Special Constables, 500 Traffic Wardens and 11,500, civilian staff.

Case 5
"The Strange Clue
Of The
Man With No
Boots"

Percy Anderson
(1935)
Murder
of
Miss Edith Drew-Bear

Illustration 2:
Percy Anderson

With Brighton and the whole country in the grip of "Trunk Murder" fever, in November 1934 an extraordinary murder took place at the East Brighton Gold Course, which had it not been eclipsed by the two trunk murders in the town in June and July, would have become a cause celebre in itself...

The extraordinary case of Percy Anderson...

On a cold November night on East Brighton Golf Course, a girl's scream is followed by gunshots and a shadowy figure running into some bushes. A patrolling policeman is found and a search of ground near the clubhouse reveals the body of dead woman in a water tank, but who has been strangled... There is an immediate suspect – the girl's boyfriend, but he has also come under suspicion as he boards a bus back to Brighton, trenched from head to toe but wearing no shoes...

The boyfriend, Percy Anderson claims no knowledge of the crime but then appears to try and commit suicide whilst under arrest by drinking a substance from a bottle hidden in his coat. However by the time of the trial the substance proves to be harmless and the court hears that the gunshots came from a toy gun built by Anderson, which was equally harmless if fired only at the body. And still, whilst Anderson admits going to the water tank, he claims no knowledge of the crime, and says he had suffered mental problems having been struck on the head by a golf ball when aged 12...

Percy Anderson met Edith Drew-Bear at the end of June 1934. She was introduced to him, through friend. They were both from Brighton in Sussex, **he 20, she 21,** and they fell for each other immediately. Ordinarily, particularly in the age that they met, they would have courted and married and may have even been alive still today, in their mid-eighties. However five months later in November 1934 their relationship had come to an abrupt end.

It was just after tea on **Sunday, November 25th, 1934**. It was pitch black and two brothers were walking across East Brighton Golf Course in the shadow of the well known Roedean Girls School when suddenly Reginald and Stanley Crane heard a girl's scream. Jokingly they said to each other that one of the older girl's had probably sneaked out to meet her boyfriend for some kind of clandestine meeting. Then suddenly a number of shots rang out and shortly afterwards the men were confronted by a shadowy figure, who rushed past them and into some bushes.

The Crane brothers were not far from the clubhouse and were now concerned fearing that a girl had been attacked. The men called out and looked around the clubhouse but it was pitch black and so they decided to walk towards the nearby village of Ovingdean, in the hope of coming across a patrolling policeman. Sure enough they had been walking for about five minutes when they came across a policeman, Constable Hayes. All three men returned to the clubhouse and aided with the officer's powerful torch, they began looking through the bushes before turning their attention to the clubhouse itself. It was a large building, but the officer said they had been reports of young couples gaining entry to the back of house and so the men went there first.

The brothers told Constable Hayes that the man appeared to have come rushing from an area a little bit further back from the clubhouse, a distance of perhaps a few hundred yards, where was located two large water tanks and small hut. The officer thought it highly unlikely the men had heard gun shots and though it most likely it had been a couple "larking about"; particular as it was a very cold evening. However Constable Hayes felt he should just check in the hut and tanks. Incredibly in one of the water tanks the officer saw the body of a fully clothed, young woman floating face up.

Despite the discovery and the sound the brothers said they had heard, no one in the clubhouse had any idea what was going on, and on entering the club, Constable Hayes took aside two older members who he recognised, Dr Robert Crothers and Mr W. Barfoot. He explained the situation and asked them to discretely accompany him to the water tank, where the five men lifted the girl's body out of the tank. By six-thirty, everyone at East Brighton Golf Course was aware something had happened as a large number of policemen, both in uniform and in plain-clothes, had arrived from Brighton.

None of the five men had recognised the girl and they could see she was probably just too old to be a schoolgirl from Roedean and there was no form of identification in her clothes. However fortunately for the police, two detectives, Sergeant Walter Collyer and Constable Maskell found two articles - a maroon hat and a girl's handbag in undergrowth near the tank. In the latter the officers found a number of documents, which clearly suggested the dead girl was Edith Drew-Bear, and she appeared to be unmarried. The documentation had a local address - 8 Ship Street, which was in Brighton itself by the sea front.

The police immediately went to the address where they were met by the Drew-Bear family: her parents and a brother, Harold. All three were horrified to hear about the discovery of a body. They told the police of Edith's relationship with Percy Anderson, who they described as a pleasant, handsome man, whom they had no untoward feelings about. They said that Edith had left her job as a cashier in a restaurant in a pub called the *Bodega* which was also in Ship Street, at just after four to meet Anderson, and it was something she did most Sundays.

An examination of Edith's body at the scene revealed that she had indeed been shot and so after all, the Crane brothers had heard a shot. However intriguingly the bullets were of such a small calibre that the police believed they could not have actually killed her, although they might have caused her to loose consciousness. The actual cause of death was strangulation and this had been carried out by a man's white scarf, which was knotted tightly around the girl's neck.

Both Edith's parents and her brother were shown the scarf and said it was very similar to one that they had seen Anderson wearing. Within minutes of this information the police were on their way to Anderson's home at 25 Lennox Street in Brighton. However unbeknown to the Drew-Bear family the police had already paid one visit to Anderson's home. Incredibly without any knowledge of Anderson the police at the East Brighton Golf Course had a followed up a clue, which had lead them directly to Lennox Street...

At the golf course the police had set up a roadblock on the main road into Brighton and were stopping the traffic and in particular the buses to see if anything suspicious had been seen. The most promising lead came from one bus driver, Mr Edward Elliott, who said that at around seven o'clock a most amazing thing had happened. A young man had boarded the bus at Ovingdean Gap and asked for a ticket to Brighton. Despite the fact that it had not been raining, the man was soaked through and shaking. Then as the driver looked down at the man wondering whether it was safe to let the man board, he noticed he was wearing no boots!

In an era when most people wore standard clothing, Mr Elliott was also struck by the fact that the man, who he guessed was about 20 and from a "good background" was not wearing a jacket, waistcoat or most noticeable, a hat! The driver asked the young man why he was in such state and he gave a convincing reply that he had been for a walk locally and had wandered into the sea. The young man gave a Brighton address. Incredibly it was the very same road that Mr Elliott lived in! The sodden traveller was allowed on the bus. It was then that the penny dropped and the driver recognised the young man - it was indeed a neighbour – one Percy Anderson.

This story was relayed to the police, who contacted Brighton police station, who told them about the identification of the scarf and that two detectives, Sergeant William Clinch and Constable Victor Patching had already been sent to the house to establish whether

Anderson was there or had fled. On arriving at Lennox Street the officers were warmly welcomed in by a pleasant middle-aged lady who said she was Anderson's mother. Shortly afterwards Anderson himself came into the living room, and immediately struck the officer with his pleasant manner.

At first Anderson said that he only been with Edith Drew-Bear on the sea front that evening. However when asked whether they walked near the golf clubhouse, Anderson said no and then said he had no idea where his girlfriend was now. Detective Sergeant Clinch told Anderson that he was not satisfied with Anderson's answers and he was asked to come to the police station. Before they left Lennox Street Anderson admitted to the two policemen that he and Edith had gone for a walk near Roedean College and they had been to the two water tanks or "wells" as he called them, by the clubhouse.

The two officers were then not surprised to hear Anderson say that the couple had rowed. However if the officers were expecting a confession they were in for a shock, because Anderson then went on to describe how he had suffered searing pains in his head, and that the next thing he remembered was being in the sea, soaked to the bone. He said he had no idea what had happened to his girlfriend.

Although the officers should have waited until they were in the police station, Sergeant Clinch felt he was on to something and said that he had to inform Anderson that Miss Edith Drew-Bear was dead. Anderson did not look shocked or surprised and then said he had taken a pistol to the golf course to shoot rats! Anderson now appeared to swoon and seemed genuinely shocked and said: "Murdered!".

At the main Brighton police station, Percy Anderson began a statement at 9.45 p.m. in front of Inspector Arthur Pelling. Anderson described how having met Edith in Ship Street, the couple walked to Castle Square in the town before catching the bus and getting off at the East Brighton Golf Course. Anderson said the couple reached the water tanks and sat on the edge of one. Anderson then said: " She brought the subject up about me smiling at another girl. Heated words passed between us and both of us lost our tempers. Then I got a pain through my head. I started swimming for my life after that."

So no mention of killing, attacking or by what route, Anderson reached the sea front. Anderson then simply described catching the bus, returning home, changing out of his wet clothes, and having his tea, in front of the fire! Anderson said that the pistol would be in his jacket, which he presumed would be in the sea. From the police point of view Anderson's statement in so far as it went was correct. He was questioned in depth by Inspector Pelling about what had happened at the water tank, but he just stuck to the same story and at 10.20 p.m. Anderson signed his statement and was formally charged with the murder of Edith Drew-Bear.

Inspector Pelling wasn't sure what to make of Anderson. He seemed calm and didn't seem to be particularly bothered about what had happened. However as the officer looked into Anderson's eyes, the two others officers, Sergeant Clinch and Constable Patching, who had been in the interview room, both saw Anderson reaching into his trouser pocket. Both men jumped forward and grabbed Anderson's wrist. On releasing their grip and searching the trouser pocket, the officers found a small bottle. When the contents were chemically tested, they turned out to be, zinc and ammonium chloride. If Anderson had drunk the whole bottle, it might have killed him, although Anderson later said he used the substance for soldering the toys he made. A further search of Anderson revealed three bullets.

With Anderson having been stripped searched and put in a cell at Brighton police station, the police then went to his home and searched his room. Here they found three more bullets, and an empty gun box. The police also took away all Anderson's wet clothing, which when forensically tested showed traces of salt. On the following day the sea front was thoroughly searched for the gun but it was never found, although one officer did find Anderson's jacket and waistcoat and his hat.

Although the case against Percy Anderson seemed cut and dry, he appeared six times before the Brighton Magistrate's before, he was finally committed for trial. By the time of his final appearance before the magistrates at the beginning of January, the December assizes had finished, and so Anderson remained on remand in prison until March 1935.

The trial of Percy Anderson at **Lewes Assizes, which lasted three days, began on March 7th, 1935 before the country's most senior judge, the Lord Chief Justice, Lord Hewart. The Crown's case was put by the eminent, Sir Henry Curtis-Bennett and his assistant, Mr Geoffrey Raphael, whilst Anderson was defended by Mr Eric Neve.**

The court was told that two days after the murder, Sir Bernard Spilsbury had conducted a *post-mortem* on the victim. Sir Bernard said that the man's scarf had been twisted twice around the girl's neck so tightly that it had to be cut away. He confirmed that this had killed Edith Drew-Bear, and it would have taken about 30 seconds to kill her. However he also described the injuries, she had sustained from the gunshot wounds. In all there were five bullet wounds in the body of Edith Drew-Bear. Sir Bernard said that the wounds were in the back, between the shoulders, behind the right ear and left ear, and two in the back. None of the wounds could even be considered serious and it was left to Anderson himself to explain to the jury the mystery of the gun. The *post-mortem* also revealed that Edith had died a virgin, and there was no evidence of sexual assault.

Earlier the court had heard how Anderson had given Edith his scarf because it was such a cold night. The gun, said Anderson, was actually a toy, that he had built himself some four or five years earlier. Anderson, who worked as a mechanic, said he had built the gun, from various different parts, and he told the jury that if fired at the body and not the head, it was relatively harmless. As in his statement, Anderson told the court he could not remember shooting at his girlfriend. Anderson was then asked by his counsel about the bottle in the police station. He said it was totally innocent, as it was a mixture he had used for soldering, and that he had absolutely no intention of committing suicide.

The defence was that Anderson was suffering from amnesia when Miss Drew-Bear died and he told the court that he had suffered from blackouts and severe headaches from the age of 12, after he had been struck on the head by, ironically, a golf ball and had then fallen on the back of his head. Anderson's mother told the court that her son was the youngest of 11 children (Anderson had actually earlier told the court, eight). She said that one of his sister's had died as a small child, having suffered an epileptic fit. However, apart from, severe headaches, Mrs Anderson said she considered her son "normal".

A neighbour in Lennox Street, Mr Herbert Southern, told the court a similar story - that Anderson regularly complained of migraines, but that he considered Anderson a nice man, who had never shown the slightest inclination to violence. Mr Southern also added that Anderson said he had become depressed after he had lost his job in May.

Mr Neve told the court that the defence would say that Anderson was suffering from a condition called "masked epilepsy" when the victim was killed. However, Mr Neve conceded that he would not be calling any expert medical witness to argue this. To underline the point that Crown totally rejected any notion that Anderson was insane, the jury heard from two doctors: Dr Hugh Grierson, the Medical Officer at Brixton Prison, where Anderson had been on remand, and Dr Joseph Nicholl, who held the same position in Lewes Prison. Both men said they could not find the slightest degree of insanity in Percy Anderson.

After summing-up by the Crown and defence, Lord Hewart told the jury that he was struck by the fact that Anderson appeared lucid and calm in the witness box. Furthermore the judge said it was poignant that Anderson made a detailed statement of all the events, except the death of Miss Edith Drew-Bear. The judge suggested the jury may wish to take a sceptical view of Anderson's loss of memory, but they could only do so in conjunction of the absence of any defence's witness, saying Anderson was insane. The jury were absent for 40 minutes. They returned to a tense courtroom. There appeared to be no real motive for the murder and in such cases jury's might have simply disregard the medical evidence and returned a verdict of guilty but insane, simply to avoid the death sentence being passed.

Percy Anderson was afforded no such mercy from the jury, who found him guilty of murder. On **March 29th** the appeal court rejected Anderson's plea. The defence had said that the trial judge had suggested to the jury that Anderson had tried to kill himself because he knew he was guilty, whereas during the trial, the Crown Counsel had accepted that the bottle was a red herring. Furthermore the defence believed Lord Hewart had been too dismissive of the evidence that Anderson was insane. However, not surprisingly the judges, **Justices Avory, Hake and Lawrence**, rejected any criticism of their senior colleague and dismissed the appeal. Shortly afterwards the execution was set for **April 16th at Wandsworth Prison** in London since executions were not longer carried out at Lewes Prison.

In the death-cell Percy Anderson put on two stone in weight. This was attributed to severe shock and his case was taken up by the well-known abolitionist Mrs Violet van der Elst, who opposed any execution and naturally portrayed Anderson as a victim. She said she was sure he was insane when he killed Miss Drew-Bear. She held a number of meetings in and around Brighton and two petitions raised an incredible 100,000 name's which were then presented to the Home Secretary, J.Gilmour.

According to Mrs van der Elst, in the death-cell, Anderson seemed in another world, and told his family that he was "quite happy". However when Edith's name as mentioned, a tear rolled down Anderson's' face. Mrs van der Elst claimed Anderson had no real concept of being executed. However the Home Secretary believed that Anderson had showed a determination to murder Miss Drew-Bear, whilst the trial judge, Lord Hewart told him that he believed Anderson had taken the girl to the water tank with the intention of killing her. He said he also believed that Anderson had made a half-hearted effort to drown himself in the sea.

Even as death approached at nine o'clock, Mrs van der Elst and her supporters protested outside Wandsworth Prison. They had been there for an hour and the police were there in force and a cordon of them prevented the crowd getting too near the gate. Climbing on to the running board of her hallmark yellow Rolls Royce, Mrs van der

Elst denounced the government for hanging an "innocent insane" man. She then made the claim that within six months hanging would be abolished in England. It wasn't and Percy Anderson was hanged by **Tom Pierrepoint and his assistant Alfred Allen**. As Anderson was hanged, the large crowd removed their hats and sang *Abide With Me*.

Case 6
"Was The 'Man on the Hill' The Riverstown Murderer?"

Patrick Kelly
[1941]
Murder
of
Mary Breheney
IRELAND

The case against Patrick Kelly seemed irrefutable: apparently damming forensic evidence and a mass of circumstantial evidence from locals in the County Sligo village of Riverstown. But for Kelly to be the brutal

***murderer and sex attacker of Mary Breheney, he had to
be the "man on the hill". But was he?***

The crowds had been waiting since the early morning to gain access
to Sligo District Court. There may have been a war on, but the
shocking murder of **Miss Mary Breheney, a 39-year-old
unmarried woman and farmer**, from Riverstown in County Sligo,
had caused the biggest sensation in the county in living memory. The
six-day hearing before Mr Justice Flattery, spread over three weeks,
was a result of the arrest of another villager from Riverstown,
Patrick Kelly (31), a farmer's labourer. The case was complex.
Miss Breheney had been murdered and sexually assaulted on
Thursday, April 17th, 1941, but although questioned by the police
two days later, Kelly was not arrested and charged until May 17th.

The body of Miss Breheney had been found at about midday on
April 18th by a neighbour, Mr John Nangle, who like most other
people in Riverstown worked the land. He had found the body by a
stream near the River Unshin, just 50 yards from Miss Breheney
home, a small cottage, where she had lived alone since her father had
died earlier in the year.

It had been well established by the police that on the early evening
of April 17th, Miss Breheney had walked into the village to buy
some provisions. On the way back she called at a neighbour's, and
she was last seen alive walking to her farm called Rossmore at about
nine p.m. In order to reach her house, Miss Breheney had to walk
across several fields, and the police were satisfied she never reached
home as scattered about in the field nearest to her cottage, were
several parcels containing the items she had purchased in
Riverstown the night before, and the house was padlocked.

Although it was clear visually, that there may have been some type
of sexual assault on the victim, by the state of her clothing, the State
Pathologist, Dr John McGrath confirmed to the police, that shortly
before death an attempt at rape had been made. He also said that she
had been manually strangled, but that the actually cause of death was

drowning. The police believed that the attack was not pre-planned and the assailant many have thought, that he had killed Miss Breheney by strangling and then had taken the body to the river to make it look like an accident. From the marks on the fields, the police deduced that Miss Breheney had been dragged by her feet.

Patrick Kelly became a police suspect because a number of locals were able to place him near to the field, and when questioned by the Garda, he made a number of contradictory and confusing statements, and indeed attempted to place himself some distance from the field at the time of the murder, sometime between eight and nine p.m. However the police believed that Kelly had left a rabbit snare in the wood nearest to the field in a panic, having managed to clear way the rest. Similarly a man's handkerchief was found near the scene, which the police thought belonged to Kelly. However the police thought they had a water-tight case against Kelly because of bloodstains on his clothing and apparently most damming of all, police photographs of footprints at the scene, which were said to match Kelly's boots.

A neighbour of Miss Breheney, Francis Higgins told the court said he saw her at about nine o'clock near the lane that went to the Powell farm, where Miss Breheney would often stop for a cup of tea and a chat on her way back from the village. In the village Miss Breheney had bought some peppermint sweets, coal, bread, an Indian meal, and some oats. She had been seen by several other villages coming back from Riverstown, but Francis Higgins was the last person to see her alive. At Mrs Katherine Powell's, Miss Breheney mentioned that a neighbour, Mr Nangle was coming to her farm to plough her garden, the next morning.

Mr Nangle lived with his mother at Emlagh Farm in an area of the village called Ross, although he also owned another farm nearby. On April 17th, having tended some cattle at his farm, he returned home at about eight-thirty. He told the police that as he walked along the road he looked up at his farm, when he saw a man on the top of a hill in one of the fields near Cooper's Hill Wood. Darkness was fast enveloping the countryside and in the half-light the man cut a sinister figure. Mr Nangle wasn't able to identify the man, but he watched him emerge in a field just some 30 yards from him, and looked straight at him, and he was aware he was wearing a "dark overcoat". Taken aback and slightly concerned, Mr Nangle looked away and turned back onto the road. When he looked back the man had disappeared.

Mr Nangle spent the rest of the night thinking about the "man on the hill". The next morning he made his way to Rossmore Farm at about ten-thirty with a brother. As they approached the farmhouse, the brothers noticed what appeared to be rubbish in the corner of one field by a small cow-shed by a well-worn path used by Miss Breheney to reach the village road, and on land owned by another Nangle brother. Despite the unusual sight, Mr Nangle ignored the 'rubbish', and went up to the cottage and called out. He saw the pad-lock and went back to the field, where he discovered the 'rubbish' was in fact shopping. Neither brother touched the items, as their attention was taken by the downtrodden path to the river, which was very clear, as the field was a meadow.

The newly created path lead down to the *River Unshin* and by following it, Mr Nangle quickly found the body of his neighbour. The body lay face downwards on the river's edge. Neither brother touched anything and Joe Nangle ran to the village police station and alerted Garda Alexander Armstrong. The officer knew the victim very-well and one of her neighbour's, the father of Francis Higgins, Mr Patrick Higgins told him that about 8.45 p.m. he had left his house for a friend's in the village, a Mr James Flynn. He told the officer the same strange tale of the "man on the hill" in the dusk, and furthermore he said he saw him in the field, next to the one where the shopping was, and where Miss Breheney had almost certainly been attacked. He too couldn't make him out; bar that he was wearing an "overcoat of a dark colour".

Mr Higgins went on to say that he left his friend's place at 9.45, for the short walk back, but on the way he saw a torch being shown near Miss Breheney's cottage. Although it seemed stationery, Mr Higgins thought it may have moved, and was at arm level, as if someone was finding their way around. It was not an unusual sight as Miss Breheney herself would use the torch if she came out of the cottage late at night, but it did make Mr Higgins think back to the "man on the hill"....

The police officer in overall charge of the murder inquiry was Superintendent Joseph Devine who was sent from nearby Ballymote. It soon became clear to him that he believed the "man on the hill" was Patrick Kelly through the statements that the villagers were giving to him. One local, Mr William Crevin, said that Kelly had called at his house "between seven and eight" to borrow a bicycle so he could go and get some snares. However it was getting dark and Kelly left without the bike. Mr Crevin said, as usual, Kelly was wearing a "dark overcoat." The next day Mr Crevin spoke about the murder with Kelly, but the latter showed no emotion at all, and asked to borrow a donkey.

Patrick Kelly was employed by a Mr Joseph Baker and it was the statements of his three children that were to put Kelly near the actual scene of the murder at the correct time. James Baker (14) said that at seven-thirty p.m. he was in the village with a friend waiting for a friend of his father's who was to give him a message. He saw Kelly coming from Mr Crevin's house and walk out of the village towards where Miss Breheney lived and towards *Cooper's Hill Wood*. All the Baker children knew of the wood as, some years back, the police had searched the wood, as part of a murder inquiry in County Roscommon. All the village children were warned not to go in to it, as it was said a man still lurked in there.

On Friday, James Baker spoke to Kelly and asked him if he were the man that his younger brother, Tommy and 16-year-old sister Mary had seen in the wood the night before, "between eight and nine". The wood was large and dominated the Ross side of Riverstown and *Cooper's Hill Wood* was right next to Miss Breheney's farm, but Kelly said that whilst he had been in the wood, he had been in *Ardcumber Wood*, on the other side of it. Indeed at about 11 o'clock two others villagers, Mr Patrick Sheerin and Mr John Tahney were walking into the village when they saw Kelly and he told them he had been in another part of the wood, *Charleton's Hill*, rabbiting, although both men noticed he didn't have any rabbits on him.

Shortly afterwards Patrick Kelly knocked on the Bakers' door to ask whether he was to begin planting potatoes tomorrow. Mr Baker asked him where he had been, and he replied he had been in *Cooper's Hill Wood*. The next day, Mr Baker noticed that Kelly had washed and was clean-shaven. During the planting, a neighbour, Mr John McCann, spoke to Kelly about the murder, and Kelly then spoke to Mr Baker, who said he didn't believe the story, as he said Miss Breheney never went that way home, i.e. by the river. However Mr Baker soon discovered she had been murdered and noted that Kelly would say nothing on the subject.

At about one p.m., Mrs Baker came into the field with the men's lunch. She said that there were many police and detectives at Miss Breheney's farm and that "were tracks of boot tracks". Again Kelly said nothing, but after dinner he was with Mr Crevin, and he began picking at his boots. For some 20 minutes or so, he worked at his boots with a penknife, and the spot where the work was carried out was later pointed out to Detective Sergeant John Feighan, where the officer found a piece of leather that Mr Crevin said Kelly had been using to help repair his boots.

One apparently important clue against Kelly was the discovery of a man's handkerchief found near *Cooper's Hill Wood*. Mr Patrick Sheerin's brother Thomas said that in March he knew that Kelly had a brown handkerchief with dark blue spots, as he used it to kneel on whilst the pair were looking for a stray ferret. Then on April 27th, Patrick himself saw a handkerchief of the same description in a field some 200 yards from the road. It was reported to the police, and the farmer, Mr Edward Boyers said he had seen several times, but had not touched it. All he could say was that it did not belong to any of his family. When Thomas was shown the handkerchief, he said it looked the same, but he would not swear it was the exact same one, that he had seen in March.

On May 15th, Patrick Kelly was again questioned by the police, as human bloodstains had been found on his clothing. He told Superintendent Devine that his hands were often scratched and smeared in blood through his job, particularly when he was rabbiting, or working on hedges. However Kelly was allowed to leave

Ballymote police station and returned to Riverstown telling one farm labourer and his wife: "People nowadays would swear your life away."

When the local doctor, Dr J.P. Kilfeather arrived at the river, he noted that the victim's underwear was across her knees and the rest of her clothes were pushed up to her face, so that she was naked from the waist up. He saw the scratches and bruising on the face, and from the fact she had clenched teeth, he believed there had been some kind of struggle, and marks from her fingers showed she had tried hard, to defend herself.

On April 19th, the police had taken away Kelly's boots and they immediately noticed that they had been roughly repaired. However it was after Dr McGrath had examined his clothing and found human blood that he was asked to return to Ballymote police station. At the police station, Kelly made a statement, which Superintendent Devine wrote down and then re-read it to Kelly, who signed it. Kelly said that on April 17th, he came home from rabbiting at seven-thirty p.m., before leaving at eight for Mr Crevin's, and eventually saying that he went to *Cooper's Hill Wood* at about nine. He said he remained there for about two hours having set the traps. He said he met no one in the way back until he arrived at the Bakers'. He said after that he went home and went to sleep at 12.45 a.m.

On a second visit to Kelly's house on April 21st, the police did find a flash lamp, although it was not in really good working order - it did not work in the house, but when the officers tried in the police station it did. One of the problems that Kelly gave the police was that he kept giving different accounts of the way he went to the wood and the way he left. However if the police could place Kelly at the murder scene, then as he had never said that he gone to the river on Friday, that would appear to be clear-cut evidence against him, and so the forensic evidence of the footprints was crucial.

Detective Officer M. Horgan from Garda Headquarters in Dublin was a photographer with the Technical Branch and he came to Riverstown on April 18th and returned on June 4th. On May 20th, he received Kelly's boots from Dr McGrath. Soon after the body had been found the police had taken a number of casts of footprints from the river and field. However it was after Kelly's statement on May 15th, that two days later he was arrested and charged with the murder of Mary Breheney. Superintendent Devine noted that the times that he interviewed Kelly, he was generally aggressive, but when he was questioned about the bloodstains, he became restive and uneasy and when he signed his statement both his hands were shaking badly. However Kelly was charged before the police believed the footprint evidence weighed heavily against him and indeed it was not used at the district court until the third week.

On Saturday June 14th, Mr Justice Flattery decided that there was a case for Patrick Kelly to answer at the **Central Criminal Court in Dublin**, and he added there was a "strong case of circumstantial evidence." Somewhat surprisingly the jury trial lasted only four days - two days shorter than the preliminary case. Kelly pleaded 'not guilty' before **Mr Justice Hanna. Mr R. McLoughlin, KC, and Mr George Murnaghan prosecuted, whilst the accused, was defended by Mr Barra O'Briain, KC and Mr Oliver Gogarty. The trial opened on Monday, October 20th, 1941**.

Opening the case for the State, Mr McLoughlin said that he would say Patrick Kelly had attacked Miss Breheney with the intention of raping her and had tried to strangle her to stifle her cries for help. Then, as the police first suspected, he probably thought she was dead, and so he dragged the 'body' to the river and put her in, hoping the police would think she had drowned accidentally. The counsel said that although Riverstown was a small community, there was no suggestion that Kelly had ever even spoken to Miss Breheney, and it was probably the case that the crime was quite unpremeditated. Indeed Kelly was a newcomer to the village, having only arrived a few months before.

Mr McLoughlin said there was ample circumstantial evidence that Kelly was in the general vicinity of the murder and at the salient time and on the following day he was seen to work on his shoes, after he would have known that the police were aware of the presence of bootmarks in the field and by the river. Then, whilst on remand in Sligo Prison, he spoke to a Mr Michael Flaherty, a neighbour of the victim, saying he could not be the murderer as he was in *Ardcumber Wood* at the time Miss Breheney was attacked. Mr McLoughlin said that Kelly then went on to remind Mr Flaherty to remind Mr Baker, his employer, that his two boys saw him, something which Mr McLoughlin said was quite untrue, and done furthermore to create a false alibi.

Referring to the forensic evidence concerning the bootmarks, the prosecutor said impressions of heels of the bootmarks found near the murder scene corresponded in outline measurements with Kelly's boots. Similarly, Mr McLoughlin said bloodstains on his clothing suggested Kelly had committed the murder. The rest of the day was then taken up by the evidence of those who had seen Miss Breheney returning from the village to Rossmore.

The second day began by Mr Crevin recalling how Kelly had left his house between six and seven, whilst wearing a 'blue' overcoat. Then the jury heard from 14-year-old James Baker, and how on the day the body was found, he asked Kelly, whether he was the man his brother and sister had seen in *Cooper's Hill Wood*. The young lad told the jury that Kelly told him he couldn't have been the man as he was in another part of the wood, despite telling others, including in a signed statement that he had been in *Cooper's Hill Wood*, and by implication nearer to the murder scene. However when cross-examined by Mr O'Briain, Tommy Baker did say he had not seen any man, but nevertheless it did not diminish the fact Kelly said he was in another part of the wood.

One strong piece of evidence against Kelly, namely the finding of the handkerchief, was somewhat belittled by the defence, when it was proved to the court that a number of village shops sold it, and it was worn by many a young man in the village in their breast pockets on a Sunday. The defence were then able for the jury to hear little Tommy say, that he hadn't seen Kelly in *Cooper's Hill Wood*, and this was followed by his sister Mary, say she also had not seen any man in the wood at the pertinent time.

Another plus point for the defence was Sergeant William Halloran, who told the court that in the presence of Superintendent Devine,

Kelly had agreed to be medically examined and when he had spoke to Kelly in a cow-shed the accused showed him his overcoat and allowed the officer to take it away. And so concluded the second day of the trial.

The third day began with Dr McGrath telling the court that Miss Breheney had stood at just 4' 8", and also that she was an albino. He said he was quite satisfied she was alive when she was put into the water. The doctor also thought that she had not simply been dragged into the river, but she had been thrown in. He said that on April 29th, he examined Kelly's clothing finding both human and animal blood on them. He said the bloodstains on the label and sleeve of Kelly's overcoat, may have come from when he was beating her around the head.

However when cross-examined by the defence, Dr McGrath admitted that, old work scratches and wounds would have also accounted for the blood patterns. Most importantly said Mr O'Briain, both Kelly and the victim shared the same blood group, as did half the population, so there was no evidence her blood was on Kelly's overcoat or clothing. The defence then moved on to completely destroy the footprint evidence, when Garda J.J. Murphy from Dublin took the stand.

The officer produced a number of footprint casts that had been sent to him, and he said two of them were consistent with heel marks from Kelly's boots, but " the cast impression lacked detail or any particular characteristic." Garda Murphy said that although the marks corresponded in measurement, he could not swear that they were caused by Kelly's boots. After the court heard from Superintendent Devine to say that he had written down Kelly's statement on May 15th, the court was told that was end of the State's case.

Mr O'Briain began the defence's case by asking that the case be thrown out by the judge as "there was no evidence to connect Patrick Kelly with the case." Mr Justice Hanna rejected this, and defence counsel said he would be calling no evidence and Kelly would not be going into the witness-box himself, but he would using his final speech to vigorously champion Patrick Kelly's innocence. Thus there the third day ended.

On **Thursday, October 23rd, 1941**, on the final day of the trial, Mr O'Briain said: " It is not the duty or obligation of the prisoner in the dock to.... prove his innocence. Any one fact inconsistent with a man's guilt, is of more importance than a dozen facts consistent with his guilt." Mr O'Briain pointed out that the victim had been wearing glossy Wellington boots when she was murdered, and yet, despite the fact the prosecution said she had been dragged to the river, there were no fingerprints on the boots. Then he asked the jury to consider a piece of wool found under one of the fingernails of Miss Breheney, which had not come from Patrick Kelly's clothing.

In his summing-up, Mr Justice Hanna said the jury must be wary of circumstantial evidence as often this type of evidence was open to interpretation and also the jury must not hold it against Kelly, the fact he had not gone into the witness-box. But he did say the jury could ask himself why he hadn't done this, as he could have answered many questions, about why he ad given conflicting versions of where he was when Miss Breheney was being attack and murdered. Mr Justice Hanna said he felt the most pertinent evidence was that of the three Baker children, who at some point, had all said they had seen Kelly in the wood nearest to the field, where Miss Breheney was attacked.

The jury retired for only just over two hours, despite the fact the case against Kelly seemed weak: the footprint and bloodstain evidence seemed non-existent, whilst two of the Baker children had said they hadn't seen any man in the wood after all. What the jury were left with, was a) the fact that Kelly seemed to be keen, to suggest to some people at least, he wasn't in *Cooper's Hill Wood*, and b) was he the "man on the hill" seen by Messieurs Nangle and Higgins. Despite this Patrick Kelly was found guilty. When asked if he had anything to say why the death sentence should not be passed, he replied: "I have nothing at all."

Patrick Kelly's appeal against his conviction but this was rejected the following month in November, and he was hanged at **Mountjoy**

Prison at eight a.m., on December 18th, 1941. Ironically the local 'paper reported that the forensic evidence - bloodstains and footprints had helped to convict Kelly.

Case 7

"Murder

In The Shadow

Of

Abbey Road"

~The Extraordinary Case
Of The
Final Round~

Arthur ANDERSON (52)
Aka
Achilles Apergis
[1942]
Murder
Of
Pauline Barker (43)[3]

---

3   b. 14-May-1899

"Rice, I may not see you any more; I am going to commit a murder'. Mr Rice said, 'Don't be a fool, pull yourself together'. Anderson said, 'All right' and left …. The *Princess of Wales* pub in West Hampstead, north-west London on the last day of May in 1942 ….

'On my honour as a Greek she is lying stone dead. My honour as a Greek means more than anything. It was a clean shot, all she went was 'ough'. I put a pillow under her head to make her comfortable.' 'Arthur Anderson' - was he Greek or English …?

" …. in every case where any question arises after the verdict, an inquiry is made into the state of mind of the person charged." - The jury had sent the judge – England's most senior judge – a note …

Extraordinary war-time murder of a woman – a minor celebrity in the world of classical music – in London - shot dead by her boyfriend of some 15 years – a man who was half-Greek, and who had a fascination with guns and who prior to the murder had visited his local, telling the landlord, he was going to commit a murder ….

T he name of **Pauline Barker** has long been lost in history, but if you were interested in classical music in the mid 1920s, she was something of a household name on the BBC …. She had been born in Islington in North London in 1899, the daughter of Frederick and Lydia Barker, who had married the year before: He was a solo harpist and she was a leading contralto with the *Carl Rosa Opera Company* …. However, Frederick, left Lydia in 1910, according to the divorce documents, because 'Her violent temper and ungovernable behaviour and constant and habitual use of filthy, disgusting and obscene language and constant disagreements for ten years which have rendered his married life most unhappy. He has continued to supply her with funds for the maintenance of her and the children, and is willing to continue to do so.' Lydia was willing to let bygones be bygones, but Frederick was having none of it. 'Dear Sirs, do not waste your eloquence. There is not the remote chance of my returning to my wife. My bitterest enemy could not wish me a worse wish! Go on with your divorce. It is the only possible remedy.'

Lydia brought up Pauline and her two younger children in a house on Highgate Hill in Hampstead in north-west London, and Frederick saw them every other Saturday. Pauline became an accomplished solo harpist like her father. Aged 18, she married 47-year-old George Longfield-Beasley (he invented the Beasley-Gamewell system, an integrated fire and police alarm used in *Windsor Castle* and by several local councils); but after just three years, George sued for divorce on the grounds of Pauline's adultery. Two years later, Pauline, married Harry Lowe, who was a viola player and later the conductor of the *BBC Theatre Orchestra*. However, in 1931, Pauline had an affair with a ship's officer and she and Harry separated, although not actually divorcing until ten years later …. This effectively ended her professional career – certainly with the BBC – Before, Pauline's work, had been flourishing: She had engagements with the Russian Ballet and the BBC and played on numerous radio broadcasts from 1924 to 1930, mostly from Belfast. And it was here that she had also met yet another man …. **Achilles Apergis** …. in 1927 …. Despite his name, Apergis, was born to an English mother in Dulwich, south London …. Brought up in a middle-class family, his father was Greek and had served in its army as an officer, and Apergis himself had served in the Greek Army too …. But Apergis' main interest was cars and he ran a number of garages in the capital …. As Apergis considered himself to be somewhat English and to help 'fit in', he re-named himself **'Arthur Anderson'** …. In 1927, he found himself in Belfast, and that is where he met Pauline Barker …. they immediately began a tempestuous affair ….

Anderson had intended expanding his garage empire all over Britain and Ireland, but his venture across the Irish Sea failed, and he returned to London, and as we shall see, this failure had a profound effect on him .... Also his Greek family did not want their name associated with a car-mechanic .... Pauline, herself, owned a property in the capital and often traveled back from Belfast, and so Anderson tried to keep in contact .... It worked, and the pair began living as 'man and wife', in London .... Anderson was working in and around Kilburn as a motor mechanic briefly running the *St John's Wood Garage* in (the now famous) Abbey Road in Hampstead: the couple lived locally, and in 1937, Pauline's mum bought a large Victorian town-house – **184, Belsize Road – in West Hampstead;** the intention being to run a guest-house .... It was virtually on the corner of Abbey Road ....

However, their decade or so long relationship was peppered with domestic violence .... Anderson drank heavily, spending much of his free time in the local pubs .... He would use 'foul language' and often treated his wife roughly, something Lydia Barker was aware off, when the couple moved into Belsize Road, where she was a frequent visitor .... Anderson didn't get on with his effective 'mother-in-law', but would stop abusing Pauline when her mother saw them, sarcastically saying, 'I didn't know you had your 'seconds' around' .... Lodgers and guests alike also witnessed the abusive relationship over the years .... but it took many years to come to a head, and it was now war-time, and almost the summer of 1942 .... postal-worker, Katherine Maher, in May of that year, often heard them arguing, and Anderson hitting Pauline and once threatening to shoot her during a 'heavy' air-raid .... By now, Pauline, would often ask other females to stay in her room at night, as she feared Anderson would seriously injure her .... Pauline's mother, who now lived in Blackpool, last stayed in Belsize Road in May, leaving on the twenty-fifth; and she noted 'as usual they were very aggressive towards each other' ....

But then, on Wednesday, May 27th, 1942, after a particularly heated row, Arthur, packed up his things and left. Pauline told Katherine, it was because he was jealous of her talking with one of the lodgers, Alan Sedgwick, who had moved in less than three weeks earlier. Pauline said she was glad Arthur had gone and hoped it would be for good, although she was surprised he left so peacefully without threatening her .... She showed Katherine bruises on her leg and thigh where Arthur had pushed her over in the kitchen the previous night. *But four days later Anderson came back to Belsize Road ....*

At about one pm on the afternoon of **(Sunday) May 31ˢᵗ**, Katherine and Pauline, were talking in the kitchen, when they heard Anderson shout 'Pauline' from downstairs. Pauline called back, 'I am just serving lunch, I will be down in a minute – what do you want?' He said, 'I want to speak to you a minute.' She went downstairs and when she came back about five minutes later, she told Katherine Maher, that Anderson had said he wanted to shoot her …! Katherine looked out of the window and saw him at the front of the house – he still had a front-door key .... He started to come through the gate again, but then changed his mind and walked in the direction of the nearby *Princess of Wales* pub on the corner of Abbey Road; whilst at the same time, his brother-in-law, a Dr Hector Apergis, had pulled up outside in his car and spoke briefly to Pauline – earlier Anderson had telephoned and then seen his brother to talk about his 'marital' problems with Pauline .… The doctor then took Anderson to see their parents, before Anderson came back to West Hampstead .… Anderson hoped his brother could persuade Pauline, that the couple should get back together again .… Alfred Rice, the landlord of the *Princess of Wales*, had known 'Andy Apergis' for the past five years, and he also knew Pauline Barker; and that although they lived as 'man and wife', they weren't married. At about 7.05 pm, he spotted Anderson in the saloon-bar and thought that he'd been drinking, but was not drunk. Anderson said, 'Rice, I may not see you anymore; I am going to commit a murder'. Mr Rice said, 'Don't be a fool, pull yourself together'. Anderson said, 'All right' and left .… Back in the house, Pauline, had told Miss Maher, that the Greek doctor had wanted her to go with him in his car, but she had refused, Miss Maher, agreeing, saying: "I am very pleased you did not go, I have a feeling something is going to happen tonight and that your husband will come back." Pauline replied: "Yes, he's got the key and is sure to come in, in one of his bad tempers again." She also knew he had a gun, which she had hidden on occasions .… Anderson had used guns to fire at birds in their garden and had erected a target to shoot at too .…

That evening, at just after seven, Mr Sedgwick, was in the lounge on the ground floor, when the man he knew as 'Mr Barker' opened the lounge door asking for Mrs Barker. Mr Sedgwick replied that she was upstairs in the kitchen. 'Mr Barker' walked out and shut the door. Two minutes later, Sedgwick, heard a loud bang, followed by someone running down the stairs and the front-door slamming. When he went up to the kitchen, Mr Sedgwick, found Pauline lying on the first-floor landing step leading to the second floor, her head on a cushion, and on her back with her legs apart: she was fully dressed and her clothing had not been tampered with in any way. There was a strong smell of gunpowder, and then a large amount of blood emerging from her dress from her chest area – by the body was a bullet and some sandwiches and milk, which the lodger had asked for .... Finding no pulse, the lodger telephoned 999, and told the police what had happened. He waited at the front-door until an ambulance and the police arrived. Arthur had gone back to the pub, confessing to Alfred Rice: 'I have done it.' Mr Rice said, 'You haven't!' Anderson said, 'On my honour as a Greek she is lying stone dead. My honour as a Greek means more than anything. It was a clean shot, all she went was 'ough'. I put a pillow under her head to make her comfortable.' Arthur took an almost fully loaded Colt-45 from a holster at his waist and handed it to Mr Rice, saying what a nice gun it was – a 'beauty' - said a very worried Mr Rice. 'I don't want to get you into trouble', he said,'so if you want, I will tell the police I threw it away – in a front garden somewhere.' In order to get the gun off him, Mr Rice, said, 'Thanks old boy, I will have it.' Arthur took the empty cartridge case out and then gave Mr Rice the gun and the holster, which the landlord locked in the cellar .... He also gave him a book of *National Savings Certificates*; 'this should cover the three or four pounds I owe you' - They were in the name of 'Arthur Henderson' .... Then Anderson said, 'Buy me a double scotch because I may not see you again, and I am waiting for the police to come.' A barmaid handed the Englishman-cum-Greek a double-scotch, which he drank at the bar. Then Mr Rice went into the office to phone Anderson's brother, and the killer followed him and put sixteen bullets into Mr Rice's jacket-pocket .... Then the landlord heard an ambulance outside and realised that something serious really had happened .... As this was happening, Anderson, said to the landlord: "Aren't you going to have a drink with me, I am going to be hanged!"

Mr Rice left the pub and met the police at the house, and told them, Anderson, was waiting in the pub-bar, before returning with the officers back to the *Princess of Wales*. Minutes later, a Dr Arthur Rees, the police-surgeon arrived at the house and found Pauline Barker had been shot through the heart. Anderson had, indeed, made no attempt to flee and was arrested in the pub and taken to West Hampstead Police-Station .... Mr Rice gave the police the gun, the bullets, the holster, and the book of certificates. The post-mortem, carried out the next day by the famous pathologist, Sir Bernard Spilsbury, showed that the gun had been fired at close range; the single bullet passed through her heart and Pauline died instantly ....

To the officer leading the inquiry, Detective-Inspector Harold Cripps, Anderson said: "The shot was good, I won't say anything now." But he appeared not to know, that his girlfriend was dead until told by the police ....

Almost exactly a month later, on **Monday, June 29th, at the Old Bailey, before the Lord Chief Justice of England, Thomas Inskip, 1st Viscount Caldecote**, Arthur Anderson, pleaded 'not guilty by reason of insanity'. In court, his brother, Dr Apergis, said there was no insanity in the family – although the accused had been in poor health for the last nine months, including suffering from a bad back and pancreatitis. The defence called two eminent psychologists to demonstrate that Anderson was insane at the time he committed the offence, but the jury was not convinced. The Medical Officer at Brixton Prison also said that in the month the prisoner had been on remand, there had been no evidence of insanity, only that he was 'intensively jealous' towards the victim – an Indian lodger in the house, Indra Das, said 'Mrs Anderson' was kind and friendly to all the lodgers regardless of their sex, but if she were friendly towards any male in Anderson's presence, he would become morose and sulk .... The jury, which included four women, found **Anderson guilty of murder, after two hours retirement; but added a strong recommendation for mercy on the grounds of 'diminished responsibility'** .... Although not made public, the jury, were divided between murder and insanity, and the compromise was the recommendation – they had asked the judge, if such a recommendation would mean, that a further inquiry would be made into the prisoner's mental state .... The judge replied by way of a note, that: " …. in every case where any question arises after the verdict, an inquiry is made into the state of mind of the person charged." The inquiry came to nothing; and there was no appeal either – the Home Office were left with a premeditated murder with a firearm ….

Arthur Anderson was hanged at Wandsworth Prison by Albert Pierrepoint and Herbert Morris at nine am on Tuesday, July 21st, 1942.

The house was demolished as part of a 1960s redevelopment in the area, and there is now flats and a park where the house once stood ….

Case 8
"The Spalding Poisoning
&
The Execution Cover-Up"

"They [the jury] have found that by your hand that woman, whom you were bound to protect, that mother of your children, has met her death." Mr Justice Lawrance at the trial of Edward Bell.

'(the) young fellow carried out his gruesome duties very efficiently'. How the local media reported the execution of Bell by William Billington (but he shouldn't have been doing the job in the first place).

".... carried out the sentence in a very satisfactory manner and his conduct has been satisfactory in every respect." The cover-up: from the letter by the Under-Sheriff to the Home Office, glossing over what had happened at the execution of Bell. However at the same time the Governor of the Prison made his report in a more fuller detail.....

Edward Bell
[1899]
Murder
of
his wife Mary Eliza

Edward Bell

In True Detective's (July 2007, pg. 48) Victorian Hanging series, a short narrative of the execution of Edward Bell at Lincoln Prison appeared. Now can be revealed the full story of the crime, a murder that shocked Victorian morals, and of the subsequent 'scandal' at Bell's hanging and how the authorities reacted to the situation....

On April 6th, 1899 Mr Thomas Clayton, a farmer at Spalding Marsh a few miles to the north-east of the Lincolnshire town of Spalding employed a young man from the neighbouring small village of Weston, just a few miles to the east of the town. **Edward Bell was 26** and began working as a farm yardman and had previously been working in the village of Gedney, which was further along the main road past Holbeach. Bell was married to one, **Mary Eliza who was four years older** than him, and they had been married for six years and had two children. They lived in a cottage at Weston Marsh and had a lodger, a Mrs Emma Butters, to whom Bell on **Monday, April 24th** said that his wife was seriously ill. Two days later the local doctor, a Dr Gilbert Barritt was sent for again but apparently after Bell's wife took some of his medicine, she died; well that was at least according to Bell.... Bell seemed devastated at his loss, and Mr Clayton said he would do all he could to help.

On the previous Sunday (April 23rd) Mrs Bell had been talking to Mrs Butters saying that she felt under the weather. Next morning Mrs Bell knocked on her bedroom wall calling for help and Mrs Butters found her doubled up in pain, and she drank some brandy. During the day Bell sent a note to the doctor who despatched some medicine but it appeared too 'strong' for his wife. That night Bell went into Spalding returning with some more medicine, but at 3.45 am (Tuesday), Mrs Butters was awoken to find Mrs Bell in terrible agony; she was vomiting and passing large amounts of blood. Later that day, Dr Barritt visited twice, gave Mrs Bell some teaspoonfuls of medicine, which she was to take every hour. Mr Clayton also helped out looking after Mrs Bell until her mother, a Mrs Fox came at about seven pm, having been informed of the situation by Bell.

At 3.30 am (Wednesday) Mrs Fox called on Mrs Butters to say her daughter was gravely ill. At 12.45 am she appeared to be dying, and Bell summoned Mrs Butters to view Mary Eliza, who appeared convulsed, drawn and as if she was in terrible pain. Mrs Fox said to Bell: "Oh Ted it must be that powder", to which Bell replied 'no' in a sharp manner: Fifteen minutes later **Mrs Bell died (April 26th)**. Mrs Butters asked Bell about the powder, as she was curious about this, as Dr Barritt had not mentioned any powder as part of her daughter's medicine and Bell now seemed quite annoyed by her talking about it, tersely saying that the doctor had sent it. Six days later Mrs Butters eventually spoke to the doctor about this, but still couldn't get to the bottom of the mystery of the powder, but was told that Mrs Bell was rather a 'delicate woman', who had been ill for a week before she died.

On the evening of the previous Saturday, the day before Mrs Bell spoke to Mrs Butters about felling ill, Bell had gone into Spalding to a herbal shop owned by a Mr Algernon Molson. At first Bell asked for two ounces of **laudanum**. At the time the drug was quite legally sold and in addition to any recreational use, it was used as medicine, and Bell had complained of a toothache and wanted to use it also for cuts. He also bought some **'white mercury'** for poisoning rats. This drug was far more dangerous but Bell assured the herbalist, he knew what he was doing and gave Mr Clayton as a reference, as his employer was a well-respected member of the town. Bell signed the Poisons Register in his own name, although he gave his address as in Holbeach.

Two days later on the Monday, Bell returned and bought another ounce of the rat poison. This time Bell also asked for **arsenic** for the same purpose, but the shop was out of stock and so Bell bought some **strychnine** on the advice of Mr Molson. Finally on **Wednesday (April 26th)** Bell came into the shop saying he had injured a dog in an accident at work and wanted to put it out of its misery and was told **prussic acid** was the best for this purpose. However Bell declined to bring the dog to the premises and in the end bought some more strychnine, and furthermore Mr Clayton was unaware of any injured dog on the farm.

Mrs Fox had been told by Bell that Dr Barritt had said that her daughter was 'passing gallstones'. On the Wednesday when Mrs Fox realised her daughter was probably dying she told Bell to fetch the doctor who injected her daughter with **morphine**. The doctor left and Bell went into the town returning with more medicine. Asked by Mrs Fox why he had been so long, Bell replied that Dr Barritt had been busy seeing to someone else. It was now that Bell produced a powder, which perplexed both Mrs Fox and Mrs Butters as the doctor had not mentioned anything about a powder, when he had been in the house. Ignoring the two women's protestations, Bell went up to his wife. He then came back downstairs saying that she had taken the powder 'capitally' along with half-a-glass of soda water. Soon afterwards at dinner, Bell said to his mother-in-law, that they had done all they could for Mary Eliza. There then was a terrible death scream....

Mrs Bell was crying out in pain and it looked as if her eyes would burst out of her head. Mrs Fox thought her daughter was having a fit. Mrs Butters also rushed into the bedroom but Mrs Bell died shortly afterwards. Despite their disquiet about the powder, the death certificate recorded 'acute enteritis' as the cause of her death, and three days later she was buried in her home village of Orby near Skegness. From his insurance 'club', Bell received 10 shillings for help to pay for the funeral etc. Mrs Fox had never liked Bell and often her daughter would ask her to come to their home in Gedney as she and Bell frequently rowed.

When Dr Barritt had first come to the Bells' house on the Sunday, he thought Mary Eliza was suffering from a severe stomach upset. He later sent some medicine in a bottle, which was later broken. He saw Mrs Bell again on the Monday evening at seven. Bell said his wife's diarrhoea was better but she couldn't take the medicine. Bell went into Spalding and returned from the doctor's with a bottle of 'bismuth and pepsine'. At six am on Tuesday, he was again summoned to Weston. Dr Barritt now concluded Mrs Bell was suffering from a severe inflammation of the bowels and injected her with morphine. He said he never said the patient was passing gallstones, but, in passing, may have said the condition may have something to do with gallstones. Early on Wednesday he saw Mrs Bell again and she was passing blood. When he heard that Bell had said he was delayed in Spalding because the doctor had another case, he denied this emphatically. However despite any misgivings about Bell, on Wednesday evening Dr Barritt signed the death certificate. But as we shall see, that was far from the end of the matter. Dr Barritt was later to say that had he spoken to Mrs Butters and Mrs Fox in greater detail and had he been told, that he'd been supposed to have prescribed a powder, he would never have issued the death certificate and would have asked for an inquest at the very least. Had he known about a young woman who was now living in Huntingdonshire, he would have called the police....

Miss Mary Hodson (22) had lived next door to Mr and Mrs Bell in her parent's home. The Bells had left Gedney because of her, for in the language of the day she and Mr Bell had been 'inappropriately intimate' with each other. Despite Bell moving away he continued writing to her, although she later burnt all their correspondence. And on April 29th, the day of his wife's funeral, Bell telegraphed Miss Hodson and they met two days later, when he asked her if she 'would have him' to which she replied yes. The girl had no idea that Mrs Bell had been ill, only that she had died. Furthermore she was desperate to marry Bell, as she thought she was pregnant. She had not gone to Spalding immediately after she knew Mrs Bell had died, as her father had forbade her. Until it emerged she was having an affair with Bell, she and his wife had always been on good terms. Bell was quite open to his wife that he was having sex with Miss Hodson but simply ignored her pleadings for it to stop until she finally persuaded them to leave Gedney after a series of beatings she had received from her husband.

Eventually all this reached the ears of the police by way of an anonymous letter saying that Dr Barritt had never given any powder as medicine for Mrs Bell. The letter had been received by Mrs Fox, and on May 9th, a Superintendent Osbourne interviewed Bell. He asked him about the powder. Bell told him it was a magnesia for her stomach and he had bought it in Spalding. However he now said he hadn't got it from the doctor and he denied ever buying any poison from the herbalist. He was then brought before an Identity Parade that evening and Mr Molson picked him out as the customer. The police were fully aware of who Miss Hodson was and Edward Bell was charged with the murder of his wife. Superintendent Osbourne then went with an Inspector Peach to the Bells' home where they took away three bottles of medicine, including the suspicious broken one.

The body of Mrs Bell was exhumed and a *post-mortem* carried by a Dr Francis Walker. He was under no doubt that she had suffered and died from mercury and strychnine poisoning. Parts of the internal organs were then sent to a Dr Stevenson, at Guy's Hospital in London. He was a scientific analyst who did work for the Home Office. He said the bowels showed clear signs of mercury poisoning, and he found traces of the same poison and strychnine in the stomach, bowels and liver. Dr Stevenson said that the strychnine came first followed by the mercury. He said that having read the statements of Mrs Fox and Mrs Butters, they were the classic signs of strychnine poising. Dr Stevenson believed eight to ten grains, as much as would fit on a six pence, had been administered. He said there was no way such an amount could be taken by accident or in error.

Edward Bell appeared at the **Lincoln Assizes before Mr Justice Lawrance on Tuesday, July 4th, 1899 in a trial that lasted just the day**. Given the nature of the supposed motive for the murder, the public gallery was packed, mainly with females. **Messrs Appleton and Bonner** prosecuted and after the former had told the jury that this was a clear-cut case of murder for personal gain, the defence began their case. Bell pleaded total innocence and his case was put by **Mr Bonsey**. He said that Bell would now admit buying the poison from the herbalist, but surely he had bought so much this would point to his innocence: here was hardly a man who'd secretly and surreptitiously intended to murder his wife. However Mr Bonsey refused to call Bell as a witness[4] and then dramatically refused to call any more evidence, and it was described by the media as a 'brief and futile defence.'

In his summing up, the judge began by addressing the curious mystery of the letter received by Mrs Fox, as it appeared that it was in the handwriting of Bell himself. It read: "I cannot bear it any longer; I am miserable. The doctor did not give the powder. Going away tomorrow." But the judge was not absolutely sure and conceded, that it could have been written by someone *au fait* with

---

4   The law allowing the accused to give evidence on his on behalf had just come
    in 1898.

the case wanting the police ultimately to believe it was some sort of 'confession' by Bell. Mr Justice Lawrance said there seemed no doubt that Mrs Bell had been poisoned by the two very same poisons her husband had bought and signed for, and that the accused had put the poison in the broken bottle that had originally come from Dr Barritt, in order to make his wife more willing to drink it. He then turned on Miss Hodson describing her behaviour as 'shameful' both before and after Mrs Bell's death. He then told the jury it was for them to decide whether that relationship was motive enough for 'cold-blooded' murder. The judge looked at the jury and nodded and they nodded back and without leaving their box found Edward Bell guilty of the murder of his wife. Bell shook his head when asked if he had anything to say before he was sentenced to death.

The black cap on his head, the judge then said to the prisoner: "They [the jury] have found that by your hand that woman, whom you were bound to protect, that mother of your children, has met her death." He said he had no doubt Bell murdered for the 'lust' of Miss Hodson. He added: "A more cruel, a more deliberate, a more cold-blooded murder, I have never heard or read of .... for that crime you must follow your victim, and I would beg of you to entertain no spark of hope that your life will be spared." The judge then said that even at this late hour that the condemned should repent his sins. Throughout, Bell remained unmoved and heard the death sentence impassively. He was then taken away to the death-cell.

Miss Hodson was once again taken from the court with police protection, as on her arrival before the trial, she had been spotted by those wanting to gain entrance to the court, and had been 'hooted and hissed' and yelled at. This affected the young woman and she continually sobbed whilst she gave evidence and after the trial, Miss Hodson was quickly taken away by the police to an undisclosed village police-station outside Lincoln, although the mob quickly discovered this was at Waddington. When some tried to follow the cab they were prevented from doing so by the police, who warned them not to travel to Waddington.

With such a murder there was no question of a reprieve and the Home Secretary, Matthew White-Ridley, declined Edward Bell mercy and his execution was set for **Tuesday, July 25th, 1899 at nine am at Lincoln Prison**. It was considered particularly treacherous that Bell had given his wife strychnine telling her, it was medicine from the doctor. The day before his execution Bell wrote a letter from the death-cell. It read:

" ..... I have enjoyed wonderfull [sic] good health, all the time I have been in prison. I have slept well and enjoyed my food. But Miss M.S. Hodson is the cause of my Death and my wife .... she will have to suffer either in this world or the next. But God knows all. I hope this will be a warning to all young people, both single and married. Women will get you into trouble, but will not help you out. She knows as much about my sad case as I do. But I do believe God [h]as forgiven me all my sins. Goodbye to all, my friends EDWARD BELL"

That night Bell retired to bed at eight pm and soon dropped off. The death-watch prison-officers reported he turned over twice in the night but otherwise slept in the same position until he was awoken at six am, by the changing over of the officers. He opened his eyes and was fully refreshed and ready for his final ordeal. A bonus for the authorities was the fact that Bell also confessed, saying that he had given Mary Eliza more arsenic than the police had found!

When the clock on Lincoln Cathedral struck nine, it meant Bell had been executed, but what the public didn't release was the 'scandal' that was behind the execution and this was to cause ructions in the Home Office in London. The local media did report that James Billington, who had originally been requested to carry out the hanging, had been taken ill and had been replaced by a son. It was reported that the 'young fellow carried out his gruesome duties very efficiently' and 'had been refused to be hurried' and indeed, it was reported he carried out the execution 'perfectly'. But what really happened?

On the day and after the execution the Governor of Lincoln Prison, Major Patrick Briscoe filed his report with the Home Office (see sheet six). The letter said that James Billington, the chief executioner since late 1891, sent a telegram to the prison saying that he would arrive at four pm (on the day before the execution). However at six pm one of his sons **William (24)** turned up saying his father was too ill to attend. This of course caused a bit of a panic and the governor spoke with the Under-Sheriff of the County, Mr Charles Scorer, who legally had to organise, witness and was ultimately responsible for the execution. He interviewed William Billington who said he'd carried out executions before, but said that he had never carried out an execution without his father being present. He said when his father had been present there had been no other assistants there. Apparently satisfied that William could do the job, Mr Scorer gave the go-ahead.

However in the governor's report (sheet seven) Major Briscoe said that William seemed not confident when tying the rope to the beam and he seemed similarly unsure what to do with the rubber washer, which secured the loop on the rope against the condemned man's neck, and had to be showed what to do by the prison-officers. This was in complete contrast to the Under Sheriff's report (sheet 13), also penned on the 25th. Whilst it clearly referred to the fact that James Billington was replaced by William, he concluded by saying, that the latter "carried out the sentence in a very satisfactory manner and his conduct has been satisfactory in every respect", and indeed William Billington was paid the £11 5s for the 'job' by the Sheriff.

With such a difference of opinion the Home Office launched an inquiry (sheets 12/13 is a summary of this part and the handwriting is great!!). The Prison Commission was ordered to trawl through their execution reports since James Billington became chief hangman and could find no reference to William ever having participated in an execution as a 'number one' or assistant. Father and Son were asked for an explanation. On August 4th, James wrote to Major Briscoe from his home in Bolton. He explained that on the night of July 23rd/24th, he was taken very ill with the flu, although a telegram was sent as he thought he might be better on the Monday. But he couldn't make it and he told William to tell the Under-Sheriff that he could carry out the execution as well as him. The next day William, who also lived in Bolton, wrote:

" I must tell you that I have never been to an execution before, and I am very sorry that I told you I had, but I should not have undertook it, if I had not been confident that I should do it in a proper manner... I was the only person that my father could trust."

William Billington concluded the letter saying he hoped he would not be looked on unfavourably in the future. Ultimately he was accepted as an official executioner, although not until he had tested the patience of the Home Office again, by assisting at a further five executions in 1899 as assistant to his father whilst not being on the official list. The explanation given by James Billington was that his other son Thomas, who had acted as an assistant before, had disappeared. Eventually in 1900 the Home Office decided to finally rationalise this system and all executioners had to be formally trained and a proper list sent to the Under-Sheriffs and Governors throughout the country, and only those on the list could participate at a hanging.

James Billington died in December 1901 having executed approximately 150 killers in Britain and Ireland. A month later Thomas died, having eventually returned to the fold: he had assisted in about 20 cases. Another son John, who had participated in over 40 hangings, died in October 1905, whilst William died in March 1934, aged 59. He had been involved in nearly 90 executions, although he alone was sacked for problems relating to drink.

Case 9
"Nottingham Shop-Keeper Attacked And Killed In Her Own Bedroom"

John Constantine
(1960)
Murder
Of
Lily Parry

A brutal murder of an elderly shop-keeper during a burglary. At the killer's subsequent trial he claimed that he was merely an accomplice to the burglary, and that a friend was the actual killer ....

April 22nd, 1960, was a Friday night and had been another night of fun for 15 year old Judith Reddish; she had been out down the pub with her friends and then it was on to a local rock'n'roll dance. At 10.45 p.m. she arrived exhausted at her lodgings, **a shop, at 14 Summers Street in Nottingham.**

Miss Reddish who had just left school was lodging in the city and enjoyed staying at **Mrs Lily Parry's small general store and greengrocers shop**. She had come from a family of 13 and liked the peace and quiet. Also the old lady didn't nag her and didn't mind if she came home late, although she wouldn't allow boyfriends into the house!

When Judith woke at seven she made her way to the bath-room, when she let out a deathly scream: blood was seeping out of Mrs Parry's bedroom, gently lapping against the landing carpet. Stealing herself with several deep breaths, nervously Judith turned the door-knob. Inside Mrs Parry was lying on the floor, fully clothed, with blood dripping from several head wounds. She was groaning incoherently.

Judith called out to the 76 year old but received no response. She then called the police. Within five minutes a team of Nottingham C.I.D. detectives had arrived. A senior policeman took Judith aside and after carefully questioning she was taken to the hospital, and then to her mother's, where she was kept for 48 hours, under the doctor's observation.

Her mother Ruby said Juddith was a 'bag of nerves' and that she was deeply upset, because the old lady had been very kind to her daughter.

The police immediately suspected a robbery, that had gone badly wrong; a back door glass panel had been broken. In addition another local shop-keeper, Mrs O'Loughlin, told the police that in the early hours of the morning she had been woken by a fight between several young men. The police investigated this but it had no connection on the attack on Mrs Parry.

Mrs Parry's next door neighbour, Mrs Burnell said that Mrs Parry had lived in the shop for thirty years and was crippled with arthritis. But despite this she worked hard to keep her business going.

Mrs Burnell also told the police that Mrs Parry had a dog, who would bark at any stranger or noise; she had heard nothing:

"I came home about 1 o'clock in the morning but the street was deserted. If there had been a bang we would have thought it was a car or lorry, many of which park in the street overnight."

Also Mrs Parry had recently moved her bedroom from a room that was next to Mrs Burnell's own bedroom. In the past if Mrs Parry needed help she would bang on the wall.

Mrs Parry who was rushed to Nottingham General Hospital was operated on but her condition was given as 'very serious'; she was clinging on to the very thread of life.

At a press conference the city's Chief Constable Mr T. Moore, said the attack had taken place between 11 p.m. and when the attack was discovered. He noted it was fortunate that Judith Reddish had not been woken by the intruder. It now also emerged that Mrs Parry's other neighbour had heard a noise at 1.00 a.m. The police also needed help to find the murder weapon: "If any member of the public comes across anything which might have been used as the weapon, it will most probably be bloodstained and may have been thrown away in a corner or back-yard.", said Mr Moore.

He continued:

"The assailant too, will no doubt be heavily bloodstained on his clothing .... likewise if anyone hands in any bloodstained clothing to cleaners or laundries, we should like to be told."

The team of detectives was led by Det. Supt. Rex Fletcher, who said he was setting-up a mobile unit in the local district and that teams of C.I.D. officers were questioning known petty criminals in the area.

Following an examination of Mrs Parry's facial wounds and the forensic evidence the police believed a crow-bar or tire-lever had been used and a description of one was given to the local press. It was said to be 15 inches long and made of hard cold steel. It was indeed a viscous weapon. The police had visited several local shops and believed it had been newly purchased.

During the weekend the police dragged the city's canal borrowing a new electro-magnet from their colleagues in the Lancashire Force. It proved extremely fruitful for a crow-bar was discovered, but was it the murder weapon ? The police had found no finger-prints at the shop and could not take any from the crow-bar.

The police also now knew that between -20 and -30(about -600 in today's money) in bank notes had been stolen, as well as some of Mrs Parry's keys.

Even more fruitful for the police was that fact that the shaking up of the local petty criminals produced a name: **John Constantine, a 22 year old box-maker**, from nearby Waterloo Promenade. Arrested on Monday, two days after the attack, he readily confessed to attacking Mrs Parry, thinking that the old lady was not badly injured. He said: "A figure loomed up from the back .... I panicked .... and hit it."

Constantine was then charged with wounding with intent to murder and on the following day made a five minute appearance before the city's magistrates at the Guildhall. Constantine was also able to confirm that the police had retrieved his crow-bar. Whilst having a cup of police tea he said: "This tastes like canal water and I remembered that I had dropped it in the canal."

He added: "I thought the bedroom was empty and as I bent down to pick up a bag a figure loomed up from the back. I panicked and hit it; I never meant to hurt anyone, honest."

The following day the brave shop-keeper died. The charge against John Constantine was now extremely serious. Not only murder, but *capital* murder, as robbery was the motive for the crime.

Constantine stood trial at the Birmingham Assizes before Mr Justice Ashworth in during a three-day trial beginning on July 20th. Defended by Mr Ralph Brown Q.C., Constantine was not simply going to go the gallows without a fight.

He now claimed that he was an accomplice to the attack on Mrs Parry and had named the actual killer. The man he accused was Joseph Colothan, a former workmate and current lodger of Constantine's, who was severely rebuked by the judge for speaking about the case to another witness; prosecuting Mr Joseph Grieves Q.C. said that Colothan would be kept under strict police observation.

Constantine had claimed that he had discussed with Colothan the robbery on Mrs Parry's shop, but cross-examined by Mr Brown, Colothan denied being in the shop. Mr Colothan was accused of talking to a Mr Andrew Clarkson about the Friday night of the murder.

Mr Clarkson, a butcher, told the court that he and Colothan had visited several pubs outside the city before returning to Clarkson's car at 1.15 a.m. It was observed that Colothan and Clarkson had been talking in the men's toilets. Clarkson said that Colothan wanted to know what types of questions he had been asked.

Questioned by the prosecution Constantine claimed he had met Colothan a few minutes before the attack at Colothan's lodgings at 166 Hayden Road. Mr Grieves said: "The evidence you are giving in the witness box is false ?"- "No, sir", replied the box-maker.

In all Constantine was in the witness box for four and half hours. He said that after he and Colothan had broken in, he remained downstairs whilst Colothan went upstairs and he heard several short thuds.

However the police had spoken to Colothan's landlord a Mr Walker who said that Colothan came in at about 1.30 a.m., somewhat drunk and had to woken at ten on Saturday morning. Mr Grieves told the jury if there had been one shred of evidence against Colothan he would have been charged with murder.

The forensic evidence now showed Mrs Parry died at about one o'clock and this proved Colothan could not have possibly been the murderer, for he was drinking in the village of Underwood, a dozen miles from the city. Mr Grieves said: "Colothan is a truthful man whose word you ought to accept on the all important matter as to where he was that night.

Contrast this with Constantine's first statement while Mrs Parry was still alive and contrast that with the evidence now being given by him. "Mr Grieves also pointed out that Constantine had tried to suggest his landlord, Mr Walker, was 'in' on the plan to rob Mrs Parry.

Mr Brown suggested that Constantine's first statement to the police was mis-interpretated and he suggested Mrs Parry's dog could hold the key as what had happened.

He said: "

If that dog could speak, it would tell you whether one or two men went into that room. You may say; "It cannot be." It cannot in sound but sometimes we speak of inference.

That little creature was there throughout the night. If there had been but one man prowling around looking for money, turning upside down tins, opening boxes, going upstairs and coming down again, do you not think that he inference is that the dog would have set up some sort of commotion.

Remember Constantine said: " I had to fuss that dog to look after him to keep him quiet." In a desperate bid to save his client's life Mr Brown said the jury could return a verdict of non-capital murder or manslaughter in that Constantine admitted being in the shop during the robbery.

In his summing-up Mr Justice Ashworth said that certain points must be taken into consideration, when listening to Colothan's evidence, namely that he had been accused of murder! But also the fact that Constantine was a liar did not make him a murderer.

The judge then picked up the crow-bar and waved in the direction of the jury and said: "Who struck Lily Parry ?"

The jury retired for an hour and three quarters before declaring Constantine guilty of capital murder. Asked if he had anything to say, Constantine shook his head and stared blankly towards the judge.

Mr Justice Ashworth donned the black cap and said: "You have been convicted, and in my view rightly convicted, of a truly brutal murder. Worse than that, in the course of your defence you have not shrunk from charging innocent young men of the crime of which you are Guilty .... You shall suffer death in the manner authorised by law."

An appeal was rejected on August 15th and the date of the hanging set for September 1st, 1960 at Lincoln Prison a small crowd gathered outnumbered by nine policemen; It was five years since the last hanging at Lincoln, and nearly a year since the last execution in England, when the infamous German police-killer, Guenther Podola was hanged.
The night before the hanging Constantine's young wife Valerie visited her husband for the last time; she left in tears and was accompanied by the prison chaplain the Rev. Geoffrey Druitt.

At six minutes passed eight the prison-gates swung open and the small crowd went home, satisfied the law had taken its course. **Harry Allen and his assistant Royston Rickard** had carried out their duties expeditiously as usual.

It is interesting to compare Constantine's fate to the previous death sentence passed in England in June. It was an almost identical murder, that of a Blackburn pawn-broker, during a robbery. But in this case Mihaly Pocze was reprieved.

Case 10
"The Dark Secret
Of
Allotment 48"

"What is all this gossip about me?" - Percy Atkins, just under a month after his wife was last seen alive ….

Percy Atkins[5] (29)
[1922]
Murder
Of
His Wife Maud (27)

---

5   Some sources have Atkin but the police file and BDM has Atkins.

Percy James Atkins Aged 29
The Murderer

Maud Atkins Aged 27
The Victim

Shocking case of a young Derby woman buried alive in a shallow grave on an allotment owned by her husband and bigamist, and a man who had told so many lies it must have been difficult for him to keep up with them all. In the end the pressure became too much as he had set himself a deadline for his new 'wife', but still had the old one ....

In **1922** it would be many years before there would be a Bank Holiday on **New Year's Day** and so Mr Thomas Gore found himself walking to work across the Highfield Allotments in the Chaddesden area of east Derby. The railway-worker was just passing the anonymously named 'Allotment 48' when his dog began scratching furiously at the earth. As there was a mound, Mr Gore assumed something had been buried, perhaps a dead dog. But Mr Gore wanted to get to work and decided he might have a look at the mound the following day.

The next day Mr Gore had the late morning off and so armed with a fork, he thought he would, after all, examine the mound on the allotments. As the railway-worker dug down he came across some clothes and thought they must have been discarded. However as he dug deeper he suddenly realised he had uncovered a body .... the body of a dark-haired young woman. Mr Gore left 'Allotment 48' immediately to look for a policeman. At the time Chaddesden was still a village, and it was not until a quarter-past twelve that he found an officer, Constable Frank Holmes. He accompanied Mr Gore back to the allotments and the pair took turns in digging out the body. Eventually they had cleared enough earth, down to about two-feet, to see that the body was clothed, but had decomposed.

By the head of the body was a hat and shawl and next to it a broken spade. Telling Mr Gore to guard the spot, Constable Holmes returned to the local police-station. A number of officers then returned to the allotments along with Dr John Southern who carried out a brief examination of the scene. He noted that the body was on its left side, the hands being drawn up to the head. The left hand lay under the woman's head, while the right lay on her face. After the body was hauled out of the ground, the doctor noted a small amount of blood where the head had been resting.

Obviously the first priority was to identify the body. One potential lead for the police was that on the body was a card, which had the name of a man and woman and address on it – could this be the dead woman? A check with the central police-station in Derby revealed that the woman's name had been on the missing persons list since November. The names on the card and the missing persons report saw the police visit a house in Francis Street near the city's race-course, a house that had once been rented by a **Mr and Mrs Percy and Maud Atkins, who were aged 29 and 27.**

The body in the grave was clearly that of a young woman and it was Maud Atkins that was on the missing persons list. She had not been seen alive since **Monday, November 21st**. To make matters more complicated, Atkins, a railway-worker, was himself now missing, along with the couple's two young children. The Atkins' had themselves sub-let rooms in the house and one couple, the Butchers, knew them well. Very quickly the police were able to determine, that the body was that of Mrs Atkins, although her features were so distorted she could not be identified in the normal way, and it was done so, by her hair and her rather large front teeth. Mr Henry Butcher, who also worked on the railways, said the couple had moved into Francis Street in the previous summer. Mr Butcher's wife,

Hilda, told the police that the boots Mrs Atkins had been wearing had been given to her by Mrs Butcher. Given the disappearance of the husband and children, the police began an extensive search and began digging in the rest of Highfield Allotments. They found nothing.

The Butchers were able to give the police detailed information about the Atkins and their domestic lives. When the Butchers had first moved in Mrs Atkins had been staying with her family in Huntingdonshire helping out on their farm in the village of Buckden. She returned to Derby in the third week of October with the children. It was clear to the Butchers that all was not too well with the Atkins' and on Monday, November 14th, Atkins told Mr Butcher that he was leaving and going to live in the Normanton area of Derby. He said he had given the owners' of the house a week's notice and told the Butchers that if they wanted to stay on they should speak to them. Five days later Atkins left leaving his wife and children to sleep on the floor.

Over the next two days the Butchers saw both Atkins and his wife, together, a few times, the last being at 2.15 pm on the Monday, when the couple left Francis Street. As they left, Mrs Atkins called out to Mrs Butcher: "I'm not going for good …. I'll call to see you again. I'll leave the irons and I'll fetch them on Thursday." That same Monday evening Percy Atkins popped back into Francis Street to collect some outstanding rent and a few pieces of small furniture.

Fortunately the Atkins' youngest child, a little girl, was found alive and well at her paternal grandmother, who lived in the same Huntingdonshire village as Mrs Atkins' family. However they had no idea where the other child, a little boy was, and on January 3rd the police took the decision to make a public appeal for their whereabouts. Percy Atkins was described as: "Height: five feet six or seven inches; clean shaven, grey eyes, long dark hair, brushed back from the forehead; stiff build; upper false teeth, two believed missing in front; tattoo resembling (a) triangle on the right wrist; addicted to biting his finger nails; recently suffered from boils on one arm. Total abstainer but a smoker." As to a possible motive for

Maud Atkins' death, the police had discovered that her husband had just recently 'married' another woman, who had been duped ….

Miss Margaret Milton, who also lived in Derby, told the police she had first met Atkins at a whist drive in the autumn of 1920. Very quickly they were seeing each other; Atkins saying that he was a *single* man living *near* to Francis Street. The deception continued and Atkins proposed to Miss Milton who readily accepted. To keep the lie going, Atkins said he had bought some new furniture for their future home and that the reason she hadn't met any of his friends was that most of them had gone abroad! Then it all came unstuck. On November 10th, Miss Milton's next-door neighbour told the girl, that Atkins was already married. Atkins immediately responded that he had, indeed, been married, but his wife had just died, although after he had met Miss Milton. He said she had died from 'galloping consumption'. Rather oddly Atkins told his girlfriend that he hadn't told her the 'truth', as he thought she would have not been interested in him.

Miss Milton told Atkins she no longer wanted to see him anymore, which caused him problems, as his son had been staying with her, albeit he had said it was his nephew! However Miss Milton was desperate to marry and agreed that if she could see the death certificate she would go ahead with the marriage. Another lie was forthcoming when Atkins said that the document was with his mother for safe-keeping, but he would immediately write to her to ask for it: Atkins had bought a few more days for himself. All seemed to be working as Miss Milton agreed that Atkins' daughter could also move in with her, ahead of the wedding, although once again, he lied, saying it was his niece.

On November 14th, despite not seeing the death certificate, Atkins and Miss Milton married. They returned to her home with the two children. However on December 12th, a problem arose. A neighbour from Francis Street, a Mrs Cook, came to Atkins' new home, along with a number of other interested parties, asking where Maud Atkins was. Atkins was at work and the obvious problem for him would be that Mrs Butcher had seen Maud on November 21st. When he returned home his new 'wife' launched into a blistering attack on him, asking him what was going on. Atkins tried a few more lies, before finally saying, that if she went to the police, he would be prosecuted for bigamy.

Atkins told Margaret that he had last seen his wife on November 21st on the Derwent Bridge, which is in the city-centre on the River Derwent and is the start of the Nottingham Road. He said that this was at nine-thirty pm. He went on to say, that they had quarreled and she stormed off. It was clear to Atkins that his new 'wife' wouldn't be standing by him and so he decided to leave. He took the children to Huntingdonshire but his mother wouldn't look after the boy and so Atkins returned to Margaret pleading with her to look after him for the time being. Despite putting herself in potential trouble with the police, she agreed to help, although she didn't see Atkins again until December 17th, when they met up in Manchester. Soon afterwards he returned to pick up his son. Margaret last saw Atkins on Christmas Eve. After that he seemed to have vanished into thin air, as no-one else could recall seeing him after that date.

However as it turned out the police appeal for information about Atkins and his son was not needed when it appeared on January 3rd, as late on the day before, the police had visited a sister of Atkins who lived in New Malden, in south-west London. Atkins was arrested in connection with his wife's death. When charged with his real wife's murder, Percy Atkins replied: "I would rather not say anything." Just over a month later Percy Atkins appeared at the **Derby Assizes on Thursday, February 16th, 1922, before Mr Justice Horridge, in a trial was to last two days**.

Opening the case for the **Prosecution, Sir Ryland Adkins** said that after the victim had been seen by the Butchers at 2.15 pm on November 21st, a Mr Ernest Cook, whose wife had left the deputation to Atkins' new address to ascertain where his wife was, saw her at two-thirty, near the Cattle Market in Chaddesden, walking towards the city-centre. Mr Cook said that on December 8th, he had seen Atkins on the Derwent Bridge and asked about his wife and had been told she was in Huntingdonshire as her father had just died. Mr Cook noted that Atkins was suffering very badly from boils on his arms.

A Mr Thomas Greasley told the court that he had helped Atkins move his furniture from Francis Street to the new address on November 21st. He didn't know Mrs Atkins and as the men spoke he saw a young woman walking towards Atkins to speak to him and he asked him: "Who's the tottie Percy?" Atkins replied that it was his wife and Mr Greasley immediately apologized. Later that evening, at half-past six, Mr Greasley went back to Francis Street to help with the last few bits of furniture. As they were finishing up, Mr Greasley saw Atkins put a small hammer into his jacket pocket …. Mr Adkins told the jury that later that night by a canal near the allotments, two men returning from a football match saw the accused and a young woman, who was a couple of feet behind him. The men could not hear what words were being said and neither of the men knew Mrs Atkins.

However Mr Adkins said that the victim was still alive at eleven pm. A railway guard, a Mr Henry Belderstone said that he had just turned onto the Nottingham Road near the river when he saw Atkins and his wife, whom he had known for several years. Fellow work colleague, a Mr Elijah Hilton, who also knew Mrs Atkins well, did not see her face but described her clothing, and it was exactly that, which had been found in the grave. Mr Adkins suggested that the couple walked from the Nottingham Road to the allotments shortly afterwards and it was here that the prisoner murdered his wife.

The court next heard from a Mr Richard Sharman who lived on the Nottingham Road and who knew Atkins well. He said that at 10.45 am on the following day he saw Atkins walking from the direction of the allotments. He said Atkins looked really rough, as if he had been outside all night, and his clothing and boots were wet through. Some four hours earlier Atkins had attempted to go into work but looked very ill and said he couldn't stay at work. It appeared to his immediate manager that Atkins had a sore throat but amazingly on November 23rd, he was at work at his usual time and appeared to have made a remarkable recovery.

It was now that the jury were told the damming evidence that 'Allotment 48' was rented by …. none other that Percy Atkins.

Furthermore the allotments' secretary, a Mr Robert Eggleton, told the police that where the grave was, had been the only area of the plot, that Atkins had ever worked on and he had been renting it since 1918 and had, indeed, been the subject of a number of complaints about not looking after his plot. When asked about the digging, Atkins told the allotment association that he was going to plant an apple tree.

A Mrs Annie Ekins, the victim's sister-in-law, told the court that she received a letter on December 2nd, from the prisoner, saying that Maud had died on the previous Sunday, November 27th. He said that she had caught a 'nasty chill' and had already been buried. When the relatives arrived in Francis Street, of course, Atkins had left. It was at this point that Mrs Cook organised everyone and they went to his new address and confronted his new 'wife'. At this stage no-one actually thought a murder might have been committed and, indeed, on December 19th, Atkins who was at his parents' home in Buckden approached the local 'bobby' Constable Richard Hodson and asked: "What is all this gossip about me?"

The officer remained aloof, to which Atkins told yet another lie saying that he and his wife had decided to move and in doing so, their bedding had become caught in the rain. That night Atkins said his wife refused to sleep in the bed, but slept on the floor instead. By the following Sunday (November 27th), she had died from pneumonia. He then told the officer that he had then married Margaret Milton, although he had actually married her on November 14th! Atkins was clearly not confused by his lying, informing the officer that were there further talk about him, he would be seeking the advice of a solicitor. To a number of people he had told different stories of when his wife had died. However the cemetery where Maud Atkins had been supposedly buried had no such records and overall it was very easy to expose the prisoner as a habitual liar.

Dr Southern, who had also carried out the *post-mortem* on the victim said that despite the advanced state of decomposition, he could see no marks of violence on the outer skin of the body, but under the skin he found small amounts of blood under the tissues of the neck and small bruises just under the left temple. Although the doctor told the court that he had initially told the police, he believed the victim had been strangled, he now said that, he believed she had been hit or stunned by a blow to the head with some type of blunt instrument and worst of all, she had been still alive when she was buried and so she would have suffocated, although it was almost certain, that she was unconscious by this stage. He said that the position of her hands had prevented soil going into her mouth, something he thought he would have seen if she had been suffocated, and so initially he didn't think she had suffocated.

Percy Atkins gave evidence on his own behalf. He said that he told Maud about Margaret Milton on November 20th, six days after they married. He said that after a heated argument and being threatened with the police, he said that Maud left him intending to catch the midnight train to Huntingdonshire with their children, but she didn't go. He agreed that on the night of November 21st, he and Maud had been walking towards the allotments. He said they had been arguing about who would look after the children, when Maud threw down her wedding ring. He claimed he spent some time looking for the ring before then looking for his wife, who now appeared to have disappeared.

The prisoner now stunned the court by saying that he then stumbled over his wife's body – she was bleeding from the nose, ears and mouth having fallen from a bridge onto a large pile of stones, he claimed. Atkins said he realised she was dead, and in a panic, he carried the body to his allotment, as he remembered digging the hole for the apple tree. He took the body and then in the cover of darkness he returned at about five-thirty am and buried her. Dr Southern was re-examined by Mr Adkins and he said the whole story was absurd, as there were no marks whatsoever on the body consistent with such a fall. Adding to the suggestion by the prosecution that the murder was premeditated, Mr Adkins also pointed out to the jury, that the accused had dug the hole before he had met up with his wife, and that the tale of the apple tree was a lie. Atkins had been **defended by Mr Henry Hollingdrake Maddocks** but he informed the judge he would not be calling any witnesses, bar the prisoner, but suggested it was open to the jury to return a verdict of manslaughter.

After just 11 minutes deliberation on **Friday, February 17ᵗʰ,** the jury found Percy Atkins guilty of murder. As he was being sentenced to be hanged, Margaret Milton was heard moaning and weeping in the public gallery. In the corridors outside the court and outside the courthouse large numbers of people had gathered and showed their approval at the guilty verdict. On March 20ᵗʰ an appeal was dismissed in London. The defence had once again suggested the issue of a finding of manslaughter had not been adequately put by the judge, particularly as the defence had felt that the judge should have warned the jury more strongly to be wary of the evidence of Dr Southern on how exactly the victim had died. Mr Maddocks said, in his opinion, it was not proven that Atkins had intended to kill his wife: indeed, if he buried his wife alive, but believed she was dead, this did not make him a murderer, unless the initial attack had been designed to kill – but no-one had shown how the blows had been dealt.

When the case was presented to the **Home Secretary, Mr Edward Shortt**, they were faced with a slight dilemma, as a sister of Atkins had informed the police, that Maud had threatened to commit suicide before. However this fell under the same area as the accident defence put forward by Atkins – and had been disproved, as there were no marks on the body. It was decided that there could be no reprieve as the crime appeared to have been, indeed, premeditated. Mr Shortt thought it most significant that Atkins had bigamously married on November 14ᵗʰ, telling Margaret Milton that he would be moving in with her on November *21ˢᵗ*. ….

On Friday, April 7ᵗʰ, 1922 Percy Atkins was executed at Nottingham Prison[6] by John Ellis and Robert Baxter.

---

6   Executions had not been carried out at Derby Prison since 1907 – the case of last person hanged there - William Slack ….

Case 11
"The Strange Request"

Piotr Maksimowski
(1950)
Murder
of
Mrs Dilys Campbell

A Pole, who having been convicted of the murder of his married girlfriend, asked the judge if he could be shot instead of being hanged, a request which was denied. Indeed the Pole had rejected legal aid at the magistrates court, only to have this request rejected too.

It was early in the morning of **New Year's Eve, 1949,** at Beaconsfield police-station and the three officers on duty were expecting no more trouble than a few people leaving friend's houses, who might be a little drunk. Indeed the officers expected nothing less and were quite happy to excuse such behaviour.

However at exactly 3.45 a.m. there was a knock at the station-door. The officers had heard no sound beforehand so guessed it wasn't any partygoers. When Inspector S. Jennings opened the door, he was shocked to see a man, holding out his wrists, which were covered in blood.

The officer helped the man into the station, noticing that he smelt of drink, although wasn't apparently drunk. The man's shoes were on his wrong feet and his face and clothes were splattered with blood. Then before the officers could ascertain his details, he spoke.

The man, who spoke with an eastern European accent, stunned the three officers by saying: " I did it with the razor. I did the same to the girl in the wood. She is dead – We both wanted to die."

Despite being cautioned that he should say no more, the man went on: "She must be dead. We both wanted to die. I cut her with a knife and razor, then she did not want to die. I cut myself and put a blanket over her. "

The man, who said he was Polish, told the officers that he and the girl had stopped on the Slough Road, midway between Beaconsfield and Slough. He said that they had walked a few hundred yards from the main road, where they decided to both commit suicide at a place called Burtley Wood.

Then the Pole gave his name as **Piotr Maksimowski**. He said he was 33-years-old and was employed by Slough Council as a dustman. He said he lived in a hostel in a labour camp in Great Bower Wood, which was a mile from Beaconsfield and would take the officers to the body. He explained that the body would be in a glade on the edge of the labour camp.

The Beaconsfield officers immediately called for help from Slough and within twenty minutes a team of officers were escorting Maksimowski to the spot where he claimed he had killed the woman, **Mrs Dilys Campbell**. Mrs Campbell, 30 was married to a local Slough man. The man later told police that he had last seen his wife between 7-30 p.m. and eight, when she told him she was going out with friends for a drink in the town. The man told the officers that he and is wife were having a ' few problems.'

Sure enough the Pole quickly showed the officers the body and he was taken, under arrest to Slough police station. Initially Inspector Jennings believed the claims that there had been some kind of suicide pact were possible true, since there were no obvious signs of a struggle on the body of Mrs Campbell, although there were scratch marks on Maksimowski's face. However a doctor who accompanied the police said that in his opinion the woman had died slowly, which was rare in suicide bids. He told Inspector Jennings that the wound to the woman's left wrist was the most serious.

This last point suggested something curious because the doctor further told the police that he believed the woman had been dead for about four hours. So what had Maksimowski been doing for those ' lost ' hours?

Using a giant searchlight, the officers noticed that the clearing in the wood showed no sign of a struggle, which partly confirmed the Pole's story. However they also noticed that such was the isolated nature of the glade, that it would be an ideal place to kill someone, since the nearest huts in the camp were over half-a-mile away, and the body had been found 200 yards into the wood from the road. They also discovered that a couple would not be viewed suspiciously from the camp and many of the Poles there had local girlfriends, which they took to the glade.

By the body the police recovered a bloodstained razor blade, the broken blade of a knife, and a woman's handbag and gloves. Curiously the body had deep wounds on both wrists, yet a wound to the neck was obviously superficially and not remotely life threatening. But why would Maksimowski want to kill Mrs Campbell and why would she have wanted to die?

Whilst the Beaconsfield officers had been waiting for their Slough colleagues, one of the town doctors was summoned to examine the cuts to Maksimowski's wrists.

Dr R.H. Kippings knew straight away that, like the wound to Mrs Campbells' neck, they were simply a token and futile attempt at suicide, although the wounds did need a bandage. The doctor suggested that, in his opinion, it would not be enough to arrest a man for attempted suicide. However the doctor did notice something peculiar about Maksimowski: his obsession with death.

At Slough police station, Maksimowksi said he been seeing Mrs Campbell since July 1949. At first he didn't know the victim was married, and he said that she would often sleep with him at the labour camp after he had smuggled her in without the warden knowing.

Although a new decade was about to be born, it was to be another 15 years or so until divorce and sex outside marriage was readily accepted by society as quite normal.
Maksimowski explained that in December, he discovered Mrs Campbell was married and had two young children. At first Maksimowski said they should stop seeing each other and he claimed the pair of them could see no way out accept for suicide. However on December 29th he wrote to Mrs Campbell asking to see her the following night.

The Pole continued that on December 30th, they had spent the whole evening and night drinking in various pubs in and around Windsor. He said the couple visited five pubs each drinking half-a-dozen whiskies and 10 shandies. At 10.30 p.m. they caught the train back to Slough.

At first Maksimowski decided to go back to his camp in Beaconsfield alone, but Mrs Campbell insisted on coming along and spending the night with him.

Maksimowski explained that the taxi dropped them off opposite the wood, where his camp was, at about midnight. He claimed he tried to get Mrs Campbell to stay in the taxi, but she forced her way out. He said he was forced to hit her, but she would still not get back in the cab, which then left without her.

Maksimowski said as they walked through the darkened wood, Mrs Campbell stopped and said if they could not be married or continue seeing each other, she would rather be dead. The Pole claimed she asked him whether he would commit suicide after her. He said to her: "I will kill you first, because you will not able to kill me first."

Maksimowski then took her wrists and slashed them, but the knife broke, so he took his razor out, and took out the blade. He claimed she said: "Finish."However he then admitted she screamed out: "Why have we done it – it hurts."

It was then suggested by the Pole that Mrs Campbell made a cutting movement across her neck saying that she wanted it over quickly and with this he stabbed her in the neck and back. He confirmed that to finally ensure she was dead he started to choke her, but this was unnecessary.

Inspector Jennings suggested to Maksimowski wasn't it strange for a man to take a knife with him and perhaps it would be more accurate to say that Mrs Campbell no longer wanted to see him, and out of anger he had killed her. The police officer suggested that perhaps Maksimowski was angered after Mrs Campbell told him she was still living with her husband. Had the Pole felt he had been duped by a married woman who simply wanted a lover, asked Inspector Jennings?

Explaining the knife, Maksimowski said every man in Poland carried a knife when he went out and that in July 1949 he and another Pole had been stabbed in a café at Slough Cattle Market by another Pole.

However the Pole then broke down and confessed that whilst the couple had discussed suicide, at the last moment Mrs Campbell had changed her mind and had tried to stop him. She had scratched his face and he had had to hold her down by the throat.

At 1.00 p.m., just nine hours after the police had been alerted, Maksimowski, his wrists heavily bandaged, appeared at Beaconsfield Magistrate's Court wearing pin-stripped grey trousers, an open necked white shirt and a jacket casually over his left shoulder. Throughout the short hearing the Pole shook violently and had to be calmed by a police officer, who stood next to him in the dock.

Maksimowski was remanded for a week but when he appeared again before the local magistrates he stunned them by turning down their request for legal aid by saying: "No, thank you. There is no solicitor or soldier in this country who can help me. I have made a statement to the police and will say nothing more. " However the magistrates decided that as Maksimowski was facing a murder charge, he would have legal aid whether he wanted it or not.

On **March 8ᵗʰ, 1950** Piotr Maksimowski appeared at the **Warwick Assizes** before **Mr Justice Croom-Johnson,** in a trial that lasted just one day.

Defending, **Mr K. Berry** said, that the death of Mrs Campbell was as a result of the large amounts of alcohol the couple had consumed since eight o'clock. He submitted that there was no premeditated design to commit murder or suicide.

Furthermore whilst there was no doubt that Makismowski had cut both Mrs Campbell's wrists, but only the left wound proved fatal, the defence claimed the verdict should be one of manslaughter since Maksimowski didn't know what he was doing amounted to an intention to kill or cause serious harm.

For the Crown **Mr Fearnley-Whitingstall** said this was a clear-cut case of premeditated murder. He told the jury they only had Maksimowksi's statement to the police that Mrs Campbell had wanted to die. Furthermore, by his own word, he had admitted to the police that he had had to hold the victim down to slash her wrists.

After a short adjournment the jury returned a verdict of murder with no recommendation to mercy. It was after the judge had told him he would ' suffer death by hanging ', that Maksimowski said that he would prefer to be shot!

The shocked judge quickly regained his composure and said:" I have no power to deal with it: it has passed out of my hands."

After the trial, Maksimowski's solicitor said that, they would not be appealing the verdict, but would be petitioning the Home Office for mercy. However this was rejected and on **March 29th, 1950**, Piotr Maksimowski was hanged at **Winson Green Prison.**

Inside the jail the hangman Albert Pierrepoint was informed by the governor that Maksimowksi had made a suicide attempt. Just three days before his execution, Maksimowski had thrown himself at the death-cell window and had thrown a punch through the window. Then he pulled his wrists over the jagged glass. Fortunately for the authorities no veins had been punctured but as precaution Maksimowki had to wear special bandages from the tips of his fingers to his shoulders. In the end Maskimowski was hanged without any incidence, the execution lasting just under eight seconds.

Case 12
"The Terrible Tale
Of The
Severed Head"

~The Body In The Clyde~

James McKAY (37)
[1927-28]
MURDER
of
His Mother Agnes (60)

" .... She died about ten days ago. I put part of her in the Clyde. The rest is in the bunker." James McKay talking about his mother ….

The crime of matricide is incredibly rare – the following is a most gruesome and extreme example of it from Glasgow in the late 1920's: the son not only robbed and killed his mother, forged her will; but he dismembered her corpse, dumping the head and other bits in the River

Clyde, where it was found quite by chance, as the water had been deliberately lowered to allow work on a bridge ....

It was the morning of **Saturday, October 15th, 1927**: it was a bright sunny day as George Geddes began his job on the *River Clyde* in Glasgow .... he was a River Warden employed by the *Royal Humane Society* .... he was taking his rowing boat and a river platform to the *Polmadie Bridge* – a bridge, since demolished, that linked two large city parks – *Glasgow Green* and *Richmond Park*, which separate the Gorbals and Bridgeton in the east of the city .... The platform was to be used by joiners, who were doing some repair work on the bridge .... In order to do this, the river authorities had deliberately dropped the level of the water by 18 inches .... As Mr Geddes pulled up to the bridge, he could see a white bundle lying on the shore, a muddy bank, on the north side of the river .... he assumed it was rubbish, but being a conscientious guardian of the *Clyde*, he hauled it in by the rope that was tied around it .... Mr Geddes thought this slightly more interesting than the normal rubbish thrown into the river, so he cut the rope .... to his shock and initially disbelieving, a human female head rolled out and along the floor of his boat .... Mr Geddes had found bodies in the *Clyde* before – that was part of his job: but never a severed head – that was new to him .... So was the fact that in the bundle were two human legs, a thigh, and an arm including the hand .... The police were soon on the scene, and the body taken to the Central Police Mortuary in the city-centre ....

The legs had been severed below the knees – the wedding finger of the left hand appeared to be missing, but was quickly found in the bundle, although without the ring: the head had been mutilated presumably to hinder recognition; the nose had been completely cut off, and half the tongue had also been removed .... what was left of the head, was black with bruising .... Andrew Smith, the Chief Constable of the Glasgow Police, ordered all his men to come on duty – both banks of the *Clyde* were searched as were all buildings along it – it was a mammoth task …. The post-mortem was carried out by Professor John Glaister one of Scotland's most eminent forensic experts at the time …. From the bits of the body that he had, the professor, told the police, that the victim was 'well nourished', and 'probably in her sixties' …. The official list of missing people from Glasgow, had no-one of that description …. The Sunday newspapers widely reported the case, and a queue of people formed outside Glasgow's Central Police Station, with information on love-ones and others, who appeared to have vanished in the city …. Initially, it was not reported what little information the police did have, beyond stating that the body of an older woman had been found in the *Clyde*; and this, of course, weeded out many people; and only a handful were allowed to see the dismembered corpse …. Then the police thought, they had a break-through …. the remains were identified …. the police went to the person's home, only to find them alive and well …. The police were back to square one ….

On Sunday afternoon, a woman came to the police-station – she had recently returned to the city and went to her mother-in-law's – the woman was not around, but most worryingly of all, the furniture in the property, had been removed …. shown the body, the woman said beyond doubt, the *head* belonged to that of her mother-in-law – a **60-year-old, called Agnes Arbuckle** …. She lived at **213, Main Street in the Gorbals** – a small top-floor two roomed flat - and not far from where the body had been found …. Officers lead by Detective-Lieutenant George Stirton quickly went to the address …. They knocked at the door – they had no more suspicions than that …. the property did, indeed, appear quite empty, so they moved onto another address given to them by the woman – 241, Thistle Street – it was just a matter of a few minutes away, and bordered the *Clyde* …. it was home to the victim's son – **James McKay (37)** ….

McKay seemed genuinely shocked and distressed at what he was being told, but then suddenly he blurted out, that he knew, that his mother was dead …. he said, that he had killed her …. He then calmly said: " …. She died about ten days ago. I put part of her in the *Clyde*. The rest is in the bunker." Under arrest, McKay, was taken to Main Street …. in the property, he pointed to a coal-bunker in the kitchen .... he then said, the saw he used to cut the body up, was also in the kitchen .... The officers first went to the bunker .... opened up, it seemed full of coal, but after a few lumps were taken out, they could see a brown paper parcel – opened, it contained a human *right* arm .... The police wanted McKay's footwear and despite now being bare-footed, McKay, was immediately taken away to the police-station, before more officers descended on the flat .... At the bottom of the bunker – deep down – were two more brown paper parcels .... in each one, was half a human torso .... Outside the victim's flat, the police found Mrs Arbuckle's wedding ring ....

Mrs Arbuckle – Arbuckle was her maiden name – but she like to be referred to as 'Mrs' - had lived in her flat since 1910 .... Married more than once, she had brought up three sons in the property: one son had died in the war; one of illness in 1921; and James McKay – her youngest .... McKay, married, had one young son .... He too had fought in the war, but had spent three years in a POW camp .... Employed as a brickie, McKay, was struggling financially – partly due to his drinking - and this was beginning to effect his marriage – his wife had just spent the Summer months working in a hotel in Rothesay on the Isle of Bute and two hours to the west of Glasgow .... whilst Mrs McKay was away, her husband had to look after their child .... McKay's drinking had become worse, and now the couple were behind on their rent .... On September 20th, he had phoned his wife in Rothesay and begged her to come home .... he said that he missed her and was suffering from depression .... McKay then next said, that if she did not come home, he would sell all their belongings and leave .... Mrs McKay put the phone down on her husband .... McKay was also causing his neighbours problems in Thistle Street; and on the next day, one of them went round to Mrs Arbuckle's, to see if she could come and help McKay .... McKay was indeed beginning to sell off the furniture, and 'behaving himself funnily' .... Mrs Arbuckle came round to her son's, but a fierce argument ensued .... McKay's mum returned home, unable to help: McKay then went round to the neighbours and told them to mind their own business and assaulted one of them .... The next day, McKay, sold off what little remained of his furniture .... James McKay then went off to the home nearby of a drinking pal – a man called Owen Watters - and explained his dire situation, and was told that he, and his son, could stay with Mr Watters and his mum .... McKay seemed happy – he would spend his time in the pubs with Mr Watters, whilst the latter's mum could baby-sit his child ....

The police investigation into Mrs Arbuckle's movements up to October 15th, revealed that she had taken out her deceased son's war-pension of 9s on September 28th – it was a Wednesday – the usual day; but she had not collected it on the next two Wednesdays – the fifth and the twelfth .... Literally, nobody remembered seeing Mrs Arbuckle *after September 28th* .... So the two weeks pensions hadn't been collected, and McKay, after the end of September had wads of bank-notes that he flashed about .... And although he had lost his latest job on September 30th, for the next two weeks, he seemed to have plenty of cash .... McKay said the reason his mother hadn't been to collect the pension was, that she was not feeling too well and was bed-bound: then, when she felt a bit better, she had travelled to Rothesay to stay at the hotel, where his wife was working at .... Naturally, as the concerned son, McKay, had to be popping back and forwards to his mum's place to keep an eye on it .... However, as the police began door-to-door inquiries, they were told that McKay, had removed all the furniture .... Some neighbours had asked McKay what he was doing, and he said that when his mum came back, she would be moving to Blantyre to the south-east of Glasgow: she would be near some relatives, and would be renting a one-bedroomed flat, and therefore didn't need all her furniture ....

In the first two weeks of October, James McKay, went twice to Rothesay to see his wife – he had plenty of money – and stayed a couple of days in the hotel .... whilst there, he showed a number of people his mum's bank deposit book, which had £80 in it .... In the book were cheque slips written out by Mrs Arbuckle, including one for forty pounds .... In McKay's home were more slips including one written out and signed by Mrs Arbuckle *on October 17th*, the day after McKay had been arrested .... Also in the home was his mother's will – made out in favour of James McKay, with his mum's forged signature .... McKay had been sitting on the cheque book and will when the police arrived ...! A man called John Russell went to the police to tell them that on October 12th, he'd gone to Mrs Arbuckle's to help McKay remove a tin trunk .... it was very heavy and had to be carried down *five* flights of stairs …. in the street, McKay, seemed to have an injection of great spirit and excitement, and put the trunk on his shoulder …. The next day, McKay, called on Mr Russell and asked him to take the trunk back to Main Street: Mr Russell was paid handsomely for his help, and noted that McKay had plenty of money on him, which was most unusual …. Whilst the trunk was still heavy, Mr Russell, told officers, that it wasn't as heavy, as when he had helped take it from Mrs Arbuckle's ….

James McKay appeared at the City's High Court on Monday, December 12th in a trial that was to last three days, before George MacFarlane – Lord Ormidale …. The prisoner offered two defences – a) not guilty by reason of insanity b) manslaughter on the grounds of diminished responsibility[7]. The court was packed with many items of furniture from the accused mum's flat, and when McKay first entered the dock he was seen to smirk …. The jury of fifteen had six women on it ….

The evidence showed that McKay had sold all his furniture between September 20th and 22nd: after the twenty-eighth, he'd paid off his rent arrears; then he moved his mum's furniture into his home …. Plaster castes of the foot-prints on the river bank matched exactly the footwear of the accused …. In the murdered woman's flat, the police also found a second tin trunk …. one contained fragments of burnt flesh and a lot of blood-staining; the other had a number of books, under which were a pair of lady's corset bones – they were stuck to the bottom of the trunk by blood …. The court heard Professor Glaister say that when he saw the body of Mrs Arbuckle, he estimated that she had been dead for between ten and fourteen days …. However, he said that the body parts in the river, had only been there between 24 and 48 hours, and they were in the same state of decomposition as those in the flat …. He added that whoever cut the body up was 'lucky' – it had only taken them about two hours, but they had no skill whatsoever in anatomy …. He said after death, there had been an attempt to burn the head and torso – as to the actual cause of the murder, Professor Glaister, believed the killer had

---

7   Not part of the law of England & Wales until 1957 ….

cut and beaten the victim to death: McKay said he had hit his mother with an axe, but no such weapon was found; however, she did have cut injuries to her face and neck caused before her death; and the indictment read that she had been 'murdered with a sharp instrument' …. The court heard no evidence that McKay was at any point mentally ill, but that he was an alcoholic …. No witnesses were called by the defence …. On **Wednesday, December 14th**, the jury were out for just 26 minutes ….

The jury were unanimous in their verdict – something not that common in Scotland in the days of capital punishment – due to the fact that 15 people sat on a jury – but it was 15-0 for a verdict of guilty of murder …. As this was being delivered, Mrs McKay, burst into tears …. McKay stood to attention, as the judge told him, he would be hanged in the **City's Duke Street Prison** on January 4th in the New Year …. As McKay was lead away, someone in the public gallery, called out: "Cheer up!" With the guilty verdict, a number of people began questioning *Mrs McKay's* role in the affair …. The police were told that on September 28th – the last day that it could be proved Mrs Arbuckle was alive, Mrs McKay, had returned to Glasgow and had gone to her mother-in-law's flat …. A neighbour, told Mrs McKay, where the victim had gone, and so she said she would remain in the flat and wait …. the neighbour said Mrs Arbuckle had gone to collect the pension …. Neighbours said the pair did not like each other very much …. they recalled the victim coming back and talking to Mrs McKay …. At one time, the mother had offered her son one pound a week, if he left his wife …. After the pair quarrelled, Mrs McKay, went to visit her husband and son at Mr Watters' …. Mrs McKay had been arguing with her mother-in-law about her husband selling off the furniture in Thistle Street, and when she arrived at his new home, that was what they continued to argue about …. That night McKay went round to his mother's …. The police noted that it was not until September 30th, that Mrs McKay returned to Rothesay – she stayed with the Watters, and did not return to Glasgow until …. mid-October …. The forensic evidence suggested McKay had placed the body parts in the *Clyde* either on the thirteenth or the fourteenth – a neighbour in Thistle Street, said McKay had called at her home at five am on the fourteenth …. he was covered in dirt – he looked like he had been working in a ploughed wet field …. such were the laws at the time on the questioning of a wife, where their husband had been accused of a crime, that Mrs McKay, was never questioned about any of this …. but the police thought it somewhat of a coincidence, that she came back the day after the body had been dumped and having left the city soon after the apparent day of the murder …. And although she had, of course, gone to the police on the Sunday (October 16th), she had actually also taken a bed from her mother-in-law's on the *Saturday*, and had it carried to their flat in Thistle Street …. When she went to the police, she told them the flat was 'clear of furniture'; but she did not initially say, that she had taken the bed …. So was Mrs McKay involved - she could not have been involved in the moving of the body parts to the *Clyde* – but she was in the city when the apparent murder had taken place …. and how did she recognise Mrs Arbuckle from the corpse and head …? It is equally possible, however, that on her return, when the body was then found, she had put 'two-and-two' together, and had then gone to the police ….

In October 1926, the law in Scotland was amended to mirror that in England and Wales in the setting up of a Court of Appeal in criminal cases …. **James McKay was the first person to appeal in a murder case** – his execution date was postponed and on **Saturday, January 7th, 1928, McKay's appeal was heard in Edinburgh** – it was dismissed …. McKay was not in court and the judges took just a few minutes to come to their verdict – they then set **Tuesday, January 24th** as the new execution date, and **hangman, Robert Baxter,** was hired by the city's magistrates …. There was no reprieve and McKay was duly executed.

Case 13
"Murder
On
The
Tottenham
Marshes"

"I can assure you I would commit no crime, let alone such an atrocious crime as this. I am innocent of it." - The condemned man.

George Woolfe[8] (21)
[1902]
Murder
Of
his pregnant girlfriend

---

8   Woolfe's surname is spelt many different ways but the official documents and the BDM has Woolfe. Likewise the victim is Cheeseman.

Miss Charlotte Cheeseman (22)

George Woolfe Aged 21
The Murderer

Superficially a simple case of a boyfriend who murdered his pregnant girlfriend at the turn of the 20th century, but beneath the surface lay a much more complex and intriguing case and in the words of the Prosecutor at the subsequent trial: "The evidence against the Prisoner is strong but by no means conclusive" ....

http://en.wikipedia.org/wiki/Tottenham_Marshes

Today Tottenham Marshes in North London is just a fraction of what it used to be. Sandwiched between the *Lockwood Reservoir* and Watermead Way, as late as the turn of the 20th century, it went as far west to what is now the Tottenham High Road and a short distance from Tottenham Hotspur's ground in White Hart Lane. Just to the east of the main road is now a road called Scotland Green and it was here on **Sunday, January 26th, 1902**, at 11.30 am, when the area was part of the Marshes, that some boys out playing football, made a truly terrible discovery ….

In the bottom of a ditch was the body of a young woman, fully clothed. There were marks on the side of the ditch that made it clear that the body had been pushed or pulled down the slope. The police were alerted and officers noticed other marks at the top of the ditch suggesting the presence of a second person and given the age of the woman and that it had been a Saturday night, the inference was that she had been in the company of a male. On looking at the body, the police could see, as the boys had, that she had been savagely hit around the face and there were wounds on her hands suggesting some sort of vain attempt to save herself. The *post-mortem* would later reveal she'd suffered 17 wounds. The weapon used was either a hammer or some type of sharp cutting instrument such as a carpenter's chisel. The victim had also been kicked in the sides of the head. By the end of the day the police had identified who the girl was and she lived in Avebury Street, Hoxton just over five miles away to the south, although on a direct route, on what is now the A10.

Miss Charlotte Cheeseman (22), a dark-haired, slim but buxom woman, had been employed in a cigar factory but had been unemployed for the past fortnight and she had a regular boyfriend, one **George Woolfe (21)**. She lived with a sister, Annie, and her husband, Mr Edward Matthews. At first there was no trace of Woolfe, a labourer in a factory in Hoxton. The sister told police that Charlotte and Woolfe had constantly argued and just before Christmas he had hit her across the mouth. One of the main sources of their arguments was that she thought she was pregnant and Woolfe suspected she was also seeing a soldier named Joseph Bruce, although it seemed that he had told Woolfe that he no longer was interested in Charlotte. To another man and work colleague, Alfred Jones, Woolfe allegedly said that since his girlfriend was expecting a baby, he wanted to "shunt" her and expression meaning to ditch her. But then such is the way with such relationships that on January 20th he told his friends he intended to marry Charlotte ….

January 20th was a significant date as Woolfe went to work and had not been back since. However Woolfe was a man who often went missing. Indeed after he'd hit Charlotte, her brother-in-law and Mr Bruce went 'looking for him'. Woolfe was seen in a pub on Boxing Day and a man called Edward Sapsford, Woolfe's landlord, said he was surprised he dared show his face, to which Woolfe pulled out a six-inch file sharpened at both ends, and said with this, he wasn't afraid of anyone. This immediately struck a chord with the officers as this could have been the murder weapon. The police were also shown a letter, dated December 30th, written by Woolfe to the cigar factory in which he alleged his girlfriend to be dishonest: Woolfe had used a false name and address. But again to illustrate the unpredictable nature of their relationship, he wrote a loving letter to Charlotte and after January 11th, they spent every night in each other's company, and witnesses told police that they had seen the couple in the *Rosemary Branch* pub in Shepperton Road in Hoxton on the night of the murder. Later a ten-thirty pm other witnesses said the pair were in the *Park Hotel*, in Tottenham, and that Charlotte was under the influence of drink and Woolfe appeared greatly annoyed. Soon afterwards a railway signalman on duty saw a young couple pass over a railway bridge and walk towards the Marshes and this was corroborated by a train-driver. The woman was slightly taller than her companion, which was the case with Charlotte and Woolfe. If it were the victim it was the last time she was seen alive ....

George Woolfe lived in Eagle Wharf Road in Hoxton. A 24 hour watch was kept on the property and numerous plain-clothes officers were looking for Woolfe all over North and East London. Officers were also told that shortly before midnight on the 25th, Woolfe was met by three men outside his home. They all went into a pub and when they came out one of the men punched Woolfe, and that man was Sapsford. However he didn't mark Woolfe's face badly and yet the next morning, Woolfe's father noticed that his son's face was badly scratched. Asked about this, Woolfe quickly responded: "Oh! It's what Sapsford did to me last night." Yet if this was correct and Woolfe had killed Charlotte and she had caused his facial injuries, he would have had to have returned to the Marshes from Hoxton. The next day Woolfe went to Charlotte's home and asked her sister if she was in. Told no, Woolfe then added that he had been out when she had called for him the night before. As we know Woolfe hadn't been to work since the 20th but he made it seem as if he was going to go to work but instead on the Monday (27th) he went to St George's Barracks in Trafalgar Square and joined the *Surrey Militia*, using the name 'Slater.' Eventually as the pressure mounted on Woolfe and his family his father went to the police and on February 6th Woolfe was arrested in the barracks. Woolfe told officers he had not seen Charlotte on the evening of January 25th, but the evidence, albeit circumstantial seemed overwhelming and he was charged with the murder of his girlfriend.

George Woolfe appeared at the **Old Bailey before Mr Justice Grantham on Monday, April 14th, 1902, in a trial that was to last three days. Counsel for the Crown were Messrs Richard Muir and Archibald Bodkin; whilst the prisoner was represented by Mr Arthur Hutton and Mr E.W. Fordham.**

Mr Gilbert Dent a barman at the *Rosemary Branch* said he had known Woolfe and the victim for some four or five months. He said the pair often came into the pub two or three times a week. When he found out on Monday who the victim was, he went to the police to say that the couple had been drinking in the pub between nine and nine-thirty pm on Saturday night. Furthermore he picked Woolfe out of an ID parade. Mr William Grier was a tram conductor and he said that he had seen the couple on what was locally called the Rosemary Branch Bridge and he said the time was about nine. They boarded the tram saying they were going to Manor House (northwards towards Tottenham). As Mr Grier was collecting fares the girl lost her temper and threw an apron onto the floor. He noted the man was wearing a cloth cap and had a coloured handkerchief around his neck. Shown a photo of Woolfe by the police on February 25th he too picked the prisoner out of an ID parade. Such a procedure is now inadmissible, and Mr Hutton suggested to the conductor that he only picked out the prisoner as he had seen the photo and Mr Grier agreed there were other men on the tram that night wearing a cap and handkerchief. But Mr Grier had already described Woolfe accurately *before* he was shown the photo.

Before the prisoner's father help turn in Woolfe, on February 2nd, a fellow soldier called Henry Monger had read a report of the case in a tabloid newspaper – *Lloyd's* – and said to Woolfe that there had been a murder in Tottenham an area that 'Slater' said he knew. It seems Private Monger had no inkling that Woolfe could be involved but was surprised when 'Slater' said: "You don't think it's me? You don't think I am as bad as that do you?" Monger replied of course not but he informed the police.

A Detective Sergeant William McCarthur told the court that he arrested Woolfe and the prisoner replied that he was quite innocent of murdering Charlotte and indeed Woolfe elected to give evidence in court, which, at the time was quite novel, as the law had only been changed in 1898 to allow it, and so there was great excitement in court as Woolfe stepped into the witness box. He said he first 'walked out' with the victim in October 1899. He said he loved her – they quarreled and made up – and indeed he said they had not argued for some time before the murder. He denied completely that he ever told anyone he was going to dump her.

Woolfe said that he collected his wages that were due on the Saturday of the murder at one pm, afterwards buying a 'paper in the City Road area in Hoxton. He had a lunch-time drink with Charlotte leaving her at 2.15 pm. He returned home staying in all day until six, when he went for a shave, five minutes from Eagle Wharf Road. He then headed for Charlotte's home as they intended having an evening out. The couple then went for a drink locally – the victim wanting to go to the theatre, but Woolfe said he was short of cash. Woolfe said this annoyed Charlotte and he walked off leaving her outside a pub. When he went back for her, she had gone …. Woolfe said he looked around the vicinity for about 15 minutes then gave up, saying it was between seven and seven-thirty pm. He told the court that Charlotte seemed disinterested in him that night and he had the impression she wanted to be with someone else. Woolfe said he decided to spend the evening at the *World's Fair* in Islington arriving at 7.50 pm and leaving at 10.35 pm arriving in Hoxton at 11.10 pm. Having visited two pubs he returned to Hoxton to see his father but as there was no light on in the house, he assumed he was out, and so Woolfe went to another pub staying until 11.50 pm. Yet again his father wasn't in when he went back home and so he went to yet another pub. However when he once again went home his father was in. After a brief chat he went back to the last pub he had been in – the *Sir Robert Peel* – and saw Sapsford and became involved in the fight.

Woolfe claimed he knew nothing about the murder until Private Monger told him. He said he panicked as he realised the police would want to speak to him. He explained that he had found the sharpened file on Boxing Day and just put it in his pocket as he thought it would be useful to sharpen knives with. He said that he'd never took it out of his house after that and that it was still there now as the police had not actually taken it away with them. Woolfe also denied ever hitting his girlfriend and said that he had intended marrying her all along. He admitted penning the letter to her employer and said it was completely untrue and that he was deeply ashamed he'd done it, adding he thought Charlotte was seeing another man. Woolfe admitted he drank frequently and said he must have written and sent the letter in that state.

The prisoner said it was quite correct that he and Charlotte frequently went into the *Rosemary Branch* but he denied ever going into the *Park Hotel* saying he didn't know of it and he claimed not to really know Tottenham that well. Furthermore and somewhat unbelievably he claimed not to know "Tottenham Marshes at all" and that he had never seen the 'Hotspur' play but he had visited the River Lea which was also nearby – a witness at his previous place of work had said that on January 20th, Woolfe had said he was leaving and going to 'ramble around the River Lea'. Woolfe admitted that on the evening of the 25th after he'd lost Charlotte he had become more and more drunk as the evening went on. Asked by Mr Muir, when he went to the victim's home on Sunday and was told she wasn't in, he wasn't concerned, he said that on some Saturdays Charlotte had stayed with some female work colleagues after a girls' night out.

Mr Hutton did produce two witnesses for the defence – one said he had seen Woolfe in a Hoxton pub between 11.15 and 11.40 pm; the other said he had seen Woolfe after the fight with Sapsford and his face was bleeding. Mr Hutton told the jury in his summing-up that even the prosecution would only say that the accused had been with the victim up to ten-thirty, and the defence would say these witnesses were mistaken. Since the prosecution had based their case on this, without their evidence, surely there was no case against Woolfe. If the prisoner had returned to Hoxton then no-one was suggesting he went back again to the Marshes to commit the murder, and the judge in his notes to the Home Office seems to agree by saying even if Woolfe had gone *directly* to Hoxton to be back at midnight, it did not leave much time, let alone going back to the Marshes. Furthermore Mr Hutton suggested that Woolfe had formed the idea of enlisting before the murder and it was done particularly as he *did* want to marry his girlfriend. However suspicion was too great against Woolfe and after just 45 minutes the jury found him guilty of murder, to which he replied: "I can assure you I would commit no crime, let alone such an atrocious crime as this. I am innocent of it." However Mr Justice Grantham said he fully concurred with the jury's verdict.

There being no appeal court an execution date of **Tuesday, May 6th, 1902, was set at Newgate Prison and the executioners William Billington and John Ellis,** hired. Woolfe made no final confession and walked firmly to the scaffold. There had long been plans to redevelop the prison and the Old Bailey and **George Woolfe was the last man hanged in the prison.**

So was it a straight-forward case after all? A hundred years later the Home Office file on the case was released and is extremely voluminous. It is clear that the Home Office considered Woolfe an intelligent man who used certain situations such as the fact he had previously been to the *World's Fair* to then describe them as if he had been to them on the night of the murder. They point out that when Woolfe met Charlotte's sister-in-law on the Sunday he did not mention when he last saw her and the *World's Fair*. The file contains a 21-page letter by Woolfe outlining the weaknesses in the case against him. One page is entitled "Some True Facts In May Favour" (Photo 129). In it he claims 'Lottie' as he called her wasn't pregnant; that he hadn't destroyed any of his clothing he had worn that night; he hadn't shaved his moustache off; that when he enlisted he made it clear he came from Hoxton and gave the name of his previous foreman at the company he worked in on the City Road.

However the Home Office could see no other explanation than that Charlotte at least had been in the *Rosemary Branch* and the *Park Hotel* and apart from the soldier Bruce she had had no other boyfriends bar Woolfe, so who else would she have gone to the Marshes with? They concluded that Woolfe was already scratched when the fight with Sapsford began and it was not noticed and that Woolfe had lied by saying that Sapsford 'fought like a woman' to then account for the scratch marks as opposed to bruises. Furthermore it appeared Woolfe and his father had tried to enlist a cousin into saying that the cousin had seen Woolfe at the *World's Fair* on the night of the murder, but the cousin had been ill in bed. However Woolfe said all he had asked his father to do was to see if the cousin, who regularly went to the Fair, had been there that night.

Perhaps the most intriguing document is a note by the senior prosecutor, Mr Muir, who observed: "The evidence against the Prisoner is strong but by no means conclusive." He had requested an exhumation of the body to see if there were traces of skin under the victim's fingernails. Sadly the body had been cleansed by the mortuary keeper, Mr Albert Plumb ....

Case 14
"Capital Murder Or Murder?"

Frank Stokes
(1958)
Murder
Of
Linda Ash

A murder committed after the victim had offered the killer 3/6d hour to do some gardening, after 4d had been original amount requested! However the crime became capital, under the Homicide Act (1957), when the killer burgled the victim's house. The fact that another murder took place only 200 yards away, on the same day, complicated the police's attempt to bring the killer to justice. But in this case was it really capital murder .... what if the intent to burgle came after the murder ...?

It is also a notable case in that it was the last murder-case that the legendary Lord Goddard was involved with. Having dismissed Stokes's appeal the 80-year-old retired.

Seventy-five year old widow Mrs Linda Ash lived in a comfortable house in Marlborough Avenue, Gosforth a northern suburb of Newcastle-upon-Tyne: Mr and Mrs Ash had run a boarding house, and three tenants still remained. One of the pleasures in her retirement was her garden. With spring fast approaching in March 1958, Mrs Ash was looking eagerly forward to spending the summer months in her garden. However due to her advanced age she could no longer tend it to a degree that would give her satisfaction, so she placed an advert in the local newspaper shop, looking for a gardener. Tragically she had actually advertised for someone who was going to kill her.

On Monday April 14th a short stocky built man in his mid-forties was looking for work, as he just been made redundant from a his job as a hotel-porter in Leeds, and had gone to the North-East looking for employment. During his working life of thirty years, **Frank Stokes, 44**, had done many labouring jobs and had also turned his hand to gardening, so seeing that a local house was advertising for a gardener was excellent news for him, so he took the five minutes to Marlborough Avenue and Mrs Ash's house.

Stokes rang the door and politely introduced himself to Mrs Ash and she showed him her garden. In the kitchen she offered him 3/6d per hour: Frank Stokes wanted 4d and was adamant and began to raise his voice. However Mrs Ash was equally determined and asked him to leave or accept her offer. Stokes then asked what gardening equipment Mrs Ash had. As the old lady knelt down and rummaged at the bottom of a cupboard, Stokes saw a hammer and grabbed it. He brutally, repeatedly and mercilessly beat Mrs Ash around the head. The old lady collapsed and past out but bravely hung on to her life.

At this point if Stokes had been arrested and charged with murder, he could not have been hanged! Under the somewhat paradoxical terms of the recently enacted Homicide Act(1957) only certain capital murders still attracted the death penalty. One such term was theft: and Frank Stokes effectively ended his own life when he took Mrs Ash's purse from the kitchen table, and searched the bedroom upstairs.

On fleeing Mrs Ash's house Stokes did not shut the back-door and after an hour a concerned neighbour called the police. At 3.30 p.m. a local police-constable entered the house and immediately 'phoned for an ambulance for the old lady was still holding on to her life.

Although Mrs Ash was rushed to hospital she was too ill to help the police and died the following day. Even hardened policemen were upset by this crime: The Newcastle police told the local press it was one of the most savage murders in Northumberland for some years.

If solving one murder was going to stretch the Newcastle and Northumberland police resources then two would create real problems and might require the services of Scotland Yard.

Less than a quarter of a mile away was the Rogerson household and when the police were called there in the early evening of Monday, the Chief Constable Northumberland requested Scotland Yard's assistance: Superintendent Davies was despatched. The two murders were completely unconnected and in May, Joseph Rogerson stood trial for the murder of his wife, though a plea of manslaughter was accepted.

At Number 41 Marlborough Avenue the local C.I.D. officers prepared the scene for Supt. Davies, who arrived at the murder scene in the early hours of Tuesday April 15th. Whilst officers searched the whole house and garden and numerous finger-prints were taken it was not obvious what the motive was for the house was not ransacked and Mrs Ash was not known as someone who kept large amounts of cash in the house. However theft was a good possibility because a bedroom in the house had been searched, and a suitcase and box opened and disturbed.

From house-to-house inquiries Davies quickly had a description of Stokes and by interviewing the local newsagent he had an excellent description. It was this description of Stokes that gave Davies his first clue as to where Frank Stokes had disappeared too. The emergence of television helped the police inform the public of Mrs

Ash's killer, because a description of him was given on him all over Britain.

Witnesses stated that the saw Stokes trying to hitch a ride on the A697: the main road from Newcastle to Scotland, apart from the A1. On Wednesday the police received definite information that Stokes was in Scotland. Mr John Kane, who owned a fire-clay business in the Scottish town of Dalkeith told the police that his nephew Thomas Kane was a driver for his firm and that he had told him of strange man that he had given a lift to at Haddington near Dalkeith.

Unfortunately Thomas Kane was a long-distance driver and was not located until Thursday. When he returned home he was taken to Dalkeith Police-Station, where Davies interviewed him where he gave the police " valuable information ".

Mr Kane told Davies that he stopped because he thought Stokes was a lorry-driver, who's vehicle had broken down. The man asked Kane for a cigarette and said he was a gardener looking for work. Kane gave Stokes a lift to Dalkeith but was suspicious of him and dropped him off. For Davies this was his best piece of evidence because although many local people were able to describe Stokes they would not tell him much more: many people were understandably frightened and remained silent.

From interviewing local people it emerged that three people were actually asked by Stokes the way to Marlborough Avenue. One of three was a tenant of Mrs Ash, Mrs Sybil Tait and from interviewing her on Friday, Supt. Davies said that robbery was the motive: Mrs Tait told the police that she could not locate Mrs Ash purse and that she normally kept it in the kitchen. Usually Mrs Ash kept about 2 (100 on today's money) in the house and usually in her purse.

Armed with this information Supt. Davies sent Supt. John Patterson of the Northumberland C.I.D. to a part of the city on the Tyne, where a man answering Stokes's description lived and had not been seen for several days.

Despite the fact that police-forces all over northern England and Scotland were looking for Stokes, Davies had another distraction on the weekend of April 19th/20th. On Wednesday Joseph Wilson, a 53 year old slaughterman from Crown Street in the city committed suicide by gassing himself.

On Saturday Davies took Mrs Tait to look at photographs of Mr Wilson: Mrs Tait did not think it was the man and Supt. Davies was sceptical. Also Stokes had a South Country- Yorkshire accent and Wilson was a man who had lived all his life in Newcastle.

Despite the fact that the police and public were furnished with an excellent description of Frank Stokes the case was not solved until Friday April 25th, when Frank Stokes walked into a police-station. However it was not a Tyneside or Scottish police-station: it was in London!

Stokes had entered Cannon Row police-station and said he might be able to help with their inquiries. Scotland Yard had been alerted for a 45 year old stocky built man and Stokes was immediately arrested on suspicion of murder. Stokes's clothing was removed and taken to the Yard's Forensic Laboratory. With Stokes's arrest Supt. Davies and one of his assistants Det. Sgt. Sydney Gentle rushed back to London. In 1958 the journey took ten hours!

Having interviewed Stokes he was not immediately charged with murder or capital murder as Davies wanted to place him front of an identity parade. On the afternoon of Saturday April 26th Davies and Gentle made the long journey back to the North-East.

On Sunday Stokes was placed before an identity parade and in the evening of Sunday was charged with murder. At this point Stokes made a statement during which he emphatically denied that theft was the motive the killing and that he had " lost his head " and did not know why he had killed Mrs Ash; he also said he found Mrs Ash's purse in the street.

On Monday April 28th Frank Stokes appeared at the Newcastle County Magistrates Court at Moot Hall held before Mr J.

McCracken. Supt. W.B. Jenner only wished to present evidence of Stokes's arrest and wanted Stokes remanded in custody until May 7th.

The problem for Supt. Davies was that Stokes would not admit that he went to Mrs Dodds with the intention of stealing; when the Homicide Bill was being debating by Parliament in late 1956 and early 1957, it was stated by the Attorney-General Sir Reginald Manningham-Buller that just because a theft took place, this would not *per se* prove capital murder and a premeditated intent to steal would have to be shown.

Somewhat controversially when the Bill became law Manningham-Buller had withdrawn from this position and stated that as long as a thought of stealing was
present, even for a few seconds, before the killing, then this would suffice for premeditation. Thus even if Stokes went to Mrs Ash's house with absolutely no intention to steal, if he thought about it, or it could be implied he thought about it after he entered the house, before he struck Mrs Ash, then he could be convicted of capital murder.

Stokes was not charged with capital murder in the furtherance of theft or robbery until Monday June 2nd, at which point Stokes still denied he killed Mrs Ash to burgle her house. However Supt. Davies felt that the evidence of the stolen purse was enough to prove capital murder.

Stokes stood trial at the Yorkshire Assizes in Leeds on Wednesday July 23rd before Mr Justice Edmund Davies. Defended by Mr J.S. Waller Q.C., Stokes's defence was to plead guilty to non-capital murder, in that he was thwarted for what he thought was a reasonable wage demand, and had a sudden and uncontrollable impulse to hit Mrs Ash, through anger.

The Crown rejected this and sought to show Stokes killed to steal. The case for the Crown was that having come in from the garden Stokes saw the purse on the kitchen-table and made up the story about wanted to see the gardening tools and he saw the hammer hanging in the cupboard, he repeatedly struck her.

The judge summed up the evidence for 100 minutes during which the law of murder and capital murder was dealt with in depth. Since Stokes admitted " murder " it was for the Crown to show beyond reasonable doubt that the motive killing was theft for capital murder. Mr Justice Davies also warned the jury not be prejudiced against Stokes because the heinous nature of the crime. He said, : " You [the jury] will approach the matter solely on the evidence and not upon prejudice. You must not say that the accused is a monster and the sooner he leaves the land the better for society. That would be a wholly unwarrantable approach. "

Retiring for just fifteen minutes the all male jury declared Frank Stokes guilty of capital murder. Accordingly Mr Justice Davies turned to him and said, : " You murdered Mrs Ash in circumstances of the most brutal inhumanity as your own evidence shows. The jury have further found that the murder was committed in the course or furtherance of theft. With that further finding I am completely in agreement. You shall suffer death in the manner authorised by law. "

Legally Stokes's hope of escaping the gallows at Durham Prison was in the hands of the Appeal Court in London. The head of court was the Lord Chief Justice of England, Lord Goddard, who held the post since 1946. Lord Goddard was a great supporter of capital punishment and it was unlikely he had any sympathy for Stokes.

Sitting with Mr Justices Ashworth and Cassels on Wednesday April 20th, Lord Goddard dismissed Stokes's appeal in less than fifteen minutes.

Lord Goddard began by saying it was a " horrible crime : No jury could have returned a verdict other than that which they did. " Lord Goddard said there was plenty of evidence that Stokes had robbed the house: only 1/6 d was found in the house by the police and there was the evidence of Mrs Tait that Mrs Ash kept money in the house.

Lord Goddard ruled that there was plenty of circumstantial evidence that theft was on Stokes's mind: Why did he strike Mrs Ash, when she was not looking ? Why did he then search through the bedroom ? If Stokes had no real motive other then anger, why did he not flee the house immediately, or even try and get help for the old lady ?

The Home Secretary, R.A. Butler, did not order a reprieve and **Frank Stokes was hanged by Harry Allen on Wednesday September 3rd, 1958 at Durham Prison**.

So was Frank Stokes unjustly hanged for capital murder, or was he cunning enough to realise that what he had done was a " hanging offence " and hope that the Crown could not prove the intention to steal.

Case 15
"The Mysterious Request"

Robert Galloway
(1912)
Murder
of
Minnie Morris

Robert Galloway

Today Walsoken (Now part of Wisbech) is in the county of Cambridgeshire, but in 1912 it was in Norfolk and in the warm hot summer of that year it witnessed, what appeared to be, a typical crime of passion resulting in murder, but may have been a genuine request from a depressed young woman to be killed ....

Outwardly **Minnie Morris was a bright and lively London girl of 21**, who had travelled up to Norfolk for the fruit-picking season. Unmarried Miss Morris soon began associating with a number of men including a man called William Turner, whom she had met in London, and **Robert Galloway, 27,** a fellow Londoner, whose last job had been in the Royal Navy, but who was also spending the Summer fruit-picking. Although Miss Morris certainly felt no real love for Galloway, unfortunately the ex-Navy lad felt very strongly for her, and was extremely jealous of Turner, though not unnaturally he strenuously denied both ....

On Sunday July 14th Galloway's calm finally broke. In the early afternoon Galloway saw Miss Morris and Turner drinking at the *Black Bear Inn*. Consumed with rage Galloway began shouted and telling Miss Morris how much he loved her. Miss Morris told Galloway in plain language that she was not interested in him, to which he replied with venom: "If I don't find you I can always find him. "

However such is the unpredictability of love that two days later on **Tuesday July 16th,** Miss Morris and Galloway were seeing each other again. The couple began the day by drinking at the *Black Bear* from opening time at 11.00 a.m. until mid-day: they then went to the town for lunch, returning to the *Black Bear* at 1.30 p.m. At two o'clock they left again and were seen by other drinkers in the pub garden walking down the road to King's Lynn.

Just outside the town was Burrett's Lane. Surrounded by the inspiring Norfolk country-side the couple stopped and began talking and lay down by the road-side on the grassy verge and continued talking: However Miss Morris was looking to Galloway as a friend and not as a lover, as an aunt had been despatched from her parents to bring her back to London. Minnie wanted to stay in Norfolk, as Galloway did; and her aunt had returned to London, her task not completed; but the aunt had made it clear that she regarded Minnie's stay in Norfolk as most definitely not permanent.

Later Galloway's first confession was to suggest that the motive for what he had done .... was passion; the second suggested that Miss Morris wanted him .... to kill her, as she was depressed at the thought of having to return to London. However Galloway also said he killed her because he was jealous of her returning to London ....

Sometime between two-thirty and three o'clock the mood in the lane had changed somewhat to that of dark and sinister, though to a passing cyclist, Mr Bertie Ash, it was difficult to tell whether it was normal or something more life threatening.

Mr Ash saw the man kneeling over the woman with his hands over her mouth and on her chest area. Since it was a beautiful sunny day Mr Ash finally thought all was in order, and that Galloway and Minnie were a playful couple: He continued on his way as he had pressing business.

When Mr Ash came cycling back past he this time saw the girl lying alone. Again Mr Ash did not feel anything was amiss, assuming the girl was asleep, as many of the fruit-pickers did: He had no idea Galloway had killed her.

Having killed Miss Morris Galloway calmly walked back into the town and visited several pubs, though he had a desperate urge to confess what he had done. In the *Bell Inn* he asked for a piece of paper and wrote what later turned out to be a confession. In the *Black Bear* he spoke to a Mr Pearce giving him another piece of paper, saying he could not fully explain the notes as: "That could be giving the game away. The next time you see me will be at the Norwich Assizes".

By the early evening Galloway was somewhat drunk and made no real effort to conceal his dreadful crime and attracted the attention of the first policeman he saw. In Walsoken market-place, at about six-thirty, he walked up to P.C. Jacobs and simply said: "I have strangled a woman in Burrett's Lane. "

By eight o'clock the police had examined the murder scene and Miss Morris's body had been taken to the town's mortuary. In the police-station Galloway expressed a great pleasure that the young woman was dead and wrote and signed a confession in the cell.

Since ancient times the Norfolk Assizes, like many rural courts, only sat four times a year, and so Galloway had to wait until the Autumn Assizes in October to be tried.

Since the facts of the case were not in dispute the trial before **Mr Justice Grantham only lasted one day on Saturday, October 19th. Galloway was represented by Mr H. Lancaster and the Crown by Mr F.T. Henle assisted by Mr J.I. MacPherson**.

When asked by the Clerk of the Court how he pleaded Galloway simply replied: "I remember nothing about it". This short sentence was to be the defence of Galloway .... that he was guilty but insane. If the jury accepted this special defence Galloway would be taken to the Broadmoor Asylum in Berkshire and not the death-cell at Norwich Prison. In addition Mr Lancaster tried to suggest that Galloway did not intend to kill or cause serious harm to Miss Morris and that the crime should be reduced to manslaughter.

Having opened the case for the Crown, in which Mr Henle, said that the accused did not express any real motive for the crime, but that passion and jealousy must be assumed to be a root of the problem, and that any thought that Miss Minnie wanted to be killed should be quickly dismissed from the jury's mind: - Mr Henle stated with vigour that Galloway was not insane and had deliberately and intentionally killed Miss Morris.

The first witness called was Minnie Stringfield, the mother of the victim. She said her daughter had left London at Easter and initially she had no idea she had gone to Norfolk.

It transpired that back in the capital, in May, Miss Morris had begun dating William Turner; and in June they had travelled together to Walsoken. Although they did not work together they saw each other two or three times a week and were apparently in love. However other witnesses stated they had seen Miss Morris in the company of Galloway also two or three times a week in the local town pubs ....

William Turner told the court of the events of July 14th in that Galloway came up to the couple and said: "Minnie, I want to speak to you. " She replied cheerfully: "I am all right where I am. " Later as the couple were leaving Galloway made his ominous threat of knowing where Turner was living.

Mr Francis Pilmby the landlord of the *Black Bear* spoke of **Tuesday July 16ᵗʰ.** He said that Galloway was friendly and seemed to be on good terms with Miss Morris, and that she seemed happy too. Mr Pilmby said he was surprised when Galloway returned and began buying men in the pub drinks, but he did say that Galloway was not drunk.

Mr Henry Newman, a gardener, told the court that in the *Bell*, Galloway approached him and said: "You had better have one, as I am going to spend it all up. I have only six weeks to live". Galloway then referred to a story in local paper of a man who had recently committed suicide .... by hanging. Galloway then told Mr Newman that he could not commit suicide and wanted to be hanged. Mr Lancaster was to later use this statement to show that it indicated Galloway's insanity. He also recalled to the jury that Galloway had once gone to *Walsoken Railway Station* to throw himself in front of a train, but that he could not muster the courage.

It was a William Fraser, a labourer who actually found the dead body. Several people had walked or cycled passed, but all thought Minnie was asleep. Fraser shouted at Miss Morris to wake up, but when he received no answer he shook her gently: a few moments later he shook her more violently. Fraser then removed her cap, that had been covering her face, and to his dread, found she was not breathing, and that a dark foam had covered her chin. Covering the body, Fraser ran to call the police.

P.C. Frank Taylor had the body removed to the *Bell Inn*. On examination of the body it was clear that there had been no sexual assault and that death had been caused by strangulation: - Knotted tightly around Miss Morris's was a handkerchief. It had been pulled so fiercely that the skin around the knot had swelled so as to actually cover the handkerchief. In the cell later in the evening Galloway told P.C. Taylor: " .... I was mad when I killed her and I felt I could have done in a dozen more at the time. After I did it I went to the *Black Bear Inn*, then to the *Bell*, then to the *Bear* again, then to the *Exchange*, and on to the *Globe*, and afterwards gave myself up to the police. "

Although Galloway made the above statement, which he signed, he then gave a more detailed one after the Coroner's Inquest had been suspended due to his arrest on July 17th to Sgt Wells, again at *Walsoken Police Station*. Galloway signed the following statement:

"I, Robert Galloway, wish to state the case of the fact to you. I and the girl Minnie Morris had been drinking heavily the past ten days. The girl's aunt returned to London last Monday night, leaving her stranded in Walsoken. I met the girl on Tuesday morning and we had several drinks in the *Bell Inn* and also the *Black Bear*. We left the *Black Bear*, as near as I can tell, at about two o'clock and went on the Lynn Road towards King's Lynn. We walked until we got to a lane on the right-hand side. She wanted to turn back and return to the *Bear*. This I refused to do and we came to high words. She said she would rather die than go back to London. She said: "Have you the pluck to end my misery?" I then said I would do so and gave myself up to the police afterwards and pay the penalty of the law for my crime, for which I ask no forgiveness. That is all I have to say. That is the truth. "

Mr Lancaster told the jury that Galloway's defence was that of insanity in that he did not know what he was doing when he strangled Miss Morris. Mr Lancaster also suggested that the argument between Galloway and William Turner and Minnie did not occur when Turner said it did – it may have been before the Sunday - if it took place at all ....

Mr Lancaster called Galloway to give evidence. Appearing calm Galloway simply said he could not remember killing Minnie but that he did not deny it. He did say emphatically that he did not know William Turner and therefore did not know Minnie was seeing him. He admitted being in the *Bell* and *Black Bear* regularly, and that he was a heavy drinker.

Galloway told the court that during a period of employment in the Royal Navy Galloway had spent some time in Lewes Prison in Sussex and that he had attempted suicide by hanging.

Cross-examined by Mr Henle, for the Crown, Galloway said after Sunday he remembered nothing. He did not remember making the confession, though he accepted he had made it. He said he was not really in love Minnie having only dated her on a few occasions.

Further for the Crown Dr Starling, the Medical Officer at Norwich Prison, said he did not think Galloway was insane: he answered all question coherently and sensibly.

Mr Lancaster asked Dr Starling whether Galloway could have killed Miss Morris during an epileptic fit. The doctor said he saw no such signs and that epilepsy did not necessarily produce a long period of memory loss.

On the defence of manslaughter Dr Groom was called by the Crown. He told the court that the knot around Miss Morris's neck was tied so tight that it had cut from the girl's neck: Mr Henle turned to the jury and suggested the death was a deliberate intention to cause serious harm at the very least, if not a clear intent to kill ....

After the summing up the jury retired for just *five minutes*: Galloway was guilty of murder. Mr Justice Grantham told Galloway that despite the ability of Mr Lancaster, he had been justly convicted of murder and sentenced him to be hanged by the neck. Galloway received the death sentence with same indifference he had shown throughout his short trial.

Galloway did not appeal to the newly established Court of Criminal Court and was duly hanged at **Norwich Prison on Tuesday, November 5th, 1912, by Thomas Pierrepoint and George Brown**.

So did Galloway actually kill Minnie Morris through jealousy that she did not love him; or did he make the story up that she really wanted him to kill her, through an after-thought, realising that what he had done was both legally and morally wrong ?

Case 16
"The 'Good Luck' Murder"

"We were turned out of our digs last night. She got on my nerves in the hut and would not let me sleep, so I strangled her." Milton Taylor, the killer [1st statement].

"I think anybody should strangle anybody if they feel like it. If they feel like it, it would be right from their point of view. The way I look at it, it was right to do it. I don't feel sad or sorry: quite happy as a matter of fact." - Milton Taylor, the killer [2nd statement].

"The only time I will come home is in a wooden-box!" - Mrs Marie Bradshaw, the victim.

Milton Taylor
[1954]
Murder
Of
Mrs Marie Bradshaw

Victim: Mrs Marie Bradshaw

A young pregnant married woman is found in an agricultural hut in rural Cheshire. Her killer quickly confessed; but did he kill, because he lost his temper with her, or did he kill for far more stranger reasons..............?

In 1948 George (20) and **Marie Bradshaw** married and began their new life in Bury in Greater Manchester. Some six years later they had a young family but these short years had seen them argue a great deal. Marie had married at 18 and one of the problems was that she was still interested in other men and *vice-versa* on the husband's side. Now aged 25, eventually she was found out in early January 1954, when her husband came home unexpectedly to find her in bed with a neighbour, one **Milton Taylor (23),** a local labourer. There was no violence towards Taylor, but when he left a terrible argument took place between man and wife, and the result was that they split up. Although their two families affected a reconciliation, it was very brief and Marie announced that she wanted to live with Taylor, who had moved to Crewe in Cheshire, after their affair had been discovered.

Initially the pair took rooms in the town and for a few weeks everything seemed to be working out fine. Then, Mr Bradshaw came to visit. On **Saturday, February 20th,** he asked his wife to return home and as if to prove he'd forgiven her indiscretion, he asked Marie to be a character witness, as he was being asked to pay maintenance by a woman who claimed he had fathered her child. However Marie then announced that she was pregnant by Taylor! However Mr Bradshaw said that he would accept the child as his, if she would come and return home to live with him in Bury, and that he had no interest in the other woman and would steer clear of other women from now on.

However Marie Bradshaw was far from willing to just up sticks and leave Taylor. By now voices were being raised and were being overheard by the landlady, a Mrs Winifred Gregory. As she took in the conversation she realised, that she'd been duped: she had taken in Taylor and Marie as a married couple. She entered the room and told Marie she would have to leave. Soon afterwards, Taylor, who'd also come back to the house and the other two, left the lodgings. They headed for the town centre, where Marie would have to make a decision.... In the end Mr Bradshaw headed back to Greater Manchester on his own, leaving the other two to look for new rooms. However by now it was evening time, and landladies were reluctant to take in new couples at this time for fear of their reputation. All this left Taylor and Marie with a problem and at ten pm they were seen in the neighbouring town of Nantwich looking for rooms. It was to no avail and they were last seen at a late night coffee-bar in the town-centre.

As eleven o'clock approached, they decided to head out of town and look for a barn or farm outbuilding to spend the night. Just a few miles to the north of Nantwich lies the village of Worleston on the

B5074 and, a mile or so away and on the main road to Middlewich [A530] by a farmer's gate was a hut, just behind a hedge; little more than a garden shed, it was used to store farm materials and by farm labourers for tea-breaks etc., and was in a field belonging to *Windy Arbour Farm*. At last they had found a building unlocked and the couple went inside for the night....

At just before ten-thirty am, Sergeant Thomas Shone was on duty in the front-office in Nantwich police-station when a young man, not wearing a tie, who looked like he might have had a bad night, came in. With the man was another young man, who said nothing. As it was Sunday, the sergeant wasn't immediately taken aback by what the man had to say, as he had heard it all before, particularly as the officer quickly recalled that he'd earlier seen the man in the town at about nine-thirty, and had exchanged pleasantries, and the young man seemed perfectly normal, and indeed he knew this man's first name - 'Milton'. The young man said: "I have come to give myself up. I have killed a woman." The sergeant paused and then asked him where this had happened and the reply was: "She is in a hut in a field off the Middlewich road and before you get to the *Rising Sun*. I strangled her with a tie and covered her up and left her." The young man then gave the officer the name of the woman and where they had been staying and that they were originally from Bury. He said he had committed the crime at eight-fifty am that morning. Asked why he had done such a thing, the man replied: "We were turned out of our digs last night. She got on my nerves in the hut and would not let me sleep, so I strangled her."

The man said his full name was Milton Taylor and he was kept in the police-station as the Sergeant and an Inspector Murray made their way to Worleston, where they were joined by a Superintendent Henderson from Crewe. They opened the hut door and inside could see what appeared to be the body of a woman lying on her back fully-clothed, and covered by a white raincoat and her face by a red handkerchief which, perversely had the words 'Good Luck' written on it, along with a number of 'good luck' symbols such as horse-shoes. Pulling these back, the officers could see it was the body of a young woman and she had suffered a bloody nose (although she had not been hit in the face), and that she had been strangled, as tightly tied around her neck, in a reef-knot, was a man's neck-tie; within six hours a Home Office pathologist from Liverpool, Mr Charles St Hill had performed the *post-mortem* and had told police that there was no question that the attacker had intended to kill the woman, and that blood from her nose and also from her ears had been caused by the strangulation. The officers returned to the police-station where Taylor readily admitted the tie was his. Furthermore he was now searched and a bloodstained lady's handkerchief was found in his pockets. Taylor was charged later in the afternoon with Mrs Bradshaw's murder and appeared at the **Chester Assizes on Wednesday, June 2nd, in a trial that was to last two days, before Mr Justice Byrne.**

Opening the case for the **prosecution Mr Frederick Elwyn Jones, QC,** said that shortly before Taylor went to the police, he had confessed to a friend, a Mr John Mann, in a farm workers' hostel in Nantwich, saying: "I am in trouble. I have killed Marie. I have strangled her." Mr Mann told the police that Taylor was in a very 'agitated state' and was constantly weeping, saying that he must go to the police and that he had blood on his hands: Mr Mann knew 'Marie' as Taylor's 'wife' and said he would come with Taylor to the police station. Mr Jones said that Mrs Bradshaw had first introduced Taylor to her husband just before Christmas, saying he was just a 'friend'. When Mr Bradshaw travelled to Crewe in the following February, the dead woman uttered the strangely prophetic words, that: "The only time I will come home is in a wooden-box!"

In the witness-box, Mr Bradshaw was asked about his marital problems. All he would say was that: "We had our differences." He said that when they discussed her pregnancy, his wife only said she *thought* it was Taylor's. He added that in the lodgings in Crewe whilst he and his wife had argued, Taylor had silently entered the room, before joining in with the argument, and then he said that he would like to see the baby when it was born, but that he seemed to accept that Marie would be going back to her husband. Mr Bradshaw also said that at one point, although his wife said she would be spending the night with Taylor in Crewe, she would be 'coming home' the next day; the day she was murdered on....

Mrs Gregory, when cross-examined by **Mr Edmund Davies, QC, for the defence,** said that Taylor and the victim had come to her house on January 30th, and that in the three weeks that they stayed there, they were very affectionate to each other, and indeed, there were never any raised voices between them. Overall they acted as they had originally told Mrs Gregory, namely that they were a 'newly-wed couple'. Mr Davies told the jury that this was a most perplexing case, as Taylor was genuinely fond of Mrs Bradshaw. He said the defence would not deny that Taylor had killed the victim, but they would suggest he was insane, when he committed the act. The court then heard from a Dr Isaac Frost, a Consultant Psychiatrist, who said that when he'd interviewed Taylor, the prisoner had kept smiling in a "fatuous and irrelevant way, not in keeping with the surroundings or in the position in which he found himself." He described it as 'child-like' and said that he would put Taylor's mental age at just 11 ½ years, exactly half his real age. Dr Frost said he would have no hesitation in certifying him as 'feeble-minded'.

Dr Frost said that when he questioned the accused about the murder, Taylor replied: " I strangled somebody some time in February. I wanted to." Then contradicting what Taylor had originally told the police, he told the doctor that Mrs Bradshaw *hadn't* upset him but that he just wanted to kill her and that he gained some satisfaction from the act. Suggesting that Taylor was a psychopath, Dr Frost then said that Taylor added: "Just felt better when I did it with a tie. When I want to do a thing, I do it, whatever the consequences. If I felt like it, I would do it to anybody else." He then made the extraordinary statement: "I think anybody should strangle anybody if they feel like it. If they feel like it, it would be right from their point of view. The way I look at it, it was right to do it. I don't feel sad or sorry: quite happy as a matter of fact."

However Dr Frost conceded to Mr Jones that Taylor agreed that other people would think such behaviour was 'wrong', and crucially Taylor agreed that he knew that murder was against the law. He explained to the jury, that Taylor had suffered from an inflammation of the brain following a vaccination[9] and that, in his opinion, this

---

9   See the case of Charles Koopman (Master Detective 1/08) who also offered a

could lead to mental instability, and he told the jury that even though Taylor knew what murder was, he did not think it wrong for *him* to do it. However to counter this argument, the jury heard from a Dr F.H. Brisby, the Chief Medical Officer at Walton Prison in Liverpool, where the accused was held on remand. He said there was no history of mental illness in Taylor's family and that he couldn't find any evidence of inflammation of the brain either. Similarly, a Dr A.V. McKenzie, who held the same position at Shrewsbury Prison, said that Taylor had been held in his prison until the end of March and he concluded that Taylor knew what he was doing and knew it was wrong. Mr Davies said that Taylor, who was wearing a brown sports jacket and an open neck shirt, would not be giving evidence on his own behalf.

On the second and final day of the trial **[Thursday, June 3rd, 1954]**, despite hearing of Taylor's peculiar view of murder, or perhaps because of it, the jury were out for just 35 minutes, before reaching their verdict. They rejected the suggestion that Taylor was insane and found him guilty of murder, and Mr Justice Byrne sentenced him to 'suffer death by hanging'. There was no appeal and despite a plea for clemency to the Home Secretary David Maxwell-Fyfe, on the grounds that Milton Taylor wasn't fully responsible for his actions, he **was hanged at 8.00 am on Tuesday, June 22nd, 1954 by Albert Pierrepoint and his assistant on the day, Robert Stewart, at Walton Prison, Liverpool.**

---

defence of insanity based on this.

Case 17 "The First Execution At Swansea And The 'Mysterious' Foreigners"

"'Foul, unnatural and diabolical murder.' .... The persons implicated in this atrocious act are foreigners, Greek sailors, whose long-bladed knives carried as daggers behind there backs makes every English heart shudder at the very sight and which are too often drawn and used on the slightest provocation." – Local media

"You are a little fool, that you do not take the cook to bed and take all his money". – The 'sinister' Greeks to a local prostitute.

Manoeli SELAPATANA & Panaotis ALEPIS

[1858]
Murder
Of
Atanasio Mitropani

PANAOTIS ALEPIS, Aged 23.　　　MANOELI SELAPATANA, Aged 28.

Swansea Port has for many centuries been a melting-pot and low-levels of violence, drunkenness, and prostitution had long been tolerated, but in early 1858 a shocking murder occurred, that railed the local media about crime and 'mysterious' foreigners and was soon afterwards to lead to the town's first ever execution….

It was February 1858 and **Manoeli Selapatana (28) and Panaotis Alepis (23)** were two "swarthy and sinister-looking" Greek sailors on board the brig *Penelope*, which had been in Swansea docks in south Wales for nearly three weeks and was now taking on coal in preparation for its next voyage. The men had just recently joined the vessel and on board the ship was another foreigner, also Greek, a cook, **25-year-old Atanasio Mitropani**, who on February 14th, had received some monies from the ship's captain, including two Turkish coins. On their arrival in Swansea all the crew, including the above three had headed for the port's pubs and brothels, where they spent most of their evenings. By the evening of **Tuesday, February 16th,** it was well known by a number of prostitutes near the docks, that Mr Mitropani had significant funds to really have a good time. And so the cook left the ship at seven pm heading for the nightlife, with a smile on his face....

Soon after Mr Mitropani had left the boat, Selapatana and Alepis followed, and various witnesses would say, they were either in his company or even that they appeared to be following him in a sinister way. At any event, at about eight-thirty pm, awful blood curdling screams of horror were heard coming from the direction of the *Penelope*, near a canal that lead to the harbour. Being a cosmopolitan seaport and at the heart of the British Empire, Swansea was used to many languages being spoken in the docks, and the cries and shouts appeared to be foreign, which was not surprising. And so the shouts and screams did not arouse that much suspicion and it was assumed it was just a fight amongst foreigners, but then there was a loud splash.... Two locals rushed to the scene and saw something floating in the water. The police were called and it was the body of a young man.

The body was fished out and what the local 'paper called a 'foul, unnatural and diabolical murder' was uncovered. The man had been stabbed all over his body in a great number of places, possibly with a dagger. The ferocity of the attack was clear, as it was still winter and the victim had been wearing thick clothing, including a sheepskin coat, and yet the blows had penetrated this, cut through a rib and deep into his lungs. The man, who was dark-skinned, had also received a number of terrible blows to his head that had fractured his skull. Witnesses spoke of two other foreigners seen running away from the spot. Very quickly news of the attack spread through the docks, and it was quickly established that three crewmembers of the

Penelope were missing. Other crewmembers quickly identified the body as that of Mr Mitropani and that the two suspects were Selapatana and Alepis.

As the ship's captain Mr Alexander Feluce returned to his ship later in the evening, speaking with an interpreter, he was told that Selapatana and Alepis had been arrested and he confirmed that he'd paid the cook two days before. As to the motive: well, an argument of some sort perhaps, but the police believed robbery lay behind the crime. The ship's cabin boy, 14-year-old Lazarus Stena told the police, that in addition to his two Turkish coins, Mr Mitropani had an English sovereign and other silver coins in his pocket. He also took a purse, said the boy, and this was found in the canal, and yet, it only contained a 'few shillings'.

Obviously a key part of the murder inquiry, were the docks' prostitutes. They were almost entirely local, and one Miss Elizabeth Phillips, said that she had 'entertained' the cook on Sunday and on Monday night too. She had been paid with the English sovereign, and so the assumption was that Mr Mitropani had been robbed of his Turkish coins. The woman also said that on the Monday, the two other Greeks had been with him, and she had 'serviced' them as well. She said that on Tuesday she just had a drink with them between five and six, and whether it was the drink talking, they told her to beware of Mr Mitropani, as he would coming off the boat in a disguise. The prostitute said she wouldn't then sleep with the cook, to which, and of course, the conversations were perhaps a little confusing given the men's knowledge of English, the two Greeks replied: "You are a little fool, that you do not take the cook to bed and take all his money".

Miss Phillips did see, but not speak, to Mr Mitropani that night: she said the time was 7.40 pm and he was indeed dressed differently. She said that, it was near the railway station and he was with the two Greeks. At nine, Selapatana and Alepis, went into the *Jolly Tar*, where they were greeted by the landlady, Mrs Eliza Lovelace, who knew the men well, as they often would spend their nights in her pub lodgings. What she saw lead to the men being quickly arrested. In the pub's back yard, Alepis or "Italius" as he was also known, took out his handkerchief, washed it, and then came inside and dried it by the fire. Seemingly unconcerned, Selapatana, who was also known as "Zelphanta", went upstairs to their shared room and returned with two coats and two hats. The men donned these and disappeared into the darkness. At the murder scene another cap had been found, which had belonged to Selapatana, and a stick by the canal was identified as belonging to Alepis. Mrs Lovelace thought she would never see the 'shifty foreigners' again, but they returned at ten and were arrested soon afterwards.....

Another 'woman of the town', Miss Elizabeth Thomas, said she had seen Alepis with the cook near the railway station at 8.20 pm., and she knew the exact time, as it was near the station clock. She had seen them at seven at the *Powell's Arms* and later in the police station, she told the officers that, Selapatana and Alepis were now dressed differently. Another witness, a waxwork exhibitor, also told police that Mr Mitropani had visited his exhibition and when he left he was joined by Alepis.

Perhaps a more reliable witness was a Mr Francis Henwood, an office-worker at a local tinworks, who between eight and nine had been watching the boats in the harbour as a part-time job. He had heard the sounds of a struggle and foreign voices between eight-thirty and nine. With him was another night-watchman, Mr Thomas Johns, and they rushed to the scene, when they heard a splash in the water. With their lantern lighting up the dark wintry night and using a boathook, they pulled the body to the harbour wall. It was Mr Mitropani and proof that it had just entered the water, was the fact that, it was still warm and steaming. Good detective work by the first officer on the scene, Sergeant William Neale revealed a knife, a large jagged stone, both of which had blood on it, a sling and shot (of strong rope and an iron ball weighing some two pounds) tied to it, and a man's cap, also blooded. All had been found on a bank nearby. The officer found a stick too. Sergeant Neale said that the knife had fallen from the deceased's body's waist-belt as it was lifted from the water, and therefore must have been put in their by his killers.

A *post-mortem* was carried out by a Mr W.H. Michael, a surgeon. He noted that the victim's hair was matted with blood and coal dust (near the canal were the docks' coal wharfs), and that there were several large wounds in the skull. In the chest area he noted four stab wounds, and that the weapon must have been a particularly strong knife: the largest wound in the chest was an inch-and-a-quarter wide. All the stab wounds had been inflicted from behind. A large amount of blood had drained away from the victim, he told the police, and any of the wounds would have probably caused death, had the victim not been thrown into the water. The sling and shot could have caused the head injuries, which were delivered from the front. Dr Michael surmised that Mr Mitropani had been hit over the head, rendered semi-unconscious, and then was stabbed to death before being thrown or pushed into the water. Given the circumstances of this and the pattern of the wounds, the doctor believed two or more men had attacked the victim. The coal dust on the hair and head suggested he had fallen head first onto the ground after the first blow, then had been picked up and stabbed. Another prostitute, Miss Frances Edwards said she had seen two men, one of whom, she knew as 'Italius', running from the canal along an area called the Strand. This was less than 50 yards from the murder scene.

At just after ten-thirty pm, Superintendent Dunn, who was in overall charge of the murder inquiry, and Constable Noah Owen went to the *Jolly Tar* and arrested Selapatana and Alepis. In the former's trousers they found a Turkish sovereign, 7s 6d in silver, whilst in the waistcoat of the latter, they discovered 20s in silver. Even more damming was evidence, that there was some blood spots on Alepis' trousers, and in the chamber pot in the men's room were traces of coal dust, sand and human hair. Some time in the previous sixty minutes, Selapatana had bought some mince pies in the shop of a Mr Charles Price, paying with a Turkish sovereign. As to the blood, all Alepis could suggest to the police was that he had suffered from a nosebleed. Selapatana claimed he had been in a 'dancing-house' all evening until arrested, but he admitted buying the cakes and washing his handkerchief. The local paper was pleased that: ".... The persons implicated in this atrocious act are foreigners, Greek sailors, whose long-bladed knives carried as daggers behind there backs makes every English heart shudder at the very sight and which are too often drawn and used on the slightest provocation." With a sense of irony, the words 'Welshmen' were added, almost as an afterthought, to those also fearful of such foreigners.

Less than two weeks later on **Saturday, February 27th, 1858 the two Greeks were tried for murder before Mr Justice Bramwell at the Swansea Assizes in a trial that lasted just one-day. After the case for the Crown had been put by Messrs Giffard, Bowen and C.B. Mansfield, the jury heard from the defence, Messrs T.Rees and Allen, who defended both men**. They dwelt on the purely circumstantial nature of the evidence; pointing out that no one had actually seen them commit the murder. They also caste doubt on the police's assertion that robbery must have been the motive, asking why had the purse with money been throw into the canal. In all, the judge summed up the case for one hour and then the jury retired. They were absent for just half that time before returning to court. They found both, Manoeli Selapatana and Panaotis Alepis guilty of murder. The men were then sentenced to hang and an execution date of **Saturday, March 20th, 1858** set. There was much excitement in Swansea, as it was decided that, given the growth of the population and importance, that the town would become a centre for executions. And of course it would be in public, the exact spot being some 250 yards from the southwest of the prison walls, on the sand dunes. The scheduled time would be eight am, and it was to be a bright and cloudless day. In all it was estimated nearly 20,000 people were in place by the allotted time.

Large crowds had descended on the town on the day before, many coming by rail and many enjoyed watching the scaffold and gallows being constructed. Many of the crowd were coalminers from the surrounding districts, as well as a good many 'loose women' and those from the 'lower orders', although it was noted that there was a sprinkling of folk from the middle-classes.

Both Selapatana and Alepis had been spiritually looked after by a Greek Orthodox Priest from London, who returned to the capital briefly, before returning to the men on Thursday night. Unfortunately for the authorities, neither man made a confession and indeed would not discuss the subject. They went to bed at eight pm on Friday, being woken at midnight, so that for the next eight hours they could be subjected to more religious instruction, although they were allowed to smoke their pipes. Then at 7.45 am, the High Sheriff of Glamorgan and his officials arrived in the death-cell, which the Greeks had shared. **William Calcraft**, the executioner, who had arrived in the port on the eight-fifteen London train the night before, quickly pinioned both men. The Reverend E.B. Squire, the Prison Chaplain, then led the procession to the gallows. The men walked the 250 yards with firmness, their route being screened from the masses. On the scaffold they fell to prayer. They kissed the Greek priest, the Reverend N. Morphinos, and asked for forgiveness from him and from the officials. Calcraft then moved them gently but firmly onto the trap-door. The rope was put around Selapatana's neck first then Alepis'. The two men then shook hands and exchanged a few words in Greek, and then shook Calcraft's hand. As the clock began chiming eight, the officials withdrew, and the hangman pulled the lever. Alepis was executed without a struggle, but Selapatana 'died hard' in agony, taking a terrible six or seven minutes to die, although Calcraft deemed it unnecessary to pull down hard on his legs to finish him off. The crowd then dispersed peacefully, even though the bodies remained hanging for another hour.

It was to be the first of 15 executions in the town, although the local media hoped it would be the last saying: " We trust the day has passed when Englishmen will resort to that deadly weapon, the knife, even to avenge the greatest insult and wrong; but by adopting legal and proper steps will show to those foreigners who frequent our land that the use of murderous weapons are un-Christian and un-English."

Case 18
"The Sad Tale Of The Withered Flowers"

Privates Stanley Boon & Arthur Smith (1939)
Murder
of
Miss Mabel Bundy

With the war clouds of Europe about to descend on England, three young soldiers looked to take advantage of an unmarried woman: Sex was what they wanted but it ended in murder; but really happened in the grounds of a Surrey hotel …?

It was very early on the morning on Thursday **July 5th, 1939,** when Scotland Yard received a 'phone-call from the Surrey C.I.D. They said that the badly beaten body of a woman had been found on a footpath in the grounds of a hotel in Hindhead, a picturesque village on the Surrey/Hampshire border. They said the woman was short in stature and had dark hair, and somewhat tragically by her body was a bunch of withered flowers.

By eight a.m. three officers had arrived in Surrey. The woman's body had been found by Thomas Mitchell a porter at the hotel at just before six-thirty in the morning, and was near the tradesman's entrance near the kitchen. He had confirmed to the local C.I.D. that the victim was **42-year- old Mabel Bundy**.

A native of Portsmouth, Miss Bundy was employed as a maid in the hotel, but also worked behind the bar, and had been at the hotel for about a year. She had a room at the hotel and was to have had a half-day holiday on Wednesday.

The first impression on the Yard Men was that Miss Bundy had been the victim of a viscous rape. She was lying on her back and her face and arms were badly bruised. Her blouse had been ripped open, and her bra straps had been pulled down her arms. Although the woman's stockings and suspenders were untouched, her underwear had been pushed aside, though not ripped.

The results of the post-mortem, carried out by Dr Eric Gardner in nearby Farnham, showed that Miss Bundy had suffered a broken nose, a bruise over her left eye, and a severe blow to the right side of her head. This injury went from right hand side of her head to her chin: It was this blow that had killed her after it had caused severe brain damage. However the post-mortem could not tell if she had been struck by an object or punched. The post-mortem also revealed that Miss Bundy had recently had sex, which considering the violent assault on her, was assumed to have been rape.

Having interviewed the staff at Miss Bundy's hotel, it emerged she had spent the evening in the bar of another local hotel, the Royal

Huts Hotel. The barman there recalled that Miss Bundy had come in about seven o'clock and had began drinking with a girlfriend. After about an hour the two women were joined by a soldier, a young man, whom the barman thought was in his early 'twenties.

After another hour or so the girlfriend left Miss Bundy in the company of the soldier. When the bar closed at just after ten, the barman said that he overhead the soldier offering to walk Miss Bundy back to the Moorlands Hotel.

All the staff at the hotel said Miss Bundy was a quiet woman who everyone liked and thought a bit shy. Everyone said that it was highly unlikely that she would simply go off for a walk with a young man she didn't know. If she did go with him, it would because she believed he was escorting her home. However the barman at the Royal Huts said that both Miss Bundy and the soldier had had a number of drinks.

Other people, including a number of soldiers, told the police that they saw Miss Bundy walking towards the Moorhead, and that following them were two other young soldiers.

It emerged that after Miss Bundy had left the Royal Huts, she bought a bunch of red carnations from a flower seller in Hindhead High Street, but the flower-seller said she was alone, but that nearby was one soldier and two others further behind him.

Only two miles from Hindhead was an army base at Thursley. The barman at the Royal Huts confirmed to the police, that he had knew that most of the young men in the bar were soldiers from the camp and they were from the 2nd Battalion of the North Staffordshire Regiment were stationed.

The Yard Men was particularly interested in one soldier who had scratches under his eyes and a deep cut in his nose, and who claimed he had fallen through a bush and who denied being in the hotel. Tall and handsome the soldier was indignant when asked would he have to attack a woman for sex.

A further two men also denied being in the hotel but their deception was exposed when another soldier recalled seeing them. To make matters worse for them one of the soldiers was picked out by three locals, two men and a woman, at an identity parade.

Eventually on of them, who stood just 5' 4", admitted all three had been at the Royal Huts and had been talking to Miss Bundy. All three were young privates: **Stanley Boon was 27, Arthur Smith 26** and Joseph Goodwin, 26. Boon, the short one, said they had been drinking in a pub before going onto the Royal Huts.

The clothing of all three was taken to London for forensic evidence and blood from the clothes of Boon and Smith matched blood taken from under Miss Bundy's fingernails. Confronted by this evidence Smith said they had gone down the lane for sex. Smith said he went first and Boon was to come next and Goodwin was also to follow. However Smith claimed that after him, Miss Bundy did not want any more sex and panicked at the thought of two more young men.

Both Boon and Smith vehemently denied that they had intended to kill Miss Bundy. They also claimed that she had been ' very friendly' with all three in the hotel and they all thought she would have sex with them.

Crucially for the police Goodwin seemed keen to co-operate and claimed that Boon had said: " We shall have to knock her out to get what we want. Goodwin also claimed that he tried to pull Boon of the woman, after he had seen him punch the woman in the face.

Goodwin said that Boon was drunk and he only went down the footpath to look after his friend.

After questioning all three soldiers separately all three privates were charged with murder.

In September 1939, the three soldiers all stood in the dock at the **Old Bailey before Mr Justice Oliver**. All three of them had been dismissed from the Army and wore civilian clothes and all pleaded 'Not Guilty.' Appearing for the Crown were **Mr George McClure and Mr R.H. Blundell**, whilst Boon was defended by **Mr Stuart Horner**: Smith by **Mr B.J. MacKenna** and Goodwin by **Mr W.B. Manley**.

Mr McClure said that all three men had been charged with murder because it was the prosecution's case that Miss Bundy had been killed during a rape on her. Consequently even though Private Goodwin had not touched her, he too was charged with murder, as it was alleged that he was party to the rape.

Furthermore, continued the Crown counsel, the blow that killed Miss Bundy may not have been delivered with the intention to kill, but if it were part of the rape, then it was sufficient to prove murder.

Of the three only Boon gave evidence. He said that Miss Bundy seemed quite happy to walk back to her hotel with all the men, although she seemed most friendly with Smith. Boon claimed that as they approached the back entrance of the hotel, she and Smith started kissing and went down the footpath.

Boon went on saying that the footpath was shrouded by trees making it impossible to see what Smith and Miss Bundy were doing, but both he and Goodwin assumed they were having sex. Boon suggested that on the way back to the Moorhead that Miss Bundy had joked with all three men and that each would have to wait their turn. After about five minutes Boon and Goodwin decided Smith had had enough.

Boon told the court that when he has arrived Miss Bundy's blouse had been undone, her bar pulled down and Smith had put his hand between her legs, and they appeared to have had sex. However Boon admitted when he arrived Miss Bundy appeared to be struggling as Smith undid undo his trousers and pull her legs apart and had sex with her. Then bowing his head, Boon effectively confessed to murder by saying that in the panic that followed, " I put my hand over her face. "

Miss Bundy continued to struggle and angered by her unwillingness to submit, Smith began punching her, said Boon. Although Boon tried to hold her head as she thrashed about her head slipped to the right and she received a fatal blow to the side of her head from Smith.

All three soldiers ran away when it appeared that Miss Bundy had become unconscious. Boon said all three of them were devastated when it emerged she had died.

Addressing the jury, Mr Horner, on behalf of Boon, said there was no 'common design' to commit rape and since there was no suggestion that Boon intended to kill he should be acquitted of murder, although he intimated they would accept the lesser verdict of manslaughter.

Mr Manley suggested to the court that Goodwin should not be facing a murder charge as he had no premeditated intent to commit rape, as when he went down the footpath he believed Smith and Miss Bundy were having consenting sex and that she would be consenting to sex with him and Boon at a later stage or even when Smith was present.

Furthermore, submitted Mr Manley, since in English law, it is no offence for one man to watch another raping a woman unless he and the rapist had agreed to commit the crime, the fact that Goodwin had not touched or encouraged the other two to either, rape or attack Miss Mundy, meant he was not guilty of *any* crime and should leave the court a free man.

On behalf of Smith, Mr McKenna argued that whilst his client struck Miss Bundy, it only amounted to a punch. Furthermore since Smith did not believe he was raping Miss Bundy and was engaging in consensual sex, he could not be convicted of murder and the jury should only decided whether to acquit him or convict him of manslaughter.

After the four-day trial had ended on **September 21st,** the jury retired for just under an hour. Both Boon and Smith were convicted of murder and were sentenced to hang, but Goodwin was acquitted of both murder manslaughter and rape.

Stanley Boon declined to appeal and informed his solicitors that he accepted his fate. However Arthur Smith felt his conviction was unjust and on **October 11th** his appeal was heard by the Appeal Court.

However all three judges, the Lord Chief Justice, Lord Hewart and Justices Charles and Humphreys, quickly dismissed the appeal saying that: " As the men were engaged in violating the woman and blows were struck which killed her, even if they did not intend to kill her, then both were guilty of murder. " Lord Hewart ended the appeal by saying that the crime was 'repulsive, ferocious and brutal.'

Although both men had been scheduled to die together the prison authorities at **Wandsworth** informed the Home Office that there was much bad feeling between Boon and Smith.

Smith claimed that it was he that Miss Bundy fancied in the hotel and that they had agreed to go off for sex on their own, but that Boon and then Goodwin followed. He claimed that as he and Miss Bundy had sex, Boon appeared wanting to have sex with her.

He claimed that in a panic he hit Miss Bundy when she tried to get up after Boon had touched her and that there was no agreement between him and Boon for the latter to hold her head whilst he punched her.

To prevent any untoward scenes on the gallows Boon was to be executed on **October 25th, 1939, and Smith the following day**.

By this time, however, Britain was at war, and there was little sympathy for the two soldiers, and they went to their deaths almost unnoticed.

Case 19
"The Terrible Weobley Murder"

John Hill & John Williams
[1885]
Murder
of
Ann Dickson

'acts of the utmost depravity'. - The Vicar of Weobley

'if they choose to hear disgusting details which came out in the administration of justice, they might do so.' - The trial judge in allowing women to be in the public gallery.

"We'll see if you laugh then" – Berry, the hangman, to one of the condemned men, when he joked about his forthcoming execution.

Shocking and gruesome case of the rape and attempted rape of two female tramps in rural Herefordshire in 1885 by two men, but was one of them really guilty of murder?

Nestled deep in the Herefordshire countryside some 12 miles or so to the north-west of the county town, lie the pretty villages of Weobley and Weobley Marsh, and they are about 15 minutes from the Welsh border. Now a tourist village, it tries hard, to hide a dark secret of a terrible murder that occured there in the autumn of 1885. The local 'paper said that at some point between ten and midnight, a "terrible deed has thrown the people of the locality into quite a ferment."

The day of the murder was **Wednesday, September 30th**, and about a month before, two women **Ann Dickson (33)** and Mary Ann Farrell (40) had met up in Worcester. The girls were little more than tramps, Ann also being known as Doughtey or Cox. They came from Irish backgrounds and would spend their years going from farm to farm looking for seasonal work. Although not married, Mary had a four-month-old baby and Ann, a five-year-old daughter. On that fateful September day, the girls, with their children, had walked the 30 miles from Worcester to Weobley. There they found work at Holme Farm in the nearby village of Dilwyn, hop-picking. As per the norm, they received a very small wage, food and a bed in a barn.

The day of the murder had seen some very bad weather: strong winds and heavy rain. No work meant no pay. The farmer lent the women some money to buy food, and the two of them had to walk to the nearest shops in Weobley, a round trip of about five miles. They took the baby with them, wrapped in a shawl, as despite the time of year, it was very cold. The grocery shop was part of the *Red Lion* in the village, and as they were there, Ann said she hoped to meet her 'husband' Daniel Cox. Cox had just been released from Worcester Prison having served a short sentence for assaulting a woman whilst being drunk. The woman was Ann. Ann had sent her husband money and a note to come to Weobley that night.

The women went into the bar, had a drink, and wondered if Cox would turn up. The girls, alone, soon caught the eyes of other farm labourers, and two, one known as 'Blackbird', came over and started chatting them up. More drink followed and flowed, and Ann began singing loudly and became the centre of attraction and attention. The men paid for the beer and Ann and Mary were enjoying themselves and soon forgot about Cox. As the evening rolled on, two other men came in, 'Sailor Jack' and 'Irish Jack'. They were also hop-picking and were well known locally. **They were aged 33 and 26**[10] and were often mistaken for brothers, as they looked so similiar.

A local man, 'Sailor Jack' had spent many years abroad at sea and was feared in the village as a bully, as he liked a fight, especially when drunk. 'Irish Jack' was more local, spending most of his life in Weobley. He lived in the village with his elderly mother and also worked as a painter and decorator. However although the pair had worked on the local farms too, they were also unemployed. 'Irish Jack' had twice been to prison for assault. The pair also had a liking for the local 'talent' and so in the *Red Lion* that night, they homed in on Ann and Mary and turned on the charm.

'Irish Jack', or **John Williams** had with him his favourite hitting stick. It was a normal stick with a nasty looking head the size of a human hand, which, as the beer flowed, Williams would wave around and thump the women he fancied. Mary Farrell joined in the fun, but was equally concerned about the welfare of her baby. She playfully took the stick off Williams, and said she would give him it back later. When that time came she sat by the pub fire and Williams came over and sat by her: Williams thought he had 'pulled'. However Williams made the mistake of being too friendly with the baby, which Mary didn't like and she left him by the fire.

---

10 Williams age on the BDM

John Williams wasn't the sort of man who took 'no' from a girl he fancied, and he began following her around the pub, and according to Mary, he sexually assaulted her, there in the *Red Lion*. In the meantime 'Sailor Jack', **John Hill**, had been chatting up Ann Dickson. At eight-thirty, Hill left the pub to go back to his lodgings to change his clothes. He returned shortly in his 'Sunday Best' and bought more drinks for Ann. Then at nine-thirty the girls said they were leaving to walk back to the farm. The weather was even worse and the clouds had completely hidden any moonlight: The 2 ½ miles back to Holme Farm would be in pitch darkness in an area, neither girl knew at all.

'Conveniently' Hill said he was going to Holme Farm anyway, and would, of course, escort the women. Mary Farrell said she trusted Hill (but not Williams), especially as her 'husband' and a son were sailors. And so the trio headed off for Weobley. As they left the pub, Mary glanced back and her eye caught Williams, who was chatting to some mates, but when saw her, he began tapping his stick. Mary said to Hill that, she really didn't like Williams and suggested they went to the village police-station to ask for protection. Hill just chuckled and told her not to be so stupid. Hill was helped, as Ann also told her to stop being silly and everything would be all right. As the trio made their way out of the village, at first Hill was walking and talking and trying to cuddle Ann, but as they reached the dark open fields, he dropped back, as the two women started chatting about their affairs. Hill, clearly miffed, kept trying to but in with tales of the sea. When this failed he upped the stakes, by telling the girls of his sexual adventures and what he'd like to do with them in particular. They ignored him. As the drink began to fade, Mary began to get annoyed with Hill and told him to shut up and that he was boring.

Half-a-mile into their journey they reached a ploughed field. Mary opened the gate and was suddenly struck a violent blow across the head. It was a blow from a stick and seriously injured her right eye. She had then fallen onto the mud. Although it was totally dark, she assumed it was Williams, who had attacked her. She was momentarily stunned, but kept hold of her baby. When her senses returned, she felt a man on top of her trying to rape her. Twice Mary pushed the man off, but she was punched and hit and returned to the ground, where the man once again tried to penetrate her. It was now, beyond any doubt, that the man was Williams, as she felt his hot pulsating breath in her terrified face.

Williams still could not rape Mary and so picked her frightened crying baby up and threw it into the field. Again trying to have sex with her, he told Mary, that he would kill her and the child, if she refused to submit. Mary, fearing for their lives, decided to pretend that she had wanted to have sex with Williams all along. She told him they would make their way to the barn, where she was sleeping, and Williams could spend the night with her. The ruse worked and the 'pair' made their way across the fields. Williams was enjoying every minute of this; Mary, a baby in her arms, had blood pouring from her eye. As they walked along, Williams fondled Mary breasts and kissed her, and she made light of her injury, even saying she enjoyed the way he had treated her.

However at the first opportunity, a shepherd's cottage, Mary broke away, banged on the door, and screamed 'MURDER'. Williams bolted and the shepherd took her in and then on to the hop-pickers' barn which was now, only a few hundred yards away. There he could see her terrible injuries: she was black and blue all over, her clothes ripped, and apart from her eye injury, all her teeth had been loosened by being repeatedly punched in the face; and indeed one fell out in the barn. Somewhat strangely she did not mention Ann, and was left in the barn that night. Even in the morning she did not tell the shepherd about her friend. Presumably her lifestyle meant she herself would make inquries about her friend before going to the authorities.

At daybreak, two local men were on their way to work in the fields. William Jones and Richard Preece reached the gate by the ploughed field, when to their horror, they saw a woman 'standing' up against an oak tree. It was a truly ghastly scene of death. The arms were half raised above her head, the fists clenched in terror, and the face beaten beyond human recognition. One eye was no longer in its socket. The clothing had been ripped and torn, muddied and blooded. The skirt had been pushed up above the stomach and the stockings down around the ankles. In the daylight blood could be seen near the tree and marks on the grass showed clearly that the woman, alive or dead, had been dragged across the ground. The dead woman was Ann Dickson. Nearby was a stick with its head, split in two, and broken off completely.

By now Mary had also reached Weobley and began making her inquries. Around the police-station, she could see a crowd developing, and despite her own terrible injuries she made her way through it and called out to Superintendent Ovens. The officer knew something awful had happened when he saw the poor beaten woman, who also had terrible scratches cut deep into her face. Having heard a brief outline of the previous night's events, Superintendent Ovens ran to Williams' house and arrested him immediately. In his room were his clothes scattered on the floor, and covered in blood. Williams seemed greatly surprised when told that Ann was dead, and he quickly admitted that he had been with Mary. The man who liked a fight was now himself terrified by Superintendent Ovens and his men, and said he knew who had killed Ann.....

With Williams under arrest in the police-station, Superintendent Ovens then went to Hill's lodgings, only to be told he had disappeared. Assuming he would head for sea, the ports of Newport, Cardiff and Swansea were alerted with his description by telegraph. Hill was indeed in the first of those ports, and somewhat brazenly on Friday night went to the central police-station, asking for a note to allow him to spend the night in the workhouse, as he was homeless. Although not using his real name, the desk constable was suspicious of him, and pushed back his right sleeve.... On his arm was a tattoo of a 'full rigged ship', exactly the description as had been sent by the Herefordshire police. When told he was being detained on suspicion of murder, Hill began trembling and weeping. By the end of the weekend, both Hill and Williams were being kept in Hereford Prison, on remand.

On the day of Hill's arrest an inquest was opened in Weobley Workhouse. The Coroner, Mr H. Moore, had overseen a *post-mortem* by a Dr William Walker. He determined the stick could have been the murder weapon: the force of the blow to the face had pushed bones into the victim's brain. Indeed identification of the body by her 'husband' Cox, was only possible as some years before, she had had, her left breast removed in an operation. Williams, himself, was present at the inquest, and was described as indifferent, and of course, on the face of it, he hadn't actually attacked the victim, or so it seemed at this stage. Also at the hearing, was Mary, who was described as a 'gypsy'. She said that she had first met Ann, in the 'Tramp Ward' of Worcester Workhouse in August. Cox, also described as a 'tramp', said he had met Ann some four years before. He was greatly effected by the crime, constantly weeping. Since Hill was under arrest in South Wales, the Coroner then decided to adjourn the inquest.

Unlike today the murder scene was quickly abandoned by the police and many people came to visit it and reduced the grassy area by the oak tree to a quagmire. It was said people came from as far afield as Hereford and Leominster. Some gathered around the shepherd's cottage, some hoping to see Mary Ann Farrell or Ann's daughter and some offered them money. That Sunday evening the Vicar of Weobley, the Reverend J.S. Crook, preached to his flock in the strongest terms, warning of the dangers of drink, pubs, arguing and 'ribaldrous behaviour.' He said there was no place for pubs in a moral and decent society, and urged his parishioners to worship instead. He added that strong drink, in particular, would lead to 'acts of the utmost depravity'. The next day Ann Dickson was given a pauper's funeral in the village.

Mary Ann Farrell was taken under the wing of the local police and with proper food, water and sleeping facilities, she quickly recovered from her terrible ordeal, at least physically, although her right eye, was permanently damaged. Ann's young daughter soon became a desired possession amongst the hop-pickers. The girl had been described by the press as 'remarkably smart ... with expressive eyes' and was therefore valuable. The girl's worth, at her younger age, was primarily for begging until she was old enough to be used for other purposes, legal or otherwise. Fortunately the police stepped in, and under the stewardship of a local woman, a Mrs Davies, Cox was allowed custody.

On the following Friday, October 2nd, Hill and Williams were formerly charged with Ann Dickson's murder, and on the Monday they appeared at Weobley magistrate's, a recently opened building. A large crowd was present and in the village high street they 'hooted and hissed excitedly' as the men arrived from Hereford. Both men were said to look tired, particularly Williams, who was also partially deaf, and who appeared to have lost weight, giving his poor clothing and even more dejected look about them. When the police case was outlined, Williams looked 'visibly moved' and when he heard how Ann Dickson had died, he turned pale. Hill, himself, soon turned a ghastly shade of white, when he heared the prosecutors, Mr Corner, senior and junior, suggest both men were *equally* guilty of murder, desite Hill saying he had attacked neither woman. By the end of the case, there was a great deal of weeping, including amongst the police, as they heard about the attempted rape on Mary Ann Farrell, how her baby was treated and how Ann Dickson was murdered. However at the end of the committal hearing the prosecutor suggested, in relationship to Mary Ann, Williams be charged with 'inflicting grevious bodily harm' rather than attempted rape. Williams in court had accused Mary Ann of lying about the whole affair.

The court heard that Hill had many deep scratches on him, and under Ann's fingernails were found human skin. Mr Corner had pointed out in court that Hill had refused to speak to the police as had Williams once under arrest. But dramatically in court, Williams began talking about the night of the murder. Both the prosecutor and a Catholic priest, Father Henry Mackey urged him to be silent. The magistrates then ordered the pair to stand trial on **Wednesday, November 4th, 1885 at the next available local assizes, in Gloucester, before Mr Justice Field.**

In the meantime the police had taken Ann's little girl out of any control of Cox, fearing for her 'prospects socially and morally' and she was handed over to the Hereford Workhouse, where it was hoped a wealthy family would adopt her, which eventually happened. Mary Ann and her baby were also allowed to stay in the workhouse. There was some anti-Irish and anti-Catholic feeling in Weobley particularly, due to the fact, that the priest had told Williams to remain silent in court. A letter to the local media also complained that the priest and a 'Papist magistrate' had paid fines on behalf of Williams before. Other letters complained of the hypocrisy of legal marriages, costing a 'few shilling's' in the Registry Office, which had meant Ann could not have a proper funeral as she was not legally married to Cox. One of the indignities in death she had suffered was only to have her initials on her coffin.

The case for the Crown, in the daylong trial at the assizes, was put by **Mr Charles Darling, QC [assisted by Mr A. Lyttleton]**, whilst a **Mr Ram defended Hill and Williams' defence was by a Mr Griffiths**. The public gallery was full and the police had earlier stopped the crowd surging into the court. The judge had also decided that women were not to be stopped from entering the public gallery, but said they must be segregated. He added the evidence would be 'obscene' but, 'if they choose to hear disgusting details which came out in the administration of justice, they might do so.'

As Hill and Williams appeared in the dock all eyes were fixed on them. They appeared in their same scruffy clothes, and whilst Williams stared to the front through the whole day, Hill could not resist but to look around the courtroom and towards the women in the public gallery. Again it was noted how similiar they looked. Once again Father Mackey was in court 'helping' Williams, and it emerged he had paid for the services of Mr Griffiths. Both men were allowed to sit, although Hill remained standing for a good period of the proceedings, in what was seen as an act of bravado.

The prosecution's case was that since both men were intent on performing a sexual assault on both women, if either of them used violence, then the other was liable, regardless of who struck who, and who raped who: it was intent that mattered above all else. However Mr Ram for Hill said that for his client to be guilty, if Williams dealt the fatal blow, he would have to have been raping or attempting to rape Ann Dickson himself, and this had not been proved. It was also a long established point of law, that what either man said about the other, was not evidence, since they were accused of the same crime. Similarly Mr Griffiths pointed out that his client was not now even facing the charge of seriously injuring Mary Ann Farrell, let alone attempted rape, yet this evidence had been heard, as the prosecution used this against Williams, in respect of evidence of the murder charge. Why had Williams not run away like Hill, the next day, Mr Griffiths pointed out. He turned to the jury and said that Hill, alone, was the murderer.

The judge's summing up was remarked on by the local press for, 'from the beginning to the end of his speech he never uttered a word, which might tell in their favour', but it was equally noted, 'as indeed he could not.' As Mr Darling had stressed many times, the intent to commit rape was as much an intent to commit murder[11], as was the obvious intent to kill, and the judge stressed what the Crown Counsel had said, namely that no juryman, with any common sense could think, except suspiciously, why else had Hill wanted to take the women back towards the farm, if not as part of a plan with Williams to have sex with them, regardless of consent. At the end of summing up, Mr Justice Field asked the foreman of the jury if they wished to retire, and he replied that he thought not. The foreman looked at each juror, who nodded, and in under three minutes they found both men guilty of murder. Both Hill and Williams appeared unmoved.

The judge, who had placed the dreaded black cap in front of him on his bench, before the trial started, then placed it on his head and sentenced both men to hang. The men were taken below by the prison-officers and Williams fainted. Under police guard they were taken by train back to **Hereford Prison and their respective death cells**. At Gloucester railway station a large crowd 'principally of the rough element' once again 'hooted' at them, and Williams was described as 'terribly frightened'. Safely in Hereford Prison, the men were soon told their execution had been set for **Monday, November 23rd, 1885.**

Father Mackey began a reprieve campaign for Williams, but regardless of whether he had actually killed Ann Dickson, he was seen as the more callous of the two. However there many people in the legal circles, particularly in London who were concerned that the men hadn't been correctly *proven* guilty of murder. No evidence of

11   This law was abolished by the Homicide Act (1957)

actual rape had been shown, and without that it would be difficult to prove the men set out with the intention of seriously injuring the women. But, since both men accused each other, it would unthinkable that both should have been acquitted, as clearly one of them had murdered Ann Dickson. In 1885 there was no appeal court and so it was with great excitement, that on November 21st, the local press published Hill's confession. Would this really explain the actual chain of events, that awful night two months before?

From Hill's version of events, he must have seen the attack on Mary Ann by Williams, for he said she spoke the truth. He said that as Williams attempted to rape her, Ann tried to run saying she was going for the police. Hill now admitted stopping her and of also trying to rape her. Hill said he had not tried to kill her, and she was still struggling with him, when Williams returned from near the sheperd's cottage. Ann was biting Hill's finger and Williams hit her across the head with his stick. Hill got up and left. He maintained that he had never once hit Ann.

In letters to his family he denied there was any premeditated intention to commit rape by the two men, and that he had not urged Williams to attack the victim. However he did accept his position had been caused by the 'demon drink' and urged his brothers to avoid it, on his family's last visit, five days before the scheduled execution. There was much sympathy in Weobley for the men's families, and it was widely viewed that, the men were simply 'two bad apples.' On Williams' final family visit, his mother had to be carried from the prison 'crying bitterly'. It seems as they waited for death, neither men blamed each other anymore, and once again turned their wrath on drink.

Aptly the man who would hang the men was himself a reformed drinker, or so it seemed; the famous Yorkshire executioner, **James Berry**. He would later claim that every man he hanged had some sort of drink problem. On arriving in Hereford Prison, Berry 'interviewed' both men saying he would 'launch them into eternity'. He described Hill as 'the worst of the two'. He said he assumed an air of bravado in the death-cell, to which Berry warned him, of his forthcoming doom, at his hands. "We'll see if you laugh then", added the Bradford hangman. Berry said he was further angered by Hill when he asked the hangman about the drop. Hill then started laughing, asking whether, Berry would be taking his weight, 10st 10lbs, into consideration. Then Hill asked whether it would 'hurt', and the executioner seized on this, as proof that Hill was a bully. Leaving the death-cell, Berry triumphantly said that Hill would be treated like all his other cases: he would die instantaneously. But he added he thought Hill did not deserve this mercy.

In Hereford groups marched over the weekend protesting about the 'demon drink' and in *Kerry Arms*, opposite the prison, temperance members warned the drinkers as they left the pub at closing time. To add his support, Berry attended the protest, and was seen to nod his approval at much of the firey sermons.

Much of the fascination with the crime was that serious crime in Herefordshire was virtually unheard off, at this time. The planned execution of Hill and Williamas would be the first use of capital punishment in the county for over 20 years. Indeed the last use; the hanging of Thomas Watkins in April 1864 had been in public.

The Home Secretary, Richard Cross declined to spare the men. As the time approached eight a.m., on November 23rd, Williams was praying fervently, along with Father Mackey. Hill remained casual in his demeanour. Berry pinioned each man his cell, and then walked each man to the scaffold. Since executions were so rare in Hereford, a new gallows was built in the prison grounds and this meant the death procession had some way to go, 50 yards in all. As they went to the gallows, Williams said: "Jesus, have mercy on me!", his face gripped with terror. Father Mackey was too upset to continue to the actual execution and so dropped away. Hill seemed disinterested in his Protestant equivalent. Berry, as ever was keen to talk to the local press, and afterwards said, true to form, Hill stood 'firm as a rock' on the trap-door, and warming to him, said he was a 'lion of a man', who didn't want a commutation of the sentence, as he could not face a life sentence in prison.

The execution actually took place at 8.02 am: the crash of the opening trap-doors being heard outside the prison. The black flag was raised and the small crowd outside began dispersing, although a few stayed behind, hoping to see James Berry; others waiting until prison-officers affixed the death-notice onto the prison-gates. Some people, opposed to capital punishment, drew their curtains shut in protest: One local publican even refused to serve alcohol until after the hanging, in case it be thought he had profited from the execution. At 9.35 am, Berry left Hereford railway station for Bradford. Unlike his many unpleasant experiences in Ireland, the crowd were appreciative of him, and bade him fare well.

At the inquest later in the day, the prison doctor said the drop was eight feet and both men had fallen like 'leaden weights' and were perfectly still. He said it as 'the most perfect execution he had ever seen'. Although Berry was keen to talk to the press, they had been excluded from the execution, and the inquest jury severely criticised the authorities for this.

Case 20
"The Deadly Curse
Of the
Wooden Chair"

Ernest Jones
(1958)
Murder
of
Mr Richard Turner

In Leeds' Armley Prison there used to be a reception area for those under sentence of death. It was a spartan area with a wooden chair for the condemned man. It was said that should anyone else, other than a condemned man, sit in the chair, then they would be cursed and too would hang one day. In April 1958 a group of prisoners were cleaning the area, when one of their numbers sat in the wooden chair. Minutes later a prison-officer told the man to keep working and then told him of the curse.

***Eight months later that man was sentenced to hang at....
Armley Prison.***

No one could accuse **38-year-old and father of two, Mr Richard Turner** of not being dedicated to his job. His job as the manager at the Co-op store in Lepton, a small village on the A642, about two miles from Huddersfield, was his life. Mr Turner had worked in the shop since leaving school and in 1948 had been promoted to shop manager. The small shop in Station Road was one of the three centres of life in Lepton. The other two were the pub and the Ashfield Liberal Club, where Mr Turner was a member. The club was just across the road from the Co-op and for about a year Mr Turner had regularly gone back to the shop after he had been in the club, because in 1957 the shop had been burgled.

Mr Turner took the burglary personally. It was almost as if it were directed against him and since the burglary he would go back to the shop after he had his tea, and before he went the Liberal Club. Mr Turner lived not far from the shop in Spa Terrace. With his visits from the club also he was virtually acting as a night watchman too and so it came as a terrible shock when, in the middle of September 1958, a burglar or burglars tried to break into the shop again. Mr Turner was at his wit's end.

Mr Turner was particularly concerned about Tuesdays, because that was half-day closing in the village. The next **Tuesday was September 30th** and Mr Turner was determined to make several visits to the shop. Mr Turner made one trip during the afternoon and everything was in order. After his late supper he returned again to the shop, telling his wife Kathleen that he would be back home at his usual time. Mr Turner also joked with his wife, that for all his security precautions, he thought he had left the safe open and so took those keys with him. Mr Turner wasn't back at his usual time.

Mrs Kathleen Turner rang the shop hoping to catch her husband in there but there was no reply. She tried again five minutes later and decided to go to the shop. On arriving in Station Road, Mrs

Turner didn't know what to think. The shop's lights were on and she could see her husband's car at the front.

Mrs Turner knocked on the shop's door and called out. She went round the back and called out. There was no reply. Mrs Turner then walked over the road to the Liberal Club to ask for help. She saw one of her husband's drinking friends, Mr John Howe, who went with her back to the shop. When they arrived they saw a couple who lived next to the shop and who had been woken by her calling out. The four of them began calling out and banging on the shop window. But still there was nothing but silence in the shop. Soon a small crowd gathered outside the shop and at intervals continued banging on the shop windows.

The whole situation was becoming distressing for Mrs Turner and she had forgotten that her husband kept a spare set of keys at home, but although she and Mr Howe walked back to Spa Terrace, they couldn't find them. Returning to the shop they were wondering whether to call the police, when one of the crowd, Mr Michael Jessop suggested they look in the car. They didn't find the spare keys but they did notice the car keys were in the ignition. Mrs Turner asked Mr Jessop to drive to the home of the assistant manager, Mr Herbert Whittle, and get his keys. By the time he returned it was twenty to twelve.

Mr Jessop and Mr Whittle went into the shop - Mr Whittle searched the shop itself, whilst the other man went upstairs where the office and safe were. When Mr Whittle heard Mr Jessop shout "Oh ho", he knew something terrible had happened and he went into car park. He didn't need to say anything to Mrs Turner. She ran into the shop.

Mrs Turner rushed to the stairs. A second later she saw the body of her husband lying by the office door and at the head of the stairs. Mr Turner had suffered a severe head wound and was lying in a pool of blood. There was no hope for Mr Turner - he was dead.

Detective Superintendent S. Foster, who was the head of the CID in Huddersfield, and his assistant, Detective Inspector Edward

Lumb, led the murder inquiry. Then on the following morning, Detective Chief Superintendent George Metcalfe, who was the head of West Riding of Yorkshire CID, took overall charge of the case, when the police were satisfied the motive was robbery and the investigations might take some time to solve, and could cover a wider area than Huddersfield.

The whole shop and office was combed for fingerprints. Once this had been done many hundreds of legitimate people had to be fingerprinted for elimination. However at the same time the police had, at least, found out how the intruder had gained entrance. At the back of the shop a window had been broken and fragment of glass lay in the shop side. The window, its frame and the surrounding walls were also fingerprinted and removed for forensic investigation.

Throughout the shop the police found a number of shoemarks but since the shop had been cleaned that morning the task was not as daunting as the search to match the fingerprints. In all there was just one distinctive prints, one of which was found in the storeroom, on a large bag of sugar. The print was easily identified because it was a common style of the time. The so-called "Avon Heel" was not only popular but it was distinctive. Judging by the marks the police were sure the shoe was new. The police also found a new knotted silk stocking, some children clothes and some cigarettes in the shop on top a rubbish box, by the door to the storeroom. When examined by the Forensic Laboratory at Harrogate in North Yorkshire, the stocking revealed a distinctive green fibre running through it.

Mr Whittle told the police that -76 pounds had been taken from the safe and various cash boxes that were scattered around Mr turner's office, and that it would have been made up of a large proportion of change. However the police were surprised that no cigarettes had been taken – although some were put into a box - and in all there were forty pounds worth in the shop by the counter both out for sale and under the counter in boxes. Crucially no where in the shop was the "Avon Heel" and the police were sure that the burglar had been disturbed or had panicked and attacked Mr Turner and decided just to concentrate on the safe. Since there was no way for the attacker to know that whether Mr Turner would have been there with his keys or not, the police were not sure whether the burglar was also a safe-breaker, or whether perhaps the thief had killed Mr Turner and then used his keys to open the safe.

The police found no fingerprints on the broken window and all the shoe-repairers in the Huddersfield area were interviewed on the following day, but none had done any work for anyone but for people who they were not suspicious of or who they didn't know. However the police were sure the burglar was local in terms of the county. The couple next door to the shop were sure no car, expect for Mr Turner's had arrived at the shop during the night. So while the police planned their mass fingerprint exercise to eliminate all the prints in the shop, they decided to look at all the local men who had convictions for shop burglaries throughout West Yorkshire, and in particular men, who used gloves.

On October 2nd the police decided they would visit all the men on their list and two detective constables made a routine call to a house in the Wyke district of Bradford, some 10 miles from Lepton, and easily accessible by bus via Huddersfield. The address in Temperance Street was the home of a **39-year-old Welshman, Ernest Jones**, his wife and baby daughter. Jones, a builder's labourer and native of Newtown in Monmouthshire, was on the list, because just five months earlier, he had been released from Leeds' Armley Prison. He had served half of a 12- month sentence for his part in a robbery at Doncaster Co-op store, in which some -1,500 had been stolen. Furthermore Jones was a habitual criminal with several previous convictions for theft and assault. However such a record applied to hundreds of men in West Yorkshire.

The two detectives, who spoke to Jones, obviously knew about his criminal record, but he was not regarded as a likely suspect, because of his age and the fact he had no record for any *serious* violent offences. In 1949 he had been sentenced to 15 months for actual bodily harm, but the assumption was that Mr Turner had been killed by blows from a weapon. Jones denied any involvement in the Lepton murder and said he had spent the evening watching television with his wife. Mrs Jones said this was true. Also Jones wasn't wearing shoes with an "Avon Heel" and a cursory glance around the house revealed no stockings, and so the two officers left Bradford.

During the next three days the police visited every house in the village of Lepton and were struck by the fact that several people reported seeing a stranger in the village. They said he was a tallish dark-haired man and one said that he had nodded to him and believed he was Welsh. Further information was the received by a criminal in Huddersfield, who said that on the evening of the murder Jones had been in the *Kirkgate Inn* in the town. Jones had been lying to the two officers at his home.

On the Sunday, a senior officer, Detective Chief Inspector Joseph Glendinning, went to see Ernest Jones. This time Jones admitted he had indeed been in Huddersfield on September 30th. However he said he and his wife had been in the town shopping and she had returned to Bradford at teatime whilst he had been for a drink in the *Kirkgate Inn*. He said he left the pub at nine o'clock and claimed he had "walked the streets" for about an hour or so. Then Jones stunned the officers by saying he had spoken to a policewoman. Jones said it had been raining and he saw her as waited in a shop front near the town centre. Once again the officers left - Jones may have been a liar but his story had to be checked.

The Huddersfield police were able to quickly to say that no policewoman would have been in the town centre when Jones was there but he could have mistaken her for a bus conductress in the rain and dark. The police had no real evidence against Jones but on Wednesday, October 8th they decided to re-visit Jones, on the ground that they wished to re-check his statement.

Detective Chief Inspector Glendinning asked Jones to say whether he could have been mistaken about the policewoman. Jones was adamant it was a policewoman. When told this could not be true, Jones was asked to come to Huddersfield central police station to help the police with "further inquiries". Whilst in the police station Jones' house was searched and it looked that Jones did know something about the Lepton murder. The police found a new knotted stocking, which was rushed to the Forensic Laboratory in Harrogate and it emerged the fibres matched those found in the stocking in the shop. Equally importantly the police found a pair of boots in the Jones' dustbin. They had apparently been burnt but the Harrogate laboratory was able to reconstruct them and tell the police they had the telltale "Avon Heel". A search of Jones' clothes in his house revealed one jacket, which had tiny fragments of paint on it, which matched the broken window frame.

This was all put to Jones and he was formally arrested for murder. According to the officers in the room Jones' reply was: " I was there. I just shoved him.". Jones may have shoved him but Mr Turner had died from a fractured skull, broken in five places. Jones was repeatedly asked if he could account for this but he denied emphatically using any weapon and the police were never to find one, although they suspected he was lying and had used some kind of cosh.

Ernest Jones appeared at the **Leeds Assizes on Monday, December 8th, 1958 before Mr Justice Hinchcliffe**. The Crown was represented by **Mr Geoffrey Veale QC and Mr Reginald Withers-Payne, the Recorder of Huddersfield, whilst Jones was defended by Mr Bernard Gillis QC (The Recorder of Bradford), and Mr Alter Hurwitz.**

Mr Veale told the court that there was no doubt that Ernest Jones burgled the Lepton Co-op store on the night that Mr Turner had been murdered. The counsel said they would hear from a man who spoke to Jones, the night before the murder, and that man would tell them that Jones told him, he was short of money and would sell the man a large quantity of cigarettes. The counsel said it was ironic that the cigarettes were the reason that Jones decided to burgle the shop and yet he had encountered Mr Turner and was able to raid the safe instead.

On the question of a weapon, Mr Veale said: " What weapon was used I can't tell you. The doctor will tell you, it could be a weapon, something like a cosh." The Crown counsel also said that Jones had broken in to the shop, using an axe and rake, and the evidence against him was "Well-nigh, overwhelming".

Dr David Price, a Home Office pathologist, told the court that Mr Turner had died as a result of *one* blow to the head. He said it was extremely doubtful that a "shove" or even a punch could do this and was more likely to have been a weapon such as a hammer, however there was absolutely no forensic evidence to show what weapon was used. The doctor said that Mr Turner's skull was not abnormally thin.

A friend of Mrs Jones' told the court that during a visit to Armley Prison to see Jones on remand, she had overheard Jones telling his wife that he had given Mr Turner a "rabbit punch", but in the witness box Jones denied this and stuck to his story that he had only "shoved" Mr Turner. Jones told the court he was surprised to see the shop manager at the top of the stairs and had pushed him out of the way. When he found out he was dead he took his keys and found that one of them opened the safe. Jones said he was so frightened by the man's death that he could not steal anything from the shop as he thought the police would soon arrive, although he had previously moved some items, and put them on top of the rubbish box.

Naturally Mr Gillis suggested to the court that the offence only amounted to manslaughter as there was certainly no suggestion that Jones intended or wanted to kill Mr Turner and Mr Gilles suggested his client had not intended to do any "serious harm" harm to the shop manager either. Furthermore since the law in 1958 proscribed the death penalty for murder during a burglary, Mr Gilles said that even if the jury believed he had murdered Mr Turner it should not be capital, because Mr Turner had been killed *after* the burglary had been completed, and therefore was not "in the *furtherance* of theft" as the law required.

As darkness fell on afternoon of **December 10th, 1958** the trial of Ernest Jones came to an end after three days. After just 40 minutes the jury returned from their deliberations. They found Jones guilty of murder and furthermore they said they believed it was during a robbery - Ernest Jones was sentenced to hang and was taken to the death-cell at Armley Prison. On **January 26th, 1959** the

Appeal Court in London dismissed Jones' appeal, making the poignant statement that if a burglar murders in order to escape justice then that that in law was "in the *furtherance* of theft."

Ernest Jones' life was now in serious danger and the prison officers on death duty made careful note of his behaviour as the new date of his proposed execution **Tuesday, February 10th, 1959,** fast approached. Jones seemed to sleep and eat well and certainly enjoyed talking to the "screws". However on February 3rd at six a.m. when he woke, it was noted that he seemed "resigned to the chop." If Jones were not reprieved he would be hanged in exactly a week's time.

Over the next three days, Jones was visited by his wife on several occasions and was most upset to learn that the police had not returned some of his property taken when his house was searched. When, on Friday afternoon, his wife told Jones, the matter had been sorted out, he became "quite cheerful".

The Home Secretary, Richard "Rab" Butler, discussed Jones' case late on Friday night. He, and his advisors, studied Dr Price's, the Home Office pathologist's evidence, very carefully and came to the conclusion, Jones must have used a weapon or had beaten Mr Turner with his fist with such ferocity that he intended to cause him serious injury – there would be no reprieve. It was decided at Armley Prison to convey this news to Jones at around 11 o'clock the following morning. "Jones did not appear very upset" – that was what was recorded in the Occurrence Book.

Jones then said: " Well it's what I expected", although later on he became more sullen and did not want any food, although he again cheered up when his mail arrived for him. The death watch officers knew the news had effected Jones, but that he didn't want to show any emotions. That Saturday night, Jones was allowed a sleeping drug. On Sunday he appeared quite depressed – he went to Church for the first time and kept looking at a picture of his wife. At three-thirty on Monday afternoon, Jones saw his wife for the last time. Understandably Jones' last night on Earth was restless. At 8.15 a.m. the Priest entered the death-cell. At just before nine a.m. the hangmen, **<u>Harry Allen and Harry Smith</u>** entered. Outwardly calm, Ernest Jones was executed a few seconds later.

Case 21
"The Man Executed On His Birthday"

~The Case of the Man With The Twitching Face~

"I don't understand court rules. I have never been in such a place."
- Arthur Osborne, the killer.

"Just to keep him quiet." – Why Osborne attacked a defenceless old man in his bed ….

Arthur Osborne (27-28)
[1948]
Murder
Of

Ernest Westwood (70)

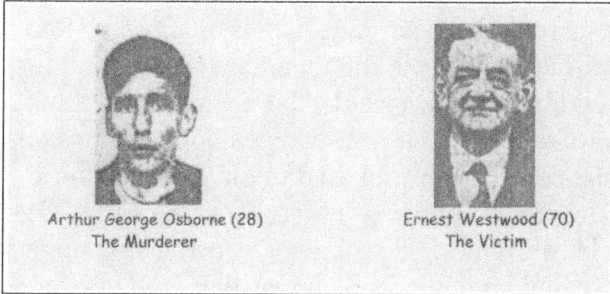

Arthur George Osborne (28)
The Murderer

Ernest Westwood (70)
The Victim

It was Saturday, September 25th, 1948 and the church was booked in Chichester, Sussex for the wedding of a 27-year-old man and a local girl called Dorothy. Unfortunately the wedding was a sham – the groom was already married and had the night before murdered an old man during a burglary in Brighouse in West Yorkshire, which lead to the most macabre of birthday's ….

Ernest Westwood (70) was a familiar figure in and around the Southowram area of Brighouse in West Yorkshire. He was a well-known Methodist and had been one since childhood and had been a former choirmaster and organist at his local church and he lived in a typical small Victorian terrace house called *Craggan* at 6, Law Lane. In such a tight-knit community routine and order was everything and so when on the morning of **Saturday, September 25th, 1948,** one of Mr Westwood's neighbours, Mrs Emily Hainsworth noticed that the curtains were still drawn at number six at *eleven* am, she went to investigate, particularly as Mr Westwood had lived alone since his wife passed away some two years prior. Mrs Hainsworth had a key

but she didn't need to use it, as the back door was unlocked anyway
....

The neighbour knocked on the door out of courtesy then went in. She called out to Mr Westwood but received no reply. There was no-one downstairs - she then made her way up the stairs calling out to her neighbour as she went. There was no need for Mrs Hainsworth to knock on Mr Westwood's door as it was open and to her horror she could see him in bed in his pyjamas lying in a pool of blood. There were a number of horrendous injuries to the back of his head, and incredibly he was still alive – just. There appeared no other struggle and so the inference was that he had been attacked in the night, and it was clearly not an accident – all the blood was in the bed. The emergency services were called and Mr Westwood was rushed to hospital in Halifax, where his condition was described as 'serious'.

The congealment of the blood from the head wounds suggested that Mr Westwood had been dead for a number of hours and it was initially believed he had been attacked around midnight. The church-going man appeared to have no enemies in the world and there was shock and disbelief in Southowram at his attempted murder. In such a small dwelling it only took the police a short time to discover an apparent motive. At the back of the property was a small downstairs window that looked onto fields and was screened from view by a stone wall. However, although it was open, and one pain broken, there was initially no evidence that an intruder had been in the house and there was no obvious evidence that robbery was the motive. For example on the living-room table was a purse containing money which had not been touched, although it looked like a tobacco pouch, and may have been overlooked. Also in his spare-time Mr Westwood acted as debt-collector in Southowram ....

The investigation was led by Detective Superintendent J. Wallace of the West Riding force and he was dispatched from Wakefield and a police head-quarters was established in the area in the *Pack Horse Inn*. On arrival in Brighouse he was told by Detective Inspector E.T. Hainsworth that he and his men were sure that robbery was the motive for the crime. There was a great deal of anger in the town over the crime as Mr Westwood was a quiet and unassuming man who since the death of his wife had grown frail and would have been no match for his attacker or attackers. One of his sons had visited him, leaving Law Lane at about nine-thirty pm. He told officers that his father was reasonably well and his usual self. Mrs Hainsworth said that her neighbour still had a job, but initially she thought he may have overslept. Normally he would catch the 7.10 am bus near his home. Despite his age Mr Westwood still worked as a foreman for a firm of stone masons in nearby Halifax, where his two married sons also lived, and they too were heavily involved in the Methodist church there. Mrs Hainsworth too had noticed the back window being open and indeed the pain being broken, and had thought it somewhat strange ….

In the afternoon fingerprint and forensic experts went over Mr Westwood's home in great detail, whilst uniformed officers scoured the fields at the back of the property looking for the weapon, whilst others carried out door-to-door inquiries. One expert found marks suggesting that the window had been forced to gain entry. However as the police investigation was on-going news came from Halifax that at 5.30 pm Ernest Westwood had died without regaining consciousness – it was now a murder inquiry and on the next day the locals joined police in looking in the fields for the now *murder* weapon. However it was the door-to-door inquiries that appeared to give the police a vital clue in the case in the hours after the crime was first discovered ….

Early on Saturday, one Mrs Edna Green who lived in New Street in a house just around the corner from Law Lane, had come downstairs to find a letter on her door-mat. Opening the envelope, it read: "I have been to your place but I see you was [*sic*] not up. I will be back on Monday or Tuesday." The letter was from a neighbour in the same road, **Arthur Osborne, a 28-year-old**, who had called a number of times over the past couple of days offering his services as a labourer and who had lived in Southowram for the last two years. He had worked for a local coal-merchant but was now apparently unemployed and always short of cash. That in itself may have meant nothing, but Mrs Green then told officers that Osborne had spoken about the deceased on September 23rd, just two days before. At that time, he had asked if Mr Westwood lived alone and remarked that he thought the old man was comfortably off .... Furthermore other neighbours said they were also aware of Osborne and he had been seen hanging around the rear of the house at around quarter past nine on the night before, perhaps waiting for Mr Westwood's son to leave ....

On the Sunday and Monday the national media published articles on the case naming Osborne. One said that the police wished to interview him and that he had been living in the Brighouse area for a number of years. Osborne had apparently vanished. He was described as 5' 6" tall, with dark hair parted at the side, a fresh complexion, grey eyes, slim and that he spoke with a 'South Country' accent as he was originally from Bognor Regis in Sussex. The appeal said that he was often seen in his working clothes – a pair of blue overalls. Osborne had married in September 1944 and had three young children but his wife was now in a mental hospital and his children were in an institution. Osborne himself saw one article on the case in a Sunday newspaper.

It appears that Osborne had gone down to the Chichester area of Sussex, where despite being married he now had a fiancée down there, a girl called Dorothy, whom he had arranged to marry on September 25th .... the day of the murder. All the arrangements had been made, the church booked and a honeymoon arranged but when Osborne sent his fiancée a telegram saying that he might be late, she cancelled all the bookings. Osborne did finally arrive and apologised to Dorothy. He then booked into lodgings in the town at the home of one Jane Stanton and her husband. It was the latter who showed Osborne the newspaper report naming him as the man police were looking for and Osborne immediately promised to return north and explain that it was all a mistake. He boarded a train but the Stantons did not like the look or manner of Osborne and the police were informed. A huge manhunt was organised across the south of England and fortunately on the next day in Sutton in South London, Osborne was found and arrested. Officers had been watching the Portsmouth to London trains and arrested him when the train stopped at Sutton.

On Tuesday, Detective-Inspector Hainsworth travelled down to Sutton and by six-thirty pm after a seven hour journey they were back in West Yorkshire on the following day, and Osborne was brought before the Brighouse magistrates where he sat in the dock with his head bowed. The court was told that when charged Osborne replied: "I did not mean to kill him. I lost my temper." When asked if he wanted legal aid or his family informed where he was he indignantly replied: "I don't understand court rules. I have never been in such a place." However, then in tears, he asked that his wife be informed of his detention. Although it was now dark a large crowd waited outside the magistrates court and police-station to see Osborne put into a police-car and driven off to Halifax police-station for further questioning. Naturally Arthur Osborne's fingerprints had been taken after his arrest and these were found to match some found on the window where Mr Westwood's killer had gained access. Osborne now made a full statement saying that he had gone to burgle the old man and had forced open the window with a large, heavy screwdriver. He found some money in a box and then went upstairs to see if he could find anything else. He heard a voice in the dark and claimed something was thrown at him. He then lashed out and claimed therefore he must have killed the victim accidentally.

Arthur Osborne appeared before **Mr Justice Slade at the Leeds Assizes on Tuesday, November 30th**, **in a trial that was to last just two days**. In the witness-box the accused swore that as he left the victim's bedroom he could see a shadow that appeared to suggest that Mr Westwood was sitting up. For the defence, **Messrs Ralph Cleworth, KC, and Harold Shepherd**, had asked for a manslaughter verdict but this had been rejected by **Mr Raymond Hinchliffe and Geoffrey de Paiva Veale for the prosecution**. The court was told that Osborne seemed to be genuinely shocked and surprised at finding out that Mr Westwood had died. Osborne said that having left the armed forces in 1943 he had worked as a lorry-driver until September 1948. As he looked for work in and around Southowram he would carry a nine-inch screwdriver around with him. He told officers that he had broken into Mr Westwood's home after his son had left and had found around twelve to fourteen pounds in a box in the living-room. He said that when in the old man's bedroom, after the object had been thrown at him, he lunged at

Mr Westwood a 'few times' with the screwdriver, but that he had the *sharp end in his hand.* Asked by his defence why he had attacked the householder, the prisoner replied: "Just to keep him quiet." Osborne said all he wanted to do was stun the victim so he could escape. He said that throughout the attack he could not see Mr Westwood in the darkness. He said he quickly returned to his own lodgings, where he lived alone, laying down on his bed trying to think what to do next. He said when detained in Sutton he had, indeed, been on his way back to Brighouse.

One of the arresting officers who escorted the prisoner back from the capital said that on three occasions Osborne broke down in tears, saying he had no intention to kill the victim. However gradually he became more composed and gave the police a clear and precise statement as to what had happened in Law Lane. Osborne had told officers where in the fields he had thrown the murder weapon, although it was never actually found. The police agreed with Mr Cleworth that Osborne was illiterate and somewhat slow, but they also claimed he was 'crafty and cunning'. When he had arrived in Chichester for his 'wedding' his fiancée's brother said Osborne looked terrible and had not shaved for at least two days. One of the officers in Sutton said he had found a bloodstained handkerchief in one of Osborne's pockets. However there was no other evidence of blood on the prisoner or on his own clothes and the forensic expert Lewis Nicholls said the blood-staining could have come from a nose-bleed.

On the second and **final day of the trial, Wednesday, December 1ˢᵗ**, the judge, in his summing-up completely ruled out any suggestion that the offence was anything other than murder. It certainly wasn't an accident, and he strongly informed the jury, which included two women, that even if Mr Westwood had thrown an object at Osborne, an armed burglar, this was not provocation. Indeed the judge had stopped Mr Cleworth when he had addressed the jury on this topic by saying, that he would be sorry if it were ever held by the courts that if a householder took steps to prevent his house being burgled and something went whizzing past a burglar's ear, it was sufficient provocation to reduce a crime of murder to manslaughter! The jury took the hint and after just 80 minutes they found the prisoner guilty of murder, although they did recommend Osborne to mercy on the grounds that they believed that he had not intended to kill.

Just a few months earlier Arthur Osborne would have been assured that he would not have been executed. In the previous February, the House of Commons had voted to abolish capital punishment, and the **Home Secretary James Chuter-Ede** had announced to Parliament that all convicted murderers would be spared execution, whilst the debates continued. However following the rejection by the House of Lords of the abolitionist bill, in November, he said this policy was now at an end. And so it was noted that as Osborne was being sentenced to hang, Mr Justice Slade had worn the dreaded black cap. He told the prisoner he had been found guilty of a 'brutal murder'. Osborne's legal team declined to appeal and he was told he would be executed on **Thursday, December 30th, 1948, at Leeds' Armley Prison – incredibly his 28th birthday.**

There was to be no reprieve. Although Arthur Osborne had indeed never been arrested before in his life, he was simply written off by the Home Office Officials, as a burglar who, if necessary would kill to escape. Outside the prison gates at nine am, there was just one member of the public, watched by a handful of policemen and pressmen. It was a dull and dreary morning and very few people were out and about, and shortly after the execution the **hangman Steve Wade from Doncaster and his assistant on the day, Harry Allen,** quickly left the prison and the city. Aside from the macabre co-incidence of the execution on Osborne's birthday, it must have struck Allen that the killer, like he, had been a lorry-driver. Allen had noted in his diary about the birthday and also that he and Wade were 'slightly' complimented by the officials on the speed of the hanging.

Case 22
"THE DEADLY SECRETS OF BETHEL STREET"

William Knighton
[1927]
Murder
of
his Mother, Ada

Although geographically overshadowed by Nottingham, Ilkeston is a small town in Derbyshire on the county border with Nottinghamshire. In 1927 an extraordinary murder took place that in recent times was investigated by the Criminal Cases Review Commission [CCRC] as a miscarriage of justice - the oldest case on their books ....

In 1927 the case was described as "one of the most sensational in the annals of crime" – A mother was found in her bed, with her throat cut, whilst her 16-year-old daughter had apparently slept through the whole affair. At the subsequent trial the girl said that her brother had come to her room for sex.... After he had been sentenced to death she and another married sister went to their brother's solicitor to tell him that their father had been having sex with them since they were 12 and that he was the actual murderer.

On the morning of **Wednesday, April 27th, 1927** there was a large crowd outside Nottingham's Bagthorpe Prison numbering about 200. At just before eight o'clock a group of factory girls ran towards the gates hoping to see the prison notice being affixed to the prison gates. The crowds outside English prisons were well aware of the significance of the tolling of the prison bell. The first bell meant that the condemned man had been pinioned in the death-cell. The second that the murderer was being walked to his doom. The third that he had been executed.

At four minutes after eight, Dr James Watson left the prison. The man had been executed efficiently. Then it was the moment the crowd had been waiting for - the affixing of the death-notice to the prison gate. It said that William Knighton had been executed. Out of the crowd of 200, none were from Knighton's family - perhaps not surprisingly as he had been convicted of murdering his Mother. There was a token protest - two women dressed in black - but the hangman **Tom Pierrepoint** was able to leave the prison later in the morning unhindered, as by then the rest of the crowd had dispersed.

William Knighton (22) had not wanted to see anyone on the day before his execution and it later emerged that after his final Saturday alive he had become depressed and refused to see anyone, even those from one of his married sister's side of the family, who did want to see him.

However there was one person who really wanted to see him, even to the extent of professing a desire be to be on the gallows with him and that was his girlfriend, Miss Florence Henshaw. She did not go to the prison but in her parents' home cried: " Oh how I wish I could stand beside him. Somehow I feel just now as if I were hanged with him."

William Knighton had been charged and tried for the murder of his **mother Ada (55)** at their home in Bethel Street, Ilkeston. The murder, extremely brutal, had taken place during the early hours of the morning of **Tuesday, February 8th, 1927**. Just *18* days later, Knighton stood trial at the **Derby Assizes** in a trial that lasted just one day. It seemed to be an open-and-shut case - Knighton's only defence was that he was insane. Indeed he had apparently confessed to the crime, and so his defence barrister made no attempt to deny Knighton had killed his mother.

Knighton was found guilty and sentenced to death. His appeal on **March 21st** was a formality and was dismissed, but then the case began to get complicated, when "fresh evidence" was presented to the Home Office. There was now no question that Knighton was insane – the defence would say he was wholly innocent. The execution was postponed and Knighton was allowed a second appeal, the first time such an appeal had been allowed, since the creation of the Appeal Court in 1907. The new damming evidence was exhilarating and cast doubt on the whole case and the events two months prior. So what exactly had happened on that night in February in Bethel Street?

Number One Bethel Street in Ilkeston was home to the Knighton family. There was Mr George Knighton, an ex-soldier and the head of the household, who since he was a cripple, slept on the ground floor, which was also the living room, and at the back of which was the kitchen. The second floor had two bedrooms, one of which was not used, the other was where Mr Knighton's son, William and a small grandson, slept and shared a bed. The house had a third floor, which had been built into the attic, and here slept Mr Knighton's wife, Ada, and his 16-year-old daughter Doris. The three floors of the house were connected by a staircase at the back the house.

With Mr Knighton unable to work it is curious why the one bedroom was not rented out and one can only assume Mr Knighton did not like outsiders. Mrs Knighton was also alcoholic and so the family's income was centred on their daughter, Doris, who worked in a local factory, and their son, William who was a miner. However William had also developed a liking for drinking and spent most of his time in the pubs with his mother. Then after turning 16, Doris had begun spending more and more time in the local pubs too.

Monday, February 7th, 1927 began like all other days in the Knighton household. William and Doris had to be up early for work – William returning after his shift at about four, Doris returning about a quarter past six. William went out at five to the pub, whilst Doris and their mother all left home at about a quarter-past nine o'clock for a few drinks before closing time, after a family meal at 7.45 p.m., intending to meet up with William. Because of her age Doris found it difficult being served some nights and this was no exception, so she returned home and was in bed asleep just after ten. Age was no bar to Ada Knighton being served in pubs and so Monday night was a heavy "session" for her and William.

Despite the spare bedroom Ada and Doris slept together in the same bed, which did cause a few problems, especially when Ada had been on a night's drinking. At just after one-forty Ada woke Doris with her coughing. This was such a common occurrence that Doris thought nothing of it, except for her natural annoyance at being woken up. Seconds later she thought her brother William had entered the room asking what the problem was. For a few seconds Doris' heart froze and her mind jumped back to the previous Saturday night.

On that night too, Doris, had had trouble being served in the pubs and had come home early and had gone to bed at 10.00 p.m. That night her brother had become so drunk that he had come home early and was in the house at the same time. Then between two and three a.m. she was woken by William calling out for some matches. William had been standing outside the bedroom and his mother shouted at him for waking everyone up. Then it went silent. Then some time later she *thought* her brother had entered the room.

Although it was dark when he came around to her side of the bed she could sense that he was only wearing his nightshirt. Doris had no idea what her brother wanted, as he said nothing. Then he stroked her hair and cupping her head pushed and then pulled her hair back. Knighton quickly pulled her side of the bedclothes back and lay on top of her in the "missionary position". Still Doris was in a state of fear as to what was happening as her brother was known to have fits and within the last week she had seen him have two but furthermore she hoped and prayed she wasn't going to be subjected to the abuse she had been suffering since she was 12.

Now on top of her William Knighton pushed his sister's nightdress up, pushed her thighs far enough apart and pushed his penis into her vagina causing such pain that Doris screamed out for help. Knighton panicked and rolled quickly on to the floor and fled out of the room. When asked by her mother, who now was awake but still effected by the Saturday night's drink, what the matter was, all the 16-year-old would say was that a man had been in the room. Doris said no more and could say no more. Ada Knighton told her she was must have been dreaming.

However undeterred by his narrow escape Knighton returned to his sister's bedroom. Whether it as to apologise or whether it was for another attempt, at what in effect was rape and was certainly incest, is unsure, for this time he woke his mother straight away, who asked what he was doing in the room. This time Knighton left the bedroom not to return.

With Knighton now *apparently* in the room again two days later, Doris became extremely wary and sat up in the bed and pulled the bedclothes up to her chin. If it were Knighton, he was not apparently that drunk and he asked what was the matter with their mother. Doris seemed quite at ease with her brother this time and asked him to light a match to see what the time was, although she did not see the man's face. It was 1.45 a.m. and Knighton looked at his sister and left the room. And that was that. At six a.m. the household arose for another day's work.

Being wintertime it was still dark when six o'clock came around and so Doris struck a match and climbed wearily out of bed. Her mother seemed to be still sleeping. However as Doris' eyes began to adjust to the early morning light, she noticed a pool of blood by the side of the bed on the floor by the toilet bucket. Ada Knighton was lying on her right side on the right side of the bed and on looking at her face Doris could see splashes of blood. Doris thought that her mother had suffered from a bad coughing fit and had lost consciousness.

As Doris rushed out of the room she saw her brother and the pair rushed downstairs to tell their father what had happened. However before Doris could speak, William had run out into the backyard, apparently to use the toilet. When William returned, their father asked him to go up into the bedroom and investigate. When he returned the general consensus was that Mrs Knighton was ill, and George Knighton's cure was a cup of strong brandy. Incredibly no one saw fit to call a doctor and so the next plan was to call on another member of the family – a married sister - Mrs Lois Wake who lived in nearby Eyre's Gardens.

It was William who went and he arrived at just before seven o'clock to be answered by his brother-in-law Mr John Wake, who let William in, offering him a cup of tea, and then listened to his garbled and frantic message that their mother was gravely ill. Moments later, armed with some blankets and more brandy, the Wakes and William trapped back to Bethel Street.

Like almost everyone else, the Wakes though William Knighton was a little simple and prone to acting strangely and spontaneously, so when as they approached Bethel Street, and William said he was off to see a friend, the Wakes thought nothing off it and proceeded alone to Bethel Street, assuming Mrs Knighton wasn't so seriously ill, after all. However once inside the house, Mrs Wake could see Ada

Knighton was very ill and even told Mr Knighton he must prepare for the fact that she might be dead. At the very least a doctor must be summoned immediately.

Meanwhile William Knighton's odd behaviour continued. He did not go to visit his friend and instead was logged at 7.25 a.m. by Constable Thomas Cowlishaw in Ilkeston police station blurting out some incredible tale and that he must see an inspector. Five minutes persuaded that Knighton wasn't completely insane, Constable Cowlishaw took Knighton to the office of Inspector James Wheeldon.

Clearly agitated William Knighton simply said: " I have done the old woman in. I have cut her throat with a razor. The razor is lying by the side of the bed." The law allows that people who make such statements be detained while the truth of the statement is checked and so Knighton was locked up in the police cells, whilst Inspector Wheeldon walked around to Bethel Street.

The senior officer was met at the house by the summoned doctor, Dr Stokes, who told the inspector that Mrs Knighton's throat had indeed been cut with a razor. Soon afterwards the police surgeon, Dr Francis Sudbury came to the same conclusion and at 9.45 a.m. less than four hours after the Knightons had woken for what should have been an ordinary day's grind, William Knighton was charged with his mother's murder. It undoubtedly seemed an open-and-shut case - what could be more simple - a full confession borne out by the *apparent* facts. On February 17th, William Knighton was committed to the next county assizes, where he appeared before **Mr Justice Branson.**

The case for the Crown was put by **Mr Maurice Healy**, and the Irishman said that it was a quite straightforward case. He said in an apparently motiveless attack, William Knighton had murdered his mother, although he intimated that the motive may have been that Knighton may have thought his mother knew about his relationship with his sister. Mr Healy said the defence would claim Knighton was insane, but the Crown would say he wasn't and there was no evidence to suggest he was remotely insane.

The court heard from Doris Knighton who told of her brother's attempt to have sex with her and how he had often come into her room since she was 12. Mr Healy said to the jury this showed that it would have been easy for Knighton to murder his mother, since Doris would not be surprised that he had come into her room. The defence **[Sir Henry Maddocks who was assisted by Mr T.R. Fitzwater-Butler]**, would use the incidents to let the jury hear of Knighton's seizures witnessed by his sister, and would suggest that Knighton did not know what he was doing when he entered the attic.

Likewise Mrs Lois Wake's evidence, of seeing a bucket filled with blood by the bed, was used by the Crown to show to the jury how brutally violent the attack on a defenceless woman had been. However to aid the defence, Mrs Wake also said that she had never seen Knighton act in any way other than affectionately to his mother and she too knew he suffered from fits and she told the jury that often he seemed dazed and distant.

The description of the attack on Mrs Knighton was given to the court by the police surgeon, Dr Sudbury. He said the wound to Mrs Knighton's throat was four inches long. He said he believed the murder took place at about four o'clock in the morning and there was a remote chance it was suicide, although the doctor said it was highly unlikely. The doctor said there was no other wounds or bruising on the body and no sign of sexual assault. The doctor said that in his opinion the attacker had lifted the woman's head by the hair and then cut her throat from left to right, which fitted with her sleeping on the right side of the bed.

When the court heard from Sir Henry for the defence they heard the first intimation that there was more to the case and it was far from straightforward. Sir Henry said his brief was to defend William Knighton on the grounds that he was insane, however he felt it was in the interests of justice to say that he had grave doubts as to whether Knighton was indeed responsible for murdering his mother.

Sir Henry said the only evidence against Knighton was his confession. It was a confession that the defence did not dispute had been taken fairly by the police, but it was just that – a confession. Sir Henry said that Knighton had gone to the police because when he had woken he had found the murder weapon in his jacket pocket. Knighton believed he had killed his mother in a fit. Sir Henry said Knighton then went up into the room placed the bloodstained razor under the bed and went to the police and confessed to Inspector Wheeldon. It was not Sir Henry's place to accuse anyone else, but there were two other adults in the house, and Mr George Knighton although a cripple, could still walk and climb the stairs, and whilst it was unlikely, it was not physically impossible for a 16-year-old girl to have also committed the crime.

However despite Sir Henry's observations the jury took only 50 minutes to find William Knighton guilty of murder and he was sentenced to hang to the sound of his two sisters crying. The appeal the following month before **Mr Justices Avory, Sankey and Shearman** was a mere technical formality and was quickly dismissed. The defence agreed the trial had been quite fair but they took the opportunity to reiterate that the crime was motiveless and there was no other evidence bar Knighton's confession.

The case was now before the Home Secretary, William Joynson-Hicks, and he was not impressed by Knighton's behaviour towards his sister, although again the evidence was her word, and it was an offence that never had even been reported to her parents, let alone the police. The Home Secretary was also told that Knighton had served in Army but had been convicted in Germany in April 1924 of sexually assaulting a German woman and sentenced to two years' Hard Labour. Furthermore the colliery where Knighton worked had told the police that whilst he was generally a good worker, he was prone to be aggressive, especially when he had been drinking.

However it was Doris Knighton that had come forward with the new exciting evidence. She now in effect accused her father of the murder. Miss Knighton and her sister-in-law had gone to Knighton's solicitor to tell him that their father had been having sex with them since they were 12, and that it was their father that had gone to the attic on February 5th to have sex with Doris.

Faced with this startling revelation, Mr Joynson-Hicks, sent the case back to the Appeal Court, the first time such action had been taken since the creation of the court in 1907. Although in the meantime he appointed two doctors, Griffiths and East, to establish whether William Knighton was sane or not. They concluded he was perfectly sane.

On **April 12th** the court, with the **Lord Chief Justice, Lord Hewart**, replacing Mr Justice Shearman, heard Doris Knighton give her new evidence. Dressed in black the young woman looking far younger than her 16 years went into the witness box. She began by repeating what she had said at the trial, namely that on the night of February 5th, she had been sleeping in the attic with her mother, and that her brother was hopelessly drunk. However now Miss Knighton said it was her father who came to the bed.

Miss Knighton then told the court that her father kept his razor by his bed in a drawer in the living room where he slept. Furthermore she said that the sounds she heard of a person moving about she now believed to be her father and since the murder she said her father had been burning clothes and on the morning of the murder had washed his shirt and trousers.... Most dramatically she told Sir Henry that she had seen her father beating her mother with a stick in the past. As a final slight to her father she now told the court that her father had told her to lie to the police and the Coroner's Inquest about the events of February 5th and the other nights.

Throughout his sister's evidence, William Knighton appeared calm, sitting forward in the dock with his chin on his hands and on the wooden ledge. He appeared to be occasionally chatting to the prison-officers that were sitting beside him and he also looked up to the public gallery that was packed. However if William Knighton thought he would be leaving the court a free man, he was to be sadly to be disappointed.

The court decided that they did not believe the girl's statement, although paradoxically the court declined to say whether her evidence in the trial was not truthful. The court decided there was other evidence pointing to the guilt of her brother. Lord Hewart told the court:

" The court has listened to the revised and amended story of the appellant's sister and every member of the court is fully satisfied that in the departure which she has made from her original evidence she is saying that which she knows to be untrue. We are so completely satisfied that, that is the case, that we do not think it necessary to offer the Father the opportunity, to which he would otherwise be clearly entitled.
We refrain from offering him that opportunity solely because we regard it as superfluous. The result is twofold. First the defence of insanity has entirely failed before this court and it failed on investigation by the Home Secretary by specialists.

The effect therefore is to establish more clearly than ever the importance of the confession which the appellant, admittedly now a sane man, made on the morning of the murder."

Emphatically Lord Hewart said: "THE APPEAL IS DISMISSED." Knighton appeared to display no emotion and voluntarily turned away from the Lord Chief Justice and began his journey back to the death-cell at Nottingham Prison.

Now the Wake family organised a petition to save Knighton from the gallows. Although Knighton's father and sister did not get directly involved in this they said would support the principal of Knighton not being executed. The petition to save Knighton was sent to the Home Secretary on **April 22nd, 1927, Good Friday**. Three days later he replied in person to Knighton's solicitors.... There was to be no reprieve.

However the case did not die with Knighton on the gallows at Nottingham Prison for nearly 75 years later the case was investigated by the CCRC [Criminal Cases Review Commission] in October 2002. The body has investigated miscarriages of justice since April 1st, 1997 and so far has had two posthumous murder convictions quashed where the accused was hanged [cf. Mahood Matten [1952] and Derek Bentley [1953]] and has referred a third [The case of

James Hanratty [1962]] back to the Appeal Court. In the Knighton case, the CCRC are investigating the case on the line that he is wholly innocent and not just technically innocent, however his conviction was upheld .

Case 23
"The Braco Murder"

~The Ghastly Affair at Blackhill Toll~

George Chalmers (45)
[1869-70]
MURDER
Of
John Miller (64)

George Chalmers

"No, I know nothing about it. I will die like a man for it, yes I will. Lord have mercy on me. Goodbye to you all for ever more. I'm quite innocent – may God have mercy on me." George Chalmers on the scaffold inside Perth Prison ….

Gripping tale from Perthshire just before Christmas in 1869 of the brutal murder of an elderly toll-keeper in a lonely toll-house, which led the police on the trail for months of tramps across large swathes of Scotland and northern England; eventually they found 'their man', but

was he the right one …? There were incredible scenes at the door of the death-cell, as some 30 witnesses broke into a hymn and prayers, as the condemned was pinioned by the executioner ….

The small village of Braco lies just inside the Perthshire county boundary, and five miles to the north of Dunblane on the A9 …. Nearly a 150 years ago, it was the scene of a terrible and brutal murder, that was to result in the **first execution inside a prison in Scotland**, and raises questions, as to whether a shocking miscarriage of justice had took place ….

As Christmas approached in 1869, **John Miller (64),** was the toll-keeper at the two-roomed toll-house called the *Blackhill Toll Bar*, which is still situated on the junction, where the road from Braco to Crieff turns off to Comrie …. Mr Miller was a confirmed bachelor – he had never married, and was now stuck in his ways …. He'd been at the toll-bar for the last five years, and was now beginning to find life a strain, and he had to walk with a stick …. He, did, however have a social life – he liked knitting his own socks, and darning his own clothes, and he played draughts etc. with his small number of friends …. Obviously, Mr Miller, did take some tolls, but since the mid 1850's toll-gates were going out of fashion, as local authorities began financing and looking after the road network themselves, and so most people no longer paid, and were simply waved through …. Mr Miller was a frugal man, but unlike many old folk, he did, at least, have the sense to keep his savings in a bank ….

At about eight pm on **Tuesday, December 21st,** local shepherd, Walter McLaren, passed by the toll, and briefly chatted to Mr Miller, who said he would not go to bed yet, as he thought a friend, Archibald McClaren might be popping by later …. When the shepherd departed, Mr Miller, left the front-door unlocked; indeed, most nights, he left the door unlocked until he went to bed, which was normally about ten pm …. This night, Archibald McLaren, a miller, took a different route home …. The miller, next day, went to the toll at six-thirty am as usual, however .... With him was a farm-servant, Peter McLeish .... to their surprise, they found the toll-house locked, and the shutters down – this was most unlike Mr Miller, who was a most reliable man .... something must have happened – perhaps old age had taken the toll-keeper away, or he had some sort of accident .... Archibald McLaren then ran to the nearby hamlet of Ardoch, where Mr Miller's sister, Mary, lived .... They returned back, and the miller cut away a pane of glass and pulled back the shutters with an axe .... inside the small building, the pair of them stood in the entrance hall – in the left-room, they immediately saw the body of John Miller – his head and shoulders drenched in congealed blood – it was a most gruesome sight .... The police in Dunblane were alerted, and by the mid-morning, a team led by Superintendent Peter Stuart, had arrived in Braco ....

The body was lying on its back and it was plain to see, that the toll-keeper had been hit once with a terrible blow on the right forehead – this had smashed through the rim of his felt hat – and then hit twice more with great force, as he lay on the floor. By the body was the murder weapon – a crowbar covered in blood and human hair .... There was no sign of a struggle in the toll-house, and the property had not been broken into .... the post-mortem suggested, that Mr Miller had lived for many hours before he actually died .... With no evidence of a break-in, it was almost certain, that Mr Miller had been murdered at some time after he was last seen alive and ten pm .... the police could see footprints running from the door to the toilet-window at the back; the toilet then leading on to the left-room and, indeed, the room could be seen through this window .... Almost certainly, the old toll-keeper had been watched as he prepared his evening supper of bread, cheese, ham, which along with a pint of ale, was untouched on the table, again suggesting the time of the attack was clearly before ten .... The killer or killers must have then rushed back round the building, through the unlocked door, and attacked Mr Miller – the first blow must have knocked the old man off his chair, the next two, were designed to render him unconscious or kill him .... In the room was a ragged waist-coat, in the pockets of which were needles, broken fish-hooks, gut, a pawn-ticket and a comb – they did not belong to Mr Miller, and their condition suggested they belonged to a .... *tramp* .... In the room was also a cap, men's leggings and some old boots - again they were in very poor condition, and didn't belong to the victim ....

It seemed beyond doubt that robbery was the motive – a silver-watch and chain had been ripped off Mr Miller's waist-coat, and the room had been searched – the sister telling officers, that approximately a pound in coins had been taken .... Whoever it was, had then left by the front-door, locked it; and had thrown the key in the garden, where it was later found by officers .... Initially, the police thought at least two men were involved – and locals told them that three *tramps* had been seen passing through Braco the previous night .... The next morning, two tramps were stopped by police in Crieff and the third in Comrie .... there's no doubt, the police thought they had found the killers, as all the men were taken to Dunblane police-station, where they were questioned the next day (December 23rd) .... In Scotland, even then, such interviews were conducted with a magistrate involved, and it soon became clear, that all the men were completely innocent; and they were all released ....

A week after the murder, Mary, told officers, that whilst going through the toll-house, she realised, that her brother's tweed-suit, a red and black shirt, and boots were missing .... Because of this, on December 29th, the police now searched the right-room!! Dramatically in here, they found a blood-splattered coat, shirt, and trousers hidden behind a large pile of firewood .... Clearly, the man who actually killed Mr Miller had taken off his blood soiled clothes, and taken some of Mr Miller's .... Although the three tramps had been ruled out of the inquiry, the clothes under the wood, suggested that they belonged to a tramp .... Even more evidence was found in the clothes - in the pockets was a knife, an awl[12], scissors, watch-key, button, hair-pin, pipe, and two pipe-heads .... However, even with all this evidence, there was no immediate break-through ....

Then, in mid-January, the investigation moved forward again .... The description of the clothes found in both rooms, was circulated throughout the country's police-forces, and Superintendent Stuart, received a telegram from his colleagues in Alloa, some 10 miles or

---

12   a small pointed tool used for piercing holes, especially in leather ....

so south of Dunblane, that officers in the town's prison, recognized the descriptions, and that they had belonged to a man called **George Chalmers (45)** .... *a well-known tramp* .... And he had been released from the gaol on .... *Monday, December 20th* .... At the beginning of December, he had received a 10-day sentence for 'exposure'[13] in the town – he had been drunk at the time, and had originally said his name was 'James Wilson'.... Under the name of Chalmers, and many other aliases, he had been in prisons and police-stations very many times; and on January 18th, a police-photo of him, was sent to all the forces in Britain and Ireland (*See photo*) .... And publicly an Official Reward of £50 was made available too .... However, despite the name, photo – the police also published a second photo, colouring in George Chalmers' beard and cheeks to represent his ruddy complexion, and reward, once again the investigation stalled ....

Towards the end of April, two more tramps were arrested, and taken in – one in Perthshire; the other in South Yorkshire – but both were innocent ..... But then, on Saturday, May 14th, a beat-officer, Constable Edward Billington, was on duty in Dundee city-centre - nearly 50 miles to the north-east of Braco .... It was 2 am and the officer spotted and stopped a tramp .... The tramp said he was heading to Aberdeen – nearly another 70 miles along the north-east coast, and that he was going to go via Arbroath .... Beyond being a tramp, there was nothing suspicious about him, and the officer let him go on his way: indeed, he didn't take his name, as he thought it would be false anyway .... Back at the police-station, Constable Billington, reported the stop to the desk-sergeant, who said it sounded somewhat like the Braco suspect – the officers looked at the photo – Constable Billington was gripped with tension – he was sure it was the same man .... Every available man in Dundee was called out – but the man seemed to have left the city .... At six am, Constable Billington, came off duty .... he immediately changed into his ordinary clothes, and began following the road to Arbroath, which was some 17 miles away .... Although the tramp had four hours on the officer, the man had not even left the city .... He was found in a farm in the Claypotts area of Dundee on the Broughton

---

13 "indecently exposing his person" ....

Ferry Road – he was carrying a sack of guano[14] .... The tramp didn't immediately recognise the officer, and said his name was 'Andrew Brown' .... When he was told the officer thought him to be George Chalmers, and was arresting him in connection with the *Braco Murder*, the tramp replied: "Na, na, there have been a few taken up for that already, you'll need to let me awa' also."

At Dundee police-station, the tramp denied he was George Chalmers, and denied he had even been in Alloa Prison .... Told officers would come from Alloa if necessary, 'Brown', eventually admitted being George Chalmers .... Then he admitted being in Alloa Prison .... he then went through a number of towns and cities throughout Britain, where he had been in jail .... Chalmers said he was now a tramp, but in the past had worked as a whaler, on a cattle-farm, and when really short of cash, he would sing in the street or even beg .... However, he did not confess to the murder of John Miller .... Chalmers was then taken to Dunblane, where he was remanded into custody, so a number of witnesses could be brought from Braco, to see if he could be identified, as having been in the area of the crime .... When arrested, Chalmers, was not wearing any clothing from Mr Miller, and had no objects to connect him to the toll-house ....

Through witnesses being brought to Dunblane, the police were able to trace Chalmers' route from Alloa .... by the night of Monday, December 20th, he was in Stirling, eight miles to the north-west .... Then on Tuesday, Chalmers, made his way north through various places towards Braco .... Witnesses also said, that the clothes and many of the items found in the toll-house, they had seen Chalmers wearing and in possession of .... The police still remained suspicious, that a second man was involved, and were intrigued to hear witnesses say, that on parts of the route, Chalmers, had been with a *second* man, a man who was never to be traced .... Police-officers in Alloa were able to positively say, that the clothes and items that Chalmers had when arrested in the town, were now the items found at the murder scene .... Similarly, the Chief Prison-Officer at Alloa Prison, William Wallace, said he had documented Chalmers' clothes and items, and could then identify most of them, when shown them

---

14   .... the excrement of seabirds and bats, used as fertilizer ....

by the Dunblane police .... Some of the items were also identified by, Mary McFarlane, whose husband was the manger of Alloa[15] County Hall .... And a journalist, John Haldon, from the *Alloa Journal*, told officers, that he had seen Chalmers in court in the town on the exposure charge, and the clothes that he had been wearing, were the ones found under the wood in the toll-house ....

George Chalmers appeared at **Perth High Court on Tuesday, September 6th, before two judges – the Lord Justice-Clerk – James Moncreiff, and Lord Cowan** .... he was described as having an 'inane expression' .... He originally came from Fraserburgh in Aberdeenshire, and seemed bored during his two-day trial .... Most observers thought him 'simple' .... Chalmers no longer denied that the clothes, and the items in them, found in the toll-house, weren't his – he said he had them taken off him, after he had left Alloa Prison .... He simply claimed that he had never been to Braco in his life, and that the witnesses, who saw him en route there, were mistaken .... He agreed, he had been in Stirling on Monday night, but then said he had walked to Edinburgh, where he stayed until the New Year .... from there, he went to Glasgow, crossed the border into Northumberland, where he had a job on a cattle-farm .... After that, he travelled across to Cumbria, re-entering Scotland via Carlisle .... He went back to Glasgow, back to Stirling; until eventually reaching Dundee .... An entry-book for a night-shelter in Edinburgh for *Wednesday, December 22nd*, showed the name of 'Andrew Brown' - were this Chalmers, it would have been difficult, although not impossible for him to have committed the murder (it is 50 miles away) – however, no-one at the shelter remembered George Chalmers ....

At 2.15 pm on the next day **(Wednesday, September 8th)** the jury retired – they were absent for exactly one hour .... The jury, **by a majority [13-2],** found Chalmers guilty of murder .... as he was sentenced to death by Lord Moncreiff, the prisoner burst into tears, almost drowning out the judge's words .... Chalmers was sentenced to die on Monday, October 3rd, **at eight am, in Perth Prison** .... A letter was immediately sent to London to contact **William Calcraft**

---

15 Alloa, at this time, was the County Town of Clackmannanshire ....

the hangman …. Once in the death-cell, Chalmers, enjoyed the unlimited access to religious advice, food and rest …. To anyone that would listen, he would constantly say, that the police and officials in Alloa Prison had lied: he said some of the clothes that witnesses said he had on, he claimed were left behind in the prison …. Overall, Chalmers, was well-behaved, quiet and didn't really cause the Perth authorities any problems …. His last meeting with two brothers and a brother-in-law were very emotional, however; and many tears were shed – Chalmers admitted that he had led a 'sinful' life; but once again, denied emphatically, having any involvement in the *Braco Murder* ….

In Chalmers' hometown of Fraserburgh, a campaign was launched to save him from the scaffold …. Two petitions were sent to the Home Office in London – one claimed, the evidence against Chalmers, was not sufficient to justify the capital sentence being carried out; whilst the other said, that Chalmers was suffering from a 'defective mental condition' …. The petitions did cause the execution to be postponed for 24 hours to **Tuesday, October 4th** …. and on Monday, the Home Office announced, there was to be no reprieve ….

And so at seven am on the Tuesday, the officials in Perth, met for the execution …. they began by gathering at the Town Hall …. they would then walk to the prison – it was over a mile away …. At the jail, they were met by the Deputy-Sheriff of Perthshire, Hugh Barclay, who handed over the death warrant to the officials from the Town Hall …. With members of the media included, over 30 official witnesses made their way to the death-cell …. incredibly, as the door was opened, they burst into a hymn, followed by a passage from the Bible read by a vicar …. The passage – from the 51st Palm - was couched in officialdom …. it read ….

"Have mercy on me, O God, according to your steadfast love; according to your abundant mercy blot out my transgressions. Wash me thoroughly from my iniquity, and cleanse me from my sin! For I know my transgressions, and my sin is ever before me …."

It carried on through another four verses and was clearly intended to obtain a confession from Chalmers …. An official then replaced the vicar, and asked the condemned man, whether he had anything to say …. he did …. but it was to ask that a letter be posted to his sister, and that it be published in the media …. In frustration, another vicar came forward, telling Chalmers ….

"It is my duty, as a minister, to tell you that, sin unconfessed, we have reason to believe, is sin unpardoned and unforgiven: and those who are guilty of it expose themselves to everlasting ruin. And if you go into the eternity, that is before you with a lie upon your lips, we have reason to fear, that you are now on the brink of ruin, on the verge of the bottomless pit; and I therefore ask you, in the sight of God, to relieve us from the very distressing position, in which we are now placed, and to say, whether or not you are guilty of the awful crime for which you are now about to suffer; because, remember you are about to enter the great eternity."

The vicar finished, by saying, that 'As you value your salvation, answer truly' …. Chalmers said he would reply, but it was to tell the gathering: "No Sir, I am innocent. I was not there at all. That is all I can say." William Calcraft had heard enough, and made his way through the crowd, and pinioned Chalmers, and led him out of the death-cell …. Chalmers was quite calm, and even helped the executioner tighten the straps …. He walked briskly to the scaffold, that had been built on the side of the east-wall, in such a position to be shielded, not only from outside, but from any of the gaol buildings …. In the distance, *St John's Kirk*, had began tolling its bell at 7.45 am, as the new law on private executions had ordered such …. On the drop, Calcraft, repeated the question of guilt to Chalmers, who once again replied: "No, I know nothing about it. I will die like a man for it, yes I will. Lord have mercy on me. Goodbye to you all for ever more. I'm quite innocent – may God have mercy on me." **The hangman pulled the lever at 8:08 am** – George Chalmers died instantaneously …. Again, under the new legislation, a black flag was raised up the prison's flag-pole …. It remained up for 15 minutes – as it came down, the tolling of the bell was also ended …. The body was left hanging for 40 minutes –

hidden, as in the last days of public executions – by a black screen …. After the corpse was taken down, it was buried in an unmarked grave in the prison grounds ….

By eight am, there were just two hundred people outside the prison-gates …. On seeing the black flag being lowered, they all left …. The next day Chalmers' letter to his sister was printed …. the tramp could barely read and could not write; and so it was beyond doubt, that not only had it been written for him, but some of the language suggested, that he had been helped with the words …. The flavour of the letter also suggested, that he had religious help in its construction …. One line said: "…. strong drink had been my ruin" …. Chalmers said he had led a tramp life for the last 12 years …. However, beyond thanking the prison-staff for their kindness, and all the religious advice he had received, and a p.s. for the help of his legal team, George Chalmers said no more ….

On October 5th, Constable Edward Billington, received the £50 Reward ….

After George Chalmers' hanging, there were just three more executions in Perth – in 1908, 1909 and the last in 1948 …. In light of this, it is fascinating that **Perth Prison had Britain's most modern execution chamber, incredibly built in 1965** …. It was, of course, never used …. After the death penalty had been abolished for murder in November 1965, it was used as a training facility, **before it was finally demolished in 2006** …. It was Britain's last execution chamber to be completely removed, although obviously, the scaffold had been taken away many years before ….

During the investigation, officers from Glasgow came to see George Chalmers in Dunblane, as on **April 18th in the city, in Stockwell Street, a truly terrible crime – the murder, sexual assault and mutilation of a 5-year-old girl, Margaret Burns - had taken place** …. Over 30 men had been arrested and released …. one of the descriptions of the killer, by a boy and girl, matched that of …. George Chalmers …. the two children were taken to Dunblane, to see if they could identify Chalmers – what struck them most about him was his …. red whiskers …. however, the police themselves, were not convinced about Chalmers, and he was released …. the murder of Margaret Burns was never solved ….

Case 24
"The Body In The Dung-Heap"

"The Case of the Last Execution at Armagh"

" ..... the evidence that was sworn against me was all lies. I swear that I am innocent: I am not afraid." - Joseph Fee.

"I only wish to warn you against cherishing any hope of mercy in this world and I would entreat you, in the short time at your disposal, to prepare to meet your doom, and make your peace with God and pray for pardon and forgiveness for your sins." - The trial judge.

Joseph Fee
[1903-4]
Murder
Of
Mr John Flanagan
IRELAND

GHASTLY DISCOVERY IN A BUTCHER'S YARD.

DEAD BODY OF A MAN FOUND UNDER A MANURE HEAP.

A dreadful smell permeated around the Jubilee and Fermanagh Street area of the County Monaghan town of Clones. This was not surprising as here was situated a badly run slaughterhouse. Eventually the authorities ordered that a dung-heap be cleared up and two men began raking and digging at it, until a foot emerged.....

For some time the good folk of the small County Monaghan market town of Clones had been complaining about a terrible smell in the town and now it was fast approaching Christmas 1903 and they wanted it sorted out. The spot where the foul odour was coming from had eventually been pinpointed to the backyard of a local farmer and would be entrepreneur, **21-year-old Joseph Fee**, who lived at the family home on the corner of Jubilee and Fermanagh Street. Many of the neighbours knew what the problem was: The Fees should never have been allowed to operate an animal slaughterhouse so near to the town centre. It was not just the smell but the noise of the animals as well. To make matters worse, the Fees had also begun piling up manure in their backyard too. Eventually the neighbours complaints looked like they were going to be dealt with, when the local authority decided to investigate....

The council ordered that the dung-heap be removed and on **December 15th,** two men arrived to begin work on it. Messrs Albert McCloy and John Farmer began plunging their pitchforks into the heap to break up the mess, so it could then be put into their cart. Incredibly by noon alone, they had filled five carts. McCloy had told his mate that they were not to take all the manure, as Joseph Fee had wanted some to remain for his cabbages, and so a small mound was pushed up against a wall. It was whilst doing this task, at about four-thirty pm, as darkness was falling, that Mr Farmer's fork hit some softish object, which was nevertheless hard to move. He prodded at it again and still it would not move and so he called out to his friend, who came over.....

They both had a go and to their shock a boot revealed itself. The men then tried to pull on it but it would not budge. Both men resolved not to be defeated and with a huge effort they prized it free: now they discovered a man's foot! Mr McCloy ran the short distance to the local police-station. Soon the whole town realised something was going on at the Fees' home, and indeed one his family's labourers, a Mr Edward Howard saw Joseph Fee, who appeared as white as a ghost, saying that the body of a *small child* had been found in their yard. This was clearly incorrect as the body was quickly discovered to be that of a young man, who was well-known in the area as an egg and butter seller. **Mr John Flanagan (25)** had last been seen in the previous April, and his sudden disappearance from Clones wasn't thought suspicious, as many people from Ireland at that time, would simply up sticks for either England or the USA without telling anyone.

The local police were aware Mr Flanagan had left and quickly discovered that he had last been seen at lunchtime some eight months ago on **Thursday, April 16th,** market-day in Clones. As usual he was there to buy eggs, and his family had become quite well-off, selling their produce on to the shops in Belfast. The father would normally give his son £30 cash and a cheque for £50, which was cashed in the town, to buy more goods if necessary. In the morning John Flanagan had taken their 'pony and trap' and had made the short journey into Clones, where he met his two assistants, Messrs Patrick Moan and Joseph Connolly. The trio then set up their stall in the Diamond next to the market. Around ten-thirty am, Mr Flanagan told his men that he was going to the local *Ulster Bank* to pay some debts off. Just as he was about to leave he saw Joseph Fee who himself owed Mr Flanagan some money, but as the men knew each other well, the latter was not that concerned about the debt and said he'd catch up with Fee later.

However Joseph Fee seemed quite keen to pay off the money and suggested that the egg-buyer come to his home at about 11 o'clock, and then suggested the pair then go down the pub, and sure enough Mr Flanagan was seen walking down the narrow street to the slaughterhouse. However when he knocked on the door, there was no reply. Witnesses would later tell the police that he remained in the street until noon, constantly looking at the property and repeatedly knocking on the door: perhaps he was keen, after all, to collect his money from the Fees. Mr Flanagan made his way back to his stall where Messrs Moan and Connolly were loading their wares into the cart ready for the one-thirty train to Belfast. The trio worked on until 12.30 pm when a smiling Joseph Fee put his hand on Mr Flanagan's shoulder and asked why he was in such a hurry. To the other men's surprise he was annoyed with Fee and snapped that he had been outside Fee's house for over an hour.

Fee continued smiling and re-invited him back to the yard. Mr Flanagan didn't want to go but eventually agreed saying he'd be no more than 10 minutes: his men never saw him alive again. As the train was in Clones railway-station ready for Belfast, a number of angry farmers swarmed around Flanagan's stall, demanding the money for their goods. Mr Moan then left the stall himself and headed off looking for his boss and for Fee. He wasn't at the Fees', nor was he in any of the 'locals'. Indeed Mrs Fee hadn't seen her son either. She too was worried, as he never missed his lunch. Mr Moan returned to the angry farmers and explained the situation. The crowd was placated when the men said that if Mr Flanagan failed to turn up soon, then they would fetch his father. The farmers then allowed the men to go to the railway-station.

At three o'clock Mr Flanagan senior and a daughter arrived in the town to speak to the farmers. Ann Flanagan said she too was desperately worried about her brother: she knew he liked a drink but overall he was very reliable and his disappearance was completely out of character. Just as everyone was mulling about what to do, who should casually walk by, but ..... Joseph Fee. Mr Moan angrily asked him whether he knew anything about Mr Flanagan and he nonchalantly replied that he'd last seen him in a local pub called *Creighton Duggan's*, where the pair had two 'hot ports'. Then somewhat curiously Fee felt it necessary to say that he had paid the two pounds he owed Mr Flanagan. As the group looked lost as to what to do next, Fee allegedly told Mr Connolly that the relatively wealthy and unattached Mr Flanagan might have gone off with a woman for the afternoon!

By nightfall the Diamond and the market were deserted. The rest of the Flanagan family had, by now, arrived in Clones and searched it from top to bottom, including every pub and bar. In every place, including the *Creighton*, they all said Mr Flanagan hadn't been seen, although being market-day every pub had been jam-packed. Eventually the Flanagans went to the police. They knew Mr Flanagan, took notes of the days events and said they'd look into the matter. Two days later Fee saw Mr Connolly near his home and asked about the egg-buyer, parting with the words that it was very odd, Mr Flanagan just leaving like that.....

The first policeman at the dung-heap was Head Constable James McKeown. A night-guard was put on the dung-heap and the next morning, he examined the body and then asked his men to fetch Joseph Fee who was in the family kitchen speechless and in tears. Suddenly he reached for a sister, Mary, who lived in the house and kissed her on the cheek. When one of the officers came in, Fee jumped back like a frightened animal. He look terrified and tried to flee, but the alarm was quickly raised and a number of burly policemen arrested him at the front of his house in the street. Handcuffed he was taken back into the kitchen, whilst the Head Constable ordered the body be removed from the manure. It was not just under the dung but under two-feet of soil too, and had been trussed up. Someone had also sprinkled it with quicklime, clearly aiming to speed up the decomposition process. Incredibly as the men from the Royal Irish Constabulary dug, they were amazed at how well the body had been preserved. The soil in the yard had neutralised the effects of the lime!

The body was then taken to the nearest pub, *Cassidys*, so that an inquest could be held. After the second day the landlord asked the police to remove it, as it was having an effect on his trade, but the Coroner initially ruled it must stay. Indeed the law in Ireland at the time was that a pub must accept a corpse if it were the nearest place to the spot where the body had been found. The Coroner did eventually agree that the actual inquest would be held in the *Creighton* though. The hearing was told by a Dr Edward Tierney that the body was somewhat decomposed, being in a 'soapy state'. It was lying half on its back with the legs sticking out at an angle. The doctor said that the killer had not buried the corpse far enough down and the protruding leg did not fit in the grave. That Mr Flanagan had been murdered was in no doubt: Dr Tierney said he had been hit on the back of the head with some type of very sharp instrument and that 'considerable' force had been used. The brain was clearly visible. The throat had also been cut and it had sliced through the Adam's Apple. It was clear to the good farming folk of the area, that Mr Flanagan had been expertly 'slaughtered' like a pig.

In 1903 in order to kill a pig humanely the slaughterer would used a long pole with a very sharp steel tip to stun the animal from behind and then cut its throat with a 'pig-sticker's' knife: as the police had moved the body this latter weapon had fallen off the body. Given Fee's attempted escape from the police, the Coroner's Jury had no hesitation in declaring him responsible for the murder. However juries in capital cases in Ireland were always loathed to convict the accused, even in so-called 'clear-cut' cases, and the case of Joseph Fee proved no different. Despite the obvious motive of robbery (the cash was never found) and Fee's behaviour when the body was found, two juries at the local **Monaghan Assizes in the March (three days) and July (four days) of 1904,** failed to reach a verdict and so the authorities took the decision to try Fee in Belfast in the following December, hoping that a cosmopolitan city-jury, would not be worried about sending a country man to the gallows. If this jury failed, then Fee would be freed, as under the common law of Ireland (and England), the prosecution would never seek to try a man a fourth time.

On **Thursday, December 1ˢᵗ, 1904,** Joseph Fee stood before **Mr Justice Wright in the courthouse on Belfast's Crumlin Road, in a trial that was to last three days.** One of the features of the case was that it had become a *cause celebre* in the North of Ireland. Even though the trial was now held in Belfast vast crowds were waiting to be allowed in, and many had travelled up from County Monaghan. Such were the numbers that the RIC had to clear a path for the accused's mother and sister to reach the courtroom. As in the previous two trials, Fee was defended by **Mr George Hill-Smith, KC**, although there were gasps in court as he intimated he might not be able to defend his client due to a dispute about fees. The prosecution was led by **Mr James Campbell, KC, MP, the Solicitor-General for Ireland (assisted by Messrs T.L. O'Shaughnessy, KC, and W.H. Brown),** who said as this was a capital case he was sure this could be dealt with and Mr Hill-Smith nodded in agreement. (Mr Hill-Smith was, at this time, Ireland's top and most expensive barrister.)

The evidence against Joseph Fee seemed overwhelming: he had even bought a new spade in the town after Mr Flanagan had apparently vanished. Local shopkeeper, Mr James Nicholl had told the police that when Fee bought it, he was in a rush, in a flush, and left in an equally hurried state, calling back as he left the shop, for it to be put on his slate. Other witnesses had seen the prisoner erecting new fencing around his property and eventually passers-by could not see into the yard. The 'pig-sticker's' knife was identified as belonging to Fee and even had some of the animals' bristles still stuck on it.

Miss Ann Flanagan said her family had spent many hours looking for the victim: Fee had even offered to help them look, and had even offered to take the girl down the pub to calm her nerves. Mr Campbell also pointed out that after Mr Flanagan had vanished, Fee's finances greatly improved. A week before the market he had bought some pigs on credit, and a week after paid off the debt: £18.00 in cash. It emerged that Fee had intended to open a butcher's shop, but had, in fact, bought poor quality pigs, many of which could not be sold in the shops, and which had to be slaughtered and their carcasses destroyed.

Mr Hill-Smith told the jury that Fee was the 'obvious subject' and thus the victim of local rumour. He lambasted the police for arresting him before the body had been fully dug up and examined. News of this arrest soon spread through Clones. He even suggested that the police had been feeding information to the media to further blacken Fee's name. Four witnesses were now produced claiming to have seen Mr Flanagan much later in the day in the town, but as the Solicitor-General informed the Belfast jury, they hadn't come forward before the first two trials. The prisoner's mother and sister told the jury that the policemen in the kitchen had lied: Fee hadn't tried to flee and had never kissed his sister 'goodbye'. Indeed things became so bad for the defence when Mr Hill-Smith informed the judge that some of his witnesses had been 'dining' too well: there was laughter in court as everyone knew this meant they were drunk! On **Saturday, December 3rd, 1904,** after the judge had summed up for some 3 ½ hours, the Belfast jury left to decide Joseph Fee's fate.....

Whatever concerns their fellow County Monaghan jurymen may have had about the evidence against the accused, this new Ulster jury seemed to have no doubts. They were absent for just one hour. They found Joseph Fee guilty of murder. The Clones man seemed unmoved and then said to the judge: " ..... the evidence that was sworn against me was all lies. I swear that I am innocent: I am not afraid." This visibly affected Mr Justice Wright as his voice trembled as he spoke the solemn words of the death sentence. He told Fee that the evidence against him was 'irresistible' and that he could not see how the jury could have come to any other conclusion. The black cap, on his head, he added: "The crime you committed was of a singularly cold-blooded and treacherous nature and was impelled by one base and sordid motive – love of money and your lust of money. I only wish to warn you against cherishing any hope of mercy in this world and I would entreat you, in the short time at your disposal, to prepare to meet your doom, and make your peace with God and pray for pardon and forgiveness for your sins."

If Joseph Fee were guilty there could be no question of a reprieve given the motive for the murder, but many in Ireland thought him innocent. Executions had long ceased to be carried out at Monaghan and so it was decided that, should Fee be hanged, it would be in **Armagh Prison and the execution date was set for Thursday, December 22nd, 1904,** such matters in Ireland being directed by the trial judge[16]. The executioner selected was to be **Henry Pierrepoint** and on the preceding Tuesday he was informed that the authorities in Dublin had refused a reprieve. The last executions at Armagh had been in 1898 and 1899 when there had been two hangings. Since then the gallows had somewhat deteriorated: they were no longer strong enough and a specialist joiner was employed from Dublin to get it ready. By all accounts Fee spent a peaceful last night, and at exactly two minutes past eight the execution procedure began. A bell was tolled and a few minutes later it stopped: Joseph Fee had been hanged.

In the famous book *"Executioner: Pierrepoint"*, Albert Pierrepoint refers to the Fee case and says that the accused, who is not named, finally told his father on the gallows that he was guilty, and in his anger Henry Pierrepoint pulled the lever extremely hard. Whilst it is true that the local 'paper reported that at the inquest held immediately after the hanging, a juryman asked the Coroner, if Fee had said anything at the last moment, the Coroner replied he would not answer as that was not to be the purpose of the inquest. The inquest heard the prison-doctor report that death was instantaneous, and the Coroner said he would allow the representatives of the media

---

16 Unlike England & Wales where the Sheriff of the County in which the crime took place would later fix the execution date.

to see Joseph Fee's executed body. It had been laid out on a table across the trapdoors that had now been closed again: but they were to never open again for a criminal, as **Fee was the last person executed at Armagh Prison.** The prison closed in 1986.

Case 25
"The Grim Secrets Of Clay Lane"

~The Terrible Death Of The 'Pigsticker'~

".... He has got all he has been asking for, for a long time." – The killers speaking of the victim ….

"....shabbily dressed, of the roadster type." – The men in the magistrates' court – worst of all neither man appeared in court wearing a jacket ….

"Yes I know all about it. Mum's the word.' – A third tramp had witnessed the ghastly murder ….

"It ought to have been done twenty years ago!" – Were the men serial killers …. ?

Oliver "Tiggy" Newman (61) & William "Moosh" Shelley (56) [1931] Murder Of Herbert "Pigsticker" Ayres (45)

Murder Scene

On the borders between the north-western London suburbs and South Hertfordshire a refuge dump had been burning for many years and in the Summer of 1931, it revealed a grim secret that lead two tramps to the gallows; and the claim that the area held even more deadly secrets ….

Notes:

Today the murder spot is in the London Borough of Barnet; at the time it was Middlesex.

Today

Edgwarebury marks the boundary between the London Borough of Barnet and Hertfordshire; but just over 80 years ago, it was still a rural area – there was no M1; but there were signs of change – a large part of the area was used as a refuge dump, and there was a railway-line to the area with sidings, known as the *Scratchwood Sidings* – they were especially used for the trains with rubbish. Yet half-a-mile or so away was still unspoiled countryside and in particular Clay Lane [it now runs between Bushfield Crescent and Edgwarebury Lane and up into *Moat Mount Golf-Course*]; although even from this point one was constantly reminded of the burning rubbish and the subsequent smoke. The fires that burnt refuge had been burning for many years …. Before the building of housing in Edgwarebury the large wooded area of Scratchwood extended even further south from the golf-course into Clay Lane and on the night of **Monday, June 1st, 1931,** a tramp, of which there were many in the area – attracted by the rubbish dump and the relative isolation – Michael McGlade left his shack in Scratchwood and walked towards the burning rubbish heaps …. He fancied an evening's smoke and wanted to light his pipe. Mr McGlade had seen a lot of things in his life and a lot of strange things being burnt; but he had never seen a human arm before ….! It was charred but there was no doubt it was human …. Mr McGlade was not the type of tramp who walked away from things; he threw his pipe down and ran down Clay Lane knowing that other tramps had hovels down there too ….

The tramp didn't see anyone that night and kept running until he reached the newly built Watford By-Pass where aptly enough he came across two policemen – they were in a police motor-cycle with side-car and happened to be in the area as there had been a number of burglaries at the local golf-course, which was also 'home' to some unwanted travellers; and the officers were going to question them. The officers followed Mr McGlade back up Clay Lane and up towards the sidings …. They too could see it was a human arm …. One officer walked back to the by-pass, whilst the other joined the tramp in a smoke. Within the hour a major inquiry was undertook by the Metropolitan Police's 'S' Division. The removal of the arm was very unpleasant work for the police as it was stuck in human waste …. But the arm revealed a whole human body, likewise suffering from burns – the right arm and feet were burnt away; and of the rest of the corpse, the left arm and chest area were the most affected …. It was a male, well built and the head was pointing north-westwards …. Around the head was a piece of charred sackcloth. The body was taken away and the police began to think whether this was a terrible accident or terrible murder ….? And of course officers had no idea who the man was ….

The next day the famous pathologist Sir Bernard Spilsbury examined the body …. He concluded that the man had suffered a severe blow to the head, which had fractured his skull. He had also had his jaw broken and had been severely struck in the chest ….. There were no clues as to what he looked like from the blows to the head, but he did have traces of a sandy-coloured moustache; and more promisingly on the bits of his arms that remained - a tattoo – a red heart pierced with an arrow. Sir Bernard believed that the body had been at the sidings for between 36 and 48 hours. But asked whether this was an accident or 'foul play', the expert told the officers he believed it was *murder* – the injuries to the man were the result of *repeated* blows from some type of blunt and/or heavy instrument …. The officer leading the inquiry, the Head of Scotland Yard's CID, Chief Constable John Ashley, wanted a local detective who knew Clay Lane and its inhabitants …. Unlike Mr McGlade most of the tramps did not want to interact with the police but one officer Detective-Sergeant Pickett knew them all …. And he knew they often sorted out 'disputes' without recourse to the police or the law; and he said there was a good chance the victim might be a tramp ….

Detective-Sergeant Pickett then made some inquiries amongst the more 'police friendly' tramps to try and enlist their help …. One agreed to look at the body and this brought immediate success – it was that of **Herbert Ayres (45)** known in the tramp community as 'Pigsticker'; and he lived in Clay Lane: the tattoos and faint moustache were a give-a-way …. The tramp said he thought he had last been seen around Clay Lane on the Sunday (May 31st); whilst another tramp who had no prejudice about speaking to the 'boys in blue', John Armstrong, said that he had been drinking in Edgware on Saturday night, before being offered a bed in one of the huts in Clay Lane …. The hut was shared by two tramps **Oliver Newman (61)**

and William Shelley (56) known as 'Tiggy' and 'Moosh'. Mr Armstrong said that 'Moosh' was of 'medium' build and very dark-skinned with black hair and black eyes. Like Mr Ayres he too had a tattoo – that of a woman. He said 'Tiggy' was much smaller; but very broad in his build – he too was dark-skinned, although not as dark as 'Moosh'. Both men had criminal records for theft, often using aliases; and all three men often worked as casual labourers on the rubbish dumps …. And what Mr Armstrong had to say made the police very much interested in these two men, who now had also vanished from Clay Lane …..; but Detective-Sergeant Pickett said they would be back – their hut was all they had in the world and a 'stake-out' was set up …. After dark, officers including the local detective-sergeant watched their hut …. The officers knew from this officer that the two tramps had three ferocious dogs that would bark if anyone came within 50 yards of their hut. Eventually Newman and Shelley did return and were, furthermore, unaware of the officers' presence in the undergrowth. The officer leading the operation Detective-Inspector Bennett decided to wait till dawn and then to pounce …. Elsewhere officers were placed in a ring around Clay Lane ….

At 7.15 am officers on the Watford By-Pass end of Clay Lane saw the two men. Detective-Inspector Bennett had placed himself a fair distance from the dogs, and so was able to stop the men personally as they approached the main road. He spoke to Shelley first and addressed him as 'Moosh'. Before he had said another word a group of uniformed officers surrounded Shelley and all he could say of Mr Ayres was: "I don't know who you mean. I know nothing about it!" Taken away to a police-car, moments later the same operation captured Newman and they were driven at great speed to Edgware police-station. With the two tramps in custody, the senior officers went back to their hut and Clay Lane … By the hut in a hedge they first noticed a heavy stick – Shelley himself called it *his* 'blunderbuss' – which had been cut from a nearby bush. It was covered in blood and attached to it were hairs of the same sandy colour as that of the victim. The grass under the hedge was heavily bloodstained …. In the hut itself under some make-shift wooden floorboards was a …. large axe; and a bucket full of blooded water. Meanwhile back at the station Newman wanted to talk …..

Newman said that he and Shelley had, indeed, killed Mr Ayres; but that it was a consequence of a fight – the two men had accused the victim of stealing some of their tea, sugar and bacon from their hut. Newman said that in order to overcome Mr Ayres, he had used Shelley's stick and the blow had rendered him unconscious …. It was now Shelley's turn to speak and he agreed to speak to Detective-Sergeant Pickett. He said it was all Newman's fault that they had been caught – he had wanted to place the corpse on the railway line to destroy any trace of the fight; but 'Tiggy' would have none of it …. He said neither man had any real sympathy for Mr Ayres, Shelley adding: " …. He has got all he has been asking for, for a long time." However when the pair were charged with murder they *both* said: "I don't understand." When the men appeared at the local magistrates' court the next day neither man had shaved and were described as 'shabbily dressed, of the roadster type.' Worst of all neither man appeared in court in a jacket …. Meanwhile with the men in custody, a number of the so-called 'Clay Lane Colony' began wanting to speak to their new friends in the police …. The police also wanted to back-up Mr Armstrong's statement …. He had said that he had retired to bed some time before Newman and Shelley had come back from their night out drinking. At about 11 pm raised voices outside the hut awoke him ….; then loud thugs and the repeated shouts of: "Oh dear!" Now fully awake Mr Armstrong looked out and in the moonlight saw the two men hitting the shouting Mr Ayres with the 'blunderbuss'. Then for about twenty minutes there was silence; then another series of thuds – when Mr Armstrong dared look out of the hut, he saw an axe being dropped into a bucket of water. Then at around midnight, he saw Newman and Shelley carrying off a body towards the railway sidings …. In part using a pitchfork; in part over Shelley's shoulders ….

John Armstrong obviously said nothing and early the next morning at 4.30 am thanked the men for their hospitality and left. However as he left Shelley approached him and said that if anyone said anything about 'Pigsticker ….' Mr Armstrong stopped the conversation and replied: "Yes I know all about it. Mum's the word." However when the body was discovered he did his duty and went to the police. Despite this the police needed to corroborate Mr Armstrong's statement – he was, after all, a potential suspect and even if he was not involved in the murder he was skirting the edges of being an 'accessory *after* the fact'. Another tramp, Richard Saunders agreed to give the police a statement – he lived in an old van off Edgwarebury Lane. He had seen Newman and Shelley in a pub in Edgware. The men looked angry and Mr Saunders asked them why, to which 'Tiggy' replied: "There will be something up if anyone comes 'mooshing' around our place." A fearful Mr Saunders thought they were referring to him, but the men said it was 'Pigsticker' that they were after …. Mr Saunders too heard cries coming from Clay Lane …. Another tramp, Frederick Cozens said he had been sitting on a bus at Edgware Station – he had been with Mr Ayres, when 'Tiggy' and 'Moosh' came on the bus as if they were looking for someone …. That someone was the 'Pigsticker' and when they saw him Newman undid his coat so that an axe could be seen …. Mr Ayres understood the message. From the police's point of view they had clearly corroborated Mr Amstrong's statement and Newman and Shelley stood trial at the **Old Bailey on Wednesday, June 24th, in a two-day trial before Mr Justice Swift.** [Just three weeks after the crime].

All the defence could try and do was convince the jury to convict the two 'old men' of manslaughter by stressing that Herbert Ayres had allegedly *repeatedly* stolen from the men's hut and that the two tramps felt genuinely justified in administering their own law; and that they had only used their fists – Newman now denied saying he used the 'blunderbuss'; and that Mr Ayres, a 'big quarrelsome man', had started the fight …. It was no good the jury were out for just 58 minutes and neither man was recommended to mercy following a verdict of guilty of murder. When sentenced to death William Shelley thanked the judge saying: "It ought to have been done twenty years ago!" As the now condemned men left the dock they began laughing. A month later the pair's appeal was rejected and they were hanged together at **Pentonville Prison on Wednesday, August 5th, 1931, by Robert Baxter and three assistants at 9.00 am. The Home Secretary, John Clynes** said he had felt some doubt as to whether this was a case for the death penalty; but having conferred with the judge he was assured this was a case of *premeditated* murder – certainly the use of the axe. Today Clay Lane still exists preserved as a Site of Local Importance for Nature Conservation …. And what did Shelley mean by his remark – after being told there would be no reprieve, he claimed there were five more murder victims buried around the sidings and Clay Lane …. However the police refused to look for any more bodies and the 'confession' was said to be stored away in a secret file in the Home Office.

Case 26
"MURDER AT MARSHALL'S WICK FARM"

Thomas Wheeler
[1880]
Murder
of
Mr Edward Anstee

In the early hours of the morning of Sunday, August 22nd, 1880, up to possibly three masked men arrived at an isolated farm just outside St Albans in Hertfordshire. They knew the owner's name and he looked out of a window, only to be blasted to death by a shotgun, on the spot. The man or men then ransacked the house, whilst the dead man's girl servant and another woman, locked themselves in their bedrooms gripped by a terror that only a female knows. However the motive for the crime was robbery and that part of the county had been plagued by a spate of robberies and burglaries and one family were the prime suspects - the Wheelers.... including one pretty 14-year-old girl, Mary, who would herself embark on a career as a "professional criminal". The girl's father, Thomas Wheeler was hanged for the St Albans murder, and almost certainly uniquely in the annals of British criminal history, so was the daughter for a double murder ten years later in 1890.

Note: The St Albans robberies and burglaries

a) June 8th at *Bernard Heath's Farm.*
b) Same day in St Peter's Street in the city (hammer stolen).
c) June 9th at *Upper Beech Hyde Farm.*
d) August 18th at *Samwell's Farm* (shotgun stolen).

On **Sunday, August 22nd, 1880,** St Albans awoke to the news of a "fearful tragedy" at a farm just outside the city in the village of Sandridge, at a 300-acre farm called *Marshall's Wick.* However it was news that that had been anticipated, as the locality had been subjected to a number of shocking robberies and burglaries carried out, in either the dead of night, or near to daybreak. However in this case the inevitable had happened and a farmer, **68-year-old Mr Edward Anstee,** had been shot dead in addition to the robbery.

The victim, Mr Anstee had been at *Marshall's Wick Farm* for some 20 years and was well known in the St Albans area, having previously been a butcher in London. Despite the size of the farm, it was run by just by Mr Anstee, his wife, a servant girl called Elizabeth Coleman and a farm boy. However, August was corn-harvesting time and on Saturday a large number of casual labourers were also working on Mr Anstee's land. Late on Saturday evening the old farmer returned to his home, a small farmhouse just off the main road into the city, and near to the home of the landowner, a local magistrate, Mr Thomas Martin JP. The farm was quite isolated and was shrouded by woodland, which meant it could not be seen from the main road.

When worked stopped on Saturday evening, Mr Anstee paid his labourers and was in high spirits as the weather had been fine and hot. The farmer was in bed by ten p.m., as was the servant girl and a Mrs Susan Lindsay, a family friend, who was staying at the farm, as Mrs Anstee was away visiting friends in Reading and London, and the farm boy was staying with relatives in St Albans. By next morning *Marshall's Wick Farm* had been robbed and Mr Anstee had been shot in the head by what was believed to have been a gang of robbers.

The terrified women told police that they were woken at about a quarter-to-two in the morning, by what they thought was a call out to Mr Anstee. This was followed by a shot against one of the farm's windows, and the police did find two holes in a pain. In the ensuing confusion the women were not sure if the farmer was shot immediately or whether a short conversation had taken place. Although Mr Anstee had been killed from a blast from a shotgun, the weapon must have been taken away by the attackers, and furthermore Mr Anstee's own shotgun had not been touched. However the police quickly discovered that a neighbouring farmer, a Mr Edward Woollatt, of *Samwell's Farm* had believed a gun of his had been stolen during the previous week.

With the farmer dead the robbers entered the house through Mr Anstee's bedroom window, the spot at which he had been murdered. Inside the room it would appear that the robbers had covered the old man's body with bedclothes. The bedroom was not as badly ransacked as all the other rooms that the robbers searched through. In an ordeal that must have seemed like hours, but probably lasted only a few minutes one of the robbers appeared in Mrs Lindsay's bedroom with a lamp. The woman, herself elderly, was told by the robbers that Mr Anstee had gone to tend a sick cow. The old lady thought that there might have been more than one man and that one of the robbers spoke to her and said that they wanted money but that she said that she didn't know where there was any, and as was later to become clear, the robber or robbers thought that she was the farmer's wife. The attackers then left the bedroom.

However the robber or robbers quickly returned to Mrs Lindsay's room and demanded money again, but again she replied she couldn't help. When they left the old lady now locked her bedroom. Incredibly the incident seemed over and Mrs Lindsay lay in her bed in sheer terror. But worse was to come, as about an hour later a man demanded she open the door and said he had hammer and would break in and hit over the head with it, and that his two accomplices were also still with him. Mrs Lindsay remained in the bed and the man tried to break in and demanded she hand over five shillings. This time the old lady pushed two shillings under the door. The man or men then appeared to have left for good, taking with them two parcels and some dining plates, although they left the hammer behind.

All this time the young servant girl, Miss Coleman, remained, equally in terror for her life and honour, in her room. She said that she thought that she heard three gunshots and that they had been at about two o'clock, and that it was Mr Anstee firing at burglars. Like Mrs Lindsay she locked her door when she realised that the farm was being robbed. Unaware that Mr Anstee had been murdered, the two women stayed in their bedrooms until daybreak and the arrival of a Mr George Bailey, who was a regular visitor to the farm, who arrived at four-thirty a.m., to deliver the milk. Miss Coleman called out from her bedroom and Bailey noticed the front door was open. Soon afterwards the trio went into the Anstees' bedroom and made the terrible discovery.

The left-hand side of Mr Anstee's face and part of his forehead had been literally blown away and the rest of the head was covered in blood. By the body was a large pool of blood and parts of the brain. The window frame was splattered in blood and with bits of human brain too, and blood had trickled down the farmhouse wall. On the ceiling were nearly 50 gunshot marks. The clear evidence was that Mr Anstee had been killed whilst looking out of the window. A note was sent to St Albans police station as well as for a doctor. A number of telegrams were sent and by early afternoon a large number of policemen from both the St Albans police and the county force were at *Marshall's Wick Farm*. The investigation was led by Superintendent William Ryder who came from Bishop Stortford and who was the county's acting Chief Constable. The murder caused a sensation in the county and soon a large crowd had descended on the farm. One of the telegrams requested that Mrs Anstee return to her home immediately. She returned at four o'clock and on hearing the terrible news was taken ill.

Although Mrs Lindsay attempted to describe the robber who spoke to her the police already had three suspects, whom they believed had been in the area to commit robberies and burglaries. Furthermore at five in the morning a witness saw a man walking back to St Albans with two parcels and inquiring the route to the city's main railway station, from where he took a train on the *Midland Line*. The police said the man was 5' 2", bow-legged, was of a light complexion and had cyst on his neck. A man was arrested by the police but was quickly released and the police issued another description. The man was fortunate to be realised so quickly as he was acting in such a such a suspicious manner that travellers and staff at the city's *Midland Railway Station* had detained him and handed him over to the police.

The new description of the new man was detailed as him being, 5' 1", of a reddish complexion and aged about 47, his hair turning grey, wearing a moustache, and with a speech impediment, but in the meantime a man was arrested on suspicion of murder in Luton, although again he was quickly released. In addition a number of person had their parcels searched, whilst on Sunday night it was believed the murderer had been arrested in Harpenden a few miles to the north of St Albans. In what was described as "from information received", Superintendent Pike went to an address and arrested a man called Henry Wheeler (42), a local farm labourer. At the suspect's house was found items from a St Albans burglary committed on June 8th at a farm, including most crucially of all a hammer stolen in another burglary on the same day in the city. A further search of the property uncovered the plates and other items from *Marshall's Wick Farm*.

Also living at the same address, was Henry Wheeler's 22-year-old son George, who was also arrested. However Mr Wheeler then incriminated his younger brother Thomas, by saying it was he, who had brought the plates and other items to Harpenden. **Thomas "Happy" Wheeler, who was 46-years-old,** was in the city on Sunday afternoon in the *Pine Apple* pub, but had been, refused a drink as he was classed as a "traveller". He returned later to the pub at the evening opening time and was promptly arrested by a large number of officers. One of the items found on him was a syringe, which it was believed belonged to Mr Anstee. By now there was an electric atmosphere in St Albans as it was believed all three men had been charged with murder. Meanwhile the police had also found other items of stolen property from the farm, in the surrounding farmlands, including some more plates and a pair of the victim's trousers, at a place called *Dead Woman's Hill*. However most importantly one officer, Constable William Sparks, found in a wood near the farm a shotgun, of which one barrel had been recently been fired, and this was later identified as having been stolen from *Samwell's Farm*.

Such was the secluded spot of *Marshall's Wick Farm*, the fact the robbers seemed to have called on Mr Anstee, and the fact the farm boy was away, it gave the police the clear impression was this was a planned robbery. It was also possible that the gun was discharged by accident perhaps when Mr Anstee tried to push the ladder away from the wall - the police had found the ladder broken in two. Such was the blood on the wall, the police believed one of the robbers, who was on the ladder may have grabbed the dead man and used him to climb into the bedroom, pulled him into the farmhouse, and then let the others in by opening the front door.

Thomas Wheeler, a native of St Albans, was actually living in Lewisham in south-east London at the time of the murder and on Monday a large number of officers descended on his home near *Catford Railway Station*. He was well known to the local police as a petty criminal for crimes such as theft and burglary. He was also employed occasionally on local farms, although he was well known as a man who did not do a lot of legitimate work. The whole Wheeler family was well known to the police in Hertfordshire and south-east London and on Monday morning Henry and George Wheeler appeared at St Albans magistrates court charged with the burglaries on June 8th in the city. The court also ordered the arrest of Henry Wheeler's wife Anne on the same charge. However despite local feeling that all three men were guilty of the *Marshall's Wick Farm*, it was somewhat of a surprise that only Thomas Wheeler faced the capital charge. Furthermore to add to the local gossip, the latter's hearing was held in secret, although it was reported that when arrested Thomas Wheeler had blood on his clothes, which he said had come from the slaughter of a pig.

Such was the local anger towards Thomas Wheeler that as he left the magistrates court and was put in the prison van, the crowd surged forward and ripped off one of the van's doors and an attempt was made to draw him in the mob. A Coroner's Inquest was quickly opened on Monday afternoon in *St Albans Town Hall,* and the first witness was Mr Bailey, who had worked, on and off, for Mr Anstee for some 12 years. He described the finding of the body and the disordered state of the farm and that in the passage leading to the front door was a large engineering or blacksmith's hammer, and he confirmed that when he last saw the ladder, at seven o'clock the previous evening, it was not broken.

Dr F.R. Webster, the doctor summoned to the farm from St Albans, told the inquest that he believed the gun had been fired at distance of between three and 10 feet, and that Mr Anstee had died instantly. The doctor said that from the blood and gunshot pattern, he believed the gun was fired close by the wall and up it. It was then decided to adjourn the inquest until Thursday. On the same day Thomas Wheeler appeared before the magistrates again, ironically with Mr Martin in the chair, the man who's tenant, Wheeler had been accused of murdering. However once again the hearing was held in private. Also on Thursday, Mr Anstee was buried in an impressive display of sympathy for the victim and his family from the people of St Albans. Mr Anstee had been a keen local cricketer and still took an interest and his local club was Bernard's Heath (the scene of one of the June 8th burglaries) and it was perhaps fitting that they were playing on the day of the funeral and equally fitting, that they stopped play as the cortège passed.

At the resumed inquest, Mrs Lindsay said that on Saturday evening, Mr Anstee had bolted the front door himself. She said she had woken by a "great banging", and she thought it might be a door slamming shut, but quickly realised it was a gun. However she said that she did not go and see what had caused it and remained in bed until she heard footsteps coming up the stairs, and she could hear them gong into the Anstee's bedroom. When the man or one of the men came into her room, Mrs Lindsay noticed he had a lamp from the dining room table. She said although the lamp as on it was not as bright as it could have been. The housekeeper said, that he appeared to be short, with dark hair, and was pale, and she did say she could recall his face.

Mrs Lindsay said that when the man returned to her room, he addressed her as "Mrs Anstee" and told her he wanted to lie down and he tried to pull back the bedclothes. She said she called out to Mr Anstee, only to be told he was out tending some cows. The man said he wanted to put out a light elsewhere and left the bedroom, allowing Mrs Lindsay to bolt the door. Later the man asked where the farmer's cash-box was kept. The woman then said that the man said that, if he did not take something from the house, he would hit her on the head, and he banged the door hard, with what Mrs Lindsay thought was a hammer. The housekeeper said she was sure she would be able to recognise the robber again. However she said she had seen Thomas Wheeler at the magistrates hearing but there he had been "muffled" up, but he did have the same voice. After the inquest heard from the servant girl, Miss Coleman, Dr Webster gave details of the *post-mortem*. He said in total he removed 37 gunshots from the victim's head, and such was the impact that none of them was in their original form.

During the following week, the police continued their enquiries into the murder and in addition to the murder charge Thomas Wheeler was also charged with robbery at *Samwell's Farm*, which included the theft of the supposed murder weapon, in the days before the murder. Whilst on Wednesday, September 8th, Thomas, Henry, Ann and George Wheeler appeared in court in relation to the St Albans burglaries on June 8th. However after this appearance, Thomas

Wheeler then faced a new charge, that of burglary on June 9th, at another farm belonging to Mr Woollatt, namely *Upper Beech Hyde Farm* at Sandridge. However on Wednesday, the Coroner's Inquest was able to conclude and they concluded that Thomas Wheeler had murdered Mr Anstee. A week later on September 15th, the magistrates committed Wheeler for trial at the next assizes to be held in **Chelmsford** in November.

The case against Thomas Wheeler began before **Mr Justice Hawkins on Friday, November 5th, 1880 and was to last three days, through to the following Monday. The Crown's case was put by Mr Talfourd Salter, QC, Mr Snagge and Mr Forrest Fulton**, whilst initially there was no counsel for the accused. It was clear that the case for the Crown was that Thomas Wheeler, and Thomas Wheeler alone had robbed and committed murder at *Marshall's Wick Farm*, a charge to which he pleaded 'not guilty' in a determined voice.

Although Wheeler had no defence counsel, it had been originally been decided to try his family at the same assize on the burglary charges, but a legal point had arisen, which meant their cases would be put back, and this left their counsel, **Messrs Woollatt and Grubbe** in Chelmsford without a brief and they took on the case. Finally at 11.55 a.m. the trial was underway and for an hour Mr Salter told the jury of a "cold-blooded murder" for the purpose of "plunder". He said that Wheeler had appeared in the St Albans area in June and from then and until August 22nd, he was "louting about", and that on nine p.m. on the day before the murder, he was on the Harpenden Road heading towards St Albans. The counsel said on Saturday he was penniless, whilst on Sunday he was drinking or trying to drink in several local pubs.

After the jury were shown plans of the murder house, the court heard the devastating evidence of Mrs Lindsay who said: " I believe the prisoner is the man who entered my room. I see nothing to distinguish between the prisoner and the burglar." However when cross-examined by Mr Woollatt she denied saying to the police that the robber was so "muffled" she couldn't see his face, although that appeared to refer to the magistrates hearing. Once again Mrs Lindsay said: " I have seen his face". In his summing-up, Mr Justice Hawkins lay great importance on her evidence, saying she had seen Wheeler's face "distinctly by the light", and this was the only direct evidence the prisoner, as the other evidence, such as the finding of the stolen goods at his brother's house was strongly suspicious, but no more than that. On the issue of the syringe, the judge said witnesses had said it was the victim's, but Wheeler said it was his, and the jury would have to decide who to believe.

To the surprise of many the jury were only absent for just 24 minutes. They had either dismissed Mrs Lindsay's evidence out of hand or believed her. It was the latter for the foreman replied strongly that they had found Thomas Wheeler guilty of murder. All Wheeler could say was: "I am not guilty". The black cap on his head, the judge then sentenced Wheeler to death. There then followed a dramatic scene as the condemned then collapsed on to his knees in the dock and recited the *Lord's Prayer*. The judge motioned to the prison-officers to remove Wheeler and some in court thought he was about to say who the "guilty" party or parties really were. It was noted by the local press that this was a "great crime" and that over 90 witnesses had appeared in court over the three days. Wheeler was taken to Chelmsford Prison, before being returned to **St Albans where he would be placed in the city prison's "death-cell",** although since Wheeler was the first man scheduled to be executed in the prison, he was kept in the prison hospital, as no actual death-cell had been built.[17]

At ten p.m. on the same evening of his death sentence a dramatic letter was released to the press from Chelmsford Prison. It had been written with the Prison Chaplain, the Reverend W. Bailey and it read:

" Mrs Anstee - It is with heartfelt sorrow that.... I did shoot Mr Anstee. I cannot ask God's forgiveness until I have asked yours.... I have been very miserable until now, but my heart feels lighter since I have told my Sin to the clergyman."

---

17 Prior to Wheeler's execution the county's executions were carried out at
      Hertford, the last one being in 1876. In fact there were only four executions at
      St Albans, the last being George Anderson on December 23rd, 1914.

Whilst the prison authorities were greatly relieved by this confession, Thomas Wheeler obligingly went further and explained the whole affair. Wheeler said that:

i) He had stolen the murder weapon from Mr Woollat's farm, and that he done so after starting a fire, which meant the occupants went to that leaving their farmhouse empty.

ii) At eight p.m. on the Saturday he made his way to *Marshall's Wick Farm*, as he said that he actually known Mr Anstee for some nine years and didn't like him, although he said the sole purpose for the murder was robbery.

iii) At around two, he (ALONE) called up to Mr Anstee's window saying a cow was ill

iv) He admitted he fired intentionally at Mr Anstee, although as it was dark, he aimed at the voice.

v) He said he took the ladder and then climbed in to carry the robbery.

vi) He maintained the syringe was his.

vii) He said he was amazed that the police did not find about the shop in St Albans, where he bought shot and powder for the murder weapon, as he thought this stronger evidence than Mrs Lindsay's.

Thomas Wheeler's execution was set for **Monday, November 29th, 1880**. There was no question of a reprieve, even more so in the light of his cell-confession. Awaiting execution Wheeler appeared to express little emotion about the murder, although he was restless, especially when his family visited him from London. Included in the family was his 14-year-old daughter Mary, who was already, an extremely attractive buxom young woman with a prefect figure and beautiful red hair. The last time she saw her father was during the week before Saturday night, when Wheeler received his last visit. Earlier in the day the executioner **William Marwood** had arrived in the city and was seen by many of the locals throughout the day and on Sunday in St Albans.

At two-and-a-half minutes to eight the execution party, numbering nearly 20, assembled in the execution chamber. Wearing his own clothes, Wheeler stood on the gallows, and asked to be remembered by his wife and children. He then said 'Goodbye' and Marwood pulled the lever. There was an enormous thud, which could be heard out in the street. It was less than 60 seconds since the condemned had stood in front of the noose. The prison clocked then chimed eight o'clock and then a black flag was raised. Wheeler's body was then left to hang for an hour before a Coroner's Inquest was held and it was recorded that he had been 'duly executed'.

And what of the pretty 14-year-old girl who visited her father in St Albans Prison - she ended her days too on the gallows as Mary Pearcey at Newgate Prison in 1890.

Case 27
"THE MYSTERY OF THE GT JACKSON STREET SHOOTING"

Martin Coffey
[1946]
Murder
of
Mr Henry Dutton

At 2.30 p.m. on November 26th, 1946, shopkeeper Henry Dutton was shot in his Manchester shop by a robber. At 4.00 p.m. the following day a young Irishman confessed to two fellow countrymen in a city centre hostel. Afterwards he showed one of the two men a fully loaded gun, in a bomb-site, which proved to be the murder weapon. The young Irishman readily confessed to the police, but claimed he had fired the gun at an armed shopkeeper and had stolen three thousand pounds, neither, which actually happened....

There was further confusion over the bullets – two were found in the shop, one on an ambulance stretcher, and a further one in the hospital. The young Irishman said he fired "two or three" times, yet Mr Dutton had been hit twice, and there was no official explanation about the bullets on the stretcher and in the hospital, although they were forensically linked to the murder weapon....

The old Victorian buildings in Great Jackson Street in the Manchester district of Hulme near the city centre have long disappeared from the skyline. The area had been severely bombed during the war and by the end of the conflict only a handful of buildings remained. Even they, to the naked eye, looked derelict and condemned, but despite this number 57 was still standing and provided an income for **Mr Henry Dutton (72)**, who loosely described himself as a "general trader".

Generally speaking Mr Dutton sold men's and boy's clothes, but he was also a pawnbroker, which meant one or two unsavoury characters would appear at his shop. On the afternoon of **Monday, November 26th, 1945**, 10-year-old James Davies reckoned he spotted one of these unsavoury characters outside Mr Dutton's shop.

Little Jimmy reckoned the man, who had a scar on each cheek and was darked hair, was up to no good, as he had paced up and down outside the shop for about two hours. It's probably that Mr Dutton didn't notice the man as he had left the shop at one p.m. for his lunch and only returned about an hour later. Great Jackson Street was a main thoroughfare into the city centre and was crowded with people and traffic, during the lunch-hour.

At just after two-thirty, Mr Harry Dixon and his assistant Mr Frank Laverty were in their truck heading towards to the city centre, a two-minute drive away, when Mr Laverty grabbed the driver's arm and told him to watch out as an apparently drunk old man staggered into the road. Mr Dixon slammed the breaks on and the truck screamed to halt. Little Jimmy looked up and watched as the two men jumped down and rushed to the old man.

Initially the men didn't know what to make of it as the old man sat on the kerb-stone swaying back and forward, but then Little Jimmy came forward and said he was a shopkeeper. It was then that the men noticed two severe wounds in Mr Dutton's stomach and thigh. Mr Dixon pulled his truck up to shield the shopkeeper from the traffic, whilst Mr Laverty did his best to protect the old man from the preying eyes of the passers-by.

Little Jimmy ran off to the corner off Great Jackson Street and the main Chester Road, where he saw Constable Frederick Magerkorth, who rushed back to the shop and then called for an ambulance from a police-box and accompanied the man in the ambulance to the city's Royal Infirmary. Whilst in the ambulance the officer found a bullet cartridge on the stretcher. When the officer returned to the shop there was a number of CID officers under the command of Detective Chief Inspector Frank Stainton but it was uniformed officer who found another two empty cartridges in the shop. Constable Magerkorth was not surprised that the CID men hadn't spotted the cases as Mr Dutton's shop was such a mess that it was not clear where the counter was. However the Constable knew the shop and knew what part of it Mr Dutton used as a counter.

Unfortunately Mr Dutton was so ill that he couldn't help with much information, although his life was not thought to be immediate danger. The shopkeeper was able to say that a young fair-haired man had come into his shop and demanded all his cash. Although the police were treating the inquiry as attempted murder and robbery, despite the help of Constable Magerkorth and Mr Dutton's wife and son, the CID officers could not actually tell if anything had actually been stolen. Privately the police were amazed anyone, especially with gun, would attempt a hold-up at Mr Dutton's shop, as even his clothing stock seemed to second hand, and much of his other stock appeared to be worth very little. Still as pawnbroker, perhaps Mr Dutton had become involved with criminals and perhaps one knew something Mr Dutton's family didn't know, i.e. he had a large amount of cash.

On the following day at teatime the Manchester police faced another hold-up, this time in the suburb of Chorlton-on-Medlock. This time it seemed more logical as the target was the local Post Office. At the time the whole country was suffering a massive rise in armed robbery and murder, as large numbers of young men returned home from the forces, nearly all of them with their service revolvers. There was also a large black-market in weapons as they could easily be bought in Germany. The post-office raid seemed to fit a predicable pattern. In this case the young man fled empty handed and the police thought the cases could be connected but that the man had not fired in the second case, as there were too many witnesses.

During the Chorlton-on-Medlock raid three young Irishmen were walking along Market Street in the city centre, when a CID officer went up to one of them **23-year-old Martin Coffey**. Coffey had been stopped in the street by a plain-clothes officer, who said he wanted to check his ID card, and who then asked him to come back to the station. The actual reason for detaining Coffey was that he was a man "known" to the police with a long criminal record for theft, burglary and who during the war, had been absence without leave, from the Royal Navy. The police officer wanted to check what Coffey had been doing with himself.

However unbeknown to the CID officer one of the other two, Mr John Irvine had been told what he thought was an incredible tale by Coffey and which quite frankly he thought was a load of "blarney". However now he had seen his friend whisked off to the police station, he wasn't so sure and confided in the other man Mr William Phelan, what he had heard only an hour before....

The three young Irishman were staying at a city-centre Salvation Army hostel in Francis Street, which was not far from Mr Dutton's shop. Coffey had joined Irvine and Phelan in a conversation over a cup of tea. Irvine was reading about the shooting of Mr Dutton when Coffey burst out laughing. Irvine and Phelan knew that Coffey was a little "peculiar" but were taken aback by his attitude. They both asked him why he was laughing. Coffey replied the description of the assailant was rubbish as apart from his hair colouring, it was nothing like *him*, and by *him*, Coffey meant himself!

Quite frankly Irvine and Phelan thought Coffey was lying. Although the men had only known each other for a few weeks, they had heard so many tales from Coffey that they just didn't what to believe and what not to. Coffey claimed he had gone to the shop at 2.30 p.m., just as Mr Dutton was returning from his lunch break. Coffey said he asked to look at a coat, which the shopkeeper pulled down and spread out on the counter. Coffey said this was simply a ruse to put the old man at his ease for Coffey said he then pulled out a gun and pointed it at Mr Dutton.

Coffey said he ordered the shopkeeper to pull out the money, and Coffey claimed it was between " two and three THOUSAND" pounds, something that no ordinary Manchester shopkeeper would have in his shop in 1945, as in today's money it would amount to between sixty and ninety thousand pounds. Coffey continued with his story, saying that he noticed the old man had become even more fidgety. Coffey said now Mr Dutton had pulled a gun on him!

Coffey claimed he fired at Mr Dutton's wrist knocking the gun from it. Undeterred the shopkeeper bravely pulled a whistle from his jacket pocket and blew down on it hard a couple of times. Coffey said he was "forced' into firing at Mr Dutton, which he said he did "two or three times". Coffey said he fled out into the crowds and made his way back to the Salvation Army hostel, which was only a five-minute walk away.

The first thing that struck Irvine and Phelan was how calm Coffey was for a man who had just tried to murder a man the day before. It was then John Irvine who asked Coffey about the weapon, but he didn't answer, but instead continued with his story about how he fled from the shop and caught a bus. By now William Phelan had heard enough and left the other two. However Irvine was curious enough to go with Coffey to a bomb-site near the hostel, where Coffey went into the shell of a house and returned with a small parcel covered by old bits of clothing, inside of which was a gun, a.755mm automatic pistol!

John Irvine still did not believe Coffey as guns were common place at that time and cheap to buy and he wouldn't put it past Coffey to have read about the shooting, bought a gun, and concocted the whole story. Thinking more of Coffey as a man with a child's mind, he took the gun from him, although Coffey warned him to be careful, as it was fully loaded. The men returned to the hostel and with Phelan went out for tea when the CID officer stopped Coffey in the street....

With Coffey and the officer a safe distance away, Irvine now told Coffey about the gun and the bomb-site. Before Irvine and Coffey had returned to the hostel, they had quickly gone to his lodgings in George Street and examined the gun and disarmed it, before Irvine hid it on top of the cupboard in his room. Now Irvine was frightened - what if Coffey had been telling the truth - would the police say he was an accessory or even worse was the fact *his* fingerprints were on the gun. A worried Irvine and an excited Phelan ran to George Street to decide what to do next.

On the morning of November 27th, Mr Dutton, although gravely ill was able to give a fuller description of the gunman and he said the attacker was said to be about twenty five years old, 5 feet 7 inches tall, clean shaven and wearing a trilby hat. Incredibly as the CID officer brought Coffey through the main entrance to Bootle Street police station, Chief Inspector Stainton was there when he was struck by Coffey's appearance. Quickly the senior officer spoke to Coffey and asked him where he had been at the time of the shooting. Coffey said at that time he was in the hostel, where he stayed until two-thirty, when he then decided to walk to Cheetham Hill.

At the time of the brief interview the police were beginning to receive information about the attempted robbery at the Chortlon Post

Office and the immediate assumption was that the two crimes were linked and so Coffey slipped to the back of Chief Inspector Stainton's mind. However the police quickly had leads on the post-office hold-up and ruled out Coffey as a suspect and so kept the Irishman in custody. However on **Friday, November 30th,** at 6.45 p.m. Mr Dutton died after peritonitis had set in the day before. The doctors told the police that his death was directly resulted to his two bullet wounds and so the police now had a case of murder on their hands.

Since Coffey had been kept at Bootle Street police station John Irvine
realised it wasn't just a routine "pull", and he became obsessed by the gun. However now that Mr Dutton had died he just could not rest and felt it was his civic duty to at least show the police the gun. The gun was rushed to the Home Office Forensic Laboratory in Preston, where Dr Louis Allen, established it was the murder weapon....

At the police station Coffey was grilled by Chief Inspector Stainton and two Detective Sergeants, Crowe and Arthur Ormiston. Unbelievably Coffey answered the Chief Inspector's assertion that he shot the "pawnbroker" with the short reply of: " You're right. That's my Pistol. I did it." Then Coffey made the even more incredible statement that he would have confessed on Tuesday evening but for the fact that Mr Dutton hadn't yet died! Coffey then shrugged his shoulders and said he didn't care what happened to him now. It seemed an open and shut case even though Coffey's assertion he shot Mr Dutton three times and stole a huge some of money didn't add up. Exactly an hour after Mr Dutton had died; Martin Coffey was charged with murder.

Indeed the only link to the murder was the gun, which Coffey clearly had, in his possession, and his "confession". A search of Coffey's room revealed nothing, the most startling omission being no bloodstained clothing - the police believed Mr Dutton's attacker would have been at least splattered, due to the small space, in which the shooting took place. Nevertheless Coffey had confessed and on the following day he was brought before the city's magistrates court.

The magistrates were more sceptical of the evidence and ordered Coffey to be remanded while the evidence was re-checked. By the time Coffey made a third appearance on December 18th, he now had legal representation and Mr George Hinchcliffe demanded the court hear the evidence against Coffey. The court was read the statement, including the fact Coffey insisted he fired *three* times. Mr Hinchcliffe said that whilst he had grave doubts about whether Coffey had even been in the shop, he said it was duty to say that Coffey now said he never had any intention of seriously injuring or killing Mr Dutton and only fired because he was frightened.

Despite any misgivings the city's magistrates felt there was a case to answer, because of the confession, and they committed Martin Coffey to the next city assize in **March the following year, where he appeared on the 12th of the month, before Mr Justice Morris** in a trial that lasted just one day! Dressed in a blue suit and blue pullover, with his hair neatly pushed back, Coffey pleaded "Not Guilty". In the ensuing three months, Coffey's perilous position had pointed out to him and he told anyone who would listen that he made the whole story up, and that he bought the gun from a Canadian soldier.

The case for the Crown, put by **Mr Frederick Pritchard, KC**, was Coffey's statement, the evidence of John Irvine and William Phelan, and the forensic evidence. The only dispute between the men's evidence was that Phelan said he could not remember Coffey saying that Mr Dutton had a gun. There was further confusion about the bullets, when the court heard that a nurse, Miss Brenda Cooke, had found one under Mr Dutton's hospital bed on the day he died. The bullet had come from the murder weapon, as did the one found on the hospital stretcher, which suggested the gun had been fired *four* times. Although this seemed to back up Coffey's claim to have fired perhaps three times, the court then heard from Dr Percy Jewsbury who gave details of the two wounds, and said he could find no evidence of a third wound, and certainly none to his wrist. As double conformation of this the Crown called Dr Charles Jenkins who performed the *post-mortem* on the body on December 3rd and who said he had found no evidence of a third wound. However the Crown made no observation as to how the bullets came to be on the stretcher or in the hospital.

The next Crown witness was Dr Louis Allen from the Home Office Forensic Science Laboratory in Preston who said he had examined the shop on the day after the shooting and had traced two bullets. He did explain why the attacker might not have been splattered with blood, because he determined that the gun had been fired by the shop door, and the assailant would have been too far away, to have been splashed with blood. Again this cast doubt on Coffey's story that he fired and hit the shopkeeper when he claimed Mr Dutton was fumbling *by the counter*. It also seemed to suggest that the gunman had not been up to the counter to demand the huge sum of money, Coffey said he had seen. Dr Allen said there was no doubt the gun found at John Irvine's lodgings was the murder weapon as the doctor had carried out extensive forensic tests.

For the defence, **Mr Kenneth Burke**, pointed out to the jury all the discrepancies - the discrepancies over the number of shots, the exaggerated or even non existent money, where the bullets had been fired from, the fact there was no evidence that Mr Dutton even owned a gun and finally the fact the gun on the bomb-site was fully loaded and yet the prosecution had not explained this. Presumably for Coffey to have fired the shots he must of either had a supply of bullets, which the police certainly never found, or he replaced them between the shooting at 2.30 p.m. and his confession at the hostel. Mr Burke pleaded with the jury not to believe Coffey's statement saying: " This sort of story is sometimes told by a vainglorious stupid man, who thinks he is hoping to achieve some measure of limelight by pretending to have been mixed up in an affair of this kind."

However Britain was an extremely violent place in the immediate post war years and the jury retired for just 43 minutes and returned with a verdict of guilty of murder against the young Irishman, who was sentenced to hang. An appeal was lodged and dismissed on **April 8th,** and Martin Coffey was hanged by **Tom Pierrepoint on April 24th, 1946 at Strangeways Prison.**

Outside the prison gates a small crowd, including Coffey's father, sister and a friend, gathered to wait the chiming of the prison clock at eight a.m.

So was Martin Coffey innocent – certainly if the man who Little Jimmy described outside the shop was the killer, then it can't have been Coffey.

Theory – I think the real killer was the Canadian, who having shot Mr Dutton, re-loaded the gun, sold (or even gave it Coffey). Coffey was suffering from what is now called a "suggestive personality" and was probably glad to help hide the gun. Then having read about the case thinks it would be exiting to be involved ....

Case 28
"THE CURIOUS CASE OF THE WOMEN'S FOOT-PRINTS"

Vivian Teed
(1958)
Murder
Of
William Williams

The brutal murder of an elderly post-master, who having run his post-office since the First World War, was killed during a robbery in a quiet South Wales village. Teed subsequently became the last man hanged in Wales.

Fforestfach is a tiny village on the junction of the A483 and A4070 some five miles west of Swansea. On the evening of **Friday November 15th, 1957** its charming tranquillity was brutally shattered: **William Williams, 73**, had been brutally killed by a shower of blows to his head that had shattered his skull. As was the tradition before the late 1960's the provincial Swansea and Glamorgan C.I.D. asked for the assistance of Scotland Yard: Det. Sup. George Miller and Det. Sgt. John Cummings were immediately despatched.

On Saturday the two experienced police-officers with a team of local detectives began examining the evidence. The most curious piece of evidence was a series of foot-prints that lead from the post-office's back, through an alley and into the village high street: curious because they were only six size. Incredible as it appeared Det. Sup. Miller pondered whether the killer could be a woman?

The victim Mr Williams had died of severe head injuries according to the Swansea Borough Coroner Mr Frances Wilson. Since the police had no immediate suspect a Coroner's Jury was not called and the inquest was adjourned until February 18th.

At the preliminary inquest in addition to the two Scotland Yard officers there was present Chief Det. Insp. Thomas Dunford, head of the Swansea C.I.D. Dunford told the inquest that he entered the post-office at 9.05 a.m. on Saturday morning and in the passage-way at the side of the house, just through the back-door, he saw the dead body of William Williams. At 11.00 a.m. the local Home Office pathologist Dr C.R. Freezer stated that death was due to, : " .... injuries to the head causing a fracture of the skull. " Mr Williams's body had been identified by a relative, Mr Frederick Camp, Mr Williams's nephew. The fact that Mr Williams lived alone and there was no break-in left Det. Sup. Miller pondering whether the obvious motive of robbery may not necessarily be that case. Perhaps Mr Williams's horrific death was due to an argument between two people who knew each other.

Local Swansea C.I.D. officers had dusted the whole post-office for finger-prints, taking particularly interest around the wooden " stable-door " in the side alley, where the attacker would have had to enter. Later teams of local policemen interviewed hundreds of locals in the village. Up to Saturday night local police stopped buses passing in and out of Fforestfach. From the harrowing injuries to Mr Williams the police were hoping that a blood covered person may have boarded a local bus to escape.

When the two Scotland Yard men arrived on Saturday evening they immediately held a local press conference at the village police-station. On Sunday Miller was forced to admit, : " I have not yet discovered any motive. No matter how small a point may seem to them, it might provide a link for us on which to work. " By late Sunday night Miller conceded, : " We are still searching for a motive. Someone must know something. All confidences will be respected. "

The approximate time of death was at 8.00 p.m. on Friday. Again Miller initially thought that a robber would wait until the early hours the morning. Eight o'clock is the usual time for friends to meet up.

From the post-office a trail of blood led past a radio shop to the cross-roads, where the local bus-stop was. However it also emerged that the local butcher's assistant Gwyn Williams, 15, had cut his finger and rushed into the high-street on route to the doctors.

Miller had also received information from the Glamorgan C.I.D. that through-out the Swansea area there had been a series of post-office robberies, though none involved actual violence.

On Monday Miller appealed again to the local public saying, : " We cannot work without the assistance of the public ..... We don't mind doing 101,000 inquiries, because we might get one that gives us a tangible lead. "

If robbery were the motive why had not the post-office safe been raided, pondered Miller: surely this ruled out any professional criminal activity. Miller was sure the killer was local.

Miller did have the murder weapon: a builder's hammer, which belonged to Mr Williams. Its shaft had been broken. Mr Williams had decided to retire and was having the post-office redecorated: for several days in August the post-office had been full of builders and decorators. For Miller the case was beginning to open up.

One of the builders was a local man **Vivian Teed, 24**. He had worked at the post-office for three days in August. He would know the whole lay-out of the post-office and appeared to have been on friendly terms with the old post-master. However on August 27th when the post-office contract was ended Teed became unemployed.

For Teed this caused a great problem because his girlfriend Beryl Doyle was pregnant. The pair had been living at a bungalow in Swansea, and to compound Teed's personal problems on October 23rd Beryl had a miscarriage. Also at this time Teed had begun associating with a local man Ronald Williams.

The pair frequented a cafe at Cwmbwria only a mile from Fforestfach. Teed began talking in depth to Williams. Teed was quite frank saying he had " weighed up " a job, and it was a dead-cert.: Teed was going to rob the post-office. Teed told Williams the night of the attack would be Friday November 15th after Mr Williams had closed the post-office. Ronald Williams thought Teed was lying and laughed at Teed.

On November 15th Teed certainly was not lying. At 6.00 p.m. Mr Williams closed the post-office. He bolted the back side-door. At 6.10 p.m. his two female assistants Miss Margaret John and Miss Nugent left. After this two expected visitors called and the third brutally murdered old Mr Williams.

The expected visitors were Mr Benjamin Davies, a local business man, and a postman Mr William Roberts, who collected some parcels. Mr Roberts left the post-office at 6.35 p.m: At 8.00 p.m. Vivian Teed appeared at the back side-door.

Teed in his own statement said he intended to force an entry. Although there were no lights on in the post-office to double-check Teed knocked at the side-door: to his utter shock Mr Williams answered.

Pushing his way in Teed struck Mr Williams with a builder's hammer, which Teed had previously stolen from Mr Williams. Although Teed claimed he was in a panic he struck Mr Williams 27 times on the head. The violence used was so great that the shaft of the hammer had snapped and parts of bone and brain were stuck to the hammer. In addition Mr Williams's skull had been forced into his brain. To compound Teed's depravity, although the man was not dead and was moaning, Teed riffled his pockets: he was searching for the safe-key. This he did not find but he did obtain the post-office door-key.

Rummaging in the dark Teed could not open the safe and within a few minutes had passed the dying Mr Williams and had fled into the night. At 9.30 p.m. Teed entered the Cwmbwria Inn. After closing time a group of men including Teed and Ronald Williams went to the local cafe.

Teed openly and without remorse told Ronald Williams, : " I have done that job Fforestfach. I hit the man. I could not find the safe keys and he was coming to, so I left him and didn't take anything. I was wearing socks. One was ripped so I might have left my prints. " The sock was actually found by the police.

Ronald Williams told Teed, : " If you have done that, you must be dumb. ". Again Williams did not believe Teed. Teed was known locally as a violent man, and did have a string of criminal offences for violence, but was also known locally as a compulsive liar. Williams did not speak to the police until very late on Sunday evening.

Because of Ronald Williams's disbelief of Teed Miss John arrived for work at 8.40 a.m. on Saturday blissfully ignorant of the previous night's horrible events. As usual she knocked at the side-door but surprisingly received no answer. She peeped through the letter-box and noticed the hall light was on. The front of the shop was also shut, which was also unusual. It was on Miss John's second look through the letter-box that her heart jumped: she saw the body of Mr Williams.

Miss John quickly ran to the police-station where she met Sgt. Hunter and P.C. Smith. She then ran for the doctor and the policemen ran to the post-office. P.C. Smith climbed over the garden wall and had to break in through the kitchen door. Once in the house he let Sgt. Hunter in.

Between the kitchen and the hall were pools of blood and blood-stained foot-prints. A Glamorgan C.I.D. Scientific Officer Emrys Davies examined the pools of blood and the angles of splashes and determined that Mr Williams had been repeatedly hit whilst lying on the floor.

Ronald Williams's information to Miller may have been one of 101,000 but it was the solving of the case. On Monday Teed was arrested and by Monday evening had readily confessed. Since Teed admitted that the purpose of the evening was robbery he was charged with capital murder, in the course or furtherance of theft. Since the Homicide Act which came into force in March 1957 the vast majority of convicted murderers were sentenced to life imprisonment, but Teed's crime remained a capital offence. If convicted Teed would face the mandatory sentence of death by hanging.

Remanded in custody Teed stood trial at the Glamorgan Assizes in Cardiff in the middle of March 1958 before Mr Justice Cyril Salmon, 54. The Crown was represented by Mr William Mars-Jones Q.C., 44, who was assisted by Mr E.P. Wallis-Jones: Teed was represented by Mr F. Elwyn Jones Q.C., 48, who was assisted by Dyfan Roberts.

Opening the case for the Crown Mr Mars-Jones told the jury, which included two women, that the prosecution would rely on Teed's own evidence to show that it was a cold-blooded killing done during a robbery and that in law was capital murder. The defence equally accepted the validity and accuracy of Teed's statement, but they were going to show that Teed was suffering from diminished responsibility and therefore the crime should be reduced to manslaughter. This defence was new being part of the Homicide Act that had recently become law.

After the case for Crown had been stated the case for Teed was laid. Mr Jones told the jury that Teed was an aggressive psychopath and that the defence would be calling expert medical witnesses to prove this. Jones told the jury, : " The defence in this case is not that this man did not kill the unfortunate post-master. That tragic fact is admitted. The defence is that when Teed did it, he was suffering from an abnormality of the mind, which impaired substantially his mentality. "

He told the jury that Teed should not be freed but that the law should label him guilty of manslaughter. Mr Jones continued, : " These psychopaths are driven to deeds of violence which are as uncontrollable as a tidal wave. "

However Mr Mars-Jones produced rebuttal evidence. Dr Marshall Fenton, senior medical officer at Cardiff and Swansea Prisons, said, : " Teed is not suffering from any abnormality of the mind. "

Dr Fenton said he had examined some 250 people charged with murder during his career. He first interviewed Teed at Swansea Prison on November 28th and observed him at Bristol Prison between January 14th and February 4th. In addition Dr Fenton received medical reports on Teed. From the medical evidence Dr Fenton said he did not think Teed was a psychopath, though Mr Mars-Jones told the court that psychopathy did not constitute *legal* diminished responsibility.

Whilst in prison Teed appeared friendly, played chess and obeyed all orders given to him. Dr Fenton said Teed did not show any outward signs of aggressive behaviour. Teed had many jobs in the building trade, which was not uncommon, and then he had joined the R.A.F. In none of Teed's history could Dr Fenton any signs of abnormality.

Thus as far as the Crown was concerned Teed had planned a robbery and fearing being caught killed the only man that could identify him. In a paradoxical way that was quite " normal ". Dr Fenton stated Teed's behaviour was the way that most violent criminals would behave, i.e. a streak ruthlessness.

Another prison doctor Dr Hugh James at Swansea Prison stated he too did not believe Teed was suffering from an abnormality of the mind. He said that though Teed appeared calm, the slightest " provocation " would cause him to become violent. Dr James interviewed Teed's girlfriend Beatrice Doyle and she stated that they frequently quarrelled and were aggressive to each other. Miss Doyle did say that although Teed was abnormal in this sense, in everything else he was quite " normal ". Thus in no way could Teed be described as insane.

Dr James concluded that Teed had shown no remorse and was a man of very bad character but one who knew what he was doing.

Summing up Mr Mars-Jones said that Teed was a cruel killer who had beaten an elderly man to death to escape being caught during a robbery: therefore he should be guilty of capital murder.

Mr Jones then gave his closing speech to the jury, : " On the facts you have heard of this crime, the history of this man, his behaviour before and after this crime, I ask you to believe that you are looking at a man who is suffering from an abnormality of the mind and that he was not fully answerable for the crime .... Teed has shown a " terrible pattern " through childhood adolescence and maturity. He has gone from one mistake to another to the inevitable fate that lay ahead of him. "

Mr Jones asked the jury whether a normal man would commit a brutal murder of an old man and then confess. Mr Jones then attempted to scare the jury by saying that the death penalty should not be hovering over Teed's head. If Teed was sentenced to death it would be on account of the abnormality of his mind, Mr Jones concluded.

Mr Justice Salmon in a fifty minute summing-up on Tuesday March 18th told the jury that Teed's confession was totally valid and might be a clear admission of capital murder. He then spoke of the defence and finally concluded by saying, : " Remember it is for the defence to prove such abnormalities of the mind. "

This question of an abnormality of the mind vexed the jury. Initially after two and half hours they retired but to the shock of the Court they had no verdict, though the foreman of the jury implied it was only one of them that was differing. Somewhat shocked himself Mr Justice Salmon told the jury, : " You are a body of 12 citizens. Each of you has taken an oath to return a true verdict according to the evidence. Of course you have a duty, not as individuals but collectively. No-one must be forced to their verdict, but in order to return a collective verdict- a verdict of you all- there must necessarily be argument and a certain amount of give and take and adjustment of views within the scope of the oath you have taken .... You are not at all concerned with the result of your verdict. What follows from that verdict is nothing to do with the conscious of any of you. "

Seventy-five minutes later the jury again returned. Again the jury could not agree. In a short note to the judge the foreman of the jury said, : " In the view of one member the prosecution has not proved the accused had not substantially impaired responsibility for his act. The remainder are quite convinced the prosecution has proved this matter. "

The judge concealing his obvious anger with that one juror said it was quite clear that the prosecution did not have to disprove diminished responsibility. It was for the defence to prove it. He finished by saying, : " If the defendant does not satisfy you the defence fails."

Despite this direction it still took another hour for the jury to declare Teed guilty of capital murder. The death sentence was by comparison an anti-climax. Teed said nothing when asked if the death sentence should not be passed in accordance with the law. Mr Justice Salmon then donned the black cap and sentenced Teed, : " To suffer death in the manner authorised by law. "

On Monday April 21st the Court of Criminal Appeal [The Lord Chief Justice, Lord Goddard, and Justices Donovan and Hilbery] dismissed Teed's appeal. Lord Goddard said there was evidence both pro- and against Teed for the jury to examine and they had decided

Teed was not suffering an abnormality of the mind: the appeal court therefore could not interfere with the trial verdict.

On Tuesday May 6th, 1958, Teed was scheduled to die at Swansea Prison. The hangmen would be Les Stewart assisted by Harry Robinson. Under the Homicide Act there would be no notice pinned on the prison gates at just after 9.00 a.m.

At 10.00 a.m. the Home Office informed the press that Teed had been executed. Later in the day the Prisoner Governor Major Geoffrey Nash said, : " I was present when sentence of death was carried out on Teed at 9.00 a.m. It was carried out expeditiously and properly. "

Outside the prison gates only two policemen were present as the prison clock chimed the dreaded hour. Across the road curious neighbours to the prison stood at the end of their gates and huddles in hushed groups. Many no doubt felt that a cruel and callous killer had met a just and fair end.

Teed did not know it but he was part of history, for he was the last man hanged in Wales.

Case 29
"Murder, Mystery & Incest at Plummers Plain House"

**James Gillon
(1928)
Murder
of
his sister Annie**

There is a libertine view that incest over the age of consent should not come within the remit of the criminal law, especially in societies where contraception and abortion are legal and freely available. However historically even the most liberal countries have criminalised incest on the grounds of public morality and because it offended their historic religious beliefs and because anecdotally it always leads to trouble and very occasionally murder ......

Just to the south of Horsham in Sussex lies the village of Lower Beeding. Just as today, in 1927 it was dominated by Plummers Plain House, owned then by Mr Godfrey Holland, a successful businessman, who split his time between his home in Lower Beeding, an office in London and the high-life of nearby Brighton.

William Matthews was his head gardener at Plummers Plain House and in the summer of 1927 he had so much work on that Mr Holland permitted him to hire an additional gardener. Mr Matthews didn't even need to advertise the job because one the servants, a pretty Scottish woman, **Miss Annie Gillon (28)** had let him and the other senior servants know that she was desperate for her brother James to come and work in the same place as her. Miss Gillon had herself only come to the house in May and had frequently spoke about her brother. The household found Miss Gillon a good worker and so her brother was employed without even a formal interview.

Mr Matthews found **30-year-old James Gillon** was a good worker and employed him more as a handyman than a gardener. Gillon was quiet and always followed Mr Matthews instructions to the letter, however when he was with his sister he was completely different, it was most mysterious ....

The staff at Plummers Plain House, especially Lillian Crouchman, the senior cook, noticed that whenever the two thought they were alone they would argue in hushed voices. On one occasion a 15-year-old gardening boy had told Mr Matthews that he thought he had seen them kissing, but not in a family way. However Mr Matthews decided that he did not wish to raise the matter with Gillon as he had not seen the incident and was overall pleased the work of his new assistant.

The household were also struck by the fact that the brother and sister never seemed to want to socialise with the other members of the staff. Furthermore at the end of every day Annie Gillon would go to her brother's cottage, which was little more than a large garden shed, and prepare his evening meal and then remain with him until late in the evening when she would return to Plummers Plain House and to her own room.

As the summer began to fade in mid September the staff were not so aware of the Gillon's unsociable behaviour and indeed they began to notice that Annie Gillon was becoming more friendly with the other members of staff and in particular George Mercer, who was Mr Holland's butler and driver. On September 19th, 1927 he had to drive to Brighton on business for Mr Holland and asked Mrs Crouchman if she wanted to come along and would Annie Gillon be allowed to, if she wished.

After seven months at Plummers Plain House, Annie Gillon was like a schoolgirl going out with her first boyfriend and spent the whole day talking about the forthcoming trip to Brighton. When she went over to her brother's cottage in the evening she told him all about the planned trip the following day. She hoped he would be pleased for her.

However far from being pleased for his sister James Gillon sank into a sullen but silent rage. Quite simply he told his sister that he didn't want her to go and said that she must not go. Despite this Annie Gillon had made up her mind and told Mercer that she would be joining him and Mrs Crouchman.

The following morning at about 11.00 a.m., Matthews was pruning a tree near the kitchen with James Gillon when his sister came up towards him and motioned him away. Matthews could sense they were talking in a hushed but tense way and barely containing their anger. When James Gillon came back to the tree, Matthews tried to pretend that he hadn't seen anything, but Gillon broke the ice by saying that he had asked his sister not to go to Brighton. Matthews said that it was none of his business, but Gillon continued by saying that he had told her he wouldn't let her go.

At just after lunch Mercer brought the car around to the kitchen and a tense atmosphere descended over those present. Both Matthews and Gillon stopped working and waited to see who would be going with Mercer to Brighton. First out of the kitchen was Mrs Crouchman and a confident look of power spread over James Gillon's face.

Mercer started up the car but didn't drive off and gradually Gillon's face went ashen colour as then as his sister emerged from the kitchen dressed in her best dress, he sank his teeth into his lips. Despite his obvious anger Gillon worked in his usual diligent manner, although when asked by Matthews what he was doing for lunch, he said he wasn't hungry. When Gillon left for his cottage at six o'clock he still hadn't eaten and walked sullenly of to his cottage.

The party returned from Brighton in the late evening, and Annie Gillon seemed a completely different person from the one that had come to Plummers Plain House in May: she was chatty, excitable and very friendly. However this mood changed when she saw her brother, whose main concern was that he hadn't eaten all day and, in his opinion, that was all the fault of sister and her selfish attitude. To the other servants Gillon was behaving, as if his sister were his wife. This was no ordinary argument between a brother and sister and was quite unnatural, which left the other servants embarrassed.

Gillon realising they were being watched, tried to rescue the situation by asking Annie to come over to his cottage and cook him a late meal but she said no and went to her room. Gillon pleaded for her forgiveness but she told him to leave her alone.

The following morning, **September 20th,** at 8.00 a.m., Matthews was once again pruning trees in the kitchen garden but did not have Gillon with him. Gillon was supposed to have been working on a broken gutter, when suddenly a shrill scream came from the servant's quarters. Matthews rushed over there and upon entering the hallway saw James Gillon staggering on the verge of collapse: he had terrible wound to the throat and blood was dripping from both hands. In his right hand he had a blood stained razor.

In the hallway was an armchair in which was Annie Gillon was sitting in a position that one would normally except to see in the dentist. Annie Gillon had, like her brother, suffered a most gruesome wound to the throat, a wound that was over three inches wide. Although Matthews could not see it, Annie Gillon had also been stabbed in the back. The violence used was so great that the knife had snapped off and was embedded in her back.

Matthews ordered Gillon to keep away from his sister and to give him the razor but Gillon was flushed with rage and threatened to "slash" Matthews. Matthews now noticed Mrs Crouchman and Mercer in the hallway and told them to keep back, whilst he returned to his workplace to fetch a rope to tie up Gillon. As he ran out of the hallway he told the cook to call the police and a doctor.

A few minutes later Matthews returned to the hallway but the rope was not needed, because Gillon was so seriously injured that he had collapsed and slumped against a wall, trying to smoke a cigarette. Soon afterwards the local physician, Dr Greville Tait arrived at Plummers Plain House and was directed to the servants quarters. Dr Tait was well averse in police matters and realised that Annie Gillon was on the verge of death and told her she must make a statement for the police - a so-called dying declaration, which Dr Tait, Mrs Crouchman and Matthews would witness and sign.

Barely able to speak and spitting and coughing blood Annie Gillon made a short statement written down by the doctor. Annie Gillon said that her brother had come over to the servants quarters shortly before eight and demanded she cook him breakfast. Annie said she wouldn't at which point James Gillon kicked her, stabbed her and cut her throat with the razor.

Soon afterwards the senior village policeman, Sergeant William Dabson arrived and the party waited for the ambulance, which took the brother and sister to Horsham Hospital, where at 9.45 a.m. Superintendent Beacher arrived. He was taken straight to where James Gillon was being treated. Although the wounds to his throat and wrist were serious they were not life threatening and as the doctors tended him the senior officer placed Gillon under arrest for attempted murder and the then offence of attempted suicide.

On September 30th, James Gillon was declared fit to be taken to Horsham Magistrate's Court where he was remanded in custody for a week. Remarkably Annie Gillon had not died and was clinging bravely onto life. The knife wound had severed her vertebrae and had left her paralysed from the stomach down. Over the next few weeks she remained in this perilous position as her brother re-appeared in the town's magistrates, until finally he was committed for trial at the Lewes Assizes in December 1927 on the attempted murder charge.

However sadly on **October 28th,** Annie Gillon gave up the fight for her life and at 8.38 p.m. the charge against her brother became one of murder. Before she died she had given the police a fuller statement saying that she had wanted to leave her brother but couldn't. She said she felt trapped by him and that he would always be with her.

James Gillon stood trial at Lewes Assizes on December 12th, 1927, before Mr Justice Horridge. He was defended by Mr Thomas Gates, whilst the Crown was led by Mr John Flowers.

The only legitimate defence Gillon could plead was insanity - certainly no jury would regard a sister's refusal to cook her brother's meal, sufficient to reduce a charge of wilful murder to manslaughter. Furthermore Mr Gates informed the court that Gillon would be exercising his right not to give evidence.

The only witness for the defence was Dr Frederick Taylor, a senior doctor at Hellingly Mental Hospital, near Hailsham, for 25 years. He told the court that in his opinion, that James Gillon was of low mentality and despite his age was suffering from dementia, and this could have caused insanity when he attacked his sister.

The Crown rebutted this and had a first class witness in none other than Dr Tait, who had been called to Plummers Plain House. He emphatically told the court that he saw no signs of insanity in James

Gillon. The Crown also called Dr John Cruickshank from Horsham Hospital, who said that in the time that he treated Gillon, he saw no signs of insanity.

The Crown called their two final and most important doctors in Dr William Watson and his assistant Dr Francis Busby. Dr Watson, who was the senior medical officer at Brixton Prison, and a prison doctor of some 35 years experience, who said he had observed Gillon for nearly two months and had no doubt he was perfectly sane, a view echoed by his deputy.

The trial of James Gillon was over just after teatime. Mr Justice Horridge only addressed the jury for 15 minutes, suggesting in his opinion there was no evidence of insanity. The jury themselves only were absent for 15 minutes and not surprisingly found James Gillon guilty of the murder of his sister. Some in the court thought a recommendation to mercy might be forthcoming, as no one knew what the motive was.

Throughout the short trial James Gillon had looked fixed at the judge and showed no emotion as Mr Justice Horridge sentenced him to be hanged at the neck. Executions were no longer held at Lewis Prison and James Gillon was taken to **Wandsworth Prison** in south-west London.

Many felt that Gillon's appeal in the middle of January would be a mere formality. However the defence argued vigorously that the judge had spent too little time explaining to the jury the law on insanity and it was wrong that the court had heard the views of Dr Tait, a mere village doctor, on the state of Gillon's mind when he attacked his sister. During the hearing the defence also gave the court a piece of information that explained the close relationship that those at Plummers Plain House had been so curious about.

The appeal court were told that in January 1921 James Gillon had appeared at Edinburgh High Court on a charge of "unlawful sexual intercourse with a woman he knew to be his sister" and that woman was Annie Gillon. The court also heard that a child had been born and Gillon was sentenced to three years in prison.

The defence also told the judges that after his release from prison the couple lived together where the continued their relationship and they had been having a relationship since 1919 when he deserted from the Royal navy. Throughout this period Gillon was also drinking heavily, although he had hidden this from his employer. The defence said that such behaviour as Gillon had shown could only be that of someone, who was mentally unbalanced and accordingly insane.

The appeal judges did not even retire to consider their verdict and added that incest was simply a serious criminal offence and not evidence of insanity - if it were the offence of incest would cease to exist.

When the petition for mercy arrived at the Home Office, the question of James Gillon's previous conviction was discussed and it was felt it added to the reason why he should not be reprieved, as he was obviously a very dangerous man. It also emerged that in 1916 Gillon had been court-martialled for striking an officer and of course he had deserted in December 1919.

Under these circumstances there was to be no reprieve for Gillon and he was hanged on **January 31st, 1928** by Robert Baxter and Thomas Phillips, and was afterwards placed in the Condemned Grave Number 51.

Case 30
"Pontefract's Extraordinary Case Of The Hung Two"

~The Ghostly Mystery Of The Oriental Restaurant~

Percy Barrett (19) & George Cardwell (22)
Murder
Of
Rhoda Walker (62)
[1918-9]

"Oh, George" - Whispered three times, what did this mean …?

"He had often asked me if I had the heart to go into the shop and knock out the man there. This I would not answer, or, perhaps I turned red and he would call me chicken-hearted, or say I had the heart of a pussy." - Percy Barrett ….

" …. they say they cannot convict a man on an accomplice's statement, but what have they convicted me on otherwise. And if that

is so I say that I have not had justice given to me." George Cardwell ….

In 1969, a local Chinese businessman in the West Yorkshire town of Pontefract, opened a Chinese restaurant, calling it 'The Hung Two' …. his decision caused a furore …. It related to a gripping and brutal murder of a shopkeeper – a frail old female jeweller – some fifty years before …. Two young deserters robbed the shop, or so it seemed – the victim was beaten and struck viciously around the head with a walking-stick and suffocated with a handkerchief and cushion …. Both men blamed the other, and what exactly happened inside the shop, remains a mystery to this day ….

The Great War may have been coming to an end, but for **Mrs Rhoda Walker (62)**, it was business as usual at her shop in the Mill Hill area of the centre of the West Yorkshire town of Pontefract, which she ran alone since the death of her husband some years before …. The shop was a jewellers and watch-makers …. By the Summer of 1918, Mrs Walker was beginning to get a little frail and had begun to think of retirement, although she continued to work hard – she was well-known in the town – she was friendly and polite and would always look to help others, and at social events, a woman of great charm …. With getting older and having money, Mrs Walker, had begun to take more and more breaks and on **Friday, August 16th**, she was looking forward to a short holiday on the following Monday, the week of which, would also include her birthday …. But Friday was a busy day – a friend, Ann Fawkes, would be in charge in her absence, and one of the many jobs they had to do was to make sure all the price-tickets could be easily read …. Meanwhile at 1.55 pm, Mrs Walker's lodger – Gertrude Lawn – went back to work - at a local bank: she said goodbye to her landlady and thought she was in good form – she had thought Mrs Walker had seemed a little tired and weary of late, and put her rejuvenated spirits down to her forthcoming holiday .... When she came back at just before four-thirty to her shock and great surprise, she noticed the shop-window display was in complete disarray .... Even more perplexing, was the fact, that the shop-door was locked – something must have happened .... Ms Lawn went round the back – it was always open during business hours, and she made her way into the their dinning-room ....

Minutes later, Gertrude Lawn, was knocking at the home of neighbour, a Miss Sykes – she was having a chat with a Wesleyan Minister George Willis .... what Ms Lawn said was to remain in the minds of the people of Pontefract for the next fifty years .... The vicar returned with the lodger and was able to bring all his beliefs to bare and remain calm: the shopkeeper was lying behind the counter in a large pool of blood .... Across her forehead was a ghastly open wound and her whole face was badly bruised and swollen and dripping in blood .... Across the shop floor were the victim's shattered dentures .... The shop had been ransacked – almost certainly burgled – everywhere there were empty trays and opened drawers .... but incredibly, Rhoda Walker, was still alive .... just .... The vicar organized medical help and that the police should be alerted .... A search of the house revealed, upstairs, a blouse and slip, which were heavily stained in blood .... Mrs Walker's clothes had not been touched in the shop, so these items must have been used in an attempt to wipe clean bloodstained hands; next to them was a bowl with a bloodstained sponge with bloody water in it .... Within twenty minutes, Mrs Walker, was in hospital .... She still had moments of consciousness, and as the doctors tended her, called out: "Don't cut me!" At 3.45 am in the morning **(Saturday, August 17th)** Rhoda Walker died .... Just before she died, she whispered to Nurse Eda Lambert, 'Oh, George' .... three times .... Realising its potential importance, the nurse tried to get the victim to speak, but she was now silent forever ....

The post-mortem revealed the full horrors of the attack on Mrs Walker, who was also undernourished and despite her age, frail .... She had been brutally struck across the head six times, one of the wounds six inches long; her whole body was bruised and battered; she had two black eyes – her left index finger broken, as was her jaw in two places …. Soon after the arrival of the police at the shop, the whole town knew of the attack – but this also showed the police how the investigation would be difficult – the shop stood on the junction of three busy roads – the Knottingley, Wakefield and Doncaster …. It seemed an almost reckless crime – a robbery in broad daylight when hundreds of people were about – why didn't the attacker break in at night …. An hour after Ms Lawn left – at about three o'clock, a fellow jeweller, Thomas Driver, passed the shop …. As he always did, he looked in at the display – he quickly glimpsed a hand open and arrange a display case – he assumed it was Mrs Walker – it didn't look like a hand that didn't belong to an older woman …. Nothing seemed amiss in the shop ….

At 3.55 pm two sisters – Kathleen Benstead and Rebecca Large passed the shop – they saw a soldier – he was almost in the doorway …. he was wearing stripes indicating that he had been wounded – they were the same as Mrs Benstead's husband – that is why she noticed them …. The sisters walked on up Mill Hill, passing by Alice Poppleton, who worked in the local post-office, and, who was going to the jeweller's as a wartime postman …. When she arrived, it was almost four – she went in and called out 'Post Mrs Walker' and put an envelope on the counter – she saw no-one …. By now the sisters were further up Mill Hill when they decided to return to the town-centre – once again, when they reached Mrs Walker's shop, they saw the 'wounded soldier' …. They too saw a hand in the shop-window, but thought nothing of it …. The soldier didn't seem nervous – perhaps he was getting married – indeed beyond the stripes, they couldn't actually describe him to the police …. At about the same time, another witness, Mary Horbury, also saw a hand in the window, but remembered that it looked like possibly a *male* sleeve …. of a dark material …. and Mrs Walker had been wearing a *white* blouse ….

By now the police were receiving dozens of statements concerning the movements of people in Pontefract town-centre, and one came from a local policeman Constable Huck …. At just before three-thirty, he was walking towards his station in nearby Ackworth – on the junction of the Barnsley and Doncaster roads, he saw two young soldiers heading towards Pontefract …. He noticed them as they were slightly running as if they were in a hurry …. The officer even thought he knew the men – their faces looked familiar …. as he discussed this with the officers in charge of the murder inquiry, he realised, they had been staying in Ackworth and working in a local pit - *Hemsworth Colliery* …. so why were they in their uniform running towards Pontefract town-centre …? Searching his mind, he said the men were called **Percy Barrett (19) and George Cardwell (22)** …. And Barrett was carrying a thick brown walking-stick …. Dr Poole, who carried out the post-mortem, said it could have inflicted the wounds on the forehead …. The men seemed prime-suspects and further checks revealed they were …. deserters …. They now became the main focus of the police's investigations …. They concentrated on witnesses, who had seen the men ….

A local farmer, John Taylor, saw the men – and he knew of Cardwell – running back across the then fields towards Ackworth …. the police soon found out where the men were staying and made their way to *Scot's Cottages* at Ackworth Top Moor …. Within minutes of arriving, the police began a nationwide manhunt for Barrett and Cardwell …. Their landlady, Anne Pratt, said the men had come to her home in June – possibly the twenty-first …. *she then told an extraordinary tale* …. the men were both strangers, *or so it seemed* …. Then Cardwell, a Lance-Corporal in the Army Service Corps, said he was her long lost brother, someone she had not seen for over 15 years! He said his mate was a Private in the same regiment; and he spoke with a London accent …. He said both men were on 'extended leave' - both injured - and that they were based at *Osterley Park* in Hounslow in west London – he quickly flashed her some official looking papers, saying they could be recalled to the capital at any moment …. Within two days they were working in the local mine …. At work, they pinned their 'wounded stripes' to their jackets …. Cardwell had six stripes; Barrett two …. When not at work, they wore their military uniforms …. Mrs Pratt said that on the Friday, they had stayed in bed until well past lunch-time, but left soon after waking …. They said they were going into Pontefract …. They came back at tea-time – nothing seemed untoward – and they ate a good meal including two pounds of sausages …. At seven pm, they left Mrs Pratt's, saying they'd be back in 48 hours …. They never did ….

On Monday morning, Mrs Pratt, received a money-order for 29 shillings – it had been bought in Halifax – perhaps a coincidence, but it was home to Cardwell's mum …. the police soon arrived at her door – the men had, indeed, been in the town …. at two am on Saturday morning …. She'd heard a young man shout 'It's Walter' - her son's second name …. Waking from her sleep, she replied 'Walter's gone back' …. As she awoke fully, she realised it was her son …! Mrs Martha Cardwell told officers that the men had stayed with her a week before – on the tenth – on one occasion Barrett had pulled a gold-ring from his finger, and asked her if she could pawn it …. he said it had belonged to a brother who had died, and Mrs Cardwell did as she was asked, obtaining 20 shillings, and being given 'two and six' for her troubles …. Having woken her in the night, the men left on Monday 'for London' …. By now, of course, the murder was big news …. On the Monday, Mrs Cardwell, was sweeping her carpets when she found …. two gold-rings …. she handed them over to a local Halifax officer – she knew where they had come from, and what it could mean …. She also told them about *Osterley Park*, and also another part of London, that the men frequented ….

Rhoda Walker was buried on the Tuesday and her funeral was somewhat controversial, as she was a Quaker, and many of her co-religionists had refused to fight in the war; but it was noted, that two of her sons had enlisted and were in France and the local newspapers took a conciliatory view of the Quaker position …. and, of course, by now, the war had been effectively won ….

The other part of London that Mrs Cardwell said the men might be in, was in the Old Kent Road area of Walworth in the south-east of the capital …. A special team of officers was told to scour the area looking for the men, and at 8.15 pm on August 20th, Detective-Sergeant George Whitmore …. saw a man in uniform, who fitted the description of Cardwell …. The man seemed nervous and did not want to speak to the officer; and he kept his hands over his pockets …. Told he would be arrested, in the police-station, he had a large quantity of jewelery and watches in his pockets .... Three of the price-tags were smeared in blood .... Cardwell allegedly said 'I know what it means' .... Asked what he meant, Cardwell, looked dejected and simply repeated himself .... Less than two hours later, and another detective-sergeant on the same special duty, Albert Sims, in the same area, called out 'Percy Barrett' .... he too quietly gave himself up .... He too was in uniform .... Barrett, who came from nearby Camberwell, said 'I suppose you've got my pal?" On Barrett were eighteen brooches, 25 gold-rings, five gold-lockets, eighteen silver-rings and seven gold-pendants .... In the police-station, Barrett said Cardwell had the best items, he the bulk .... The officers noted that as the questioning went on, Barrett sought to blame his accomplice .... And now it was time to ask him what happened in the shop in Pontefract ....

Barrett told officers: "Cardwell and I went into the shop to buy a watch-key. There was no one in the shop when we went in, so we took the stuff and cleared (out). I went out first. I saw a woman in the back-room, but I did not hurt her."

Returned to West Yorkshire, the pair were 'booed and hissed' when they arrived by cab in Pontefract .... So far, both men did not deny being somehow involved in robbing the shop, but neither had said anything about the murder .... Then on September 3rd, Percy Barrett, asked to speak to the Chief Warder at Leeds' Armley Prison, Alfred Covell – despite being told that he should speak to his solicitor, Barrett said he wanted to write it down immediately, and when he finished, he said: "Now I am ready to go to a higher court." This is what Barrett had said:

"We went to Pontefract on the night of August 15th and Cardwell put it to me that we should break into the shop the same night. I agreed. We did not venture near it that night but went back to Ackworth." The men came back the next day with the same intention, Barrett saying of Cardwell: "He said he would go in for a watch-key and see how things were inside at the same time, and then if everything was alright, would I go in while he looked out. I agreed."

He added that Cardwell was in the shop when the postwoman came in – Barrett said this frightened Cardwell, who went to hide behind the counter, when he encountered Mrs Walker, who had clearly come to the shop area in response to the call by the postwoman .... he said his friend's clothes were covered in blood and they washed them the next day ....

So were this true, at first Cardwell was in the shop and Barrett was the 'look out' .... Barrett then said that Cardwell then looked through the shop-window and beckoned him to come inside .... Barrett went on:

"And when I got in he told me to lock the door. He had Mrs Walker on the floor, gagged with his handkerchief. He asked me to get something to put over her mouth and I went into the parlour and brought a cushion, which he pressed on to her mouth and this seemed to stop her breathing. She was covered in blood and I could not see what he had done to Mrs Walker."

Outside Barrett said that Cardwell had given him some of the stolen items to put in his pockets .... Leaving the shop-keeper for dead, Barrett added, that Cardwell had gone upstairs to try and wash the blood off his hands ....

Just as Cardwell's mum called him by his second name, so Cardwell called Barrett by his - 'George' .... Barrett said that when Cardwell asked him to find something to further gag the victim, he said 'Keep low *George*, there's someone at the window.' Thus it was explained, why the dying Mrs Walker had said 'Oh, George.' And finally to downplay his role, Barrett, further said: "He had often asked me if I had the heart to go into the shop and knock out the man there. This I would not answer, or, perhaps I turned red and he would call me chicken-hearted, or say I had the heart of a pussy."

Barrett said neither man thought the shopkeeper would be an older woman, as Mrs Walker had employed male assistants before .... He added that Cardwell's walking-stick had been thrown out of the train between Hemsworth and Wakefield as they fled South .... Barrett said he had not touched Mrs Walker, but as the police-officers, who read his statement realised, he had signed his own death-warrant by saying *he had gone and fetched the gag and watched his accomplice use it* .... He also wanted the authorities to know, that he was only nineteen, as the media reported he was 23 ....

The two deserters appeared at the **Leeds Assizes on Tuesday, December 3rd, in a trial that lasted just a few hours, before Judge Horace Avory** .... Both men pleaded 'not guilty' to murder: George Cardwell took to the witness-stand to tell a completely different story to the one, that Barrett had already given ....

George Cardwell said that he had simply asked Barrett to go into the shop to buy a watch-key: he said that whilst he was waiting outside to his shock and horror he saw a bloodstained hand appear in the shop-window and take a pad of rings .... Shorty afterwards, he claimed, that Barrett came to the shop-door and said 'We'll have to get away from here, I believe I killed the old woman.' As they fled, Cardwell said Barrett told him what had actually occurred inside .... Barrett had said that when he had tried to steal some rings from the display, Mrs Walker, turned around and tried to stop him .... Cardwell claimed that Barrett had his walking-stick and Barrett said he had hit her around the head with it, adding ' .... when I saw blood I must have gone mad, and I hit her several times.' The court heard from Constable Huck, who, of course, had said it was Barrett, who was carrying the stick, when he saw them; and no-one could recall seeing a soldier outside the shop with a walking-stick .... They recalled this soldier had six 'wounded' stripes, as Cardwell had – and Cardwell said he hadn't gone in the shop as he was a deserter and there was a distinct possibility, that whoever was working in the shop, or indeed, were Mrs Walker around, they might recognise him as a local man .... But in court, Cardwell, admitted that in 1915, he had been sent to borstal for theft ....

The judge, in his summing-up, said that in terms of Barrett's statement, it was not evidence against Cardwell, but given the circumstances of the crime and its build up, did the jury believe that Cardwell was completely innocent of the plan to rob – and merely an intent to rob was enough to prove murder .... **The jury were out for**

just seven minutes – they found both men guilty of murder and there was no recommendation to mercy …. The pair were sentenced to death …. **An appeal was dismissed on December 20ᵗʰ** ….

In the death-cell, Cardwell, wrote to his dad:

" …. I expect you know that my appeal failed. I did not think it would be any good when I set up for it, but as there was a small chance for me I took it, and it failed; so there does not seem any chance now; so I suppose I shall have to go.

But I swear to you that I am innocent of this charge, and I say that I am convicted on a coward's statement; otherwise they could not have sentenced me to death. My counsel asked the judges what evidence to convict me other than Barrett's, and not one of them answered me. They said they were sorry for me, but I don't want their sorrow, I wanted justice, but they did not give it to me. They say they cannot convict a man on an accomplice's statement, but what have they convicted me on otherwise. And if that is so I say that I have not had justice given to me."

The letter went on: " …. I shall send all my belongings to you and you must keep what you want and give the remainder to my relations; and you must write to Woolwich and get what there is to come to me from there. I am sorry I cannot see you before I go, but I think it is better that you should not see me in these clothes, as I think it would break your heart and mine too! I don't want you to worry about me, as you know they cannot prove me guilty of murder – not by fair means anyhow, so try and keep cheerful.

If I have to face this disgraceful death you can always say that I fought in France, and that no man can call me a coward that has ever been led by me in action out there. As I think this will be my last letter to you, I will wish you all good-bye, and may God bless you and keep you all for the good you have done me. Your loving son and brother, Walter." XXXX

PS – Dear Dad, I think you said you were going to make a case to put my things in that I brought from France. If you do, I should like you to put it on the mantelpiece."

Lance Corporal George Cardwell and Private Percy Barrett went to their deaths on the **gallows of Armley Prison on Wednesday, January 8th, 1919, at eight am – executed by Tom Pierrepoint and Robert Baxter** ….

Fifty years on, a local Chinese businessman, Yuk Shing Chan, opened a Chinese restaurant in the building where the murder had took place …. A man with a sense of humour, and being local, he knew all about the crime and so called it '*The Hung Two*' - The case was still fresh in many people's minds in their sixties and over, and Mr Chan changed the name …. to the *Oriental Restaurant* – it remained for nearly the next fifty years until 2017, when the property was boarded up; and as of October 2018, it remains derelict ….

MATTHEW SPICER

FEBRUARY 2024

Printed in Great Britain
by Amazon

8/8/24

45303239R10165